monsoonbooks

CIRCUMSTANCE

G000075294

Rosie Milne lives in Singapore, where she runs Asian Books Blog (*AsianBooksBlog.com*). Her three previous novels are *How To Change Your Life*, *Holding The Baby* and *Olivia & Sophia*.

CIRCUMSTANCE

ROSIE MILNE

monsoon

monsoonbooks

Published in 2019
by Monsoon Books Ltd
www.monsoonbooks.co.uk

No.1 Duke of Windsor Suite, Burrough Court,
Burrough on the Hill, Leicestershire LE14 2QS, UK

ISBN (paperback): 9781912049301
ISBN (ebook): 9781912049318

Cover design by Cover Kitchen.

A Cataloguing-in-Publication data record is available from the British
Library.

Printed and bound in Singapore.

21 20 19   1 2 3

For Aurelia and Maximillian

PROLOGUE
The District Officer's bungalow
Kluanak, April 1924

As Frank made his way along the path to the landing stage, night still hung in fluttering tatters from the branches of the trees and, in the uncanny light of pre-dawn, the ribbons of mist swirling from the river looked to him like ghostly arms stretched in dreadful welcome. But then he puffed out his chest, and he flexed his fingers, and he told himself not to be a damn fool: he mustn't let Nony's hoodoo give him the jumps; mist was only mist, and soon enough it would be burned away by the blowtorch of the sun; there was no such thing as black magic; if Nony thought she could chant a bit of hocus-pocus and thereby curse him then he must remember he was an Englishman, that's all, and not a fellow to fall for any of your native nonsense.

Still, he quickened his step, and he was relieved to see the higgledy pile of his *barang*, his luggage, loom out of the dimness. It was loosely stacked on the wooden landing stage, and beneath it, in the water, he could make out a patch of shadow denser than the surrounding darkness: it was the boat, a native *perahu*, awaiting his arrival. Three crewmen were sleepily lounging within it but, at his approach, they all bolted upright and straightened their shoulders.

Once Frank attained the barang, two of the crewmen jumped

up on to the landing stage to meet him. Frank had Boy, his servant, trotting along beside him. Boy and the crewmen set to loading the trunks and cases; though the air was still cool and fresh, they were soon huffing and sweaty with effort.

Frank smoked as the Malays worked; the tip of his cigarette scribbled the air like a firefly. Only once the last of his things was safely stowed did he toss the glowing butt into the river. The two crewmen jumped back down into the perahu, making it rock beneath their weight.

The head boatman, who'd never stirred from his perch in the prow, waited until the perahu had steadied, and then he reached up and he offered his hand to Frank, but Frank didn't take it. Instead, he too hopped nimbly aboard, and again the perahu set to rocking. He momentarily lost his balance, but as soon as he'd regained it, he waved Boy closer. The servant stepped forward, to the very edge of the landing stage, and he leaned down. Frank adopted a friendly tone, or so he intended.

"Well, goodbye," he said. "Serve the next man as well as you've served me, and I dare say you'll profit from it."

He feared Boy had prepared a parting address, both overwrought and wordy, so to prevent his delivering it, he turned and he inclined his chin to the head boatman, who nodded back. Frank sat down on a seat fashioned from a rough wooden plank; the head boatman lifted a long bamboo pole from the bottom of the boat, and then he used it to push off.

After a moment or two, the perahu was swept into the central current, where the water flowed fastest. Frank resolutely kept his face set away from the riverbank, and away from this dashed entangled life he was quitting. He looked straight ahead, downriver, towards fresh fields and pastures new, he thought, with the grim relief of a man who felt he'd been trapped in post for far too long, with a millstone round his neck. He refused to acknowledge he knew damn well Nony was squatting like a frog on the verandah of their former home, watching him go, and quivering all the while with malevolent intent focused on him.

Nony was indeed stationed at the top of the short flight of stairs that gave access to the raised verandah of the District Officer's – the DO's – bungalow. She was sitting quite still, with First Daughter sleeping in her arms, and her face was so blank it appeared as serene as her child's. She was determined to watch until the perahu, and with it *Baba,* Husband, had shrunk to such a speck she could no longer distinguish it, or him, from any other flotsam washing down the river. So, he was really going, was he? Then on his head be it! She was not in the least fooled by his apparent disregard of her. She was certain that at this, their ending, she and he each felt a prickling spark of awareness arc between them; she was certain Baba knew she was watching him go, and it consoled her to think he must be unnerved; he must fear he was condemned, notwithstanding the fool scoffed at magic. As if his scorn could save him! She allowed a smile to breach the passivity of her face: by the grace of the spirits, and thanks also to the help of their earthly intermediary, the *pawang,* it could be, at most, only another few weeks before Baba, her ensorcelled doll, would find himself tossed from the brilliantly shining human realm into the fainter, drearier one of the ghosts.

Yes, later this morning she'd cast the spell the pawang had taught her, and thus consign Baba to destruction. Dead, safely distant somewhere miles out in the blue vastness of the sea. Dead, thanks to ceaseless, violent, uncontrollable laughter. Terminal laughter, literally terminal paroxysms so convulsive they shook him apart: shook his bones from his sinews; the blood from his liver; thought from his mind; his soul from his body. But still: merely laughter. Laughable, so onlookers must find its horror funny, and smile behind their hands at the victim of this, the most humiliatingly ridiculous death she and the pawang had been able to conceive.

1

The Ryton Cove Hotel
Dorsetshire, August 1924

Four months was not long for a man to find himself a bride, especially when he was under the pressure of a bet, and Frank was horribly aware that two of his had already passed. Indeed, he was feeling rather dispirited as he pushed through the door into the tearoom: he'd been mistaken, perhaps, to have left London for Dorsetshire. Granted, the sea air was as bracing as he'd hoped it would be, so already, after only three hours of breathing it, he could feel it rinsing the lingering damp of Malaya from his lungs, but if first experiences were any guide, then the company threatened to be sadly lacking in delicious young topsies. He swept his gaze from tea table to tea table, intending to confirm to himself that nobody in here would be under sixty – but half a minute! There was one young woman; one young woman in all these talcum clouds of old ones he kept encountering everywhere.

Some sixth sense caused Rose to turn her head: there was a man standing just inside the doorway and he was looking at her. For a long moment their gazes snagged. Under the force of this man's gaze, Rose felt electrified and terrified in equal amounts. The intimacy of it was too much, so she looked away. Nonetheless, she remained as aware of the man as she would have been of a wolf in the corner of the tearoom. To her great chagrin, she felt her cheeks grow warm.

Daphne noticed the blush spreading across her daughter's cheeks. She twisted in her chair. Well! A man! A man standing alone, a rock of youth and masculinity in a room awash with old women. A whole man to boot, she noted, one in possession of all his limbs. Furthermore, nothing about his behaviour, or his demeanour, immediately suggested that his mind was scarred: no jerky movements; no waving his fist at the ceiling, and shouting. In the vicinity of 30, she judged, and tall enough for a girl of an unfortunate five foot eight. It was too bad he didn't have the looks of a Rudolph Valentino, or a Douglas Fairbanks, but then, who did, in real life, in England? And in any case, the shallow luxury of aiming for a handsome catch was one no girl could afford these days – and no more could a mother. After all, apart from the newcomer there were only – what, four? – yes, four other men in the tearoom, not counting the pianist, a sad-looking specimen, middle-aged and drab in shabby tails, and three of those four must be seventy if they were a day, and the fourth, though young enough for Rose, had a flabby hole where his right cheek should have been, and his right eye was quite gone, the socket closed, now, by a flap of skin, and who knew what injuries he bore to his soul? She twisted back and she met her daughter's eye.

"I say! He must be a new guest, don't you think?"

Rose attempted to look oblivious.

"Who must be, Mummy?"

Daphne ignored such an amateurish attempt at dissembling. There was a tiered glass stand of tempting pastries at the centre of the tea table, and she happened to be holding a strawberry tart, as yet untasted, which she'd just selected. She now regarded it a moment, admired the glossy scarlet of the shiny berries. She said, "And no little woman tucked under his arm."

"Mummy!"

Daphne shrugged.

"It doesn't mean, of course, he has no little woman waiting for him at home."

Rose, at 23, shared her mother's despair that her real life, her life as an adored wife, was never going to get started. Nevertheless, she had her pride, and she now felt both humiliated and furious. But what could she say? Since nothing occurred to her, she reached for her teacup – a pretty one, the icy white porcelain decorated with a design of blue flowers. She took a sip of tea, hoping this would somehow discourage her mother from further presumption.

Daphne took a bite of her strawberry tart, one so neat it scattered no crumbs and set no juice dribbling. After a pause for eating, she said, "You'll want to meet him, won't you. After all, it's dull for you there are so few young people in the hotel."

Duller than a dun-coloured dress, agreed Rose.

"I don't mind."

Daphne again ignored her daughter's attempt at dissembling. She ate another bite of strawberry tart and then she said, "Well, we most hope he's suitable, that's all."

Rose continued to sip her tea. She knew her mother meant suitably dynastic. The current sad shortage of men notwithstanding, it was clear that Mummy simply wouldn't allow her to marry just anybody – a wrong sort of person. A man whose people were grocers, say, or railway engineers, that kind of thing. It just wouldn't do.

The Ryton Cove Hotel was a ponderous monument to the dated Victorian Gothic style. The faux-baronial morning room was gloomy and chilly, even in August. For now it was empty apart from Rose, who was sitting at a desk by one of the windows, reading a letter from her cousin Beatrice – the two of them were as close as sisters, and they corresponded daily. Beatrice was spending August in a house her parents had rented for the month, in Suffolk, and as Rose read yet another account of parties and picnics, all of them attended, it seemed, by one Mr Edmund Marchmorant, she couldn't help resenting that dear Bumbles appeared to be having a much jollier time of it than she was.

The morning room door was of dark oak panels liberally sprinkled with iron studs; it looked as if it should creak, but the hotel management kept the hinges well oiled, and it opened silently. So when Frank pushed through it, he did not attract Rose's attention; he was able to observe her a moment, without her realising she was being observed: what a stroke of luck! It was that girl again, the one from the tearoom yesterday, the one who'd so flatteringly refused to meet his eye, except for the briefest moment. Well! It would be jolly rude to ignore her in this otherwise empty, and echoing room. He squared his shoulders.

"A fine morning," he remarked.

Rose glanced up, saw who was speaking, and, as so often, she felt herself betray herself by blushing – drat her traitorous cheeks. She put down Beatrice's letter, hoping that the eagerness with which she did so was not too horribly ill-concealed, and then she glanced out of the window, as if to check whether or not the morning was indeed fine, but really to give herself a moment to compose herself. The window was a tall, arched affair with a stone frame, and leaded panes; beyond it was the terrace which gave onto the formal gardens.

"Yes," she said, to the shrubs outside. "A fine morning."

Frank noticed the effect he was having on Rose; nobody could call him conceited, but really there wasn't a fellow alive who could have resisted feeling smug. By Jove, if only Slinger could see him now!

"Sunny," he smirked. "But not too sunny, a breeze, but not too breezy."

Rose dared to shoot him another glance: he was wearing a tweed jacket and plus fours.

"For golf?"

"Waiting for the fellows who're going to make up a four with me."

By now, Frank had walked across the morning room. He was looming over the writing desk, and, wordlessly, he and Rose appraised each other.

This girl was perhaps not the jammiest bit of jam, thought Frank, but even on the very closest inspection, nothing about her suggested any delicacy of constitution. She was slender, but not so thin she looked ill, and her complexion, though pale, was healthily clear. As to her features? Her nose was retroussé, which rather appealed. Her eyes were green, unusually so, and attractively large and round. Her coppery auburn hair was shingled, and though he thought the style unfortunate, he could nonetheless imagine it: he could imagine his hands in her hair ... though such imagining was perhaps best avoided before tiffin, by a fellow on his way to golf, and certainly he must not let his eyes linger on this girl's bosom, where it swelled invitingly full beneath the bodice of her cotton frock.

For her part, Rose felt for a moment as if she were wheeling into the limitless blue of this man's blue eyes, falling, flailing, through an icy sky ... Not that she was one for nonsense. She reined herself in, and she told herself, with protective prissiness, that the stranger had about him a delightfully boyish air, a blonde and carefree air, to match his colouring. Open. He looked open. Candid – not at all a tortured dark prince. Alas, she could not judge him conventionally handsome. He was tall, six foot or very nearly, but he wasn't attractively rangy: he had about him a softness and a fullness that suggested in a few years he'd run to fat; the lines of his face were too round for male beauty, his features were somewhat doughy and his complexion was marred here and there by pock marks. Still, she found his looks touching; after all, she knew what it was to confront the world from behind a face judged ordinary. And in any case, how marvellous it would be to sink into his manly arms ... not that she could let herself think about that just now; it would be worse, even, than fancying herself tumbling through the boundless sky.

Frank knew he had to push things along, and Rose saw no need to slow them down, so although it was only a few days since they'd first talked to each other in the morning room, they were already on first-name terms – and, indeed, almost inseparable. Now they were playing tennis. The hotel's court was badly sited; there was only open ground, and no wind brake of trees between it and the cliff half a mile away, so the slightest sea breeze set tennis balls bobbing and swirling until they became unplayable. But on a calm day, such as today, with the sky like a blue blanket spread to dry in the sun, there could be, thought Rose, no prettier spot for tennis. And certainly there was no one in the world she'd rather be playing than Frank whom, she thought, looked edible in his tennis whites. Likewise, Frank thought Rose, in her own tennis whites, looked as lickable as a vanilla ice and he admired her graceful athleticism just as much as she admired his.

Frank was much the better player. Though in each game he'd given Rose fifteen, she'd barely troubled him at all on his own serve, and she'd only held her own because he'd let her. Now, he was serving for the match. He dawdled before he tossed the ball, relishing this chance to show off. Then: up went the ball; thwack, his racquet connected. The ball made a purposeful parabola through the still, warm air. Rose darted across the grass court, a flash of white against green. Thwack, her return went straight into the net.

"Oh, rotten luck!" cried Frank, delighted to have won.

Rose was eager to compliment him.

"Luck? Not at all. It was a splendid serve."

The two of them left the court, laughing and panting. They swung their heavy, wooden racquets as they walked to the welcome shade of a canvas awning; beneath it were a couple of cane chairs, and a table set with glasses and a big jug of lemon barely water. Rose flopped down into one of the chairs.

"So hot!" she said, fanning her face.

Frank began to pour the lemon barely water.

"Hot?" he echoed, with exaggerated incredulity, as he passed over her glass. "This would be a cool afternoon in Saramantan."

Frank delivered the word *Saramantan* casually. Nevertheless, Rose seized on it as a clue in a treasure hunt. She assumed, of course, that Saramantan must be someplace somewhere in the Empire, some otherwise sad and benighted patch of the globe, where, luckily enough for the natives, Britannia now held sway.

"Where's that? Africa?"

Frank shook his head.

"Malaya."

Rose consulted the personal chart of the world she carried in her head and she found … nothing. Malaya was nowhere marked, not even as *terra incognita*. After a telling beat she giggled in what she hoped was a winningly disarming way.

"And where's that?"

Frank generally found his fellow countrymen's ignorance of geography irritating, but in Rose's case he was prepared to be indulgent.

"I'll show you on the map."

The two of them smiled at each other, each of them imagining their two heads bent over an unrolled map, his finger pointing, hers following. Rose broke the stretching silence.

"I gather you have been there?"

"More than that: I live there."

Rose flinched. For a split second her face revealed her distress;

but then she shifted in her chair, which was scratchy against her legs, and she mastered herself.

"An Empire builder?"

"Yes. With the SCS. The Saramantan Civil Service. I go back in September."

Rose gave an inner wail. She asked, as calmly as she could, "How long have you lived there?"

"My entire life. My people were stationed there."

"You were born there?"

Frank nodded.

"An English son of the Malayan soil. My earliest memories of colour and heat."

Oh dear, thought Rose, this was another rotten blow, one just as awful as the distance to Malaya, and the brevity of Frank's leave. Not that she minded, but Mummy was of the firm opinion that no Englishman born in the colonies was a proper Englishman.

"Gosh," she said.

"Yes. My father was an SCS man before me, served for nearly thirty years." Frank paused, and then he added, "I've never lived in England, apart from school. Hinchford. Soon after my seventh birthday I travelled back in the care of one Mr and Mrs Shields, a missionary couple returning to Scotland, to retire after a lifetime of service."

Rose blinked, and then she blinked again. What a pang it gave her to imagine Frank as a boy, small and lost-looking, arriving, solitary, on the shores of what must surely have seemed to him a strange and lonely new life. And though it was necessary, what a sacrifice for his parents, to send him away.

"Boys need Latin and Greek," she sighed.

"Boys need playing fields and bracing games."

"Indeed ... But when you arrived England must have seemed so foreign?"

"Yes. And I seemed foreign to the other boys. I spoke Malay better than I spoke English – I certainly wrote it better. I preferred rice to bread, or potatoes ... the other fellows thought I had some peculiar ways, they called me *jungle boy* ... It was autumn, coming on for winter, and yet I couldn't get used to coats, gloves, scarves. I refused to wear Wellingtons – I often went shoeless in Saramantan. And the English too cold-mannered for me."

"I say!" Rose chaffed him. "You think I'm cold-mannered?"

"Frightfully," nodded Frank, deadpan. They took a moment to enjoy their teasing, and then he continued, "I was used to running wild, climbing trees, roaming the jungle ... Did you have a pet as a child?"

"A beagle."

"A beagle! Once, I was allowed to keep a tiger cub, and there were generally a few tame monkeys around the bungalow, a parrot or two, snakes ... All that, then school. Prayers in the abbey every morning and Euclid every afternoon."

"Were you very unhappy?"

Frank shrugged.

"I was sustained by the thought that one day I'd go back." He paused. "And I did. I returned home as soon as I could, immediately after I left school."

Rose wondered whether she could ever think of anywhere abroad as home. But then it occurred to her home was perhaps not a place, but a person. The thought made her blush. Frank smiled at her, and her blush intensified.

"Your parents must have been delighted to have you back," she said, in some confusion.

Frank shook his head.

"They were dead by then. Mother died soon after I was sent to school. Fever. Three years later Father followed her to the grave. I never saw either of them again, after they passed me into the care of Mr and Mrs Shields."

Rose's swelling heart now seemed almost to burst with pity. She longed to reach out to take Frank's hand, but it was impossible of course; she'd have to make do with touching him in some other way.

"My father's dead too," she offered. "Thrown from a horse when I was twelve."

"What rotten luck."

"Yes. Rotten luck."

For a long beat they met and held each other's gazes. Rose looked away first. She was feeling ever more flustered, and she spoke a little wildly.

"Do you have brothers? Sisters? Were there cousins you could go to in the holidays?"

Frank shook his head.

"Oh, no. I've got no family. So far as I know I haven't a relation in the world. I spent holidays at school."

Rose felt her eyes grow hot and moist; what a privilege it would be, she thought, to be the woman lucky enough to pierce Frank's solitude.

By now, when it came to Rose and Frank, all the women at the Ryton Cove Hotel had their fingers crossed – all apart from Daphne. Notwithstanding her initial eagerness to effect an introduction between Mr Langham and her daughter, she was, contrariwise, becoming steadily more uneasy about their friendship. Oh, she admitted Mr Langham was charming all right, and that was part of the trouble: he was too much of a charmer for her taste. She suspected him of untrustworthiness; she couldn't quite put her finger on why, except that the things Rose said she admired in him – his artlessness, his candour – she found overdone, and hence suspicious. He was too blatantly candid to be sincere. Or so worried Daphne.

And then again, there was the matter of Mr Langham's people. Nobody seemed to know a thing about them. Daphne had been conducting investigations, of course, via letters dispatched to her friends in London, and to her sister, Louise, Beatrice's mother, now holidaying in Suffolk, but all her enquiries had drawn blanks. She found this terribly worrying. So much of her mental energy was expended on social mapping – who was connected to whom, and was it by birth, or by marriage? – that she was confident if she could plot no co-ordinates at all for a man, then in all likelihood he had no co-ordinates worth plotting.

Such was her concern, she had decided it would be irresponsible to tolerate the uncertainty any longer; she must tackle the problem of Mr Langham's people head-on. She and Rose were in the chilly morning room, sitting with Mrs Hamilton-Whitney, a large lady of fifty, and the two Misses Templeton, tweedy, ageing, spinsters. Daphne was sitting on one of the sofas, next to the younger Miss

Templeton; Rose was sitting on the opposite sofa, between Mrs Hamilton-Whitney and the elder Miss Templeton. For the last twenty minutes, the quartet of older women had been discussing millinery trimmings, and now they were disagreeing on whether or not it was too much for ladies past their prime to have silk violets dangling by their ears: Mrs Hamilton-Whitney rather thought not, although she could persuade neither Daphne nor the Misses Templeton to her jaunty opinion.

Rose was bored out of her skull. So she was more than ever delighted when Frank walked in with Mr Hamilton-Whitney, both of them dapper in their plus fours.

Mr Hamilton-Whitney nodded towards the stone-framed window.

"Raining," he announced. "No golf."

Frank and Rose took the chance of this little distraction to smile at each other unobserved. Or so they thought. In fact, Mr Hamilton-Whitney was the only one in the room unaware of their telltale smile; the women no more missed it than they'd have missed a horse falling out of the sky and landing five feet in front of them.

Daphne reached up and pretended to pat her hair back into place, as if it had been ruffled by a momentary breeze.

"Oh, Mr Langham," she said, with no attempt at guile, "I've been meaning to ask: are you by any chance one of the Somerset Langhams?"

Frank was wary of Mrs Fitzgilbert, whom he regarded as something of a tartar. Nonetheless, he was keen to ingratiate himself with a woman as important in Rose's life as her mother, so he bestowed upon her what he hoped was his most irresistible smile.

"No," he said. "Never been to Somerset."

"No? Then perhaps the Lincolnshire Langhams?"

"Nor Lincolnshire."

Daphne knew of no other Langhams but these.

"Then where are your people?"

Frank was surprised. He looked at Rose.

"Oh," he said. "Oh, you didn't tell her?"

Daphne likewise looked at Rose.

"Tell me what?" she demanded of her daughter.

Rose blushed. How she wished the ground would open up and swallow her! She was just steeling herself to admit that Frank was one of the Saramantan Langhams, when Frank himself beat her to speech. He had composed his face into a solemn mask and he spoke in his most churchy voice.

"My people are in heaven. Mother, Father, both dead these twenty years."

There was a beat of uncomfortable silence.

"I'm so sorry," said Daphne, not a bit sorrowfully. She knew she shouldn't, but she decided needs must, she'd better pry. "But before that … ?"

"Before that they were in Saramantan." Frank paused, "That's in Malaya." He added, considerately. "It's where I'm from."

"From?" Asked Daphne, as if the word were new to her.

"Born there." Frank clarified.

Daphne dismissed colonials as black sheep and remittance men – men paid so much each month by their families to keep them out of the country. Or else they were small-minded suburbanites transplanted to the tropics, where they became far too cocksure for their own good. In any case, they were terribly inferior sorts, the lot of them.

"I see," she said, in an icicle voice.

Frank sensed the chill, and he even understood it, nonetheless he soldiered on.

"I live there still. I'm on Home leave between postings."

Mr Hamilton-Whitney rubbed his hands together, jovially.

"Langham's a jungle-wallah. A District Officer deep in the jungle, don't you know."

Daphne looked severe. She couldn't approve of jungles, and she could only suppose a District Officer must be something akin to a District Nurse, which was an admirable thing to be, but scarcely manly. She raised an accusatory eyebrow to Mrs Hamilton-Whitney: why didn't you tell me this? Mrs Hamilton-Whitney looked back at her with apologetic innocence: this is news to me. But though Daphne was cross with Mrs Hamilton-Whitney, she was far crosser with Rose. She turned to her daughter: the infernal girl would not meet her eye. Huh! She bestowed upon her a glittering glare, and she said again, in a tone just as wintery as before, "I see."

Rose and Daphne continued to stew over, as Daphne saw it, her daughter's underhand and unjustifiable refusal to share significant information about Mr Langham, and, as Rose saw it, her mother's snobbish and unjustifiable disdain for all colonials, but especially those named Frank Langham. About a week later they again had words about him.

For the sake of economy, mother and daughter were sharing a room. It was a big room, well able to accommodate, at one end, two single beds, a wardrobe, a washstand and a dressing table, and, at the other, a stone fireplace, empty in the summer months, with armchairs arranged at right angles to it. A few side tables were dotted about. The heavy, and heavily carved, mahogany furniture harked back to the 1890s, as did the fussily fringed brocade curtains. Though the lighting was electric, the gilded wall lights were old-fashioned homages to curlicues and twiddles.

For the past hour Daphne had been in the hotel's library, reading *The Times* – such terrible events in Asia Minor – but now she had returned to her's and Rose's room to change for dinner. When she pushed through the door she found her daughter curled up on one of the armchairs, looking miserable and with a letter unfolded on her lap.

"Are you moping?" she accused.

Rose was startled out of her reverie.

"Moping? No."

"Well something's the matter."

"No it's not."

Daphne looked at Rose a long moment, and then she nodded to the letter in her lap.

"Who's it from?"

Rose saw nothing else for it.

"Beatrice," she sighed, "I expect there's one for you from Aunt Louise somewhere in the mail."

Daphne flinched as she saw, immediately, the lie of the land.

According to Louise's letters from Suffolk – almost unbearably gloating letters – Beatrice, dratted girl, had quite made one Mr Edmund Marchmorant her victim. Indeed, Louise's last letter had talked of little but this Edmund, of his house, Raddington Court, of what little dears his sisters were, of how delightful was his mother.

"Dear Beatrice," she said, bracing herself, "what news?"

Mother and daughter exchanged a significant look.

"Mr Marchmorant has proposed," confirmed Rose. "Uncle Thomas has given his permission; they're to be married as soon as can be arranged."

Though, when she thought of how Louise would now condescend to her, Daphne felt desperately sorry for herself, she felt sorrier still for her daughter, and she spoke as gently as she was able.

"You poor old thing."

Rose looked shocked.

"Mummy! I'm very pleased for Beatrice."

"Of course you are."

"I am!"

"But still."

Rose dropped her gaze to the letter in her lap. She re-read a line of Beatrice's looping scrawl: *My ring is set with three garnets, each as plump as a red currant* ... for a moment, her whole being flared with fury. It was too bad! It was too bad Beatrice was engaged, and she wasn't. It was too bad she was pitied and patronised by her mother.

"You should know something!" she flashed. "I believe Frank

is going to propose."

Daphne was aghast.

"What? You can't mean it, surely?"

"Yes I can. I do."

Daphne berated herself as a fool, an absolute fool: much against her better judgement she'd persuaded herself nothing could come of Rose's and Mr Langham's friendship – not when he was going back to Saramantan in another month or so. She wrung her hands and she said, with anguish, "I quite blame myself. I knew it! I should have nipped all this in the bud. I should have bundled you home. I told myself: it's a flash in the pan, Daphne, a flash in the pan."

"But all you've ever wanted for me is that I marry."

"Marry well."

"I know you don't like colonials, but ..."

Daphne interrupted her daughter.

"Our family has never had anything to do with those sorts of people."

"Such terribly bad form," said Rose, facetiously.

Daphne narrowed her eyes.

"Form has nothing to do with it. You can't frisk off to Saramantan; you've never even been to Scotland."

"The great world out there. The vast, wide world all waiting to be discovered."

"Don't be silly! Abroad is bloody!"

"But you've never been there!"

"I've never broken my leg, either, but I know I wouldn't want to. I mean, to say: Malaya! The distance! How many thousands of miles is it, between England and Malaya?"

Rose's anger began to cool. She warned herself: be compassionate; be grateful. She thought how resentful she'd have been if her mother hadn't been upset at the thought of her removal to Saramantan – or to anywhere distant, for that matter. And she was an only child. Her mother was a widow. She wanted to ask: you worry you'd be lonely, Mummy, if marriage whisked me far away? But her courage failed her, so she asked instead, "You worry I'd be lonely, Mummy?"

Daphne gave a dismissive toss of her head.

"Of course you'd be lonely ... I worry you wouldn't cope. Life in the jungle."

"I'd be interested to see how I overcame the challenges."

"Heat? Malaria? Too many hairy creeping things with too many legs? Nothing but leaves and leaves and trees and trees for miles and miles and miles. No shops. No social life to speak of. What would you do all day? Who would you see? The tedium! And once you were imprisoned by the forest there'd be no turning back."

Rose flinched, as it hit her, at last – and oh, God, too late, perhaps? – that she and her mother were horribly tempting fate. She flapped her hands, as if to flap away any loitering god of retribution.

"We should stop this, Mummy, we're getting all forward of things. Frank may not propose, after all."

"But you said you think he's going to."

"Perhaps I was mistaken."

Daphne was scarcely falling for that. She stared a moment

at some stone acanthus leaves carved into the fireplace surround. Never mind that Mr Langham could so easily remove Rose to some distant shore, and there trap her in a life of boredom and loneliness, what about her suspicion of his character? Was he kind? Generous? Loyal? How could she know, when he looked at her with such damning guilelessness? Tact was not her forte, and yet she did try to be tactful.

"Think ahead!" she said. "Once the springtime blossoms of first acquaintance had dropped their pretty pink petals, I fret you'd all too quickly become exasperated by his boyish ways."

Rose took umbrage.

"I doubt it; I do so admire him for them."

Unusually for her, Daphne was at something of a loss; she retreated to her habitual directness.

"Well in any case, he looks me too fully in the eye."

"What?" Rose jibbed, "What do you mean?"

"It makes me think he must be hiding something."

"Mummy!"

"I find him too charming to be trustworthy. Only a fool would trust charm."

"Thank you!"

"It's too easily switched on and off. It's so horribly presumptuous."

"You'd prefer me to marry a boor?" Rose's voice was rising. Nonetheless, she flinched again at her own hubris. "I mean, if Frank proposes," she added, hastily. "If he does."

Daphne spoke harshly.

"If he does, you must turn him down, that's all. You can't

condemn yourself to life in the middle of nowhere with a jungle-wallah. My only child! My dearest girl!"

One side of the formal gardens at The Ryton Cove Hotel was bordered by a yew walk, a roofless outdoor corridor carpeted with grass and with high walls of dark glossy green. The far end was open to the view across to the sea, the end nearest the main building was hidden from the terrace by a curve of the hedge. This curve enclosed a pretty white marble rotunda; within the rotunda Rose and Frank were standing entwined, kissing.

For Rose, this was the first time she'd ever exchanged a kiss on the mouth with a man. It was unspeakably exciting. She felt terribly sophisticated to be kissing like this; she felt giddy with her own dangerous daring. And this kiss contained within itself the promise of so many other firsts, of lips, hands, flesh, of carnal joys to come ...

Frank, meanwhile, thought this kiss was very pleasant, very pleasant indeed.

The two of them pulled apart. Somewhere in the hedges behind them, an unseen blackbird began to sing. Rose thought he was singing words of broken air: note-by-note his song changed tone, as if with emotion; she felt he was singing for her, that more than having meaning his song had meaning for her. But what was its meaning? She looked deeper into Frank's blue eyes, willing and hoping.

As he'd been leading Rose to the rotunda, Frank had been feeling supremely confident, but once they were actually standing beneath the white marble canopy of its roof he'd begun to feel unaccountably nervous. Their kiss had steadied him, and now he saw the longing in Rose's eyes, he once again felt assured of success. He relaxed and he took her hands, as if he were preparing to swing her around.

"I'm awfully fond of you, you know. Awfully. And I rather hope you may be becoming awfully fond of me?"

Rose's heart began to thump.

"Oh, awfully."

"But you know I must go back to Saramantan at the end of my leave."

"Yes."

"Do you think you could be happy there? I mean with me. If …" Frank's nervousness returned and momentarily jammed his tongue.

Rose's thumping heart thumped harder.

"If?"

"Well, I was thinking … we're awfully fond of each other. I thought perhaps, if you weren't appalled by the idea of moving to Saramantan – or, for that matter, appalled by the idea of me … I mean I thought we may …" Frank took a deep breath. "Oh darling, it is yes, isn't it."

In the background, the blackbird continued to sing and for a moment Rose felt her being merge with his reedy music; for a moment she became nothing but the purity of his sound.

"Yes it is," she said.

OUTBOUND MAIL, NOVEMBER 1924
LETTERS SENT FROM THE EUROPA HOTEL,
BB, SARAMANTAN

From Rose to Beatrice

Dearest Bumbles,

What a treat! I found your lovely long letter waiting for me in Singapore – we stopped there two weeks, to rest after the voyage out, before leaving again for Saramantan, where now I find myself. It was blissful to read of your wedding and honeymoon, though your letter made me regret anew I could not stay in England long enough after my own speedy marriage to see you married in your turn. Mrs Edmund Marchmorant of Raddington Court!!! Are you yet used to the change from a girl with one name to a wife with another? I begin to be, I think – the slow weeks of my shipboard honeymoon acclimatised me somewhat to my elevated status just as much as they did to the increasing ferocity of the sun. In any case, I concur wholeheartedly that married life is wonderful. It is indeed very satisfactory to be a wife. (Married love!!! What a thing!!!)

I must apologise I failed to sit down sooner to write back to you, but there were so many diversions in Singapore, that busy, sinful city, that whilst I was there I swirled about all day in a whirl of parties and dances and picnics and shopping, and it is only now I am removed to Bandar Baru, an altogether quieter backwater, that I can devote myself to the pleasures of friendship, and of letter-writing. I do hope any letters you sent to me after the one to Singapore you remembered to address to me here, care of Government House, and the same until I can send you my permanent address. Out here we call it BB, but do not write that on your envelope for fear of confusing your postman, even supposing he knows Bandar Baru is the capital of Saramantan Island, which I doubt; this scarcely being on a par with knowing Paris is the capital of France.

A little coasting steamer brought us here from Singapore. I promise you not a patch on the P&O for grandness or for comfort, and the captain a much rougher fellow than would be acceptable on any ocean liner. We have been here now three days and the British people have made me most welcome, so when I haven't been lounging indolent in the prostrating heat, I've been taking tea with various of our officials' wives, or drinking gin pahits at the Club – gin and bitters, I mean, a drink deliciously pink, the colour of much diluted raspberry cordial, and I'm told the Old Hands believe it protects against malaria. In any case it is terribly popular here – except with Frank, who says he is a whisky-wallah, and he never found a gin cocktail he could drink all night.

BB is a pretty little town, a dozing sort of place set at the mouth of the Saramantan River – a sluggish, muddy thing. There is only a small barracks – called here a *cantonment* – housing barely enough soldiers to put down anything but a half-hearted riot, Frank says, and not much in the way of a civil district, either. Everywhere the jungle presses close to the streets, so you catch a flash of green and a glimpse of trees wherever you go – not unlike Suffolk, or so I should imagine? Except these trees – towering things – shoulder into the world with far more swagger than any

English oak and, ever present at the edge of my vision, they are a constant reminder I'll soon be living in the jungle. Although where in the jungle is anyone's guess as Frank is yet to receive his posting, which I think awfully unfair. Notwithstanding my idea of one upriver outstation is as blank as the next, I itch to know where he and I will make our first home.

In the meantime, I must report the natives here form a fearful hotchpotch. Most of them are Malay, but there are also numerous Chinamen, who originally came here to trade, and Indians, who arrived sometime in the last century as indentured labourers. Rather thrillingly, there are also to be found wandering the unpaved streets many Dayak – aboriginal people from a great variety of the different primitive tribes that populate the interior of Saramantan Island.

These Dayak spare nothing for an English lady's blushes. Even in town the best dressed men wear little more than loincloths, and some of them go naked, all except for stringy belts and ornamental pins they stick through their *things,* and if they have piercings even *here,* you can no doubt imagine the state of their ears! The women are no better. I saw a bare-breasted woman on the very steps of the courthouse, and grotesquely swollen to boot, for she was That Way.

Will you be alarmed if I tell you all the various Dayak were until recently keen headhunters? My dear husband, who sometimes likes to frighten me, says even today they sneak a head, now and then, when chance arises. He adds when he was a boy, some of them were even man-eaters!!!

What about the natives of Suffolk? Do they eat each other?

Write soon to tell me!

With that plea I must finish this to you, and steel myself to write to Mummy. You know how she is about Frank – how lucky you are your own mother approves your match – and her latest to me I find outrageous. It's a rambling tale of an ancient crime she got from her friend Miss Bellington, a terrible know-it-all, in which a bride newly arrived in the colonies discovers too late her husband is a fraud. I can only think Mummy intended this yarn to deliver a stiletto thrust between my ribs, and though she may not like Frank, to send me a letter as good as saying she thinks he is not the man he seems to be, I judge altogether too much. I have decided to pretend I missed her letter's point entirely, which should irritate her no end, or so I hope.

Your loving cousin, Rosebud

From Rose to Daphne

Dearest Mummy,

Thank you for your last, which was waiting for me when I arrived in Singapore, but such were the demands on my time there I could not reply at once. Still, Frank and I have now safely arrived in BB and I have leisure at last to pick up my pen.

I am pleased for you Miss Bellington has returned from the Isle of Wight, although I must regret that on learning I had leapt headlong to the altar, and with a jungle-wallah to boot, she should regale you with a tall tale of crack-up in the colonies. I should quite agree the whole thing shows such frightfully bad form, if only I believed a word of it.

Well, I do believe some of it. I don't doubt this Enid of Miss

Bellington's married an Old Africa Hand who'd served his whole career in the middle of some desert nowhere. I can quite believe, as well, that as a bachelor Walter took to drink to help him cope with the hardships of life bounded by all that stretching sand, and the sun striking down on him like a weapon, no doubt. Moreover, when he took his fateful Home leave I'm sure he was indeed at great pains to disguise his dissolute nature. It was only sensible that through temporary sobriety he kept from E (and from her mother) he was nothing but a lousy drunkard. So much would any man do, however reprobate. And it's only natural that any bride, arriving in the dusty middle of miles of arid emptiness, and making the vile discoveries her new husband was both a liar and a sot, would be so shocked and humiliated she'd decline to mention a thing about it in letters Home. But that one day when W was dead to the world in a drunken stupor, E, deranged by heat and despair, only went and shot him, I think stretches credulity. And as to the authorities believing her when she claimed W had shot himself in a fit of *delirium tremens*, this I find doubtful. Can a man hold a gun to his heart when he is overcome by the weakness and confusion of a shaking fever? Still, if E got away with it locally, then I suppose it holds together that in letters Home she'd claim W had died respectably, of a fever, since how would those in England ever learn the disreputably damning truth? I can swallow too that after she'd returned to live with her parents, she'd guard her terrible secret down all the long years from W's death to her own. Even the simplest lady could summon the requisite reserve and cunning if she were absolutely petrified for her own neck. But I find it hard to believe that almost with her last breath, E whispered all the thrilling details of her horrible crime to her sister, in a final act of repentance. A story such as this would take too long to tell for a deathbed, and require too much energy of the departing. Or in any case, that's what I think.

It's better than a penny dreadful! Where did Miss B find this exciting tale? Is Enid's now doddery sister a close friend of hers? For that matter, why did the sister tell all? If I'd had a sister, and she'd confessed to me she were a murderess, I can't think I'd scatter the news. I hesitate to ask, Mummy, for fear you'll take umbrage, but are you quite sure Miss B is reliable? Is she perhaps in her spare time an authoress convinced her readers' appetite for crime, treachery, murder and general infamy is nothing short of something terrible?

Your sceptical daughter, Rose

From Frank "Langers" Langham to Robert "Dandy" Dabney-Dent

What ho, Farmer Dandy,

What a turn up when I arrived back from leave, only to discover you've quit the SCS for the delights of farming with your brother in Suffolk. They say at the Club you departed at the behest of your little woman, who was missing her people worse than ever now she's presented you with a son and heir. Can it be true? If so, I must call you a sentimental fathead and I do hope my own little woman never tries anything like that.

Yes, you read those words aright: my own little woman. From which you'll gather I won my bet with Slinger; I've now joined the two of you in holy deadlock. Respectable domesticity at last for Yours Truly. Slinger hasn't been in BB while I've been here, so I haven't been able to collect my winnings, but I shall jolly well write to claim them. Oh, if only I could see his face when he learns he must now stump up $500!

My bride, Rose, is a ripping girl, and unlike your Violet, I doubt she'll miss her people as her mother is a veritable gorgon. A crashing snob, too. The haughty maternal does not disguise she thinks her precious daughter could have done considerably better than Yours Truly, and she makes it plain not only that she thinks I am an utter bounder to have snatched her only child, but also that said child is nothing but a terrific ingrate and terribly disloyal to go so far away from her – she's a widow, and determined to extract much more than her full portion of rightful sympathy for it. Thank God I'm separated from her by half the globe, and I'm sure my Rose thinks the same.

I know penmanship could be, to you, as garlic to a vampire, nonetheless, I would ask you write to let me know how you get along with the wheat and beans and barley in Suffolk.

Yours, Langers

From Frank "Langers" Langham, to Charles "Slinger"
Slightman

What ho, Slinger,

How go things at Relunas? You'll gather from the head of the paper that I'm back from my leave. Alas, I was met by the news Dandy has returned Home. So the Three Musketeers are reduced to two. A pity, and we'll have to put on a bit of a riot to make up for his absence next time we go carousing.

I had a ripping time in England, although not so ripping I regret returning; on the contrary, I'm delighted to breathe once again the tepid and vegetal air of Saramantan. Home! There's no place like it, as they say.

You'll understand if I want to report instanter that I did as you so rashly bet I'd never manage to do during my send-off. What a night! I can remember nothing after I was chaired around the room. And what a piece of luck you and Dandy were both in BB to share it with me. But I mustn't lose myself in thickets of nostalgia. The point is: I proved myself Dandy's equal in the matter of speedy romantic footwork. Yes, old man, I bagged a wife in England, notwithstanding my ugly mug. So, that's $500 you owe me, and don't think I'll let you off the debt just because you were roaring drunk when we shook on it.

My Rose is devoted to me and I think she'll make me very happy. She's awfully sweet and pretty, but not a bit drifty – a cool-headed girl, and I trust she'll be just as robust, resilient and resourceful as she needs to be to make a go of things out here.

I await your amazed congratulations, and your money. My warmest regards to Maude, and I trust young Peter thrives.

Yours, Langers

PS Hollingworth is to tell me tomorrow where I am to be posted.

2

GOVERNMENT HOUSE AND THE CLUB, BB
NOVEMBER 1924

Frank, clueless, wasn't in the least bit worried. Although he'd omitted to tell Rose that when he'd departed Kluanak for Home leave he'd cast aside a *nonya*, a native concubine, and four children he thought of as hers, not theirs, he didn't fret she'd stumble on the truth in BB. He knew well enough the capital was a bubbling pot of rumour and intrigue, but he was confident his bride could not be enlightened by the local gossips, since, thank God, none of them knew a thing about his former life of far-from-monastic bachelordom.

Who was he kidding? There were few, very few, secrets amongst the British community on Saramantan, and many, very many, open secrets. Everybody knew that. And everybody deceived themselves that never mind other people's secrets, their own were safe enough. Poor Frank! When he'd been living with Nony he'd convinced himself geography would keep him safe: Saramantan was a big island; Kluanak was two days upriver from BB; isolation would protect him from wagging tongues and pointing fingers. Or so he'd argued back then. And when he'd visited town he'd been tight-lipped about his domestic affairs; he'd confided in no one at all down the years, debarring only Slinger and Dandy, but they were good fellows and they'd always promised not to tell.

Alas, their promises had been empty, at least once they'd married. Although neither Slinger nor Dandy had ever kept a nonya, in their time they'd both spent plenty of sweat on local girls. But, as Frank had been increasingly insistently aware, in the year before his Home leave, their days of careless pleasure were now behind them. Slinger's Maude, niece of the director of BB's little hospital, had arrived in '21, in need of a husband. She'd quickly decided on Slinger, and that, for him, had been that. Meanwhile, in '22, Dandy, had returned from his own first Home leave after the War with Violet on his arm – she was the daughter of a family long known to his people. Naturally, the two men had sworn their new wives to secrecy and dished Frank's dirt.

After Maude and Violet were in on the skinny, it was only a matter of time. Though both the outstation where Maude still lived, and also the one where Violet had until recently lived, were just as isolated as Kluanak, they too had visited town, now and again, and when they had, they'd chattered. Moreover, Maude, in particular, had quickly developed a network of correspondents on Saramantan. There were gaps in their knowledge, of course – neither Maude, at Relunas, nor Violet, now in Suffolk, knew, for instance, that Frank's native mistress had ever threatened to curse him – and even what they did know they'd always edited freely as they saw fit. Still, the gist of Frank's story – a nonya, children – had slowly drifted up and downriver from them to all the ladies of the island, who'd passed on the scandal to their husbands.

Indeed, for well over a year now, there had been only one Briton anywhere on Saramantan unaware of Frank's transgression:

Mr Hollingworth. He was the head of the SCS, a being god-like in his ability to dispense as he pleased the lives of his officials, and one much feared and disliked by them. In the way of unpopular chiefs everywhere, he was tacitly excluded from the gossip, even when the gossip concerned only trivial matters such as Mrs A's speaking sharply to Mrs B about some nothing-at-all. As to gossip such as a man's keeping of a nonya? Nobody in BB, not even the most incessant rattler, would dream of breathing a word to the chief about something so serious.

And it was serious. However far-flung their postings, Empire builders, and their wives, all understood Britannia ruled more by prestige than by force, ergo her representatives should behave at all times with the utmost propriety. It was pointed out to every new recruit to the Colonial Civil Services that if he took to native women, then that would have an adverse effect on his ability to fulfil his duties: how, he'd be asked, rhetorically, how could a magistrate dispense justice fairly if he were sleeping with a relative of the aggrieved party? Moreover, he'd be given a standard letter warning of the official disgrace and ruin which would certainly follow should he enter into arrangements of concubinage with females belonging to the native populations.

Yes, for Empire builders concubinage meant the sack. In theory. In practice these things were generally not noticed, if no one drew attention to them, and concubinage, though officially disallowed, was tolerated, in some places even almost sanctified by custom – the custom of the concubine-keepers, if not that of the concubines. But in Mr Hollingworth's colony? No. No, he firmly believed that if the white man's burden was to save the native from the consequences of his childishness, then the white woman's burden was to save the white man from going native, and, certainly, he was not a man to bend the rules or to turn a blind eye to nonyas. Granted, it was dashed difficult to stamp out such entrenched immorality, dashed difficult, but that, he thought, was no reason not to try.

It was mid-morning, and Mr Hollingworth had spent the last hour touring a school with his Native Education Officer, but as he walked back to his office, his thoughts turned from the teaching of chemistry in Malay to the vexing problem of filling the DO's post at Kluanak. The post Langham had vacated in April was still unfilled, and though it couldn't be helped, Mr Hollingworth felt the irregularity to be something of a personal affront. Still, he commended himself, with a tight little smile, it wouldn't remain unfilled much longer.

Mr Hollingworth's office was the biggest and the most imposing in the whole grandiose pile that was Government House. It was entered through a smaller office occupied by his secretary, Mr Pinner, a middle-aged man with a mournful air and a neat toothbrush moustache. Now Mr Hollingworth, his own white moustache voluminous and curling, paused by Mr Pinner's desk. "Don't forget Langham's coming in this morning," he said, and then he added, with his customary casual authority, "I'm posting the fellow back to Kluanak, don't you know."

For a moment Mr Pinner felt cold, despite the dripping heat: though there was still no DO at Kluanak, he hadn't expected this. During the War there had been no new men travelling out to

Saramantan from England, indeed for much of it no travel at all between the colony and the motherland, so while it had lasted, those already in place had found themselves stuck in their posts. But the War had been over these past six years and, despite the lingering lack of manpower, for the past two or three years things had reverted to the peacetime norm. And in peacetime DOs gave up their postings when they took Home leave; on their return they were assigned new ones. Since his appointment in '13, Langham had completed two much-extended terms at Kluanak. For him to be sent back for a third time would be unprecedented, as far as Mr Pinner knew.

But that wasn't why he now felt as if an ice cube were melting down his back: the new Mrs Langham! Mrs Langham's feelings! Mrs Langham's dignity! The dignity and the feelings of an Englishwoman!

Manifestly, Mr Hollingworth knew nothing of Langham's quondam domestic arrangements – and Mr Pinner really didn't fancy enlightening him. Notwithstanding the chief missed so much, he prided himself on having his finger on the pulse; it was his boast nothing happened in his colony except he knew about it. Only a fool would now say: bit of a rum do, sir, but there's something you should know about Langham's former set-up at Kluanak. Or so thought Mr Pinner. And not forgetting betraying another fellow to the chief would be a rotten thing to do. Still, Mr Pinner steeled himself, and he dared to venture, "Back to Kluanak? Langham may not like that, sir."

Mr Hollingworth bestowed upon his secretary an arctic stare.

"I'm not offering him a choice," he said, and then he walked through into his own office, closing the door behind him.

As Mr Pinner stared at the chief's closed door, he wrung his hands above his blotter: when Langham arrived, should he take it upon himself to warn him what was doing? But how could he? He was horribly aware he wasn't supposed to know a thing about Langham's nonya, the children, all that. So how could he pipe up: a word in your ear, Langham ... The poor fellow would be humiliated to learn his life was fodder for gossip. Mr Pinner shuddered: it would be more than dashed awkward, it would be too ghastly for words, letting on that he knew what he knew full well he wasn't supposed to know. In any case, it was none of his business, this whole hugger-mugger: he shouldn't interfere in what didn't concern him. Let Langham speak if he would! As for him? Best to keep his head down. Yes, reiterated Mr Pinner, as he reached for a manila folder from his in-tray, it would best this morning to keep his head down and get on with things.

A little later, Mrs Pinner, a timid, mousy woman, was trying not to feel too intimidated by Mrs Alford. A couple of nights back, both women had been introduced to Rose over bridge at the Club, and now they had run into each other again, at this same Club – there weren't many other places to go in BB. It was a jolly little place, at the centre of British social life, housed in a charming white-painted bungalow, with an arched and airy verandah all around, set in the middle of an immaculately maintained garden and occupying a hilltop site that gave good views of the town.

Mrs Alford and Mrs Pinner had come upon each other in what was rather grandly called the reading room. Though it was lined by walls of mouldering books, little reading took place in it and the rule of silence was rarely enforced. As usual, Mrs Alford wanted to chat, with purpose. She was a woman all in shades of straw, but her personality was forceful. She lived for the Club, and for seeing and gossiping about other people, and now she was quite determined to fillet the question of the moment amongst all but one of the ladies of BB: was or wasn't the new Mrs Langham aware that before he'd married her, Mr Langham had kept a nonya?

Mrs Pinner was the exception: gossip made her as uncomfortable as an unwelcome caress; she didn't in the least want to speculate about the Langhams, but she couldn't think how to say so without appearing most frightfully rude. And she could not disregard the social necessity of flattering Mrs Alford whenever the chance arose – the old trout had been in Saramantan since the turn of the century, and her husband, nearing retirement, was the head of the Forest Service, meaning she was amongst the most senior wives of the colony.

Mrs Alford swept back a strand of her hair, which had come loose from her bun.

"Even if he didn't properly own up, he must have given her some idea, don't you think?" she boomed, in her hearty way. "Novels to read. Highly romantic and unreliable, but hinting she should at least accept the existence of nonyas."

Novels? thought Mrs Pinner. Stories full of exotic temptresses with starry eyes and jetty tresses? She gazed at the bookshelves a moment. When she'd come out a bride before the War she'd certainly had a romantic view of Malaya, she supposed, but for sure she hadn't known a thing about nonyas. Not a thing. John had told her about them only when he'd had to, after she'd learned of their existence from other wives and had confronted him. He'd had a devil of a job to persuade her he'd never kept a nonya in his own bachelor days; they'd had quite a scene about it.

"Accept nonyas?" she echoed, uncertainly. "It would have turned me upside down if I'd learned when I arrived John had once kept a native girl."

Mrs Alford felt – she very strongly felt – that this was unutterably wet. She bestowed on Mrs Pinner a condescending smile.

"But it's such an eminently sensible arrangement. No need to create about it."

Mrs Pinner let a beat elapse, and then she both reproved and just slightly taunted, "I suppose you're right."

Mrs Alford felt nettled. Mrs Pinner's self-effacing manner was a lot of bosh, she thought. Indeed, she suspected Mrs Pinner of thinking she was better than the rest of them in BB, though why she should think so she didn't know. In retaliation, she said, stiffly, "She must be reasonable. If she doesn't know now he kept a nonya, then, when she learns about it she'll just have to accept it as something that was there, and happened, and is past."

Mrs Pinner thought the past was never past; the past was always present. But she didn't say so. And nor did she correct: *if* she learns about it. In the steaming cauldron of Saramantan there could be no doubt that if Mrs Langham were now ignorant of the truth she wouldn't remain so much longer.

"Although I suppose the discovery he's a father may take a

little bit of sorting out?" She suggested.

Mrs Alford considered the point a moment.

"There's that," she conceded.

Mrs Pinner imagined her own daughters, Emma and Harriet, whom she'd left in the care of their *amah*, their nurse, at home. When she'd first arrived in Malaya, and she and John had visited bachelor households together, then if she'd heard a baby crying not far off, she'd believed what she was told: this was the cook's child. You fool! She disparaged now, the cook's child! The nonyas never appeared, of course – it saved a lot of embarrassment if they remained out of sight – but that scarcely excused her gullibility.

"Difficult for her," she said, "if she's easily shocked by this sort of thing."

Over at Government House, Frank was dreadfully nervous. Mr Hollingworth had kept him waiting a disconcerting fifteen minutes, so by the time he was summoned unto the presence, his nerves felt all unstrung. Now, as he shook the chief's hand, he did so hope his appearance measured up. Once, one wringing evening before an official reception, he'd been foolish enough to remark to the chief he wished he could dress for dinner in the native toggery of *baju*, jacket, and sarong, loose and light, rather than in a stiff and starchy shirt with a scratchy collar. Mr Hollingworth, his white dinner jacket his only concession to the closeness of the equator, had looked most unimpressed.

"I make no surrender," he'd said. "The very best way for an Englishman to nurture the proper pride he should have in himself is by dressing properly for dinner."

Hence, today, Frank had taken great pains: he was smart in spotless white; his shirt was white; his ducks; his patent leather shoes.

Mr Hollingworth was generally more on the lookout for chances to put a man in his place, than to put him at his ease, so it didn't worry him he had a limited fund of chit-chat. Small talk? He even avoided the Club, where he'd feel compelled to lower himself to the semi-official, because he was above that sort of thing. But since there was now a glaringly obvious topic to hand, he saw no reason not to avail himself of it. Men of the SCS were not permitted to marry until they had completed at least two four-year stints in the administration, and even after that they could marry only with his permission; last April, before Langham had left for his much-postponed Home leave, and with the identity of his bride-to-be as yet unknown, he'd asked for such permission in general, and in advance; Mr Hollingworth had granted it. So, as Langham settled himself in the chair on the wrong side of the shiny expanse of his uncluttered mahogany desk, he unbent a little, and said, "Took advantage of my permission, and married, I hear?"

Well, this was all right, Frank thought.

"Yes. Rose is looking forward awfully to being introduced to you, sir."

Mr Hollingworth did not bat back, *and I to her*. A bachelor, he himself was quite content to traverse the terrain of his life alone.

"Good, good, better by far to marry a white girl when you can, and to bring her out to fulfil the wifely duties."

Frank had no need to ask: better by far than what, sir? He was a little uncomfortable at the chief's allusion to native concubines, but he replied, cheerily enough, "One must never forget one is an Englishman."

Mr Hollingworth, safely from Surrey, knew Frank had been born on Saramantan, and he smiled a smile that wasn't a smile.

"Quite, quite. I take an exceedingly dim view of young men out here taking native women as companions."

Frank blinked, but he didn't miss a beat, "Oh, absolutely, sir."

"Connections of that nature I think unseemly. An affront to Britain's dignity."

Frank's complacency wobbled a little. Was it possible Mr Hollingworth were toying with him? Had the chief lit upon the truth about Nony and the brats? But how? Frank was blowed if he knew. Still, he spoke more warily than he had before, "Quite so, sir."

Mr Hollingworth nodded vigorously.

"Englishmen abased! And faced with an Englishman's abasement, you may be very sure the natives under his charge will withdraw from him their respect. What follows? I'll tell you: chaos."

Christ! With his inner eye, Frank saw an image of Nony's face condense from the air in front of him; it hung there, like the mask of a ghost ... Still, disconcerting apparitions could go to hell! He pulled himself together, sharpish.

"Well said, sir." He shifted in his seat and he made a nervous, and unwise, stab at jocularity. "Although perhaps a man should be free to make a fool of himself if he chooses."

Mr Hollingworth looked at him as if he were something unpleasant he'd only narrowly avoided eating – a sandwich spread with fish paste past its best, perhaps.

"Not at all. A man is unworthy of the SCS if he lets a native temptress make a damn fool of him. I cannot allow it."

Frank reddened, and swallowed. He couldn't think of anything to say so the silence stretched, like the rubber which was such a mainstay of the local economy.

Mr Hollingworth was used to young men becoming tongue-tied in his presence, but he couldn't let this dragging silence drag much longer; he had important things to do. He picked up, and needlessly squared off, a neat sheaf of papers lying on the desk just in front of him.

"Enough of this. No doubt you want to know where you're next to be posted?"

Frank felt momentarily giddy with deliverance.

"I do, rather, sir. And Rose is ever so keen to know."

"I'm sure she is," said Mr Hollingworth. "Well, you can tell the little woman you're taking her back to Kluanak."

Frank was aware his old post remained vacant, but he'd no more anticipated this than had Mr Pinner. His eyes widened – went very wide. Christ! To think of seeing Nony again! He flinched to remember, really for the first time in months, both her and her stupid hoodoo. And what of his wife? Rose! Oh, Rose!

"What?" he baulked. "Going back?"

Mr Hollingworth looked disapproving.

"Unusual, I grant."

"I assumed I'd get a new posting. I assumed you'd send some new fellow to Kluanak."

Mr Hollingworth didn't care tuppence what Frank had assumed. He bestowed upon his subordinate a glittering glance.

"Nobody to send. Even now the Colonial Office can scarcely get anyone out. You know that."

Frank gulped, and his inner eye again started conjuring images. This time he saw the path along the river from the DO's bungalow at Kluanak to the *kampung*, the native village. He imagined Rose and Nony walking that path from opposite directions. Pausing. Appraising each other. He imagined recognition passing wordless between his wife, and his quondam nonya; recognition flaring dangerously bright in Rose's eyes ... Christ!

"But, sir, I've already had two terms there. Extended terms, too."

Mr Hollingworth gave Frank another frigid stare.

"Are you questioning my judgement?" he asked, his voice a warning.

"Not at all, sir. But ..." Frank floundered for a moment, and then he clutched for the only straw that came to mind. "But, sir, Kluanak isn't a place where an ambitious man can make his mark."

Mr Hollingworth had never considered Langham particularly ambitious. He raised one eyebrow.

"Come, come, three hundred square miles in your power."

Three hundred square miles of nowhere, thought Frank – not that imagining Kluanak's great expanse of barely inhabited jungle explained why he could now feel sweat pooling beneath his armpits, and trickling down his back. Still he persevered with his line; he had to, he could think of no other.

"I don't want to get stuck, sir, and there must be somewhere else I could go?"

"Where do you have in mind?"

Frank ignored the chief's facetiousness. He knew Dandy's district had been amalgamated with the neighbouring one. Nonetheless, "Perhaps I could have Taman Juah."

Mr Hollingworth frowned to be reminded of that idiot Dabney-Dent's irresponsible and untimely desertion of his post. "Damned fool!" he said. "Dabney-Dent. No loss to the Service in the long run, but mark my words: he'll live to regret letting his little woman wear the trousers."

"Yes," said Frank. "But Taman Juah?"

"Cooper's managing perfectly well."

Frank thought: blast Cooper! He said, "Then perhaps I could do something here? In BB?"

"There are no openings at present."

"Perhaps someone would be willing to exchange postings with me?"

Mr Hollingworth was much amused by this novel suggestion. "Gregson, perhaps?" he said, again speaking facetiously. Gregson was chief inspector of police on Saramantan.

Frank knew he should stop arguing, but he couldn't help himself.

"But ... Rose!"

Mr Hollingworth's eyes momentarily sparkled with icicle humour at the folly of love-struck young men.

"My dear fellow!" he said. "You worry for your wife's safety? You think upriver is dangerous for white women? What? The climate, is it? Fevers? How touchingly uxorious. But this isn't the Victorian era. We know very well now how to cope." He made a steeple of his fingers under his chin. "It can't be the headhunters, can it? You know Saramantan's peaceful now, even the deepest interior. You know it's years since the headhunters gave any real trouble at Kluanak."

"I wasn't thinking of Rose's head, sir. But at Kluanak she'll be light years from the nearest white woman."

Mr Hollingworth didn't try to hide his astonishment.

"You can hardly expect me to arrange the affairs of Saramantan in order to furnish your wife with amiable society. The little woman will just have to cope, that's all." He again picked up, and squared off, the neat sheaf of papers on his desk. He didn't look at Frank as he said, "I don't think there's anything else, thank you."

Frank and Rose had arranged that after his interview with Mr Hollingworth, they would meet for *tiffin* – luncheon – at the Club. The Long Bar, on the upper floor, was indeed a long one, of polished mahogany, and the shelves running the length of the wall behind it were as well stocked with bottles as any bar in London. Native barmen, very smart in red sarongs, white bajus with shiny brass buttons, and jaunty red caps, mixed drinks for assorted servants of Empire. All the tipplers were male, as ladies were not admitted to the Long Bar. Some of the drinkers were growing rowdy, in groups, some of them were solitary and morose. Not so very long ago, the fans that stirred the cloying air had been hand-operated by servants kept for just this purpose, but now they were electric, though they revolved so slowly they may as well not have been.

Frank had positioned himself well away from anybody else, to deter conversation, and directly under a fan, in the hope, more or less unrealised, of a cooling breeze. He was quickly becoming sozzled. Now he picked up his tumbler and downed a stiff three fingers of neat whisky in one burning swallow. Hell! Why hadn't he told Rose about Nony and the brats? He didn't know why he hadn't, really; he hadn't ever precisely decided to keep mum, he didn't think, he'd just never got around to speaking, that's all. Why'd he been so reticent? Rose wasn't a simpleton; she must know he'd had women before her. Indeed she must have been grateful one of them had known what they were doing on their wedding night, and no sensible egg would be jealous of what a fellow had got up to before he'd met her. For goodness' sake! Before he'd married, he'd lived with a woman; what was so terrible about that? It was better than visiting cat houses at every chance. Then again, after he'd safely arrived in England, he'd as good as forgotten his nearly-wife and his disreputable little family in the jungle. He now felt their connection was not with him, but with some other man; their reality seemed to him to be more akin to the reality of people from the eighteenth century than that of a woman who'd shared his bed, or of children he'd fathered. Why should he have risked the most frightful stink by admitting to his bride a former connection with shadows? Why, when he'd been so sure there wasn't the slightest chance she'd ever learn those shadows even flitted? But now? Now, when he must so soon take her to Kluanak? Christ! What on earth was he going to say? Because he must speak instanter, he knew that ... Oh, God! Rose would be so much angrier, so much more aggrieved than she need have been, for having been kept so long in the dark. She'd feel as if she'd been played for a fool.

When Rose arrived at the Club she was disappointed her husband was not waiting for her, all ready with the news of where they'd soon be setting up home. They'd arranged to meet in the foyer. The area was dotted with rattan sofas blooming with colourful cushions, but she would have felt self-conscious sitting there alone, where anybody passing could see her, so she wandered into the little reading room, intending to find a chair where she could be inconspicuous as she flipped through one of the magazines to which the Club subscribed – they were six weeks out of date before they even arrived from London, but no matter.

Mrs Pinner and Mrs Alford were just leaving the reading room as Rose entered. Mrs Alford was delighted by the encounter: what a stroke of luck! She took Rose's arm and she did her best to ooze warmth.

"We're going to the verandah. Do join us!"

"I can't. I'm meeting Frank. He's going to tell me where we're to be posted."

Mrs Alford was not about to let slip this chance to have another go at discovering what, if anything, Mrs Langham knew about her husband's past.

"How marvellous. Well, come and have a quick lime juice

with us before he arrives and we head home for tiffin – so terribly refreshing."

The three women walked together from the reading room out onto the verandah. Here they chose chairs giving a view over the Club's beautifully kept garden – it was intended as an approximation of an English country garden, but the vegetation was far too bounding and lushly exuberant to disguise that this was the tropics, and not the Home Counties.

Mrs Alford summoned one of the waiters and ordered the terribly refreshing lime juices. As soon as they'd been served, she began her fishing.

"We're all thrilled Frank returned from Home with you as his bride."

Rose thought Mrs Alford was looking at her with an archness that was quite unnecessary.

"So am I."

"What has he told you of life here?"

"Oh, heaps of things."

"He's explained it's lonely for our bachelors, tucked away on their jungle outstations?"

"He says he's so glad he won't be lonely any longer."

Mrs Alford raised her eyebrows in a way Rose thought affected.

"There are of course ... distractions."

"Yes," nodded Rose. "Frank says he often takes his gun and goes for a tramp in the jungle, and now he's got someone to play he's looking forward awfully to a game of tennis, assuming there's a court, of course."

Mrs Alford took a long, slow sip of her lime juice; she kept her shrewd gaze on Mrs Langham's face as she did so. Well, she thought, if she did know, then this young person was an actress worthy of the stage – and plainly she did not wish to let on that she knew. Which was such a pity, for it meant that she, Mrs Alford, could not do as she so dearly wished to do: offer herself as a sympathetic confidante, should Mrs Langham need to unburden herself of worries about her husband's former liaison. She had already prepared her invitation: she would point out that she was an older woman and one long experienced in the ways of the East. And the ways of the East were not the ways of Medway Park, she'd say, if Mrs Langham ever gave her the chance.

Meanwhile, Mrs Pinner thought it certain Mrs Langham was as oblivious to the existence of nonyas as she had been when she'd first arrived, and she felt excruciated. She looked at the newcomer through eyes full of anguish. The horror of it, she thought. The horror of being compromised by a so-called secret everybody knew but you. It was too ghastly. Oh, to be talked about, and not to know that you were being talked about! She felt she ought to find some way of conveying to Mrs Langham the truth. And yet how could she be the one to importune, or trample? They scarcely qualified even only as casual new acquaintances, and then again, what if Mrs Langham were a woman who preferred not to know? That she herself should hate to be ignorant of some dark secret that, unbeknownst to her, shadowed her entire life, did not mean that every other woman should hate to be kept in ignorance, too. Perhaps Mrs Langham preferred evasion over confrontation, lies over the truth?

Rose glanced from Mrs Alford to Mrs Pinner. They were each looking at her in a different way, and yet she thought that each of them was looking at her in a way which was awfully strange. She rather wondered whether there may be some meaning she was missing here? Would it be rude to ask: is there something you two wish to say to me? She took a breath, preparing to risk it, but before she could speak, Frank called out to her in a thick and heavy voice. She turned, and she saw her husband approaching; he was swaying across the verandah with the telltale care and deliberation of a man for whom the ground had become unsteady.

Yes, by now Frank was drunk – but not stinking drunk. He was not beyond regretting, at first, that he should find Rose in company. Oh, Mrs Pinner was all right, he granted, but that notorious rattler, Mrs Alford, was absolute poison.

But half a minute! It occurred to him, through the fog of his blurred consciousness, that his regret was misplaced: he couldn't possibly tell Rose what he must tell her in front of any witness, and certainly not in front of an astute and nosy busybody like Mrs Alford; her presence gave him the perfect pretext to delay the horror of confessing.

Such was his relief at the reprieve that Frank was all whisky-fuelled bonhomie as he reached Rose and her companions.

"Ah, ladies, ladies," he said, with an exaggerated, and not fully successful, care not to slur his words. Alas, he could do nothing about his eyes, which were glazed with alcohol, nor about the boozy fumes he wafted with every exhalation.

Neither Mrs Alford nor Mrs Pinner was particularly judgemental: almost everybody in the British community of

Saramantan drank like a fish: the heat, the loneliness, the boredom, the easy availability of booze, its cheapness, its perceived medicinal advantages. But Mrs Alford, for one, doubted that Mrs Langham, newly married, newly arrived from Home, and so still in thrall, probably, to the high standards of Home, would be quite so lenient. She swivelled her head once, twice, from Mr to Mrs Langham, and then she sat back, preparing to enjoy the show.

Rose was staring at her husband. Her mind flew to her mother's beastly letter: the one about that silly bride who'd discovered, too late, her husband was a committed sot. Her skin prickled all over as it occurred to her that *this* was the meaning Mrs Alford and Mrs Pinner had been attempting to semaphore a moment ago, that *this* was the reason for their mysterious looks. The two ladies had been attempting to tell her that her new husband drank. That she'd married a drunkard. It was too humiliating! Must she now face that Mummy had perhaps had a point? Horrors! But what, really, did she know of Frank? Of his inclinations and habits? Oh, it was mortifying! Worse: it was frightening.

But never mind any of that; Rose, proud, was determined not to let on to her distress. She wanted to hiss at Frank: How could you? Drunk, before luncheon? I hope this is not the common way with you. But instead she summoned her resources and she affected a radiant smile.

"Dearest!" she cried, "What did Mr Hollingworth say? Where are you to be posted? Tell me! Tell me! I'm on tenterhooks to know."

Frank prevaricated as best as he was able: he pulled over a chair as slowly as a man of eighty; once he'd lowered himself into it, he waved over one of the waiters and asked for a glass of water; he took his handkerchief from his pocket, shook it out showily and used it to mop his face, which was sweaty with drink, heat and nerves combined. And then, at last, he spoke.

"I'm posted back to Kluanak."

Mrs Alford and Mrs Pinner both stiffened. Mrs Pinner was filled with pity. Poor Mrs Langham. And, yes, poor Mr Langham, too, he must be distraught. What a rotten start to their married life. Perhaps John was even now trying to persuade Mr Hollingworth to countermand this dreadful posting. She did so hope so – but, come to think of it, on what grounds? He could scarcely explain to the chief quite how he was putting the cat amongst the pigeons. In any case her husband never liked to meddle and who could blame him for that?

Mrs Alford was electrified. The adoring young bride met on the doorstep by the mistress? My days! No wonder Mr Langham had been hitting the bottle hard. How deliciously unfortunate he should be sent back to Kluanak. Notwithstanding many a bride new to Malaya learned she was replacing a nonya in her husband's bed only after she'd arrived, in all her years in the East she'd never before heard of one being forced, by circumstance, to live in quite such isolation, in quite such close proximity to her predecessor.

"Fancy that!" she said, with relish.

Neither Rose nor Frank paid Mrs Alford any attention: Frank was staring at a monstrous plant, bursting from a flower bed out in the garden, and Rose was staring at him through eyes gradually softening with the confidence, the generosity, and the indulgence, of new love. Oh, she couldn't – she'd never be able to – stay cross with him for long! If he'd been drinking then of course it wasn't habitual; he must have had his reasons, and he did look so miserable, the lamb. Moreover, she knew Mr Hollingworth made him nervous; perhaps his interview had shaken him? Perhaps he even perceived being sent back to Kluanak as some sort of slap, as the chief delivering some sort of obscure rebuke, or punishment?

"So?" she consoled. "That's surely not so bad?"

Frank kept his bleary gaze on the thrusting plant, and though its leaves appeared to him all fuzzy and smudged, he remained sharp enough to remind himself to be careful. Mrs Alford was far too observant for her own good or for anybody else's either; the rattler would pounce on any slip. He again promised himself he'd tell Rose later, of course he would, but for now … but for now … well, for now, let sleeping dogs lie, and the less said the better, and all that. He turned to face his wife.

"You're right," he nodded, and then he fell back on the line he'd earlier used on Mr Hollingworth, for all it had met with so little success. "The old ambition, don't you know. I wanted to stretch myself against somewhere new, that's all."

OUTBOUND MAIL, NOVEMBER 1924
SENT FROM THE DO's BUNGALOW,
KLUANAK, SARAMANTAN

From Rose to Beatrice

Dearest Bumbles,

I trust this finds you well – I must trust it, since I cannot know it, having received no mail at all from anybody since I left Singapore, so I now grow quite desperate for news, and though I have barely got here I feel compelled to write to ask for it.

As to the question: where is here? Let me direct you to the address at the top of this paper: Kluanak! The significance of the name may escape you, but Frank and I have finally arrived at our outstation, and this backwater I must henceforth call home, even though what I see around me now is nothing but foreign.

Of course, there's nothing foreign to Frank hereabouts. Indeed, far from being strange to him, Kluanak is the same place where he served his last two terms, so if he is now bewildered it is at being sent back, and not at finding himself living in a riddle. My poor lamb is awfully cut-up about returning – he was awfully subdued on the way upriver, at times even almost gloomy. He says this district offers too few opportunities for a man of his energy, drive and ambition so he wants a bigger challenge. A matter of visibility, too, he says – visibility to the bigwigs in BB who will determine his future prospects, for he doesn't want to be just another Englishman doing his duty in a place where no one who was anyone could want to be.

Alas, I know so little of the ways of the SCS or of those of

Malaya that when my husband's mood begins to darken I scarcely know what to say, and feel myself become a little choky – I do trust you'll say none of this to your mother, for she would certainly talk to mine and the last thing I want is for Mummy to think that Frank is disappointed, or that I am.

In any case, Frank must, I hope, cheer up now we are actually here. We arrived only this afternoon, from which you'll gather I make great haste in writing, a necessary haste, for on their departure tomorrow the boats that brought us here will carry back to BB the official letter announcing our arrival. They leave at first light and I dare not have my own letters miss them, because Frank says it will be hard on Christmas before he again sends a boat downriver, on a mail run.

Perhaps you are surprised I must rely on boats if I am to communicate with the outside world? We shall have no postman here, my dear, no newspaper boy, no morning delivery and no afternoon delivery either. Instead, the coasting steamer that brought us from Singapore calls at BB the third Thursday of each month, and Frank has told me he will each month make sure to send a boat to meet it, to collect from the captain our letters from the great wide world beyond our little outstation. In this way we will receive also the Singapore papers, English newspapers and magazines, terribly out of date, and Frank's official correspondence from Government House.

After it has called at BB, the steamer continues to Penderang, the only other town on Saramantan, on the northern coast. There it turns around and heads back to Singapore, putting in at BB on the way, not a week after it has left from there. Frank says he will likely as not send a boat with our outbound mail to meet the steamer on its homebound run, so our letters can get off to Singapore as quickly as possible. I must say it all seems to me pretty hit-and-miss and laborious, and even when I am not as rushed as I am now, I will have only a brief window to write my replies if I want them to meet that steamer.

With all my talk of boats and rivers, are you asking yourself: what of the roads? I should explain the jungles of Malaya are everywhere so densely overgrown and tangled, in short, so frightfully jungly, that the rivers here are the roads: everybody uses them as they move about, and boats must do here instead of horses, carts, buses, trams or motors.

Indeed, we had such mountains of *barang* – luggage, see how I adopt already the local lingo? – Frank ordered two boats to bring us upriver. Do not imagine boats such as one may see on the Thames, for these were in the native style, so you must picture some type of large wooden punt, or canoe, which vessel is here called a perahu.

Each perahu had an awning woven from palm leaf, but even sitting beneath ours the glare of the sun and the heat and humidity were enervating. I confess I felt quite feeble as we were rowed along and I worried submerged snags may at any moment tip our boat over, and us into the water. Still, when I put from my mind the heat, my fear of capsizing, and the unwanted attention of mosquitoes and other flying biting things, it was rather romantic to glide through the water, hearing nothing but the splash of the oars and the assorted animal sounds of the jungle. Before I arrived, I imagined the jungle as a silent place, but wherever did I get that idea? It's one of the noisiest things I ever heard! A symphony of screeching, cawing, grunting, howling, chirping, sawing and whining – when I remarked on the racket, Frank chaffed me that henceforth the sound of a monkey being throttled by a python would be a natural accompaniment to breakfast.

Debarring the regiments of annoying insects, the wildlife responsible for the din was most interesting and entertaining. From my seat in the perahu I saw monkeys galore, and colourful birds and butterflies like trembling jewels. I half-hoped to see, and half-feared seeing, a tiger, but Master Stripes kept himself to himself and refused to appear – Frank said if he had risked it, he'd have seized his gun and shot him. He added if I wanted danger I should know crocodiles lurked beneath us. Later, he pointed out a cobra swimming in the water, making elegant S-shapes as it moved, and deadly as death itself, he said.

I am told that tomorrow it will take the boats only seven hours to go down the river from here to BB, but it took two days and a night to come up, against the current. We camped last night on a mud flat formed in a bend in the river. I must say I did not like imagining the creatures which may be observing us and even the forest itself seemed to have its watchful eyes. The crew had brought with them servings of steamed rice wrapped in banana leaves. This rice (cold), washed down with water (warm from the sun) served as our rather unpalatable evening tiffin – *evening tiffin* is what we call *dinner* here.

As for sights along the way, I saw barely anything but trees. I think there can be at most half a dozen native villages all the way from BB, and we saw no evidence at all of Europeans until, in the late afternoon, we at last pulled up at the landing stage below our bungalow, which sits proud a little way back from the edge of the river – *bungalow* is what we call all the houses here, so do not think of those little boxy things now sprouting in every seaside resort at Home.

The river here does not have a proper bank, instead it drains into the land through a swampy, brackish margin filled with mangrove trees which grow directly in the murky water, so they seem to be walking upon it, their trunks held aloft on tangles of roots.

With which walking trees I'll leave you, as I must write to Mother.

Your loving cousin, Rosebud

From Rose to Daphne

Dearest Mummy,

I have at last arrived at the outstation that is henceforth to be my home: Kluanak. It's the funniest thing, but it's the very same outstation Frank quit in April, when he travelled from Malaya to England and to me. On our arrival the servants' astonishment that their new *tuan* (master) was the same man as their old one was comical to behold, although needless to say they were delighted Frank is returned to them. They made a great fuss of him, and also a quite flabbergasted one of me. As Frank introduced me as his wife, they seemed so absolutely astounded you'd almost think they knew nothing at all of the institution of marriage. Such was their amazement I could only suppose they'd none of them ever seen a white woman before, and Frank agreed they may find whiteness linked to femininity a novelty.

We have six of these servants, so you can see it's quite a household I'll have to manage. They are all men: cook (Cookie), gardener, day watchman, night watchman, whom I've not yet met, water-carrier, and the houseboy (Boy – not a boy at all, but a grown man with two wives and five children, I'm told). Boy has tolerable English or I don't know how I'd get on, since none of the other servants speaks a word, and my Malay improves annoyingly slowly – in any case the Saramantan dialect is nothing like the Malay of my grammars, which I think most awfully unfair to me. We have no need of either a groom, or a driver, as we have here neither horses nor a motor – I saw motors in Singapore, but Frank says there's not a single one on Saramantan, not even for the luckiest of blighters.

The kitchen is in an outhouse hut entirely separate from the bungalow. There are quarters for the servants next to it, but they are now used as storerooms, as jammed with all sorts of junk as any attic in England, as none of the servants lives in. No, they live in the local *kampung* (village)*. They arrive very early, before we are awake, and they go home in the evening after they have cleared away our dinner – Cookie and Boy in any case. I expect the water-carrier slopes off earlier, and the gardener of course cannot work after dark. Meanwhile the day and night watchmen each works a twelve-hour shift, they change over at about 7.30 each morning and evening.

I cannot think you'll approve this living-out, and nor do I; it seems to me the servants have been accustomed to take advantage of Frank in this matter, but he says let them be, everybody is used to the arrangement by now and it's no use upsetting the apple cart by changing things.

Boy and the others have evidently been terribly slack whilst the bungalow has been unoccupied – empty since Frank left in April – as everywhere I look I see evidence of sloppiness, disrepair, mess and dirt. And not forgetting bats hanging upside-down from the verandah's rafters, like hellish fruit, and everywhere multitudes of horrible little house lizards who cry *geh-ko*, *geh-ko* all day and all night. There is nothing to be done about either bats or lizards, I don't suppose, but their droppings are everywhere, which less than thrills me.

Well, the servants will soon learn what it is to work under a mistress' firmly guiding hand, that's all! Mistresses out here are called *mems* – memsahibs, you know – and to help me make a good fist of being one, I'm reading *The Mem's Own Handbook*, a useful little guide I bought in Singapore.

Your fondest daughter, Rose

*PS our local kampung is called *Kluanak*, just like the district, although whether the village gave the name to the district, or the other way around, I don't know.

From Frank "Langers" Langham to Robert "Dandy" Dabney-Dent

What ho, Farmer Dandy,

This is just a chit to let you know where I'm posted, so you'll know where to write to me, should you so choose. And – Oh Lord! – look at the address! Do you believe it? I can scarcely believe it myself, but it's true: I'm posted back to Kluanak. Do you tremble for me? I certainly tremble for myself. Wish me luck, and do write back if you want to know how things turn out here, as I don't much fancy squandering stamps on you unless you bestir yourself to return the favour.

Yours, Langers

From Frank "Langers" Langham to Charles "Slinger" Slightman
What ho, Slinger,
You are a gentleman, and a sport, and I thank you for it – which is to say I received your draft for $500 in the nick of time, the morning I left BB, and I cashed it, instanter.

Less happily, I am not sure I approve you shared my last with Maude. Indeed, I find it hard to summon sympathy in the matter of the "unfortunate altercation", since, to my mind, you brought Maude's wrath entirely on yourself. If you had not shown her my letter, she should never have known you'd bet me $500 I would not find a bride in England. Ergo she would not have been angry with you, either for making such a "disgraceful and intolerable bet" or for wasting "inordinate amounts" of your money on a man who was "no better than he should be". And I must say I think it was rather rotten of you to pass on such an unkind and unjust description of Yours Truly, but from friendship I forgive you.

You are no doubt surprised to receive a letter from Kluanak? But not half so surprised as I am to be here. Yes, old man, Hollingworth, the fathead, got a notion to send me back here and so here I am, and what can I do? Deuced bad luck, it quite gives me the jim-jams to think of Nony and the brats lurking in the kampung. And the worst of it is I can't quite bring myself to spit it all out to Rose. I tell you, I was as miserable as anything all the way upriver from BB, dreading what the future may hold.

Arrival has not much improved my mood. It was dispiriting to see again the sly phizzes of the servants who said goodbye to me last spring. And for their part, they greeted me with theatrical astonishment – not least because they no doubt thought I was dead. Nony's curse, I mean. Notwithstanding you were drunk when I told you the sensational news, I think you must remember the little witch intended to hex me. Though I'm still indisputably here, I'd lay any money she went ahead and hexed her bloomin' socks off.

Mind you, we both know hoodoo is the least of my problems. Alas, as I helped Rose from the perahu, Boy & Co grinned with the obvious and insolent glee of men relishing the dramatic possibilities of my unexpected return with a mem on my arm, a creature certain to annoy and provoke the aforementioned little witch in the kampung. Even Rose noticed their excitement, but fortunately she lit upon the explanation she must be the first white woman they'd ever seen, an error I did nothing to correct, indeed, I encouraged it.

Drat those servants! It's something, I suppose, that I know none of them would ever dare to raise with Rose the subject of my quondam domestic arrangements, even if they had the English to attempt it – which none of them does apart from Boy, a sensible fellow I trust to keep his mouth shut. Still, I'm sure one or other of them has already hot-footed it to inform Nony what's doing. Do you think the crackpot may now try to curse me again? I wouldn't be surprised – and I wouldn't put it past her to try to curse Rose as well.

Even leaving aside Nony's gathering herbs by moonlight malarkey, I cannot doubt she's already plotting ways to make trouble for me, egged on by everybody else in the kampung, I fear. You know how it is: the villagers regard goings-on at the DO's bungalow as a most interesting entertainment, laid on especially for them. Deuced irritating, but then what else do they have to do but stick their noses in each other's business, and in mine?

Keep your fingers crossed for me, and, as ever, remember me to Maude, notwithstanding she thinks me a chump.

Yours, Langers

PS I'm not at all surprised you've heard nothing from that near illiterate, Farmer Dandy. He always did think the only proper use for ink and paper was in the production of the sports pages.

3

THE KAMPUNG, KLUANAK
LATE NOVEMBER AND EARLY DECEMBER 1924

Like every other house in the kampung, the one Frank had provided as a sop to Nony was a windowless, one-room affair, raised on wooden stilts above the ground to protect the inhabitants from flooding, snakes and insects. The frame was of wood, the walls were made from panels of woven *atap* – palm leaf – and the roof was of atap thatch. The dry, shady space beneath the house was called the *ruang*. Here Nony was now squatting beside her youngest full sister, Intan. First Daughter was asleep on a mat by Nony's side, and her three sons were not far off; they were tending a bonfire in which they were baking clay balls to use as ammunition in their slingshots.

Nony was weaving for her house a new wall-panel to replace one that was leaking. There was an enormous bundle of long, slim leaves piled beside her, which she rhythmically plucked up and incorporated one-by-one into her panel. Intan was busy too. She had brought along a basket filled with a local nut called *kerampai*, and her nimble fingers were busy shelling: the oily brown nuts she placed in one shallow basket; the papery shells she tossed into another, she'd use them for cooking fuel later. Now she shelled another nut, and then she bestowed upon her sister a beady look.

"So, you didn't kill him," she accused.

Everybody in the kampung accepted that everybody knew everybody else's business. Indeed, the villagers would have been surprised to learn there were places in the world in thrall to the idea that people may want to keep each other at a distance. So Nony was scarcely taken unawares by her sister's accusation, nor was she resentful of her eager interest in her affairs; nonetheless, she found herself disconcerted. She continued to think of Frank as she always had done, as *baba*, not as *tuan*, and now, at Intan's words, she felt again a portion of the shock she'd first felt yesterday, to learn he wasn't dead. Oh, she'd been so sure he was! Birds were ever messengers of the spirits, and she'd been so sure the wild serpent eagle's dropping of a dead whip snake on to her roof on the festival of *Bulan Penuh*, in the sixth month, had been a sign her curse had worked and Baba had become a ghost. She scowled, and she said, "No, I didn't."

Intan was not deterred by her sister's brusqueness. She continued brightly, "Fancy him coming back here, when he said he wouldn't. Why d'you think he did it?"

"Beats me."

Intan shelled another nut.

"And this mem! It only goes to show you were right at least to try to kill him."

Nony shrugged. She'd never felt abused by Frank whilst she'd been his nonya; she'd never felt like killing him then. But when he'd made it plain he no longer wanted her, she'd of course argued he shouldn't get to enjoy anyone else; obviously, if she couldn't have all the boons that were his to bestow, then no other woman should get her hands on them either. Now, she tugged another long, slim palm leaf from the pile and as she pulled it between her thumb and forefinger she remembered when she'd decided his behaviour warranted a death sentence.

This had been a few evenings before Frank had quit the DO's bungalow for good – or so both he and Nony had thought back then. They'd been sitting together on the verandah at sunset. A slice of orangey red had glowed golden across the sky. The frogs had just started up their nightly chorus. Somewhere, a monkey had given a mournful howl. Nony had been sewing; Frank had been dangling a cigarette in one hand and nursing a whisky in the other.

Nony had put aside her work and she'd steeled herself to broach, yet again, what had by now become the only topic of conversation between them. She'd not asked Frank – she'd never asked him – *can I come with you?* Wherever it was, *Kampung Inggris*, English Town, seemed to her as alien as the moon; she'd no desire to go there. Not to mention she'd known as well as he had it would be a social impossibility for her to accompany him to his lunar motherland, and it had no more occurred to her, than it had to him, that social impossibility was not literal impossibility. No, she'd asked, "Must you abandon me?"

Frank had spread his hands. His cigarette had curved to the left and his tumbler to the right, in an expansively mocking arc.

"Oh, Lord! We've been over and over this. I told you: you'll be all right. You'll have the house, your plot of land."

"I don't want to move back to the kampung, nor into a one-room hut with walls of woven atap."

"I don't suppose you do but you always knew this must end –

it would have ended already if I hadn't got stuck here on account of the War. It's gone on a good deal longer than you can ever have dreamed."

It was true Nony had known all along her position was precarious. Indeed, she'd been convinced Frank would leave her after the births, twenty minutes apart, of their middle children, their identical twin boys, for not even the pawang could tell her which was the good spirit person, and which the bad, so these two were, she thought, as much dangerous curse, as beloved blessing. Still, anticipating being dumped didn't make being dumped any easier.

"But why can't we be together after your leave?" she'd said.

"I've told you: it's over. Be grateful for your ten years of high living."

"I wouldn't mind shifting to your new posting."

"It could be anywhere on the island, miles from here."

"I wouldn't be homesick. And you could so easily send for me once you're back, once you reach wherever it is you go next."

"How many times do I have to tell you: I won't be able to send for you, it's impossible."

"Tuan Simpkins sent for Yati when he moved to Bukit Coklat."

Simpkins had been Frank's predecessor as the DO at Kluanak and Yati had been his nonya.

"Don't drag him into this!"

"Why not? Why won't you be able to do the same? Why won't you be able to send for me?"

Frank's cigarette had by now burned into a long column of

ash. Sulkily, he'd ground it out in the ashtray balanced on the arm of his chair. Christ, he'd thought, Nony did go on so. On and on – it quite wore him down. He was properly fed up with it, and it was dashed unfair: after all it was purely out of consideration for her feelings that he'd kept his plan to himself. His plan to get married during his Home leave, he meant. Yes, it was from kindness he'd kept mum. And this nagging was all the thanks he got. Perhaps he'd been too kind? He probably had. May it not be fairest to Nony to remove all grounds for hope and dreaming? And certainly it would be fairest on himself to shut her up.

Frank had sighed a martyred sigh and he'd given Nony a long-suffering look. In a voice at once both cool and petulant, he'd said, "This endless whining! Whine, whine, whine. Will you put a sock in it if I tell you that whilst I'm on Home leave I intend to find for myself a wife – a proper, English wife."

Intan was unaware her sister had zoned out. She reached for another nut to shell.

"Have you seen her yet?" she asked. "The mem."

Intan's voice yanked Nony back to the present.

"No. Have you?"

"No. But Douri has. He says she's so huge and ungainly it must be like bedding Raksasa Wanita."

Douri was Intan's much older husband, and Raksasa Wanita was the ogre-woman who feasted off the unlucky humans she kidnapped from their homes. Nony shortened a palm leaf by snapping it in two with quite unnecessary violence.

"The fish he spears is up to him."

Intan started to giggle, but then she thought better of it and she turned her giggle into a cough.

For a few moments the sisters worked on in silence, each of them continuing to think about the new mem. Like all the villagers they assumed she knew about Nony. Why would she not? How could she not? On Saramantan, marriage was polygamous if resources allowed and the triangle between the tuan, the mem and Nony wasn't so very different from the triangle between any husband, his first wife and his concurrent second wife. Granted, Nony had only ever been the tuan's convenient wife, but that was detail, and even if he set them up in separate households, how could a man keep from his second wife the existence of his first wife, convenient or not? How, in a kampung where people's houses may as well have had no walls for all the privacy their walls provided? A man would have to have been as blur as a *belalang* to try to keep such a secret. And four children running around? Their father could no more hush up their existence than he could hush up a howler monkey.

Intan popped a nut into her mouth. She chewed it contemplatively. Once she'd swallowed, she said, "D'you think she's terribly jealous of you?"

"The mem?" checked Nony. She gave a bitterly mocking laugh. "Are you jealous of Elephant and Water Buffalo?"

Though the local *padi* fields – rice fields – were wrestled from the jungle only with the greatest difficulty. Intan's husband, Douri, managed to wring from his enough rice to fill numerous rice bowls. Intan, for the moment still childless, was Douri's third wife and by far the youngest of his spouses; for the time being she glowed with the confidence of the favourite. *Elephant* and *Water*

Buffalo were her private names for Douri's two older wives. Now it was her turn to laugh, but her laughter was not at all bitter; it was the casually cruel laughter of a woman at the height of her power, at the expense of sad old bags who were past it.

"You see," said Nony.

"See what? That earlier wives are jealous of later ones, and not the other way around?"

Nony nodded. But then a thought struck her. She tossed her hair.

"Not that I'm jealous of the mem," she said. "I don't covet her husband, in any case."

"And Douri doesn't covet Elephant and Water Buffalo," said Intan, smugly. "How could he? Those two are old and shrivelled. But you're not. That's my point. You're not ancient. You're not as tough and leathery as a dried fish. And I bet she is."

"The mem? Leathery as a dried fish?"

"No, silly. Jealous. Of you. I bet she worries you're why the tuan came back."

Nony gave her sister a disparaging look and she said, with exaggerated patience, "You forget, I tried to kill him. I told him I'd curse him. He must've known I'd go through with it. He must've told his mem all about it, even if the idiot laughed as he spoke. He'd want to puff himself up. A man worth fighting for. Think! She must assume he'd no more want to take up with me now than he would if I really were a dried fish."

Intan twirled her hand airily and engaged in a spot of wishful thinking.

"The cursing stuff? Water under the bridge."

Yes, since the tuan was not only still alive, but, moreover, had returned, Intan had begun building castles in the air. There were obstacles, but – Oh! – wouldn't it be lovely! Her whole family, from her granny, to her littlest cousin, had shared in the spoils when Nony had been the tuan's nonya. Intan herself had revelled in having a sister at the DO's bungalow: a sister who could buy her lengths of machine-made lace, and factory-made cosmetics, and glittery hairpins, and even glitterier pins for her *kebaya*, her blouse, all from the Chinese merchant who sometimes moored his boat at the kampung's landing stage; a sister who furnished her brothers with factory-rolled cigarettes and commercially brewed spirits from the same source; a sister who regularly slipped her tins of condensed milk from her kitchen, and who gave her bags of rice and sugar to take home to their mother, now deceased; a sister who had even been able to hand over to her family a few coins now and then.

Since yesterday, this past of riches had become to Intan a beautiful, if improbable, dream of the future. She looked at Nony through sideways eyes.

"You wouldn't say no, would you," she cajoled. "You wouldn't say no, if he wanted to take up with you again."

What? Nony would jump, if only Frank had the grace to beckon? Intan wasn't ashamed to make this suggestion and Nony didn't go ballistic to hear it. The feminist insistence that a woman should consider her own self-esteem when deciding whether to consort, once more, with a man who'd previously humiliated her. The feminist ban on a woman nicking another woman's man – a ban so often ignored, even in times and places when and where women need not think of men as meal tickets. Love, romantic love, and the lovely idea of it; the lovely idea that a man could be a woman's life in a relationship of equality, in which she was likewise his life. What had any of these to do with subsistence living? On Saramantan, debarring only their closest full-blood relatives, women couldn't afford to treat other women as anything other than vipers, and when men and women married it was because they had a duty to their families and to their clans to procreate. Men took as many wives as they could support because they wanted women to cook for them, weave for them and fulfil all the other one-hundred-and-one day-to-day tasks reserved specifically for women. Women married just the once because they needed a man to fish for them, hunt for them and fulfil all the other one-hundred-and-one day-to-day tasks reserved specifically for men.

Nony plucked up another leaf and she began to weave it into her wall panel. She was certain Baba would never again look at her through come hither eyes; she was positive he wouldn't now want her caresses, but his revenge. And since he had previously applied, in Kluanak, and would no doubt henceforth apply again, a legal code that was very much his own, he could so easily have it. Yes, there were alarmingly many ways in which an antagonistic DO could make a village woman's life hell. Through brooding on that, Nony had already decided her best strategy for dealing with Baba's unfortunate return would be to try to avoid him altogether – him and his wife both. Her plan now was to lie low and hope to avoid attracting either his attention or the mem's. But she didn't say any of this. She said instead, matter-of-factly, "Of course I wouldn't say no. Of course I'd return to Baba's bed given half a chance. But let's stop dreaming, Intan, it isn't going to happen."

Frank was less concerned with how he could readmit Nony to his life, and more concerned, indeed, wholly concerned, with how he could erase her from his life entirely – all without Rose ever having learned of her existence. And far from considering she may wish to avoid him, he simply couldn't get out of his head the idea that she must be out to cause him trouble. Spiteful. That's what she was – and there were so many ways she could cause mayhem. Never mind she couldn't speak English, and Rose's Malay was, for now, quite outstandingly appalling, what if she flaunted herself at the bungalow? Worse: what if she paraded the brats in front of Rose? His traitorous brats with their tattling pale skins; their telltale fine noses; their giveaway light hair. Yes, panicked Frank, if Rose got one look at the brats, then for sure the penny would drop and he'd be for it.

Right-o: the brats must leave the kampung, and so must their mother. Or so Frank had decided: Nony must agree to take the children and move elsewhere – anywhere would do, any other kampung, as long as it was suitably distant. Moreover, he had a plan to make sure she'd toddle as he desired, and now, a few days after his return, he was walking the path from the DO's bungalow to the kampung, intent on setting it in motion. He had told Rose he was off to get a spot of sport in the jungle, and so, as he side-stepped roots and brushed aside tendrils from the vines hanging from every tree, he had a gun slung over his shoulder. He was whistling, but he couldn't quite keep his spirits up: it was sordid work, he couldn't deny it, this saving of his own skin.

Nony was again squatting in her ruang, where she did most of her food preparation – she cooked on a brick grill just beyond the covered area. Her boys, First Son and his twin brothers, Second Son and Third Son, were off laying fish traps in the river, and she was alone, apart from First Daughter, who was pottering about. She prided herself she managed to ensure her children got a taste of chicken every now and again, and she was plucking a cock she'd freshly killed. She'd already decapitated it, and bled it out into a bowl; she'd later use the blood to make delicious blood cubes. She'd soaked her headless, bloodless cock in hot water for a few minutes, and now she was pulling off his wet feathers – bedraggled memories of his so recently ended pomp. She was tossing them into a wooden bucket: once they were dry she'd give them to the pawang who had her uses for them.

First Daughter squealed delightedly, so Nony glanced up from her work. In the same instant she felt both a dart of pleasure to see her daughter chasing a butterfly, and also a thunderbolt of dread to see Baba striding along the path that led through the kampung. He was wearing that silly hat, the one that looked so much like a titty slapped on top of his much-prized, thin-skulled head … He was making a beeline for her house... Alamak! She tried to hope he was coming merely to gloat her curse had failed, and far from being dead he was married now, but she very much feared he was instead coming to exact on her his iron retribution. So much for avoiding him! So much for remaining no more visible to him than an ant on the forest floor! What a fool! She should have expected this; she should have known lying low would be difficult; that

Baba would seek her out.

As Frank covered the final few yards towards Nony's house, he was still whistling, but he fell silent as he dipped into her ruang, which was just high enough to enable him to stand without stooping. He did a double take to see Nony squatting over a bloodied chopping board, on which lay a half-plucked, decapitated cock; there was a bowl of blood next to her and a bucket of feathers too. Flies were thickly swarming about the carnage. Revolted, he turned away and spotted his littlest brat toddling about; she was as naked and as grimy as only a native child could be. He scowled at her; it was ghastly to think this funny little thing could so easily betray him. He turned his back on both of them and made a great show of slipping off his gun. As he leaned it against one of the piles supporting the house, it crossed his mind too late that displaying his gun like this may perhaps tempt Nony to grab it and shoot him. Not that the danger was great; no doubt using a murder weapon as obvious as a gun would be too simple for her taste. He took off his solar topee and tucked it under his arm. Slowly, reluctantly, he turned around.

At last, Nony and Frank met each other's eyes; each of their gazes was as implacable as the other's. For a long moment they were locked into a circuit of warily hostile looking.

Frank thought Nony was far less attractive than he remembered: she was short, even for a native woman; he'd forgotten her stockiness, her sturdiness. Her features were coarser than they ought to be, her eyes smaller, her hair rattier. Her complexion seemed to him now as dark and as dull as recrimination, and she was unkempt too: she looked as grubby as the littlest brat; her sarong and kebaya were more than shabby. As to her mouth? All the local women chewed *sirih*, a concoction of spices and betel that stained their gums and teeth bloody red. Frank could scarcely believe, now, he'd ever brought himself to kiss Nony's discoloured maw.

Nony thought Frank loomed over her like a demon: his pockmarked face was all red and damply shiny. And how greasy it was, his white skin – which wasn't white at all, really, not the way a puff of cloud was white, but some oily fungal-sallow colour you'd normally expect to see on a toadstool. And where his tallow hair was plastered to his head with sweat it looked like congealed goose fat. His khakis were sweaty too, wringing dark in cloud-like patches, and the stalks of his legs, where they descended from his shorts, were disgustingly hairy.

As they appraised each other, like merchants appraising shoddy goods, Frank and Nony both remembered the last time they'd been close enough to reach out and touch the other's strange skin; they both remembered their last, difficult conversation. It had taken place the evening before that misty pre-dawn in which the river had carried Frank away from a load of trouble, as he'd thought, and ever closer to an imminent death for which he'd have only himself to blame, as Nony had thought.

That night, for one last time they'd been sitting together on the verandah at the DO's bungalow. They hadn't lit the paraffin lantern, since the sky was cloudless and the greater lantern of a gibbous moon shone bright. Beyond the verandah's rail, fireflies had flickered in the trees and, all around, the pressing jungle had been its usual night-time racket of creatures mating, gorging, killing, dying.

Frank had been thinking how much he was looking forward to jawing with Slinger, Dandy, and some other fellows in the Club at BB the next day. He'd taken a long drag on his cigarette and he'd said, "Well, old girl, this is it, I suppose. Or almost."

Nony had shaken her head.

"No. You can still agree to send for me, once you return from Kampung Inggris. You can still change your mind."

Not this again! Frank had rolled his eyes, and he'd said, "Must you make things so terribly difficult for me?"

"Tuan Simpkins sent for Yati when he moved to Bukit Coklat."

"Spare me."

"Spare you?" Nony had looked at Frank steadily, through unblinking eyes. "Your fate is up to you."

"Cut out the riddles, old girl."

"I've been to the pawang. She gave me a spell."

Frank had thought: By George! I'll be glad to be shot of all this native mumbo-jumbo.

"I'm all ears."

"It's a curse to ensure you never reach Kampung Inggris."

Despite himself, Frank had flinched.

"A curse? What curse?"

"If I call it down on you, the spirits will ensure you die at sea. Far, far out at sea."

Frank had tried to convince himself this would make a ripping yarn for Slinger and Dandy. Nonetheless, he'd been rattled.

"What? And now you're giving me one last chance to save my

skin? An ultimatum? Unless I agree to send for you after my leave, you'll use this bally spell to do for me?"

Nony had continued to look at him steadily through sorrowless eyes, "Yes."

Frank had thought about lying, then. He could so easily have said: Oh, all right, Nony, you win, after my leave you can join me wherever I'm posted, I promise. She would have believed him, he was sure, she was as credulous as a six-year-old. But he had his pride. If he appeared to crumble in the face of Nony's threats, she'd think he was afraid of her native sorcery. And even if they were about to part, perhaps especially because they were about to part, he couldn't have her thinking that; he couldn't have her thinking she had the upper hand.

So instead of lying, Frank had set to belligerent blustering.

"Look here! We've had a useful arrangement, but tomorrow, it ends. It *ends*. You've no grounds for complaint, we both know I've treated you handsomely."

Nony had shaken her head.

"I will use that magic, Baba," she'd said, "If you leave me tomorrow, I will cast the spell. Death will come for you on the sea. There will be no English wife. Your body will be cast into the depths, cold waters will close over your lifeless head, your eyes will become food for fishes."

Now, half a year or so later, and unexpectedly thrown once more into collision with Nony, Frank remembered how badly he'd had the jumps as he'd crossed the Bay of Bengal on the Homebound P&O. During a particularly bad storm he'd even considered that perhaps Nony's malevolence was such she'd sink the whole damned liner just to be rid of him. What a fool he'd been! What a damned fool ever to have let her hocus-pocus make him uneasy. As for trying to curse him a second time now he was back? He'd like to see her try! What? Her? A sorceress? He swept over her an amused glance: if she had magical powers, then he was the King of Sweden. He thought about taunting: failed to kill me off, you see. But he decided against, he wanted the little fraud to do his bidding, there could be no benefit in crowing.

As for Nony, though she'd withheld from Baba the specific nature of her curse, its gallows gleefulness, meaning it was unlikely he'd worried each time he'd chuckled during the voyage back to Kampung Inggris, she did so hope each time he'd sneezed or coughed he'd asked himself: does this herald something fatal? Still, pride prevented her mentioning her damp squib of magic. She'd paused in her work but now she resumed plucking the cock. Despite her fear that punishment was coming she couldn't bring herself to adopt the cringing manner of a woman trying to dodge her fate. Instead, she challenged, "What are you doing back?"

Frank was painfully aware that the privacy of the kampung was even less than the privacy of a glasshouse, so he kept his voice low.

"Doing?" he said, in his fluent and colloquial Malay. "It's not as if I asked to come. I'm not doing anything. I just got sent." He paused. "Dashed awkward, wouldn't you say?"

Nony made no reply to that.

Frank swiped his forearm across his sopping brow, and, with resigned certainty, he stated, "You know I'm married."

"Your wife must be so eager to meet me."

"Don't flatter yourself! She ..."

Frank had been about to say *she doesn't know a thing about you*. But then, in the nick of time, he realised Nony may not have guessed he'd kept her secret from Rose. Christ! Why hadn't he thought of it sooner? Why had he until now so unthinkingly assumed his quondam nonya assumed his bride knew all about her? Christ! To discover otherwise would present the dipper with a horrible opening. She'd have him over a barrel! Parade the brats in front of Rose just for the spiteful hell of it? No, she could instead threaten havoc for financial gain. She could extort: pay up, or else the brats visit the bungalow ...

Frank's face darkened. He glanced away from Nony, who was looking at him expectantly, and when he glanced back, he did his best to sound robust, in charge, on top of things.

"She thinks all this must be so difficult for you."

Nony was disbelieving and disparaging, but not suspicious.

"Good of her."

Frank scowled at her tone and decided the quicker he got out of here, the better. He'd say his piece and be gone.

"Look, here! I came to say it can be no good for you, or for me, or for her – for any of the three of us – to live all higgledy-piggledy on top of each other. My mem agrees. So I've got a proposal to put to you. Why don't you take the children and move to another kampung? Far away. Somewhere you could make a fresh start, away from ... well, from me, I suppose. Away from the mem and me. Much better for both of you than bumping into each other all over the place. Blushes spared all round."

Nony and Frank were not of one mind on much, but they

were united there was no more reason for parents to consider their children's wishes when deciding what to do about this or that, than there was to consider the wishes of the family livestock. So Nony didn't look aghast and protest: it's outrageous! Never mind what I'd want, how could I ever uproot the children like that? No, she calmly continued plucking tomorrow's dinner and she smiled to herself, just a little. After all, this was quite a turn up. What, Baba was here neither to gloat, nor bent on vengeance, but as a supplicant? He wanted to ask a favour of her, and a big one to boot. Well, well, well ...

"Sorry, but I don't want to move."

"You've changed your tune. Before I left, you were forever telling me you'd follow me anywhere on the island."

Nony was disdainful. It would have been one thing to trail in the wake of a powerful man who'd have been able to ensure she was treated respectfully by strangers, at least to her face. It would be quite another to shift kampungs as a mother who night after night had only her children for company on her sleeping mat.

"That was then. Things change."

Frank's eyes became crafty.

"I'd be willing to give you a lot of money to go. And of course I'd build you a house in your new kampung. You'd be all set up."

"I wouldn't know anyone."

Frank thought, yes, well. But he said, "One hundred Straits dollars."

It was more cash than Nony usually handled in years. Even when she'd been Frank's nonya, he'd been the one to settle their household accounts with the merchants in BB and the pocket money he'd given her whenever the Chinese merchant moored his perahu at the landing stage had never amounted to more than enough to enable her to indulge the odd whim of her own, as well as standing her family the presents they'd so enjoyed. Still, she really didn't want to leave the kampung. Not to mention that if she were going to sell herself, then she certainly wouldn't sell herself cheap for the opening bid.

"You gave my parents double that for me and that was over 10 years ago."

Frank had expected her to beat him up, which was why he'd started low.

"Two hundred."

"More."

"Three hundred."

"More."

Frank sighed, he'd earmarked the money he'd won off Slinger for this necessary piece of grubbiness, and now he laid it all on the table.

"All right," he said. "All right, five hundred dollars. That's my final offer. It's a sum I'd be sorry to lose and one we both know you'd be glad to accept."

Nony's eyes lit up. She paused in her feather-plucking and she felt the world glitter golden all about her ... Not that you could eat gold; true riches lay in sacks of rice. Everybody in the kampung knew that – sacks of rice pushed up against the walls of their one room houses. Mind you, thought Nony, how many sacks of rice could she buy with $500? Enough to feed multitudes, for sure; no matter if her brothers' and half-brothers' harvests failed, $500 would be a bulwark against hunger for years, for her, her children and her wider family.

"Show me," she said.

Frank shook his head.

"It's back at the bungalow."

"But you have it? The cash?"

"Yes. In my safe."

Nony had seen Frank's safe often enough. It was a metal strongbox, painted a dull grey, with a large, clunking handle to its heavy door, and it squatted on the lowest shelf of the wardrobe in the little dressing room off his bedroom. But she'd never seen inside it – just about the only secret he'd ever been able to keep from her, and from the servants, was where he kept the key. Still, she'd always thought of it as a sort of magically refilling treasure chest, stuffed with gold, pearls, diamonds, rubies, emeralds and sapphires, as well as with paper dollars. Now, she could imagine the treasure-chest-safe's gorgeous treasures winking at her; they beckoned shiny in her mind.

But she was not so dazzled she failed to remember how lonely she'd be if she moved to some distant kampung. She scowled and said, "I told you. I don't want to move."

Frank spread his hands.

"Five hundred dollars," he repeated.

Nony plucked a few more feathers. Which did she want more: to stay in the kampung, or to have $500? Which did she want less: to lose her home and with it her sense of belonging, or to lose $500 and with it the freedom of riches for a few years? She wasn't sure – and why should she be rushed? For once, Baba was the one doing the begging. For once, he could wait.

"I'm not saying no," she said. "Perhaps. I'll think about it. Give me a bit of time and I'll let you know."

OUTBOUND MAIL, DECEMBER 1924
SENT FROM THE DO'S BUNGALOW,
KLUANAK, SARAMANTAN

From Rose to Beatrice

Dearest Bumbles,

At last, a precious letter from you, and just in time for Christmas – the best of gifts. I promise you that when the perahu carrying the mail arrived, I almost jumped off the verandah, so keen was I to run down to the landing stage to grab the packet. As we opened it, Frank remarked that were it not for our letters, he should sometimes think the world beyond the jungle had ceased to exist, and I could not disagree. He added our letters out must likewise be received as proof of our continued existence, so let this one reassure you I have not sprouted leaves and turned into one of our jungle trees.

I am pleased you have had at last my letter from Aden. Until you jogged my memory I had forgotten the charming Arab boy who sold me the fresh dates on the dockside. The slowness of the mail! I still struggle to accept that to send a letter from here to you, and to get your reply to me, is an exchange that must take about three months – such gaps in thought and conversation. And the newspapers? That they are called the "dailies" seems to me now one of God's little jokes. They take so long to get here that what is news to me must ever be old news to you, so you'd almost think time in England were not at all the same thing as time in Malaya. Indeed, I learn only now of that grisly murder in Nottingham. You have no doubt already forgotten it, but if not you'll surely agree with Frank who said it only went to show members of the English lower orders could be just as frantically demonic, unnatural and depraved as any native.

Luckily for my husband, his own correspondents are mostly on Saramantan and he generally receives replies to his local letters in the next mail after he sent them, so I find myself a little jealous of him on that score. Still, how can I complain I am badly done to when I have such a cheery letter from you to boost me.

How exciting that Edmund has given you freedom to redecorate Raddington Court as you like. However, I must in conscience advise I do not think it a good idea to paint the oak panelling in the drawing room purple, this I worry may look a little eccentric in the country. But I'm terribly jealous of your plans for the bathroom. A shower! Too lucky! Our own bathhouses here are primitive – amusingly so. Frank and I each have our own; the bungalow is raised above the ground, so it catches every welcome breeze, and they are in the space beneath. They have floors of beaten earth, and they contain neither baths, nor showers, nor sinks – there is no running water here – but each one is furnished with a large ceramic pot, called a *tong*. This the water-carrier fills each morning with water from a spring. The tong stands in the middle of a square laid with wooden planks, so the area around it does not become a quagmire, and, to wash, one sluices oneself down using a bamboo ladle hanging from the side of the pot. This is bathing in the Malay style, and we must take several of these peculiar baths each day if we are not to stink. (Meanwhile, all one's business one does on a commode called a thunderbox ... I will say no more!!!)

I fear you would think little better of the rest of my bungalow than you would of my bathhouses, now you are mistress of Raddington Court. My jungle home is a simple, rustic place, built of wood, and thatched with palm leaf. There is a wide verandah all around, and the roof overhangs it for shade; the windows contain no glass, but are closed with slatted wooden shutters. We have no electricity – at night we must make do with paraffin lamps.

I confess when I arrived my bungalow appeared to me quite charmless, so I knew at once it never had a woman's touch. Poor Frank! He seems to have lacked all creature comforts during his bachelor days. The furniture, of local manufacture, was supplied by the government PWD – the Public Works Department, they build things, and all that kind of thing – so you can well imagine it is more utilitarian than elegant. Indeed, when I first walked through the rooms I teased Frank he seemed to have done his best to make everything as dreary as possible. There was clutter everywhere. When he left last spring, he decided it would be too much trouble and expense to pack up and take with him more than a small selection of his things. He decided it would be easier, as well as public spirited, to leave behind the bulk of his knickknacks and so on, to be used by the next man arriving on the station, never thinking that come the day it would be him reunited with the pictures and curios and odds and ends he'd so nobly shed.

The walls would be better called partitions. They are of bare wooden planks, very thin and gappy, so if Frank is in his room, and I am in mine, and we raise our voices just a little we can talk to each other through them. When I arrived, these excuses for walls were hung with wavy-bladed native knives called *krises*, and other knives called *parangs* (machetes) and Dayak blowpipes. There was also a rather barbaric wooden shield embellished with jet-black human hair – Frank told me, with relish, that in former times, the local headhunters kept count of the number of heads they'd taken by the number of clumps of hair sprouting from their shields.

On account of the climate, we mostly live on the verandah. It is furnished with the table where we eat, scattered side tables and my writing desk. There are also the most ingenious local chairs called "planters' chairs" – long things, of rattan, half couch, half deck chair, with footrests and wide wooden arms adapted to form tables for holding drinks, and these chairs first used by rubber planters, I must suppose.

All our rooms open off the verandah. Though we barely enter them, we have a drawing room and a formal dining room. When I arrived, there were on the floors of both disintegrating mats of woven palm leaf fit for nothing more than tripping feet. I decided at first sight: they must go! I found in the drawing room a small bookshelf holding no books, only a jumble of empty whisky bottles and discarded cigarette tins – tobacco tins too – on which discreditable bottles and tins I forbore to comment to Frank, although I assure you I had words with Boy for failing to throw them away. There were no cushions on the shabby chairs, and the tables were covered by grubby native cloths in the depressingly dark colours favoured in these parts: blood-red, brown, navy, purple. Frank left behind quite a collection of Brunei brassware and Malay silver, with numerous bits and pieces scattered about, but every item tarnished and filthy.

Still, I have already begun to make this bachelor den more comfortable with cushions and flowers, so it becomes a proper home. I threw away the tatty matting, and instructed the water-carrier to polish the floorboards to a glossy shine – he scrubs the floors and does the laundry as well as fetching our water. I also had Boy remove the native cloths from the tables and the native artefacts from the walls. Where once there hung that barbaric shield, there is now a group of our wedding photographs. I scolded Boy he'd been slack about polishing Frank's brassware and silver. Many of these pieces I had him pack into one of our trunks and this I've had placed in an outhouse storeroom. The remaining pieces now positively gleam. And though this is a terrible climate for books, as those not mildewed are attacked by page-devouring insects, the bookshelf in the drawing room now holds my Malay grammars, a collection of battered old travel books I found in Frank's bedroom and a few detective novels we brought out.

As a finishing touch, I make my house gay with big vases of orchids I cut from the garden; the vases were most of them wedding presents, and orchids grow here in colourful profusion, though we have no roses, or honeysuckle, or daisies, snowdrops, bluebells, daffodils ...

Oh, it is difficult not to feel homesick as Christmas approaches. This unseasonable heat! I yearn for cold – to think that in England now you are cosy round the fire! And what I wouldn't give for a mince pie! On Christmas Day I shall imagine you sitting down to dinner, as Frank and I eat our evening tiffin. I have asked Cookie to procure a goose from the kampung, though how he'll roast it I don't know, as the kitchen here has only a little charcoal grill and a tiny, primitive clay oven. Not to mention Cookie seems to know only about three dishes, each as uninteresting as the last.

Still, a very merry Christmas from this distant tropical clime, and never mind that by the time you receive my greetings it will be weeks since Christmas. Let's hope 1925 is as exciting for both of us as was 1924!!!

Your cousin, Rosebud

From Rose to Daphne

Dearest Mummy,

Thank you for your last, dated November 1, which with happiest timing arrived today, so I have letters from Home to cheer my first Christmas in Malaya. I hope, and trust, that this finds you well. I was happy to learn you are invited everywhere and are as busy as anything.

You are quite right in your expectation I cannot myself claim to be gadding about – or not now, in any case, although when you were writing I was in Singapore, and gadding about no end. As to what on earth I find to do all day, let me tell you …

At six, I am woken by Boy bringing a cup of tea and then Frank and I breakfast together on the verandah, enjoying the early-morning cool. It's still dark when we sit down to breakfast, for all year round day breaks here like a lid being lifted on a pot at about seven, and twelve hours later night likewise falls quickly, with no lingering twilight.

After breakfast, Frank walks over to his office in the courthouse – it's within the compound, just a stone's throw from the bungalow. He's so busy, I find it difficult to catalogue his multiplex activities. It's no exaggeration to say he is in himself the complete local government. He's collector of taxes, police officer, magistrate, treasurer, post master, forestry officer, naturalist, PWD officer and a hundred other things all rolled into one. And he has nobody at all to help him, except a trio of native clerks, whom he claims are so lazily inefficient he's better off doing things himself than relying on them. Indeed, even thinking of all my husband does makes me tired, but he refuses to bask in my admiration. Instead, when I try to praise his industriousness, he laughs it's a terrible thing to be an Empire builder, no man has the right to be such a nuisance to his fellows as a DO in Malaya.

I usually resist visiting Frank at his desk, though it would be easy for me to do so, for I would not be a hindrance to him. Instead, I devote the mornings to studying my Malay grammars or to some other useful activity.

Frank returns to the bungalow for tiffin, and after we have eaten we have our lie-off (the customary nap of this country) so we doze through the swelter of the most stifling hours. Later, when it begins to cool, Frank returns to the courthouse for an hour or two, and I again undertake some useful activity – such as my present occupation, writing letters.

When Frank finishes his duties for the day, we play tennis – there's a court within our compound, although I must say, it's a court only by the skin of its teeth. After tennis there's evening tiffin and after that, when the air is cool again, or in any case cooler, I love to sit and talk with Frank on the verandah. Night-flowering bushes scent the breeze with incense sweetness and above the forest hangs a forest of stars. Here below, Frank and I watch the fireflies as we talk. Fireflies are as common as anything here and after sunset they turn the otherwise pitchy jungle into the prettiest flickering lace of light – at this time of year they must do as my Christmas candles, just as banana leaves must do as my holly and my ivy combined.

At around eleven, the fireflies light us to bed, and I find in the jungle I sleep like a top.

Does it all sound desperately dull to you? I suppose it does, but I seem to say just as often here as I did in London: there are not enough hours in the day.

As to your idea that I will in any case be busy enough once a baby comes along, I grant the point, though I must disappoint you on that score.

I don't suppose that even on Christmas Day Frank and I will much vary our routine, but it will be Christmas in Malaya, just as much as in Kensington, and I wish you the joy of the season, notwithstanding it will be at the earliest the end of January before you can know it.

Your loving daughter,

Rose

From Frank "Langers" Langham, to Charles "Slinger" Slightman

What ho, Slinger,

Thanks for your last. Blow me down! Was it really news to you Nony ever threatened to curse me? Perhaps you were drunker than I realised the night of my send-off – or else I mumbled incoherently in my cups. Indeed, perhaps I was so blind drunk

I omitted altogether to tell you about it, though I'd swear I gave a full account. As to Maude never having heard anything so blankety ridiculous in all her blankety life and the less said about such blankety eyewash the better, I assure you I share the sentiment.

Since you evidently insist on treating my letters as newspapers to be shared across the breakfast table, there seems nothing for it but to profess myself touched I have become such an object of concern in the Slightman household. Viz: your pointed and scarcely unexpected question of whether, in the matter of the nonya, I have by now stiffened my resolve and revealed all to my little woman. Will it surprise you if I have to report non confessus sum, old man, non confessus sum?

I gather my reticence won't please Maude. She wishes me to remember truth will out, does she, and in the long run it only makes things worse if you attempt to hide them. I'm afraid I cannot agree. Surely many a hidden truth remains forever hidden? Not to mention: what you don't know can't hurt you. Surely Maude will not deny that? Surely even she will not deny that from consideration for his bride's feelings, there are some things a newly married fellow had best keep under his hat.

Which is all by way of saying that not only have I not as yet confessed a thing to Rose, I now intend never to breathe a word unless I jolly well have to. Perhaps I'm a damned fool to keep silent, and I suppose I agree there should be no secrets between man and wife, but the longer I go without speaking, the harder it becomes to speak. I've now kept silent for so long, I'm persuaded it must be better – kinder – to say nothing at all, ever, to the little woman, than to distress her by so belatedly spilling the beans.

I expect you're thinking: this is all very well, but the beans may spill themselves if Rose catches sight of four suspiciously light-skinned brats careening round the kampung.

Never fear! Yours Truly has thought of that – more, he has a plan to ensure his little woman never catches so much as a glimpse of the incontrovertible evidence. As plans go, I trust it's both cunning and simple, and in any case I've already activated it: I've offered Nony that $500 I won off you, in exchange for transferring herself and the brats from the kampung to somewhere far enough away for safety. I trust you think I've put your money to good use, and you can be sure I am now more than ever jolly grateful to have won it.

Alas, Nony hasn't yet accepted my offer; she says she's thinking about it. But despite her shilly-shallying, I'm sure she'll toddle, and the sooner the better for all concerned. After all, it can't be very nice for her to remain in the kampung now Rose is the mistress here at the bungalow.

But we should not wallow in my miserable problems this season. I shall raise a glass to you as Rose and I tuck in to our Christmas tiffin, and all the best for 1925, old man.

Yours, Langers

4

THE DO's BUNGALOW AND THE KAMPUNG
KLUANAK, JANUARY 1925

Rose and Frank were breakfasting by the light of a paraffin lamp which Boy had set upon the table, it was haloed, as ever, by airy clouds of insects. Beyond the verandah's rail, the jungle was emerging from the silvery dimness of the evaporating night and the river could be sensed as a brooding presence slithering through the condensing day. The dawn chorus was loud, and a cock was crowing nearby. Rose wondered: had his hens perhaps provided her egg? It was boiled, and now she tapped at its delicately speckled brown shell with a teaspoon.

"So what does your day hold?" she asked.

Frank sprinkled salt over his own already opened egg.

"I've had reports of dynamite fishing at a kampung about thirty miles upriver. Completely illegal of course, but the Malays think it's great sport."

"You're going there to investigate?"

"No, no. I'll draft a stiff warning to the village headman, then I'll send Fitri to deliver it." Fitri was his most trusted native clerk. "You?" Frank added. "What are your plans for the morning?"

Though Rose was dissatisfied with Cookie, he could at least bake the bread she and Frank would otherwise do without – it was not a staple of the native diet. Now, she reached for a slice of toast from the rack, and she began spreading it with butter, which came from BB in tins. She was beginning to realise her mother had perhaps had a point when she'd implied in her last letter that it may be something of a struggle for her to fill her days – at least until a baby came along. And, oh, Mummy's impertinence there! Rose felt momentarily cross to remember it; this crossness in turn made her cross she had nothing at all to do about the bungalow this morning. She ought, of course, conscientiously settle to studying her Malay grammars, but the idea didn't appeal. As to her diary, she had nothing to report, and her sketchbook was already half full of drawings of Frank, of the servants, of the bungalow. Furthermore, life at the outstation could be awfully stifling; she was beginning to feel awfully cooped-up in the compound. How pleasant it would be to get away for an hour or two. Not that there was anywhere she could safely go ... Well, apart from one place, she supposed. She smeared more tinned butter across her toast, and she put down her knife with a decisive clatter.

"I think I'll explore the kampung. I rather think it's about time I did. It's ridiculous I've not even seen it yet."

Frank felt himself go pale, so he was grateful for the wavering light of the paraffin lamp and for the shadows rippling across the breakfast table. Drat Nony's indecision! Why hadn't she taken his money and toddled already? When he spoke, he did his best to keep his tone neutral, but he suspected he'd failed: certainly in his own ears, his voice sounded all edge.

"It's not much of a place, you know."

Rose, trusting, noticed nothing strange, or strained, about her husband's tone, or about his manner either.

"I'm sure it's not, but at least it's somewhere."

"But is it wise to go by yourself. It'd be awful if you became lost on the way."

"Isn't it a single path from here to there? And doesn't the path hug the river?"

"Well, yes. But walking in the jungle can be terribly dangerous without a guide."

"You're forever taking your gun and setting off for sport."

"I was brought up in the jungle. I've lived at Kluanak for over ten years. I know the forests hereabouts like the back of my hand." Frank paused, and he too reached for the toast. "I met a chap once, in BB, at the Club you know. He was just passing through. He was an inspector of schools somewhere, I forget where. In any case, he told me how he'd once got lost in the jungle. He'd taken a track from one village to another, but he must have taken a wrong turning. He was lost for a whole day and a night. Imagine him plunging hither and thither! Eventually he found the trail again, but when he arrived at wherever-it-was, he was in an exhausted condition and covered with mud and leaches. It was years later that I met him, but he said he'd never forget the terror of thinking he was done for."

Rose was touched by her husband's concern. But her mind was quite made up: she would explore the kampung. She poured them each another cup of tea, and as she did so she said, "Silly boy! I don't intend to go plunging hither and thither. Truly, I can't get lost following a path by a river for a mile or so in broad daylight."

Frank looked as he felt: agitated.

"What if you came upon Master Stripes? Or stepped on a snake … And the wild pigs. This whole area is infested with them – they can be very aggressive."

"Pigs!" hooted Rose. "I'm not afraid of pigs, however aggressive, and you've told me often enough Master Stripes is a shy creature, more afraid of me than I am of him."

"You could stumble over a root and break your ankle."

"My sentimental lamb!" said Rose, her affection rippled with exasperation. "This is terribly sweet, but I assure you I'm capable of walking for a mile on a much trodden path without meeting with an accident."

Frank wanted to smash something. But instead he sipped his tea, and he deliberated: if Rose were determined to visit the kampung, then he couldn't see there was much he could do to stop her without making her suspicious. The bungalow wasn't her gaol. He wasn't her gaoler. And the last thing he wanted was to see her eyes narrow as she accused: darling, anyone would think there was something in the village you didn't wish me to see.

"I could come with you," he offered.

"I don't want to keep you from your work."

Frank appraised his half-eaten egg. Dare he insist? And if he daren't, perhaps Boy could be trusted, through his natural tact, without anything actually being said, to steer the little woman clear of Nony and the brats just as carefully as he would have done himself? He tried to speak casually.

"If you must go, at least take Boy. Show you the way. Act as your interpreter when you get there."

Rose gave her husband a haughty look.

"Oh no," she said. "No, no. Boy has things to do around the bungalow."

Frank racked his brains a moment. Nothing came to him; he had quite run out of strategies to sabotage Rose's desire to explore the kampung on her own. He pushed away his plate.

"All right," he shrugged, hoping he'd managed a semblance of indifference. "Walk down to the kampung if you must, I'll look forward to hearing all about it at tiffin."

Rose, in a wide-brimmed straw hat and a floral print cotton frock somewhat at odds with her sensible lace-up shoes, walked determinedly towards the bungalow's landing stage. The courthouse was to her right: it didn't look much like her idea of a courthouse; not at all the sort of place from which Britannia defied the jungle; a most unimposing building of wood and thatch. Nonetheless it had attached to it a small, bare cell where Frank could order the odd miscreant detained. Though it was generally empty, Rose thought there wafted from this cell a most minatory miasma, and she hurried past it. She very quickly reached the landing stage, where she turned left on the riverside path. She walked past that other court from which Britannia defied the jungle: the tennis court. When, in England, Frank had said wherever on Saramantan they were posted, they'd in all likelihood be able to have a game of an evening, she'd quite failed to consider how extraordinary it would be to find a tennis court in the jungle. But when she'd arrived at Kluanak and seen how densely and exuberantly the vegetation everywhere thrust and burst, she'd expressed some astonishment to her husband that anybody had ever had the audacity to create a court here, and also that he'd kept it maintained through all the long years when he'd had nobody to play. Frank had shrugged, and said it would have been unfair to the men who'd come after him, if he'd let the court go to wrack and ruin; he'd added that even when he was alone at Kluanak he'd got a game every now and then, when some or another white man happened to be passing through. Just beyond the court was the simple wooden gate which closed off the compound from the jungle. As she opened it, Rose noted there was no sign of the day watchman – a doddery codger whom she judged terribly slack about his duties – and come to think of it, nor of the gardener.

Beyond the compound the path was at first almost as easy going as a bridle path in England, and quite familiar to her for she and Frank often took a stroll to the first bend and back. But despite her insouciance at breakfast, Rose had never walked alone in the jungle before and once she rounded the bend and struck out into what was, for her, new territory, she became uneasy. Though the river flowed reassuringly to her right, the incessant sawing of the insects set her nerves jangling. The way became harder going: the path narrowed, became more thickly overhung, more tangled with roots and undergrowth; the earth here was slippery, slick with mud and rotting vegetation. Soon, her skin was just as slick with the exertion of walking through the sweating air. She caught her foot and she stumbled. Here and there on the left an animal track tunnelled off into the deepest forest – these, she supposed, must be the tracks Frank followed when he went hunting with his gun. What if she took a few steps in the wrong direction? Horrors! Within moments she'd be hopelessly lost. She remembered all the warnings Frank had issued at breakfast and she shivered to think of that poor inspector of schools, confused and afraid. She imagined him wandering for hours and hours, walking and walking, darkness falling, him becoming more and more worried, getting scratched and bitten and bruised, realising he was running out of time. Panicking. Shouting. Screaming for help which never came ... Oh, it was awful ... Or in any case it could so easily have been awful, if he'd not had the luck to stumble back onto the trail. He could have gone quite mad in the jungle's green maze. Indeed, it occurred to her, with a thrill of terror that was too real to be delicious, that the clotting forest was itself as impenetrable as a madman's mind.

She'd alarmed herself so thoroughly even a dead branch lying half on the path looked, to her, like a skeletal hand, its twiggy fingers beckoning her to doom. She was about to turn around and dash back to the bungalow, so far as the trees allowed of dashing, when to her relief she came to a cultivated area: flooded padi fields, scrappy little things, she thought, though prettily hazed by dragon flies. From this evidence of man's patchy, limited mastery of the jungle, she correctly gathered she was about to reach the kampung and so she soldiered on.

The kampung straggled a couple of hundred yards along the bank of the river. Rose thought it terribly picturesque. Here or there stood a tethered water buffalo; goats roamed; chickens pecked about. The houses, perhaps thirty of them in all, appeared to her delightfully ramshackle: the kampung houses were built on piles higher than those of her own bungalow; if she squinted, they looked to be floating quite free of the earth. Some were built out over the river – charmingly amphibious, Rose thought. Others, fully on land, were surrounded by small kitchen gardens; she recognised pepper vines, tufts of lemongrass and coffee bushes, although the villagers appeared to grow few vegetables, which surprised her. The raised houses had steeply pitched roofs, no chimneys and no windows; each was accessed by a rickety-looking bamboo ladder leading up from the ground. The entryways had removable panels for doors and most of them were now open. Rose was tempted to scramble up one of the ladders, to have a good peer around the interior of somebody's home, but she reminded herself she was the DO's wife and as such she must behave with a dignity incompatible with either nosiness, or scrambling.

As she moseyed about, Rose quickly noticed that the villagers used the spaces underneath their houses as living areas. Many of these spaces had matting spread upon the beaten earth floors and on some of the mats villagers were at work. Under one house, two women were sitting together weaving at primitive looms; under another, a woman was making something from palm leaves – a basket? A fish trap? Beneath another house, three men were mending fishing nets. When Rose stopped to greet them in her pidgin Malay, which was in any case so different from the local dialect, they simply stared at her through blankly uncomprehending eyes.

But though these men couldn't understand Rose, they were

riveted by her; she was, to them, as fascinating as a Dayak woman would have been to young bucks on Park Lane. And the same went for the many other villagers who were staring at her, through sideways eyes, from various hidey-holes about the kampung. It was 14 years since a Mat Salleh woman – a white woman – had last lived in the DO's bungalow; few of the villagers had caught sight of one since then. Now Rose caused a sensation. She was so strange. Her ghost pale skin! And that hair so plainly visible beneath her hat. It was red! Red? Was she a demon? Red was after all a colour strongly associated with evil spirits. And she was so skinny. Not as skinny as a hungry peasant, not pot-bellied like a hungry child, but still much skinnier than any rich woman had any business being – no doubt the tuan intended to fatten her up, after all he could afford the food. As to her height? So tall! What a giantess! Her hands and her feet were enormous! Her nose! What a thing! It was horribly sharp and pointed, not snub and flared, like lovely, squidgy Malay noses. Her feet were neither bare, nor shod in woven-straw slippers, but encased in those ugly shoe things the Mat Salleh liked to wear – those things that made their feet look like hooves.

Nony was one of the villagers furtively watching Rose. She was doing so from the shadows behind the open entryway to her house. First Daughter was playing with coconut husks at her feet, whilst First Son and the twins were somewhere or other with their friends. Nony, seeing the mem for the first time, watching her blunder and lumber, felt again the humiliation she'd felt on learning she'd been replaced in the DO's bungalow by a woman who could be compared to Raksasa Wanita. What, *this?* She'd been abandoned for this grotesque creature? Her cheeks burned with shame, and when she thought what the other village women must be saying they burned even hotter.

Even when Rose moved out of sight a kind of ghoulish fascination compelled Nony to continue looking, so she crept closer to her entryway in order to keep her in view. She saw Rose walk into the small grove of coconut trees between her house and the jungle – between the realm where man could sometimes kid himself he mostly held sway, and the realm where, indubitably, the spirits ruled. Everybody in the kampung appreciated the way the wavering ranks of slim, branchless palms, with their kindly bounty of nuts, offered a buffer against the more menacing trees beyond. And though, in the course of their busy days, the kampung's children slipped in and out of the jungle as easily as fever slipped through the air, the grove was one of their safest, most favoured gathering places. This morning there was a noisy group of them in there, watching Abanawas, the snake catcher, setting his trained serpent eagle to its work: killing serpents.

Abanawas was one of the kampung's oldest residents – 250 years old, at least. Nony bestowed upon him a casual glance, and then she squatted down and transferred her attention to the children. Alamak! She flinched and gasped aloud: First Son and the twins were amongst the children in the coconut grove. She assumed that the moment the mem spotted them, she'd realise these half-castes must be Baba's children – her own husband's children, the ones he'd told her about. Nony's heart jumped into her mouth to think of what the mem would do when realisation dawned. After all, she must hate Baba's bastard offspring as an affront to her own dignity, and to her own position, and as a threat to the children she herself must one day bear, unless the spirits, fingers crossed, had blighted her with barrenness. But barren or not, perhaps the devilish red-headed mem had at her disposal powerful black magic? Perhaps she'd curse her husband's bastards? Such was her concern, Nony almost called out to her boys to come home at once. But even as she formed the cry, she realised uttering it would reveal to the mem – to the witch – where she lived, and thus invite her to direct her darts of black magic at this, the house her husband had provided for another woman, when he ought to have been hoarding his money to spend on her. So she stifled her warning, and, still trembling, she offered a quick prayer to Providence – to Allah, to the spirits and to nature combined – to wrap her children in a cloak of beneficent care. And also she came to a decision: she couldn't live within spitting distance of a witch who hated her and hated her children. This settled it, the mem's appearance in the coconut grove was a sign that however reluctant she was to move, she must accept Baba's money and transplant herself and the children to some distant kampung.

Down in the coconut grove, Rose was by now making a beeline for a raucous gang of jungle urchins watching an ancient, crookedly diminutive man flap about with a screeching bird – a falcon, or a hawk, or an eagle, she wasn't sure which. It was a biggish thing, bigger than a barn owl, and even from this distance she could see its beak was a scimitar and its talons razors. Its plumage was rather drab, she thought, mostly dingy brown, but its head was a startling yellow and its eyes too glowed yellow across the grove. Its ancient keeper, or trainer, or whatever he was, had the thing hopping about on his gloved fist, but now he gave a whistled command and he shot out his arm. The surrounding children shrieked and ducked. The bird tore skyward. It soared and then in a blur it arrowed to the ground. It was aiming for a spot at the edge of the grove. When it landed, there was a brief and silent tussle in the undergrowth before it again surged skyward. This time it had something in its talons: something long, and thin, and thrashing. A snake! Rose gasped and she put her hands to her face in surprise and dismayed dislike.

The eagle circled the grove a few times, while the snake's thrashing became writhing and then wriggling. At last, even the wriggling stopped. The ancient man held out his gloved fist again, and gave another whistled command. Now the bird swooped towards him. Just as it was coming in to land, it banked and dropped the snake right in the midst of the group of noisy, chattering, cheering children. One boy successfully jumped for the body; the moment he'd caught it, he began yelling and swinging it around his head. His laughing friends whooped as they dodged the whipping snake.

Rose was momentarily terrified for the children. She could see now that the snake was a cobra, black as a bicycle tyre, and she remembered all the warnings Frank had given her about its kind. He'd told her if a fellow were bitten by a cobra, there was no point in calling a doctor, far better to carry him to the closest church, or mosque, or temple, or pagoda, or sacred grove there to let the poor chap die in the presence, perhaps, of some or another divinity. But even as she told herself she hoped the cobra was well and truly dead, she realised that certainly it was. As the snake's body swung, it was scattering drops of red; the children were becoming spattered with its blood. By George, the bird had decapitated the cobra! Its thrashing in the sky must have been nothing but the reflex action of dying muscles. Her terror for the children turned to disgust at their horrible game.

The bird, now hopping about once again on its keeper's gloved fist, had recommenced its screeching. The ancient man stroked its back to calm it. He then retrieved the dead cobra from the yelling boy and hung it from an attachment on a loop of leather encircling his sarong like a belt.

Rose had been so absorbed by the bird, the snake and then by her fear, that she hadn't yet really looked at the children, but now she swept her gaze around them. The oldest looked to be about 7 or 8, the youngest was perhaps 3. Few of them were wearing anything more than a dirty, raggedy loincloth. They were all grubby and as stringy as spaghetti – brown spaghetti. Brown spaghetti bodies; brown spaghetti limbs. The only way she could tell the boys from the girls was by the length of their hair. But whether they wore it long or short, each of them had hair like a chocolate topping ... except ... good heavens! Rose blinked, and then she blinked again. Two of the boys – no, three of them – three of the boys had fine, mousy hair, distinctly different from the coarse, dark hair of their fellows, and their skin was a much lighter shade of brown, the colour of milky coffee. Gosh, thought Rose, these boys must be half-castes! Were they brothers? She supposed they must be.

Though Rose had correctly surmised the boys' relationship

to each other, she failed to notice that the two younger ones were identical twins – in her eyes, all the village children looked roughly the same. And it did not occur to her, even as an outlandish possibility, that the boys could be the product of a union between a white *woman* and a native. Such a union was so far beyond her experience she could not even think it may occur. Instead, she assumed, correctly, and at once, that the boys' father must be a white man and their mother a native woman. How strange, she thought, how extraordinary to find such mixed breeds so far from BB, or any place where white men dwelled. Perhaps their mother had once lived in town? Perhaps BB was something of a fleshpot, and there some local girl, gone off to try her luck in the bright lights, had formed a liaison with a European. Perhaps, when her catch had tired of her and of their dalliance, he'd sent her back to her native kampung. Yes, that must be it – something like it, anyway.

Well here was opportunity! If the half-castes' mother had been a town dweller, then no doubt she knew English, and if that were the case then so too did her sons, perhaps? Rose, feeling adventurous and open-minded, decided she would ask.

It was very pleasant to think of herself as a woman who'd attempt to converse with native children, to find common ground with her improbable interlocutors. Rose, tingling with self-congratulatory good intentions, called out, in English, and stepped forward. This caused the buzzing children to notice her for the first time: they all fell silent and froze. None of them had seen a white woman before. None of them had seen such a ... such a *what* before. Even the twins, sons of a white man, thought:

what *is* this? What monster? But their older brother, First Son, recognised at once both that this was a human woman, and also who she was.

First Son was a bold boy; he wasn't afraid, he was angry. As he glared at the new mem he accused: so that's her, is it? He wanted to summon a magic knife and send it flying into her buttocks right up to the hilt! After all, she was the reason Baba – father, the same word for husband, father and head of the household – she was the reason Baba had booted *Bu*, Mum, out of the DO's bungalow and back to the kampung. Or so blamed First Son. Mind you, for himself, he hadn't too much minded the sudden relocation. He thought back to the morning last year when Baba had gone – left forever, as everybody had thought. That morning, even as day had broken and he'd trudged behind his mother along the jungle path from the bungalow to the kampung, along the path from his old life of relative privilege to his new one of mucking in, he'd been far from distraught at the loss of the father he'd barely known. And who'd barely known him. Indeed, Baba had rarely noticed him, except when he'd wanted to punish him, to wallop him for this or that. So why should he have wept on this journey of a mile, of miles, between one life and another? Even at the time, he'd consoled himself that though he no longer had a father, he had something much better: a gang. A gang to stop him noticing that his younger brothers, the twins, had their own hurtfully private gang of two. Yes, from the moment he'd moved to the kampung, First Son had much preferred being one of the crowd, living cheek by jowl with the village children, to lording it in the chilly isolation of the bungalow. This was the life, he'd thought, as he'd rough-and-tumbled with his friends, here was belonging. And this notwithstanding that as soon as he'd moved into the kampung, his peers had begun ribbing him mercilessly about his fall in the world and about his supposed airs and graces. Not to mention his odd looks: his light skin, funny hair, strange eyes, pointed nose. Alas, even now, when he lived amongst them, First Son too often felt different from the other village children, and he sensed he was as often excluded from their games, as he was from the twins' conversations. But the times when he wasn't excluded made up for the times he was, and, generally, he was now reasonably content with his lot.

But he knew Bu wasn't content with hers. She complained often that she now had to use the communal latrine pit in the kampung, and that she missed sleeping on a soft bed under jungle curtains, and that she hated having to fetch her own water, and that it was too bad she hardly ever now got even a bit of beef. And, blazed First Son, as he stared with defiant insolence at Rose's large and redly perspiring face, this bitch was the reason for all Bu's losses, her deprivations; *she* was the reason Bu had been so snappish and unhappy these last few months. He was too young, yet, to feel anything other than an overwhelming love for his mother; for now, he loved her unconditionally, fiercely, protectively, painfully, blindly. And this passionate love led him to hate Rose on first sight; he was a generous, imaginative boy, not prone to hatred, but he hated this bitch for what he judged she'd done to his bu and the pain she'd caused her; he hated her with all his heartbreakingly undefined, developing heart.

Rose was oblivious to both the terror she'd caused in most of the children and also to First Son's despairing fury. She pointed from him to his brothers, who were standing together a little apart from the others.

"You three!" She commanded, now making a theatrically sweeping gesture to wave them over, so they'd understand her mime, even if they couldn't understand her English, "Come here!"

All of the children, even First Son, were alarmed by the gabble. And all of them, except First Son, jumped to huddle together, leaving him isolated, exposed like a solitary water buffalo faced with a gaping jaw filled with feline teeth.

Abanawas too was becoming nervous: what on earth did the new mem want? Well, whatever it was, it would no doubt lead to trouble for him. He held out his gloved fist and whistled his serpent eagle to the top of the closest coconut palm. This time the bird's movement was lazily gentle; with a sighing noise like falling silk, it took wing. He watched as it settled amidst the nuts – smooth plump orbs of fresh, juicy green protected within a crown of elegantly frondy leaves – and then he doddered over to the mem. His back was already so bent he had no need to bow and he adopted his most obsequious manner. Malay was a language with myriad ways of addressing other people, depending on the speakers' ages and ranks relative to each other, with different forms of "you" used to convey respect, courtesy, familiarity, insult and so on. Abanawas used the politest form of Malay, a manner of address the lower orders used with their social superiors. He mumbled through his toothless gums, "Yes? Can I help you?"

Rose had no idea what the grimy and desiccated little bird man was mumbling and she was revolted by the headless dead snake dangling off his hip. She batted him away and then she approached closer to the huddle of children, veering at the last moment to swoop on First Son, where he stood alone. She bent down to his level, and she looked him in the eye, intending to communicate her kindliness and her good will toward him. She noted that his eyes were occidental hazel, not oriental brown, and as round as her own, but she quite failed to see they were as hard as agates with loathing for her.

"I say!" she said. "Do you speak English, young man?"

First Son thought the mem was making noises as senseless as a monkey's hoo-hooing. But never mind her gibberish, he now properly noticed her demon-red hair. Help! Was the new mem a she-devil? And her eyes! Whoever heard of a human with green eyes – reptilian eyes, eyes like those through which the dead cobra had so recently surveyed the forest floor, eyes like a crocodile's, or a lizard's. Though First Son was a brave boy, he began to feel as thoroughly afraid as the other children. He was too proud to cry, nonetheless, he felt his eyeballs were bursting with tears. At last he could bear the pressure no longer. He shouted as loudly and as rudely as he could, using not just an impolite form of Malay, but gutter Malay he wasn't supposed to know at all, sewer Malay of the local dialect, so coarse he only ever heard it when he crept up on the village men at night and listened in to their chat about women as they drank themselves into palm-toddy stupors: "Go away! *Pukimak kau!* Nobody wants you around here!"

As his words echoed, First Son jumped to rejoin the other children and then the whole flock of them turned as one and ran towards the pawang's house – she lived beyond the coconut grove, just where the kampung's cultivated land met the jungle, at the threshold where man must abandon his pretensions of dominion, and accept the dominion of the spirits.

Rose gathered from the boy's tone and manner he'd shouted something it was better she didn't understand. Well! This was the thanks she got for her generous impulse to commune with him. She flapped her hands after him a couple of times – after all the children, in a half-hearted attempt to wave them back. But it was hopeless: wave them back? Huh! She was waving *to* their backs. She stood a moment longer, watching them run as if in fear of their lives, and then, ignoring the ancient bird man, who appeared to wish to detain her, she wheeled about and, decidedly grumpy, she headed back towards the path along the river to the DO's bungalow.

Up in her house, Nony was still squatting on her haunches in the shadows behind her entryway, watching events in the coconut grove unfold. Although it was known in the kampung that the mem could not speak Malay – the general opinion was that she must be terribly backward, since even children not yet three years old could manage it – she'd been terrified when she'd heard First Son's yell of *pukimak kau* ringing clear across the coconut grove. After all, unless the mem had rice porridge for brains she must surely have understood that First Son had insulted her. Still, despite her dread, Nony hadn't realised quite how tense her body had been until now when she saw her children flee. But now they were getting away she relaxed, so she almost tipped over on top of First Daughter, who was next to her and still bashing coconut husks together. Nony steadied herself and then she stared hard

at the mem. She saw how she flapped her large, pink hands after
the disappearing children: she seemed confused they were running
from her, bemused they were off. But any witch worth her brew
would have had it in her power to stop children fleeing, if that
was what she'd wanted ... With this thought, Nony's fear of the
mem began to fade, like cloud fading to the horizon. Honestly! A
witch? What had she been thinking? *Pukimak kau?* For goodness'
sake! None of the village women would have tolerated her son's
rudeness: if he'd cheeked any of them the way he'd cheeked the
mem, he'd have received a quick slap to the chops, if not a proper
belting. But the mem hadn't flashed out her hand to slap him;
she'd just taken it. No witch would be so supine, not even one too
dim to speak Malay. Nony felt ashamed, now, of the fear she'd
felt earlier: how could she have feared a woman who'd let children
run rings around her? Not to mention that now her children were
safe, she remembered something she'd forgotten when she'd
thought they were in danger: the Mat Salleh scoffed at magic.
They rejected anything they couldn't understand; they disdained
respect for the spirits as absurd; they didn't believe in witchcraft,
or ghosts, or anything like that. The mem a mistress of curses?
She wouldn't even believe in curses! Well then, Nony stiffened
her resolve and reversed the decision she'd made not ten minutes
back: let herself be bounced into leaving the kampung by fear of
the mem? No, not at all, her decision need not be influenced by
fear of one such as her; she needn't make up her mind just yet
about whether or not she was willing to make things easy for
Baba; she could continue to weigh the pros and cons of taking
his money or not; she could continue to take her own sweet time.

When Rose and Frank reconvened on the verandah for tiffin, they found that, as on almost every other day, Cookie had steamed a tasteless river fish; neither of them felt much enthusiasm for it. Frank, nervous and on edge, prodded at his fish's spongy grey-brown flesh and he asked, with a studied nonchalance that did, in fact, deceive, "So, did you go for your walk through the kampung?"

"I did. Fascinating, if rather horrible. I saw a man set a bird to kill a cobra."

Frank relaxed, a little.

"A serpent eagle," he said. "Astounding agility."

"Astounding," Rose agreed. She added, "A crowd of children was watching too."

Frank had just taken his first mouthful of fish, but now he choked on it. Christ! Had Rose collided with his brats after all? He gave her a sharply appraising look: she didn't seem like an egg who'd stumbled upon a dangerous secret; she seemed entirely her usual self. He said, carefully, "Yes. The kampung is chock full with brats, some tame, some wild."

Rose used her fork to ease a fish bone to the side of her plate.

"I noticed three who were evidently half-castes. All boys. Brothers, I thought. The oldest looked about 7 and the other two a bit younger."

Frank's sons were actually aged 9 and 7, not that the Malays kept close count and not that Frank thought now was the time to explain to his wife either that two of the boys were twins, or that native children often looked younger than their years. The fine hairs on his forearms rose and bristled stiff as tiny wires and he threw another sharply suspicious glance across the table: no, Rose no more appeared to be acting now than she had a moment ago; she appeared to be tackling her fish in the manner of a woman sincerely in the dark. Still, he could not feel reassured: was his wife leading him into a trap which would spring shut any second now and snap his head off?

"There are a couple of half-caste brats amongst the full breeds," he croaked.

"Frog in your throat?" asked Rose. She reached for his water glass and began to refill it. "I hoped they may perhaps speak English so I tried to speak to the oldest of them, but he shouted something I couldn't understand – in Malay, I mean – and then he ran off, taking all the other children with him."

Frank was so overcome by gratitude for the linguistic gulf between his wife and First Son that all he could manage to say was, "Oh."

Rose replaced the water glass by his plate.

"I suppose their mother lives in the kampung," she said.

For a moment, Frank couldn't breathe. Could he lie, he wondered? Could he deny he had any idea who was mother to the half-castes or where she lived either? He was still debating with himself when Rose smiled at him and said, "She must have lived in BB."

Frank startled so badly at this lucky misapprehension he knocked over the glass of water Rose had just refilled.

"What?"

Rose passed him her napkin, so he could dab at the spilled liquid.

"The boys' mother," she repeated. "She must once have lived in BB, don't you think? To have born children fathered by a white man. I suppose she must have returned to her home village when he chucked her."

As Rose spoke, she met Frank's eye. Her expression was as trusting as ever. With a great effort of will, Frank forced himself not to look away; instead he held her eye levelly, directly. But he couldn't bring himself to speak. Again, Rose smiled at him.

"Or perhaps she's still in town. Perhaps when their father grew bored with her, she sent her little mementos home to live with her mother, or her sister, so they wouldn't be an inconvenience as she cast her net for another fish."

Frank swallowed, but, at last, he found his tongue.

"It's an idea," he said, intending to convey the parentage of the kampung brats was none of his concern.

Rose nodded.

"Silly thing!" she said. "You'd have thought she'd have realised such a doubtful liaison could only possibly end with her left holding the babies."

Frank felt as if he were being wound in a python's killer coils. He made a noise somewhere between a grunt and a groan. But Rose was by now too absorbed by her own thoughts to notice his unease. She said, her voice soggy with distaste, "And what sort of man can he have been? Her ... her ... inamorato ... to ... to ... consort ... with a native."

The python coils began to squeeze, hard, then harder. For a long moment, Frank said nothing. Eventually, though, he pulled himself together. He mentally crossed his fingers and he indicated a dish of chili relish, just out of his reach across the table.

"Pass the sambal, dearest, this grub's as bland as anything."

The distraction worked. As Rose complied with his request, she rolled her eyes.

"Cookie!" she said and then she launched into a tirade about the useless man's shortcomings.

5

THE KAMPUNG, KLUANAK, JANUARY 1925

Nony was squatting in the shade of her ruang, gutting fish, small perch-like things, for *asam pedas*, a sour and spicy stew she planned to cook for dinner. She had three fly-swarmed wooden buckets in front of her: one held unprepared fish; one held the fish guts she was extracting; one held prepared fish. First Daughter was doodling about, poking at things with a stick. Meanwhile, First Son and the twins were off after ants' nests in the jungle – ant larvae mixed with rice made a delicious meal.

A hornbill flapped by, calling with its distinctive, squeaky caw. It was an especially sacred bird, so Nony looked up from her work, hoping to receive its blessing. But, alas, it seemed to be bringing her ill-fortune: for the second time since his return, she saw Baba approaching her house. This time she was scarcely taken unawares, she'd realised he'd probably respond to First Son's behaviour yesterday. In any case, she knew by now he must be impatient to know whether she would refuse his money and stay, or accept it and go. Indeed, he was impatient for everything; like all the Mat Salleh, he seemed not to understand that the passage of time was something to be enjoyed slowly, so the slowness of enjoying it in turn slowed it down. But however much he harassed her, all she'd be able to tell him was that she remained in two minds about whether or not to allow herself to be seduced by dollars into leaving the kampung.

Frank dipped into the ruang and at once he wrinkled his nose against the stench of fish. Nony did not acknowledge his arrival, and he did not proffer a greeting. In silence, he watched her slit a fish from its mouth to its tail; the silvery steel of her knife flashed against the silvery steel of the glittering scales. He was tempted to ask her to stop gutting whilst they talked, but he felt that to do so would in some obscure way disadvantage him. Hell! It was ridiculous that he, the DO, was negotiating with a native for a favour, and never mind if the native in question had once nightly stroked him to joy. Still, he mustn't give any hint he felt the weakness of a petitioner prostrate before a potentate, so to speak, he must swagger through this encounter, just as if he were a potentate himself.

He'd already noticed First Daughter busy with her stick. Now he barked, "Where are the boys?"

Nony scooped out a fistful of fish guts, a bloodied red mash, and she tossed it into the correct bucket.

"Not here."

"I hear they encountered my mem yesterday."

Nony shrugged and she tossed the cleaned fish in with the other ones.

Frank tried not to show how much he resented her stroppy, unhelpful attitude.

"That's why I've come," he said. "Look here, Nony, stop dithering. This whole set-up – it can't continue. Don't you see: you *must* leave the kampung! I can't have the children colliding with my mem all over the place. Much better for everybody if you move." He paused. "How about going to your aunt's kampung?"

Nony spoke with obvious disdain.

"Which aunt did you have in mind?"

Frank ignored this. The breast pocket of his khaki shirt was bulging, as if he had a tin of cigarettes in there. Now he put his hand to the bulge.

"I've even brought the cash." he cajoled. "Want to see it?"

"All five hundred?"

"All five hundred."

Nony cleaned her bloodied knife on a rag, before laying it aside. She used the same rag to wipe her hands, but when she held one out it remained slimy and wetly red with fish blood.

"Give it here."

A-ha! thought Frank, now I've got her.

"No," he said. "I'll show it to you, that's all."

"But you'll give it to me, if I say I'll leave?"

There were no flies on Frank, or so he preened. He knew the crafty ways of the natives; he knew if he were to pay Nony to leave before she'd gone, then she'd never go and he'd never get his money back either. She'd immediately spread amongst her relations any cash he passed over; he'd lose it for good.

"Not if you say you'll go, no. You go – actually go – and I'll send it on to you later."

"How much later?"

"A month." Frank paused. "And you'd better not try to cheat me any other way, either. No monkey tricks. No taking my money, waiting a few weeks and then sneaking back. I'd have you arrested. Stealing. You'd have to appear before me in the courthouse. I'd toss you into gaol."

This was a bluff. Frank could probably have tossed Nony into gaol on a pretext, although if he'd tried such high-handedness he'd have risked a kris in the back from one of her aggrieved cousins, but he feared he could not risk becoming embroiled in a public spat with his quondam nonya: if he did, then what the deuce would he say if his wife demanded all the damning details of what had led to the spat in the first place?

Still, Nony was intimidated. But her intimidation was spiked by infuriation, both with herself for being intimidated and also with Frank for blocking the more obvious tricks for getting the better of him – because of course she'd cheat him, if she could, of course she would. Who wouldn't?

"All right," she said sulkily. "Show me! Let's see it, the money."

Frank unbuttoned his breast pocket and he extracted the fat wodge of folded notes. All of them were used, greasy and creased and crumpled from passing from hand to hand; some of them were torn. Still, they represented salvation, grieved Frank, who felt, already, the pain of their loss. He unfolded them, as one stack, and then he skilfully flicked through them, as a bank teller would, or a card sharp preparing to cut the cards. They blurred with their various colours, brown for 50s, red for 10s, green for 5s, and blue for singles.

Nony, who'd rarely handled paper money of any denomination, only coin, was almost hypnotised by the flicking notes. Lightly floral above the strong whiff of fish, she fancied she could almost even smell it: the sweet smell of money. She imagined the softly sensual feel of the notes beneath her caressing fingers, their silky crumples and creases and tears.

But what about the smell of home? Nony didn't mean the damp rotting-leaf smell of the jungle, or the mingled smells of cooking and people she sensed with every breath. She meant something else, some elusive base perfume beneath the top notes she could name. And what about the feel of home, so consoling, if also so indefinable? Scent, texture, they were both of them necessarily tied to *here*. Yes, Nony reconfirmed, Kluanak was where she belonged; Kluanak was where the rhythms of life were familiar to her; where she knew her place; where she knew how to place everybody else; where she knew the *adat* – the law, the way of doing things, the norms, the customs.

Frank knew full well Saramantan was an island where time and geography played strange tricks, so kampungs only five miles apart could sometimes seem to be separated by oceans, and centuries. Moreover, if pressed, he'd have admitted belonging could not be bought, that home was not was tradeable, like coconuts or rice. But he really couldn't see any of that was reason for Nony to refuse to cave.

"Well?" he said, in a studiedly neutral tone.

Nony bestowed on the money another yearning glance.

"I don't want to leave my family, my clan, my friends."

By way of reply, Frank once again flicked through the bills. Once, twice, he flicked through them. They were as tempting to Nony as the palm sugar paste she boiled up in the palm sugar season.

"The adat," she said.

Frank now made a fan of the notes and he held it out to her; it pulsed between them. Nony couldn't bring herself to reach for that pulsing fan of money, but she couldn't bring herself to reject it either.

"Tomorrow," she said. "Or the next day. I still need time. Another week. Just give me another week or so to think it over, and then I'll tell you whether I'll go or not."

Frank was furious. He'd liked to have challenged: accept now or I withdraw my offer. But how could he?

"All right," he said, through gritted teeth. "All right. I'll give you one week."

The following morning Nony and Intan were squatting side-by-side in Nony's ruang, shelling beans – later, they'd spread them on mats laid in the full sun and hope the rain held off long enough to let them dry. They were throwing the discarded pods into that useful waste bin, the undergrowth beyond the ruang. First Daughter was helping them. That is to say, she was hindering them, and they broke off from their conversation now and then to chastise her for mangling the pods, or squashing the beans, or eating them. First Son and the twins were just outside: they were busy with their parangs, clearing the vines that threatened to engulf Nony's coffee bushes.

Intan paused in her work and she circled back to the topic of the hour, "So then, what's it to be? Five hundred dollars and shifting, or nothing and staying?"

Nony ran her thumb nail along another bean pod to split it, thus revealing three plump, pink-veined white beans lined up like jewels in their casing of vivid green. She eased them out and she let them plop one by one onto the heap sprawled on the mat between her and Intan.

"I don't know. I want that money, of course I do, but if I left home I'd be like a tapir forced to swing from the tops of the trees like a monkey."

Intan chucked another empty pod into the undergrowth beyond the ruang.

"Have both," she said insouciantly.

Nony looked sceptical.

"If only I could. But I told you: he said he'd throw me in prison if I tried to cheat him."

"That's if you took his money and didn't go," said Intan, "or if you took his money and then came back. But I'm sure there must be other strategies for having the best of both worlds."

"Of course there are," mocked Nony. "Such as?"

Intan grinned and shrugged.

"I've no idea, but why don't you go to the pawang?"

The pawang didn't only mediate, or negotiate, between people and the spirits, the living and the dead, the living and the unborn, via her magic and her trances; she was also the villagers' confessor, counsellor and all-round sage.

"What?" asked Nony. "For advice, you mean?"

"Exactly. You could ask her if she'd got any idea how you could both relieve the tuan of his five hundred dollars and also stay in the kampung. Not either-or. Both. Both, Nony. I'm sure she'd be able to think of something." Intan paused. "Perhaps she could give you another spell?"

Neither sister's faith in the pawang's mastery of magic had been shaken by the failure of the laughing curse the old woman had taught Nony to rid the world of Frank. No, instead of taking his continued existence in this, our colourful world of things and happenings, as evidence that the pawang's powers were perhaps not all they were cracked up to be, they took it as evidence that Nony was an idiot: she must have made some elementary mistake as she'd attempted to damn Frank; she must have jumbled the magic words; she must have sacrificed a diseased cock; she must have omitted some vital herb from the bundle she'd burned. Or something.

So, no, Nony didn't reply to Intan: I've tried her magic and it didn't work. Instead, she paused in splitting a pod, and she looked at her sister blankly.

"Another spell?" she echoed. "To do what?"

Come to think of it, Intan wasn't entirely sure. But she still cherished hopes of seeing Nony reinstalled in her deliciously spoiled former life of well-fed ease and riches up at the DO's bungalow, and of herself once more able to share in all sorts of little ways in her sister's good fortune.

"Kill the mem, perhaps?" she suggested, dreamily.

"Kill her?" baulked Nony. "Don't be silly! Think! Afterwards, her ghost would be hanging about far too close for comfort. I'd never be so reckless."

Nony was referring here to something everybody knew: if a person were killed by witchcraft then their ghost would not sleep easy but would be condemned to wander the earth bent on retribution, meaning the murderer would never again be able to feel safe. Likewise it was common knowledge that ghosts could not cross water, meaning if Nony's curse had worked as she'd intended then the sea would have made a watery barrier preventing Frank's ghost from returning to wreak vengeance on her; the sea would have become a salty cage containing the danger. But as to killing Rose now? No, it was far too risky.

Intan nodded, more to herself than to her sister.

"All right. Not kill her, necessarily. Just get rid of her. A spell to make her disappear."

Nony frowned.

"I proved myself utterly useless at cursing; if I asked the pawang for another spell, she'd no doubt have to explain she couldn't risk letting someone so incompetent at magic loose on the world a second time." She paused. "In any case: to what end would I make the mem disappear? My chance of five hundred dollars would disappear with her; if she went, Baba would no longer think it worth paying me to go."

Intan's eyes gleamed, and she shook her head.

"You aim too low. Never mind five hundred dollars, with the mem gone you'd be free to reclaim everything she pinched from you. Move back into the DO's bungalow. Become the tuan's nonya once again."

Nony loved her sister and she was prepared to be indulgent of her nonsense; she did not accuse, even in the privacy of her own head, that Intan had crossed a line from harmless make believe to cruelly taunting her with impossibilities. No, instead of taking umbrage, she rolled her eyes. Then she threw back her head and she laughed, as at something properly funny.

"What? I'd just go to him, and say: 'Here I am!' Honestly! This idea you've got that I could ever get back with Baba. It's crazy!"

"Don't be so sure. You could always prepare a philtre – slip it to him so all he could see was you."

All the village women knew how to prepare love potions, and Nony had tried plenty of them in her time. But, like more arcane magic, they were notoriously hard to get right, either in their preparation or in their administration. And in Nony's experience, after she'd fallen pregnant with First Son, just a couple of months after she'd become Baba's nonya, they'd never really worked. Now, she looked dismissive.

"If the mem suddenly disappeared in a puff of smoke, then even if I squeezed *ubat cinta* into Baba's eyes, while he slept, he'd take Adik or Mahsuri, not me."

Adik and Mahsuri were unmarried girls in the kampung.

"Adik has a sharp tongue, and Mahsuri is as blur as a belalang."

"And both are as pretty as orchids, and as juicy as ripe mangosteen."

Intan couldn't deny it. But it was so hard to relinquish a lovely fantasy. Sulkily, she eased another bean out of its pod.

"Well, in any case go to the pawang," she pouted. "That's what I think. Unless you have a better idea, which we both know you haven't, have you."

The next day found Nony walking through the coconut grove with First Daughter balanced on one hip and with a bowl of rice and fish in her other hand, on her way to pay the pawang a visit. Apart from its slight suggestion of isolation, the pawang's house, from a distance, looked nothing out of the ordinary. But up close her ruang was unlike any other in the kampung. On the ground, its borders were marked by lumps of white quartz, alternating with coloured stones. Feathers, snake-skins and skulls of all sorts – human, bird and animal – hung from the ceiling. Bunches of dried leaves rustled from pegs on the supporting piles. Three tin pans, larger and shallower than cooking pots, stood to the left, one contained the sleekly black oil the pawang collected from an area of oozing tar pits not far off in the jungle, and which she used for divination. The other two she used for preparing her medicines – she was the village physician in addition to her other duties. To the right of the pans was an enormous and ornate brass incense burner, always stuffed with lighted incense sticks, so the ruang was ever smoky and scented. Next to it was a locked trunk; here the pawang stored her especially powerful amulets, the ones she brought out only at funerals.

As everyone knew, a woman's ability to control magic, rather than being controlled by it, was in inverse proportion to her sexual potency, meaning magic was much safer in the hands of a crone than a nymph. The pawang was even older than Abanawas, 300 years old, reassuringly ancient and by now as sexless as a stick. She was tiny, scrawny, wizened and hunched. Unusually for a woman, even for a 300-year-old woman, she wore her silver hair cropped short. She had no teeth, just the odd decaying stump, and her gums were stained by sirih. She always dressed in plain grey: a grey kebaya and a grey sarong.

Despite her great age and decrepitude, the pawang remained famed for her eyes; they were as enormous and as lovely as a tarsier's and they shone with intelligence. Moreover, thanks to a combination of good health, of the rejuvenating potions she brewed, and of the blessings of the spirits, she could see through them just as well as she'd been able to when she was 20. Or so she claimed.

When Nony stepped into the pawang's unnerving ruang, she found the old woman squatting on the mat, skilfully rolling incense evenly onto splints. The two women exchanged greetings, and then Nony set First Daughter down; she at once began to explore the unfamiliar space. She toddled straight over to the trunk where the pawang kept her funerary amulets and she began patting it, happily, as she sang to herself a little song.

The pawang watched First Daughter hungrily, greedily. The village children, boys and girls alike, tended to be afraid of her; they generally ran past her house as fast as they could. Most would be far too afraid even to enter her ruang, let alone to approach the trunk containing the funerary amulets. Was First Daughter's fearlessness an indication that she was spirit-chosen? The spirits bestowed the ability to commune with them only sparingly; they chose those who'd serve them only grudgingly. For years the pawang had been keeping an eye out for a girl distinguished by evidence of the spirits' favour, one she could train as her successor – after all, every old woman who could be trusted to handle magic safely had been young once, and you had to start somewhere. You had to start them early and hope for time. Time for both of you, shaman and novice. Time which was rapidly running out for her, as the pawang was so distressingly aware. Now, as she watched First Daughter unsuccessfully try to lift the lid of the trunk, she thought: I wonder ... Mind you, First Daughter was a mixed breed, meaning many of the villagers looked at her askance, and even the most tolerant would surely baulk at accepting her in a role of spiritual power. Not that anybody would have much choice, if the spirits so disposed things. And, mused the pawang, perhaps the spirits were less anxious about blood tainted with white than were humans?

Nony was still hovering at the edge of the ruang. She assumed the eagerness with which the pawang watched her daughter was simply that of the very old for the very young: the craving of a person near the end for the special magic of a beginning. She cleared her throat.

At last, the pawang transferred her attention from First Daughter to her mother. She nodded. Nony walked over and squatted down beside her. She placed the bowl of rice and fish between them. The pawang eyed her payment a moment and then she nodded again, before she took up another bamboo splint from the pile beside her and began rolling it with incense. Her rolling board was a plank of wood; the lump of incense looked like gritty grey dough. Nony picked up a splint too, and then, as she lent the pawang a helping hand, she began to talk.

Frank's return had surprised the pawang just as much as it had any of the other villagers, notwithstanding her preternatural insight into the future. She blamed Nony for this slight lapse in prophecy; her faith in herself was no more shaken by the tuan's unexpected return, his continued survival, than was Nony's faith in her. No, when it came to her curse, she too assumed Nony must have messed up the killing magic. The silly child! And if it were her fault the tuan was still alive, then obviously it was her fault too he'd turned up once more in Kluanak quite without psychic warning.

Mind you, if the pawang had known before his return that the tuan was still alive, she could of course have predicted his revised marital status; any of the village women could have done so. And from the moment she'd learned he'd stepped onto the landing stage at the DO's bungalow with a new mem in tow, she'd been certain Nony would soon enough pay her a visit. The poor child must be as discombobulated as a honey bee deprived of its flower, and a good chinwag always helped. Furthermore, she'd thought the child may very well demand another killing curse, directed at either the man who'd shamed her or the woman who'd replaced her. If Nony had now been intent on murder by black magic, the pawang would no more have remonstrated with her about the morality of it all, than she had done when she'd asked for a spell to kill the tuan in the first place. The ancient shaman knew the soul-expanding power of revenge; in her line of business she had to be non-judgemental towards people who were vindictive or vengeful, or who brooded, or who nurtured grudges. But for all that, Nony had been quite right when she'd anticipated the pawang would never have been rash enough to entrust her with another curse, and also why: Nony's incompetence at magic and the danger for her, and for that matter for all the other villagers, in having a furious ghost loitering in the vicinity of the kampung.

So it was fortunate indeed, the pawang now thought, that

Nony merely wanted practical advice. She nodded along as Nony continued to speak, and she made encouraging grunts, occasionally. When at last Nony fell silent, she summarised, "You want me to tell you how you can have your *kuih* and eat it, too."

She was difficult to follow because her lack of teeth made her words indistinct and she spoke in an insect-y mumble, dry as a cricket's sawing. Nony took a moment to process what she'd heard. But then she nodded.

"Please, I hope you can."

Fortunately, the pawang rather thought she could. Three days ago, she'd been weeding in her kitchen garden in the morning sunshine, when, out of the corners of her enormous eyes, she'd seen the new mem entering the coconut grove where the tuan's boys had been larking with their gang as Abanawas busied himself with his eagle. Like everybody, she'd assumed that on seeing three boys with light skin and fine hair, the mem would recognise at once: these are my husband's sons. Naturally, she'd paused in her work and leaned on her hoe to watch this most significant meeting. Despite the distance between herself and the action, she'd been confident she'd see all there was to see, just as she always had done.

Now, in her ruang, the pawang dropped her chin to her chest and closed her eyes; she sat still and silent for a long time, looking inward to the things she'd seen the other day. She'd seen, for a start, that the mem had been unselfconscious in her approach to her husband's children. And that was odd, she'd thought. It was odder still the mem had at first maintained an easy casualness through the awkward social encounter. Not to mention her placid passivity when First Son had cheeked her. The pawang's ears were as sharp as her eyes and she'd plainly heard his anguished, aggressive cry of *pukimak kau*; she'd been just as astonished as Nony by the mem's dimwit lack of reaction to what was so obviously an insult. She herself may have been wrinkled and crinkled but any child who'd sauced her like that would have felt the back of her hand, sharpish. But the mem hadn't seemed in the least bit angry with First Son – not about the insult, not about anything. Wasn't she angry with him simply for being him; for being her husband's child? Apparently not. But surely anger would have been a commoner reaction for a woman in her place than inert neutrality? Yes, yes, it was true enough a man's wives sometimes loved each other's children, but far more often they didn't. Far more often the first wife detested her own children's rivals – the second wife's children – and schemed against them, and the second wife detested her own children's rivals – the third wife's children – and schemed against them, and so on down through the family. True, Nony had only ever been the tuan's convenient wife, but would the nicety make an official wife any better disposed to her rival's children than she otherwise would have been? By the spirits, the pawang couldn't think so. No, she'd puzzled, surely it wasn't quite normal, the mem's indifference to First Son?

After the children and the mem had departed the coconut grove, the pawang had returned to her weeding. As she'd hoed out a particularly stubborn patch of a vigorous bindweed, it had occurred to her the mem's weird composure could perhaps be explained if she hadn't twigged just now that First Son was her husband's child. But inability to speak Malay was one thing, and this was quite another. How could anybody be so stupid? Such dimness must be impossible for a normally intelligent woman – unless she didn't know her husband had children at all.

Alamak! The pawang had jerked upright against her hoe. Was it possible the mem didn't know the tuan was a father? Come to that, was it even possible she didn't know she had a predecessor in the kampung? But no. No, the tuan couldn't have refrained from telling his new wife everything – not unless he were so cocky he'd fooled himself she'd remain forever in the dark, and surely even he couldn't have been so arrogant?

The pawang had frowned to herself, and recommenced attacking the bindweed. As she'd grubbed at a pale tangle of roots, she'd thought about the tuan marrying in far-off Kampung Inggris. Perhaps from this place, miles across the oceans, he had indeed assumed it would be impossible for his bride ever to discover he'd once kept a nonya so he'd decided he need not say a thing about her. Then again, he'd believed he was never coming back to Kluanak, the kampung – *this* kampung – where his former nonya was secreted. Safely secreted, he must have thought. Had he perhaps thought: why speak, if I can get away with silence? He was a man after all, and if a man thought he could pull off some useful deception of a woman, then he'd no doubt do it – especially if he were a powerful man, one used to throwing his weight around. And keeping from his second wife the existence of his first wife would have been a deception any man at all would have found most useful: why would a man poke a stick into the cobra's nest that was female jealousy if he didn't actually have to? Not to mention Mat Salleh men took only one wife. One at a time, in any case. The same woman: the first wife and the last wife, debarring only her early death. So what kinds of expectation did that arouse in the minds of Mat Salleh women? The pawang didn't know – but unrealistic ones, probably. Could they perhaps be so unrealistic they'd render a Mat Salleh man afraid to speak? … Well, well, well, the pawang had thought. Well, well, well …

And now here was Nony, offering rice and fish, both of which were very welcome. At last, the pawang raised her head. She opened her eyes and looked directly at the child. She smiled broadly, thus deepening all the crevices and wrinkles of her face, and then she clicked her tongue against her toothless gums.

"Everybody thinks she knows, you know, but she doesn't know, I know it."

Nony had continued making incense sticks all this time, rolling patiently whilst the pawang had been thinking. She was relieved the old woman had spoken at last, but she was momentarily lost in this thicket of knows. When she'd unscrambled them, she was none the wiser.

"Who doesn't know what that you know about what?"

The pawang blinked her enormous eyes a couple of times, like a frog blinking when it swallowed a fly.

"Think, child, what if out of fear of the cobra the rat avoids the padi field entirely?"

Nony imagined a rat, even its whiskers paralysed by terror, eyeing a cobra swimming silently black and purposeful between rice plants thrusting like spears of emerald merit from the flooded expanse of glinting fields … But, no, she quite missed the pawang's meaning.

"I don't understand."

"Men like a quiet life."

Well. Yes.

"And ... ?"

"Men often withhold information from women if they can, for fear of the consequences of telling."

"True. But ... ?"

The pawang relented.

"What if the tuan hasn't told the mem a thing about you?"

Nony shrugged.

"He must have told her."

"Why?"

Nony shrugged again.

"Stands to reason. He couldn't keep me secret. He had no reason not to tell."

The pawang picked up a bamboo splint, and recommenced rolling incense sticks.

"On the contrary," she said. "What if he had no reason to speak? What if he argued the mem would never find out about you?"

"But she would find out. She'd see the children. He'd know that."

"He thought he was never coming back, remember?"

"So?"

The pawang met and held Nony's eye. She didn't say anything but she blinked, slowly, and then she blinked again: blink, blink.

By a kind of psychic osmosis, Nony understood. She rocked

back on her heels and her mouth fell into a wide O.

"What?" she breathed. "You think he kept her in the dark?"

Blink. Blink.

"You think she failed to realise the other day my sons are his?"

Blink. Blink.

"Risky, though ... She'd be furious if she ever found out, wouldn't she. All other things aside, to realise she'd been hoodwinked like that."

Blink. Blink.

"Well, that would certainly explain why he's so keen to see me quit the kampung."

"To *pay* you to quit the kampung," said the pawang, with heavy emphasis. "To *bribe* you to quit the kampung."

Again, the pawang met and held Nony's gaze. This time, the pawang didn't blink; she kept her eyes round and wide and glittering. Nony again understood by psychic osmosis; she understood the ancient shaman was telling her a man's offer of a bribe could so easily flip into a woman's demand for hush money.

"He's made himself vulnerable, hasn't he?"

Blink. Blink.

Nony reached down to place another incense stick on the growing pile of finished ones.

"He's at my mercy. He's in my power."

Blink. Blink.

As with vengefulness, neither Nony nor the pawang had any qualms about blackmail: undoubtedly it was sometimes justified, especially if the victim were a Mat Salleh who'd himself attempted a bribe. Nony laughed.

"What you're suggesting is, I say to him: I'm not going anywhere. I'll have that five hundred dollars, thanks, *and* I'll stay in the kampung, too. You pay up or else I see to it the mem learns the truth."

Blink. Blink.

Nony began rolling another incense stick.

"Even if she does know all about everything – me, the children – there couldn't be any harm in threatening him with it, could there. With threatening revelation. I'd have nothing to lose. If she knows, there'll still be his offer of five hundred dollars to move, even if I choose not to take it."

The pawang was too old to take offence at Nony's use of *if*.

"Nothing to lose," she echoed. She held up and examined the bamboo splint she was working on: the incense wasn't rolled as evenly as she'd have liked. She replaced it on the rolling board and began evening out the lumps. "But you'll see. I'm right. She doesn't know. And so he'll have to keep on paying, won't he. On and on. You can say: five hundred today and then so much every month, or I make sure the mem finds out." The pawang began to cackle; it was a rustling, papery sound. "The two things you want. Money – oodles of it. Staying put. Yes, child, this is how you can have your kuih and also eat it."

6

THE DO's BUNGALOW AND THE KAMPUNG
JANUARY 1925

Nony and her children had just finished their rice porridge
breakfast in the ruang. Outside, First Daughter was already busy
stripping leaves from one of her mother's coffee bushes. First Son
and the twins were preparing to disappear for the day. They'd
arranged to go hunting spiders in the jungle with their friends,
but now Nony intervened. She nodded at Second Son and then
at Third Son.

"You two can go," she said. She nodded at First Son. "You
can't."

First Son was most put out; barbecued spiders were a great
delicacy and he'd been looking forward to his share of the feast.

"It's not fair!"

Nony shrugged.

"I need you to do something for me."

The twins exchanged a gloating grin and then dashed off at
top speed, before their mother had a chance to change her mind
and rope them into whatever it was. First Son watched them go.
He turned back to his mother.

"What?" he asked sulkily.

"You know Baba will be in his bathhouse for his midday
bath. I want you to go and hide yourself in there, so you can give

him a message from me."

First Son had been nowhere near the bungalow in the nine months since he'd left it, and as for his father? Well!

"Baba?" he jibbed. "In his bathhouse?"

"Yes." Nony frowned to herself a moment. If the mem had not yet cottoned on that First Son was her husband's child, then she certainly didn't want her cottoning on now. After all, if everything now hidden, or so she hoped, were out in the open, then her power to blackmail Baba would drift away like smoke. But if the mem saw one of the half-castes she'd seen in the coconut grove skulking about the bungalow, or even actually talking to her husband, she may be prodded to wonder. She may even take it into her head to ask Baba a few pointed questions – ones he'd find it difficult to evade. She spoke decisively. "It doesn't matter if one of the servants sees you, they won't rat, just don't let yourself be seen by the mem. That's important, understood?"

First Son nodded that he'd got it.

"Listen carefully, this is what you're to say: I need to see Baba at once, today, to discuss the offer he made." Nony swept her hand around the ruang. "I'll be waiting for him here after lie-off time. He'd better come. He'd better bring the money ... Repeat that back to me."

"What offer? What money?"

"None of your business. I asked you to repeat my message."

First Son scowled. He knew there was no point in pressing his bu, there never had been; it was just like the morning when Baba had left last year. Almost the moment they'd arrived back in the kampung, Bu had ordered him and the twins into the jungle to help her gather herbs. They'd asked why, of course, but she'd shrugged and said they didn't need to know. He'd had to learn from his friends, later, that the herbs he'd helped her gather were ingredients in a spell she'd used to curse his father. He'd neither worried overly much whether this curse would succeed, nor thought Bu needed forgiveness for laying it; if he had done, he'd have granted it, such was his love for her. But he'd been hurt she'd dragged him into her murderous plotting without giving him any clue at all what was going on. And now he resented her refusal to trust him even more than he resented being denied a day of poking sticks into spiders' holes. He sighed, heavily, but there was nothing else for it: dutifully, he parroted back her message.

It seemed to First Son he'd been squatting patiently on the bare earth of Baba's bathhouse floor for ever and ever. He'd been humming to himself to help pass the time, but now he stopped: someone was clattering about in the bedroom above his head. It must be Baba. Only he would be booted and be that noisy; he'd begun whistling one of his strange Mat Salleh tunes; no doubt he was undressing. In a moment he'd be down for his bath. How surprised he be! And, probably, how angry! For a moment First Son felt tumbled by dread. But then he jumped up; he stood as straight as he could as he girded himself for the coming encounter.

The bathhouse was a Spartan place. The wooden thunderbox was at one end – it was literally a box, with a hole in the top and a large chamber pot within, which pot the water-carrier emptied twice daily. At the other end there was the area laid with planks where stood the ceramic tong, and beside it were a towel rack and a table, where Frank's shaving bowl, his razor and assorted toiletries were set out. There were no windows, since the rough wooden walls extended neither all the way up to the low planked ceiling, nor all the way down to the floor, instead there was a gap at the top, and another at the bottom, to let in light and air – also snakes, spiders, ants, rats, bats. Despite the constant ventilation, the bathhouse was never entirely free of the whiff of the thunderbox which now, as ever, gave off its sewer smell.

Frank was still whistling as he stepped through the bathhouse door but he jumped a mile at the sight of his son and his whistle died on his lips. Willy-nilly he let go of the door, which groaned shut behind him. Just as First Son had anticipated, he'd stripped off his sweaty khakis upstairs and now he was wearing nothing but a white towel wrapped around his middle.

Meanwhile, First Son was as usual wearing nothing but his once-white, now greyly grubby loincloth. The pale-skinned father and his darker-skinned son each froze for a long moment; each stared at the other with a kind of horror, as though they were not each other's flesh but as if each were to the other an apparition.

First Son broke the stretching silence.

"Baba," he said. He was glad now, he supposed, that his father was not dead. But, golly, it gave him a funny feeling to be addressing him again after such a long time. He could not fully articulate the thought, but he half-understood he could use it correctly, this word *Baba*, but in so far as it referred to a relationship between himself and the man now standing so close to him, he had no idea what it meant. And he still could not feel it; he could no more feel today, when he saw his father again, than he had on the morning Baba had left last year, that in his relationship with him, or in his lack of one, he was missing out.

As likewise was his father. But for his part, Frank felt no pain at all at the sight of First Son, this child to whom he'd always been more-or-less indifferent. Instead he felt appalled: Christ! What if Rose were to spot the brat? But notwithstanding his shock, and his fury, he didn't forget himself so much as to shout; he was horribly aware his wife was now on the verandah somewhere above him, waiting for him to come up for tiffin; any row down here would be audible to her up there and the last thing he wanted was for her to come to investigate.

"Damn cheek!" he hissed. "Waylaying me like this."

First Son really, really, really didn't want to attract the monstrous mem's attention either. But neither fear of the mem, nor fear of his bu's anger if he were careless enough to let the ogress catch a glimpse of him when she'd told him not to, explained why he too spoke quietly. Baba's presence seemed to have muffled his voice so he could summon no more than a whisper.

"Bu sent me."

Frank gave a curt nod.

"So I presumed." He paused. "A message, is it?"

First Son remembered the insulting obscurity of that message. He scowled as he nodded and said, "She says to tell you this: she needs to see you at once, today, to discuss the offer you made her. She'll be waiting for you in our ruang, after lie-off time. She said to tell you you'd better come. She said to tell you to bring the money."

Frank noted his son looked truculent, but then truculence was nothing less than he'd expect of the lad. As for himself, though his own face did not change, his mood began to lighten. This was splendid! He was to bring the money, was he? That could mean only one thing: Nony had at last accepted his offer. She'd take his $500 and toddle off out of his life. He'd been right all along: it had only ever been a matter of time before she'd succumb to temptation and agree to go.

"Very well. Tell her I'll be there, all right, but I'll be damned if I'll hand over the money today. Remind her: not until she's gone." Frank assumed First Son would take this as a dismissal and he took a step towards the tong, all ready for his bath. But his son remained standing exactly where he was, staring at him.

"Gone?" he asked, with evident alarm. "Bu, gone?"

Frank saw no reason to explain.

"Just tell her." He jerked his head backwards, towards the door behind him. "Now shoo! Shoo, and make sure the mem doesn't see you!"

In preparation for delivering her ultimatum to Frank, Nony had changed into her best sarong and kebaya – the sarong was woven with a pattern of stylised white birds on a blue background and the kebaya was of white lace. She'd delivered First Daughter into Intan's care for a couple of hours. The twins were off somewhere, and she'd indulged First Son by saying he could head off for his own spot of spider hunting in the jungle. When Frank panted all sweaty up to her ruang, she was, unusually, alone and doing nothing more than squatting on her mat. And also she was relishing the idea that, even more unusually, between her and

Frank she'd be the one now running the show.

Frank was so sure Nony had come round to his way of seeing things, he was prepared to be almost friendly. He squatted down beside her.

"So then, old girl, you've decided."

Nony was determined to enjoy herself. She'd toy with Baba and linger over her toying to boot.

"I have."

"Good girl. I knew you would."

"But First Son said you wouldn't bring the money."

"You've seen it. You know I have it."

"I want it today."

"I've told you: you can't have it until you've gone. I'll send it along to your new kampung."

Nony laughed.

"I've decided I'm not going."

Frank was thrown; this was so unexpected he thought he'd misheard, and he asked Nony to repeat herself, which she did. When it was clear she'd said what he thought she'd said, he reddened.

"Not going!" he accused. "Not going! What d'you mean? Why not?"

Nony bestowed upon him a smile of bridal radiance.

"Because I don't want to. But I'll have it anyway. My five hundred dollars."

Though he was squatting, Frank began to wave his arms.

"Now look here! You can't have it, if you don't go, you know. That's what it's for. Moving to another kampung."

"No, Baba," said Nony. "That was what it was for before."

"Before?" jibbed Frank. "Before what?"

Nony paused to relish her moment.

"Before I discovered your *pelacur putih* doesn't know about you and me, or about our children."

Pelacur putih. White whore. Frank, infuriated, momentarily failed to recognise the danger he was in, and he focused on quite the wrong part of Nony's reply.

"I say! I won't have my mem referred to as *pelacur putih*." No, it wouldn't do. It wasn't just an insult to Rose and to him, but also, he felt, to Britain. He was, after all, Britannia's representative in Kluanak, and Rose was his wife.

Nony looked at him with contempt.

"She doesn't know," she repeated.

It began to dawn on Frank where this could be leading. Christ! Had his worst fears been realised? Had Nony cottoned on that by letting things drift – by failing to confess to Rose – he'd left himself wide open to blackmail? But she couldn't possibly know, he reassured himself, she couldn't possibly know Rose didn't know. At best she could only have made a lucky guess.

"Stuff and nonsense!" he blustered. "I told her everything."

Nony narrowed her eyes.

"She knows already, does she? So, then, you won't mind, will you, if I visit her, to discuss with her our history. Yours and mine. The children. All these things she already knows."

How dare she! Frank remembered who he was, and who she was.

"You can't discuss anything with her," he flashed. "You can't speak English. She can't speak Malay."

"Come *on*!" jeered Nony.

Frank had to grant she'd find a way. He tried to tell himself Nony may have the gall to threaten him, but she'd surely never have the audacity to go through with her threats. Nonetheless, he began to feel sick.

"You know she's seen the boys. You know she knows they're mine."

"I know nothing of the sort. She's seen them, yes, but did she recognise them as yours?"

"Half-castes in the kampung? Of course she did."

"Then I'll send them round to introduce themselves properly. Only polite." Nony smiled a smile so sweet it could have rotted teeth. "You can act as translator between your sons and your wife."

"N-o-n-y." Frank's tone was some blend of threatening, afraid, warning, begging, bullying and humble.

Nony tossed her hair.

"You know my price."

"You want me to buy your silence?"

Nony held out her hand, palm up, all ready to receive the dough.

"Five hundred dollars. If you want me to keep my mouth shut, you'll give me what I ask, no quibbling. And as I said, I'm not leaving the kampung. I'm not going anywhere now."

Frank's nausea intensified so he almost gagged. For a long moment he looked at Nony's outstretched hand and then he caved.

"I can't give you anything right this minute. Didn't I make

myself clear? I left the money at the bungalow."

Nony was cock-a-hoop.

"So you admit it! You admit she's in the dark about everything."

Silence.

Nony, still gloating, became briskly business-like.

"First Son's out hunting spiders. When he gets home, I'll send him over. You'll give him the money so he can bring it to me. I'll tell him to wait in your bathhouse again, before evening tiffin."

Anger rose in Frank, hot and bubbling, like volcanic mud rising through the earth's crust.

"This is the thanks I get for keeping you like a queen for 10 years!"

Nony met his anger coolly.

"And another thing: from now on I want one hundred dollars per month. A regular payment."

"Preposterous!"

"If you pay me that on time each month your pelacur putih will continue oblivious. But if you don't …"

Frank forgot both himself and the public-private nature of the ruang so thoroughly that he began shouting loud enough for the birds in the padi fields to hear.

"Impossible terms! Impossible sum!"

"One hundred and fifty dollars."

"I don't have a tree I can shake every time I need cash."

Nony considered a moment: had she overreached herself? Would Baba really have trouble paying her $150 per month? She summoned her idea of his safe as a magically refilling treasure chest stuffed to the brim with ropes of lustrous pearls and gold coins and a sparkling rainbow of jewels. She spoke flatly, "Five hundred dollars today, then one hundred and fifty in a month. One hundred and fifty every month. You can afford it."

Far from holding pearls and diamonds, the safe in Frank's wardrobe actually contained important documents, such as his and Rose's passports, their marriage certificate, his cheque book, usually a little cash and, for now, the $500 he'd won off Slinger. Later, after his and Rose's game of tennis, when he was again naked but for a fresh towel wrapped around his waist, all ready for his evening bath, he did what he must to save himself from exposure: he opened his safe, and, it seemed to him, he raided it; he plundered it as easily as if it were made of cardboard.

On the way down to his bathhouse, he clenched the $500 tight in one fist and he tried to kid himself Nony would have had second thoughts about blackmailing the DO. But of course she hadn't chickened out. Of course First Son was waiting for him. Frank didn't greet the boy or give him a chance to speak, instead, as soon as the door had creaked shut behind him, he held out his clenched fist and one by one he unfurled his fingers; thus he teasingly revealed the slightly squashed stack of folded notes lying on his palm. As earlier, he kept his voice low, fearful that Rose, up on the verandah, would overhear proceedings down here in the bathhouse.

"This is what your mother wants."

First Son watched his father's fingers unfurl; he thought they looked like petals slowly unfurling from a flower. He still didn't know what was going on. He still didn't know what he'd become embroiled in; he couldn't catch the rules of this game between his parents. But he knew he hated being used as their go-between. He felt his involvement in all this cloak and dagger stuff brought him under suspicion of something or other, and no matter that he couldn't quite specify what it was, this thing he judged to be his supposed crime. Still, for the moment, he forgot his simmering resentment, his confusion and his distress. They were all equally obliterated by the awe he felt in the presence of so much money. He'd never before imagined that such a fortune existed even in the whole entire world and now he didn't have to imagine it: he was looking at it! He'd have been shocked into speechlessness, even had he felt inclined to speak to his father, which, in fact, he didn't.

In silence First Son raised his small, slender brown hand and he held it, palm up and flat, towards his father. Frank reached across and he deposited the money on his son's upraised palm. Neither of them moved. Instead, they both looked at the dirty wodge of notes resting on First Son's palm. Frank thought, regretfully, of all this money could have bought: all the booze and cigarettes and meals at the Club in BB. For his part First Son had only the haziest idea of the things that money could buy. He had no idea, really, what anybody at all could buy with the fortune he now held, let alone what he could buy with it. But he understood well enough that money meant power; that money was some sort of protective talisman; that the Mat Salleh used it much as the villagers used the pawang's amulets to stave off disease, distress, danger. At last, in conscious imitation of his father, and now thinking of a flower open during the day but closing for the night, he slowly furled his fingers one by one round the notes; he could scarcely believe he'd been entrusted with anything so precious.

But what a pity they felt so horrible! They felt grittily greasy, so First Son wished he could wash them before he took them home. Or else wash his hands. Yes, the notes made his fingers feel as if he'd dunked them in a pot of the bluish-black indigo Bu used to dye the threads she used in her weaving. And it wasn't just his fingers that felt stained, it was him. All of him. Which wasn't fair. And he knew who to blame for his misery: it's all your fault, his eyes silently accused, as he blazed out of them at his father.

Frank was taken aback by the force of his son's glare. What had got into the ungrateful lad? Well, whatever it was, it was outrageous. And though the brat now had the money safely in his grasp, he'd still made no move to leave. Frank pointed to the door.

"Do you intend to take root? You've got what you want ... *She's* got what *she* wants. Now bugger off!"

OUTBOUND MAIL, JANUARY 1925
SENT FROM THE DO's BUNGALOW,
KLUANAK, SARAMANTAN

From Rose to Beatrice

Dearest Bumbles,

Oh, I did so enjoy reading of the bonfire Edmund lit at Raddington Court for Guy Fawkes Night, and the toffee, and the gathered village children's happy faces lit by firelight as they watched the guy go up in flames.

Lest you pity me for missing out on the fun, I should like you to know that we too have here in the jungle our own bonfires and our firecrackers – or rather they have them down in the kampung. And not once a year, but once a month! Every night the full moon rolls round – Oh, the beauty of a full tropical moon and her stars all swarming around her – every full moon the natives hold a most terrific celebration. It's called bully penny, or billy penoo, or something like that. All the villagers go, and we even have to give our night watchman a holiday, so I worry a tiger may wander in from the jungle, and, on finding no resistance at all, mount the steps onto the verandah with predatory intent.

I've never actually attended this bully penoo – that wouldn't do at all, for the mem – but I've heard it, for it's a very noisy affair, and the music keeps going all night – drums and xylophones and gongs, all most irritating when one is trying to sleep. Frank tells me the whole to-do is dedicated to the villagers' deceased parents and grandparents, for, in thoroughly Saramantanese fashion, our natives, though Mohammedan, worship as well as their god the spirits of their ancestors. Apparently, they believe that on the night of the full moon, the ancestor-spirits return to visit the world of the living, and so their descendants hold a party for them to forestall their making trouble – feasting, music, bonfires, and everyone very jolly on palm toddy. Frank says the imams (Mohammedan priests) in BB would put a stop to our natives' drinking just as much as to their expansive reverence, if only they could, but the religion that blew here on dry, dusty winds from deserts far to the west, has to date penetrated only so far up the rivers of Saramantan's rainy jungle.

Of course, our natives do not burn on their bonfires straw-stuffed guys in remembrance of failed plotting. No, they burn votive offerings for the dead, little models of things they'll need in the next life, such as fishing nets and cooking pots, or so Frank tells me – all these things woven from the natives' endless rattan, he says, and their smoke as useful to ghosts as the real things to us.

So you see what a fantastical, fairy tale world I live in, so different from your own of dogs and church and village things – English village things, I mean. Oh, English villages! I'm not at all surprised your vicar's idea to introduce sheep into the churchyard next spring, to keep down the grass when it starts to grow, has caused something of a sensation; I do hope they don't eat the flowers people leave. As to your Good Works, I found your account of taking soup to decrepit villagers too hilarious.

Write back to me soon with more tales of rural life, and next time there's a full moon, try to catch sight of it in water. Our natives believe to see the full moon reflected in water is the most terrific good luck, and even my sensible Frank insists we view her reflection in the river here, the night of bolly ponoo. Hand-in-hand we walk down to the very end of the landing stage and the silver disk rippling liquid beneath us makes a most romantic sight I must assure you.

Your loving cousin, Rosebud

From Rose to Daphne
Dearest Mummy,
Thanks for yours, of December 1. I was sorry to hear you'd been poorly with a shocking head cold, and I trust you are by now fully recovered.

When I arrived at Kluanak, didn't I write to you of my servants? I seem to remember I did – I am sure so – but I cannot think that when you sat down to write, you had yet received mine to you. How strange our two letters on the same subject should have crossed in the mail.

Please pass on my thanks to Miss Bellington for her advice. I quite concur servants are the most frustrating people; mine always have some very good reason why something wasn't done, which I know, and they know that I know, to be an absolute lie.

I have heard before that Chinamen are hard-working servants, but not to be trusted to do the marketing, as they are unreliable about money, and I grant this would be most useful information if any of my servants were Chinamen, but mine are all Malay. Likewise Miss B's advice on appointing my lady's maid: I would certainly follow it, if such a creature ever came my way, but ladies' maids are as rare as hen's teeth in the jungle.

I quite agree I must lead my servants by example, and that if they perceive my conduct is regulated by high and correct principles, then they will not fail to respect me. Indeed, mine are already much livelier about their duties than when I arrived. It is most satisfactory that they begin to understand I miss nothing.

Still, I can't deny I find their manner often insolent. Not to mention their nosiness. Frank says it's hopeless, trying to hide anything at all from native servants, he says they're worse even than servants at Home for knowing all, and I fear I cannot disagree.

Cookie, meanwhile, I begin to judge entirely a lost cause.

Your fond daughter, Rose

PS You are quite right I must do without a hairdresser and so my shingle is growing out. My hair is below my shoulders now, and begins to curl, annoyingly.

From Frank "Langers" Langham, to Charles "Slinger" Slightman

Christ, Slinger, what a hugger-mugger,

So, Maude insists that obviously what you don't know can blankety well hurt you. What you don't want to know. What you are frightened to know. What others are afraid to tell you. I suppose I agree. And I can understand why she urges I should blankety well get it all out in the open, despite the lateness of the day. Yes, I suppose her advice I should come clean to Rose is sound, but I can't seem to bring myself to speak and that's all there is to it.

On the other hand, I certainly cannot agree with your little woman I was a rotten cad to offer Nony a bribe to move. Who said anything about a bribe? I merely proposed to make a gift to the dratted egg to do something that it was all along in her own best interests to do. And a rotten cad? I cannot prevent myself objecting this is another horribly unfair description by which Maude chooses to slur Yours Truly, and another one which, from friendship, you may have done better not to tell me. But no matter, I'm a forgiving man; from friendship I yet again forgive you.

In any case, none of this matters now. There have been developments, old man, developments. Nony is refusing to leave the kampung. This would of itself make life dashed awkward, but, worse, she's somehow guessed Rose knows nothing of our quondam connection and she's realised, too, that this leaves me as exposed to her as a lamb to a wolf. The dipper's got the gall to blackmail me! Yes, the cat wants paying to keep the kittens in the bag.

Perhaps best not to tell Maude, but she's already had the $500 I won off you, and now she wants $150 per month in return for her continued silence. Damned impudence! Does she think I'm as rich as Croesus? I wish I were, but you know I only have my salary and as a regular thing I can't possibly afford to bung her hush money. Indeed I've quite made up my mind: that's it! She's bled me already as much as she ever will. I'll no longer play her games, and to hell with the consequences.

But, oh, the possible consequences! I tell you, black ideas now flap about my head like bats about the jungle. And I confess I've been hitting the bottle pretty hard these past couple of evenings. I dare say I'm soused now, for I knocked back three whiskies before telling Rose I must deprive myself of her delightful company for an hour in order to write my letters. The little woman was not above raising her eyebrow and pouting at the speed with which I downed my drinks, and I suppose she was right to look askance. I hope you can read my writing. It never was the best, even when I wielded the pen stone cold sober, and now I fear alcohol makes my words spiders on the page.

If only Nony would drop dead overnight. Wouldn't that be the sweetest payback after her ridiculous attempt to curse me, but no such luck, I suppose.

Yours, Langers

PS Doubtless Maude will say I have only myself to blame. Do a chum a favour and implore her to refrain from instructing you to tell me: I told you so.

7

The DO's bungalow, Kluanak, February 1925

From the eaves of the DO's bungalow, at the outer edge of the verandah hung chicks, blinds made of thin strips of split bamboo, which could be raised or lowered to provide shade, or to let in a breeze, or to keep out the rain. Today, the heat was syrupy and the chicks were lowered against the glare of the sun. Thus the verandah had acquired something of the feeling of a tent; it was dim with the sort of filtered light so often found under canvas and the trapped air was almost musty, it was so warm and still, and as soporific as anything. Or so Rose had tried to tell herself, as she'd nodded off at her desk over one of her Malay grammars.

After all, it was far safer to blame the opium effects of heat and *Colloquial Malay: a simple grammar with conversation*, than to tempt fate by dwelling on her hopes. But, oh, her hopes! There was no denying her monthlie was by now a month late. And she'd been so tired so much of the time, recently, not to mention her body dragged with a new kind of heaviness ... Mind you, she could be late for all sorts of reasons or for no reason at all, and even if she were late for the obvious reason, the ordinarily miraculous one, then that was no excuse for sleeping in the middle of the morning.

Or so Rose had chided herself, even as she'd dozed off. But now something, some intrusive awareness, caused her to stir and she hung for a moment between waking and sleeping. And, neither awake nor asleep, suspended as she was between the reality of her dreams and the reality of her physical surroundings, she was washed by a most uncanny feeling: she was being watched by ghost-like eyes; a pair of eyes fluttering about her head like an insubstantial butterfly, like a gossamer moth. Sleep-blurred, she fancied she was being watched by an unborn child, its eyelash existence pressed up close, aching, against the window of this our loveliest of worlds ...

But then sleep loosened its grip on Rose a little further, and a little further, until she jolted awake. What? Watched by an unborn child? Gossamer moths? Eyelash existence? What had got into her? Rose sat up and she glanced about the verandah, half expecting to see Boy grinning at her, so unbearably insolently, from a doorway, but there was nobody there. She decided she was being too silly for words. This would teach her to doze off as she studied. Verbs were the thing! She picked up *Colloquial Malay* and she tried to return her attention to the future tense: I will drink milk, *saya akan minum susu*; you will drink coffee, *anda akan minum kopi*; he will drink tea, *dia akan minum teh* ... Alas, her attention wandered. The future tense, she thought: he will be. God willing.

In fact, as she'd slept, Rose had indeed been watched by a child, although not an unborn one and not hers either. The intrusive awareness prodding her to wakefulness had been caused by First Son beaming on her his pitiless disdain: Bu was using him as her go-between again; she'd told him he was again to wait in Baba's bathhouse at midday, there to deliver another of her distressingly mysterious messages. As before, Bu had said it wouldn't matter if he were caught by the servants, but she'd skin him alive if he let himself be seen by the mem.

Well, there was fat chance of that! First Son had only paused to look at the ogress, as he'd made his otherwise fleet and flitting way across the compound because she was safely snoring. She'd been framed by the gap in the chicks, where the stairs gave access to the verandah and she'd been facing towards him; her cheek squashed hard against an open book on the desk. Her face had looked flabby and crumpled, and her alarming red hair had tangled about it in a messy mass. Her mouth had drooped open and First Son had even fancied she drooled; he hadn't been able to see clearly whether or not she did, but he'd seen no reason to give her the benefit of the doubt. He'd stared at her a long, long moment, a time-stopping moment sticky as cobwebs, it had seemed to him.

But then the mem had stirred. First Son had been scared rigid: what if she woke up and opened her strange green eyes? He'd shot off, his heart pumping just as fast as his legs. He'd thrown himself into the safety of the shadowy space beneath the bungalow – the cobwebs here were literal ones – and then he'd crept towards the entrance to his father's bathhouse, where he was now sitting on the thunderbox, pretending it was a sultan's throne, and waiting, waiting.

Though he was naked but for the white towel wrapped round his middle, Frank didn't feel the least bit cool; the midday heat was itself like a hot, damp rag pressed close to his flesh. By George he was looking forward to his midday bath! How good it would be to slosh off the sweat of the morning. He walked into his bathhouse cheery with anticipation. But he jibbed in the doorway: Christ! First Son! Drat the brat! And drat Nony! He knew what this intrusion was about of course: the dipper's deadline for the first of the monthly down payments on her silence was already a week in the past; evidently, she'd decided today was the day to milk him. Though he'd expected something like this, he nonetheless felt taken unawares by his son. His sweaty flesh became sweatier, and the heat began to prickle him as bad as ant bites.

First Son jumped off the thunderbox and stood staring at his father. Behind Frank, the bathhouse door slowly creaked shut on its rusty hinges, thus enclosing the two of them in the slightly smelly, not quite private space – this space where they were hidden from view, but not, as Frank was so horribly aware, free from being overheard by his wife. He hissed,

"So, Bu's press-ganged you again as her apprentice in racketeering, has she?"

Though First Son still didn't understand what his parents thought they were up to, and though too the words "press-ganged", "apprentice" and "racketeering" were new to him, his father's belittling accusation caught him on the raw; it reminded him how grubby he'd felt as he'd closed his fingers around that payment of $500 he'd carried from his father to his mother a month ago, give or take. What had Bu done with the money? Here was another adult puzzle to make him feel puzzlingly fraudulent. He was no dodger or schemer! He was an honest boy! So why was Baba jeering at him? Well, whatever his reasons, First Son felt the special disappointment of a boy failing to fulfil his own expectations of himself. Not that he was entirely sure what it was he expected of himself, but in any case: not this. Not to run between his parents, as if he were the butt of some joke of theirs he didn't get. Naturally, he resented Baba, his father, for making him feel so soiled and baffled, and he even resented Bu, just a little. But resenting his mother upset him further, so he felt he was spiralling down and down and down into misery.

Frank thought First Son looked quite unnecessarily sullen. He waited for him to speak, but the lad just gazed at him like a mental deficient. He jerked his thumb over his shoulder to the door.

"I don't care about her demands. Tell her my answer's no." He paused to let that sink in, and then he added, "Now scram!"

First Son didn't move.

"She says to remind you: you were supposed to pay her last week. She says you know the price."

Frank looked his son up and down. The brat was as usual shoeless and naked but for a grimy loincloth; his scabby brown legs were smeared with mud; his hair was matted; his face was grubby. Well! He would not be humiliated by this ... this ... urchin, this *goblin*, that's all.

"This won't do," he said. "I won't have it!"

"She says I must take the money back with me, she wants it today."

"She can say what she pleases. You tell her this: her terms are ridiculous. You tell her even if all she asked were one dollar, I wouldn't pay." Frank flung out his arm and pointed at the door. "She can go to hell. Now be off and tell her that!"

This time, First Son duly scarpered. But as the bathhouse

door groaned shut behind him, Frank could not feel relieved.
He momentarily dropped his head into his hands before telling
himself, sternly, to pull his socks up; he must bathe and get upstairs
for tiffin before Rose became suspicious. He let his towel slide to
the floor. Naked, he walked over to the tong, picked up the ladle
and began to sluice himself down with tepid water. But it was no
good, he may as well have been rinsing himself in dread. Now he'd
torn it! He was tempted to hotfoot it down to the kampung to tell
Nony he hadn't really meant it, he'd pay up after all ... But no.
No. He shouldn't have lost his rag like that, but he'd had to reject
Nony's ultimatum. Of course he had. Pay up or else? He'd had no
choice; he couldn't let Nony make him her plaything, he'd had to
choose or else. He again dipped the bamboo ladle into the water
and he told himself he must speak to Rose instanter, he really
must ... He poured the ladleful of water over his head and he
changed his mind about that: though she'd not yet wavered, now
push had come to shove, surely there was still an outside chance
Nony would be too afraid of him, the DO, to carry through on
her threat to expose him? He dipped the emptied ladle back into
the tong, refilled it and then sloshed water across his chest. Yes,
he'd keep silent just a little longer, he decided, just long enough to
see if Nony would let him off the hook.

Nony's face was like thunder as she listened to First Son's account
of his exchange with his father. Huh! Baba surely hadn't meant
what he'd said when he'd told their son he wouldn't pay her what
she'd asked. And whatever he'd meant, she'd teach him! She'd
show him!

Or rather, she quickly corrected herself, she'd show the mem – and what she'd show the mem would be herself. Yes, even as she learned Baba intended to play silly buggers, Nony began to formulate a plan to flaunt herself in front of the new mistress up at the bungalow. How would Baba like that? There'd be a tiny risk, of course, that the mem would realise how the two of them – the three of them – were connected, and thus bring an end to her own career as an extortionist, but she judged this risk to be so small as to be not worth bothering about. Why would a Mat Salleh woman too stupid to realise the pale-skinned children she'd spotted in the coconut grove must have been fathered by the only Mat Salleh man for miles around, think to connect some or another Malay woman sauntering round the compound with her husband? But for sure it would give Baba a fright to learn his wife had seen her hanging about the bungalow. With luck, he'd be scared into paying up.

And so at first light the next morning, Nony instructed her sons to keep an eye on their little sister, and then she walked the path from the kampung to the DO's bungalow. She waited in the jungle just beyond the compound until she saw Baba walk across to the courthouse to start his working day. Once he'd disappeared into the building, she slipped into the compound. She waved to the two watchmen, night and day, who were chatting together as one finished his shift and the other started it, and then she hid herself in Baba's bathhouse.

Rose had fallen into the habit, now, of walking through the bungalow every morning to check that Boy had not been slacking.

This morning, she as usual started her tour in the barely used drawing room. She ran her finger along a table top and it came away clean, with no dust, which pleased her. She checked whether the water in the vases of flowers had been changed: it had. The bits and pieces of silver and brassware she'd not had packed away were all highly polished, as were the floorboards; she'd now expect no less.

Satisfied, she walked across the verandah and into Frank's bedroom, where her expectations were likewise met: the bed, where he rarely spent the whole night now that he was a married man, was neatly made, and there was no dust on his writing desk. She lifted one corner of the rug: no, Boy had not lazily swept the dirt under the carpet. Frank's little dressing room was orderly too; all her husband's clothes had been put away, she saw nothing of which to complain.

Frank's bathhouse was next on her itinerary. The steps leading to it opened directly off his dressing room. Down she went. The wooden staircase was short, only six or seven steps. On the third step, she got a shock: a Malay woman was coolly strolling out of Frank's bathhouse, just as bold as brass, as if she had every right to do so, as if she were mistress of this house. Well! Rose was outraged.

"I say!" she called sharply, in English. "What are you doing?"

Nony had been hiding in Baba's bathhouse a good hour already and she'd walked out now just because she'd heard Rose's tread on the stairs. She knew it could only be the mem's footsteps she'd heard, the servants moved silently on shoeless feet, and Baba, who stepped particularly heavily, must still be at the courthouse.

Rose called again, "What are you doing?"

Although Nony couldn't understand the mem's words, she knew that in the high-handed way of the Mat Salleh she'd think she was in charge of this encounter. Well, the bitch was wrong. *She* was running it; *she* was in control. She turned around unhurriedly, almost languidly, with deliberate hauteur and she bestowed upon Rose a disdainfully dignified stare.

And so, for the first time, Rose and Nony met each other's eyes. Just as Nony had anticipated, Rose failed to grasp what relationship they bore to each other – why should she? But although only one of them knew how they were linked, they stood equally pinioned as each silently appraised the other.

Alamak! thought Nony. The mem seemed even larger and more ungainly close to than she had when seen across the coconut grove. Her devilish hair looked redder, her face looked shinier with sweat. And it was true what they said: her eyes weren't properly brown but an inhuman green. Moreover, her teeth were like an animal's: bestial white, not stained beautifully red by sirih, as a woman's teeth properly should be.

Rose, looking down from the staircase, at first felt nothing but the continuing force of her righteous indignation at the native woman's effrontery in invading Frank's bathhouse. But then something about the quality of the intruder's gaze caused her to shudder. This woman's eyes put her in mind of the eyes staring up at her daily from her plate at tiffin: steamed fish eyes. Except steamed fish were past caring about what they saw; they regarded her, or failed to, with indifference. But this woman's gaze, though blank, seemed to be charged with something quite the opposite of indifference ... they were blank with hostility, she may even say. Pointed and personal hostility. Hostility for her. Goodness! Rose felt for a moment as if she'd been caught in a searchlight beam of darkness, dense with disgust and loathing.

But, half a minute! Rose reminded herself she was the tuan's wife, an Englishwoman, and she got a grip. She was being too silly! Why on earth should this stranger feel anything in particular for her? There was nothing personal between them. Beams of darkness? Fiddlesticks! It was far more likely she simply couldn't read the other woman's alien gaze. And eyes aside, the intruder looked more matronly than vituperative, too comfortable about the hips to harbour hatred, too cosy for loathing. What a ridiculous little thing! Dumpy, and probably approaching the lower slopes of middle age. Rose thought her rather ugly: she had the broad flat face, fleshy lips and squashed nose so typical of the Malays, not to mention a mouth horribly stained by that vile sirih. She was shoeless, in the native way, and dressed in a tatty sarong and kebaya. Her loose black hair fell to her waist in lankily greasy hanks.

Rose decided it behoved a daughter of Britannia to break the stretching silence.

"What do you want?" she demanded, in the ringing tone she'd already learned to adopt with the natives, the tone of a woman accustomed to being obeyed. But the words were barely out before she realised the intruder almost certainly couldn't understand English, so she tried again, in Malay ... except: how did you say *want* again? Despite the difficulties, she did her best.

"*Apa yang kamu mahu?*" she asked, pausing between each word to search for it. She used exactly the same ringing tone she'd used when she'd been speaking English and the same intonation too.

Nony realised that the mem was trying to speak Malay, but even when her words could be distinguished as words, they were so heavily accented they could have meant anything. She shrugged theatrically. In silence she turned and in silence she sauntered towards the gate that gave access between the compound and the path to the kampung.

Rose was pleased how easily she'd seen off an audacious trespass. She stood on the steps, watching until the dumpy little woman had let herself out of the compound. Though she had an ugly gait, heavy and flat-footed, there was a most exasperating impudence about the sway of her hips. Only once the intruder was lost to sight, did she continue down to Frank's bathhouse, where she found everything shipshape, just as she'd trusted she would – although the rusty hinges to the door still needed oiling, despite her repeated requests that Boy jump to it. Still, debarring only that minor niggle, she was jolly pleased with her skills in household management.

Meanwhile, Nony too was well satisfied: so far, so good. But what if the mem omitted to tell her husband she'd seen a native woman hanging about? Nony realised this was a potential weakness in her plan to frighten Baba into paying up; to make certain he learned of the encounter, she intended to tell him of it herself. So after she'd let herself through the gate, she squatted just inside the jungle until she judged the coast was clear and then she made her way back to Frank's bathhouse. She stepped silently and stealthy to avoid attracting Mat Salleh attention, though again she trusted the servants would turn a blind eye. Once reinstalled in the bathhouse, she squatted on the floor and she settled down to wait. She didn't mind how long she sat there; what better use could she make of this time?

An hour or so after she'd seen off the Malay woman, or so she thought, Rose was lounging indolently in one of the planters' chairs on the verandah – she excused herself of laziness on account of her Certain Suspicions. She had already bathed and now she was waiting for Frank to return from the courthouse for tiffin. Although Boy had positioned himself by the steps leading up from the garden, watching for her husband's return, Rose barely noticed his patient presence; she may as well have been alone. As usual, the chicks had been lowered against the searing dazzle of the midday sun; Rose was grateful for the shade, but she had raised the one closest to her chair, to let in both the breeze and a view of the river: a broad and sluggish ribbon swirled with every earthy shade known on Saramantan, from the colours of coconut husks and coffee grounds to those of cinnamon bark and the local gooey red laterite mud.

Soon enough, Rose heard Frank come whistling from his duties. She watched him bound up the wide, shallow steps onto the verandah. At the top he stopped whistling and he exchanged a word or two with Boy as he passed him his topee. She called out a greeting. Her husband turned to her and grinned.

"I'm running like butter," he said. "My bath will be jolly welcome."

With that he walked across the verandah, entered his bedroom and banged shut the door behind him.

Inside, he again began to whistle. Rose could hear him clearly: *It's a long way to Tipperary*. She sometimes found the thin deficiency of the bungalow's walls exasperating but now she smiled indulgently. She heard her husband walking through to his dressing room. She imagined him stripping off his sweat-drenched khakis and dropping them to the floor for Boy to find. For a moment, she couldn't help imagining him naked but she knitted her brows at her own audacity and she refused to linger over the image she'd just conjured – not before tiffin, for heaven's sake, and not when she was a woman with Certain Suspicions. In any case, she knew Frank wouldn't remain naked for long, in a moment he'd take the clean white towel which had been laid out for him on the table and wrap it about his middle, so he'd look something like an Ancient Egyptian, painted millennia ago, his portrait only recently revealed on the wall of King Tutankhamen's tomb. After a little while she heard him descend to his bathhouse, still whistling. Even shoeless his footfalls were loud, they cracked against the wood with a sound like plates breaking, she thought with affection.

When a moment later Rose heard the door to Frank's bathhouse creak open, she barely had time to be irritated the hinges still hadn't been oiled before her husband's whistling abruptly stopped, and she heard him start shouting – unfortunately in Malay, meaning she couldn't understand what he was yelling. A woman replied, much more quietly.

A woman? Rose's mind flew at once to her earlier encounter:

that intruder she'd seen off must have had the sauce to return. Well! It was typical of a Malay to sneak back so stealthily. This one must have some grievance she wished to bring to Frank; she must have crouched in wait for her poor husband. Outrageous! And in his bathhouse too! How shameless! Had the impudent madam no modesty? Rose had a good mind to go down to the bathhouse herself, to upbraid the hussy. Except, she wondered, may that not have looked, both to the Malay woman and also to Frank, like an affront to her husband's authority? Or what if one or other of them, or both of them, judged that her motive was nothing more than nosiness? No, thought Rose, it simply wouldn't do for the tuan's wife to be suspected of stooping to anything so base. Indeed, she wouldn't even walk across the verandah to raise the blind that would have given her a view down to the doorway of Frank's bathhouse; even that would have been to betray herself, by indulging a vulgar curiosity unworthy of her position. Instead of meddling she would remember her dignity and her husband's; she would stay exactly where she was, lounging in her planter's chair, watching the river flowing on past the bungalow – on and on it flowed, on and on and on ...

Meanwhile, down in the bathhouse Nony was delivering the blow.

"I engineered for your pelacur putih to see me this morning," she said calmly. "You'll have to ask her about it when you go back upstairs."

Frank recommenced swearing freely in Malay, at full shout.

Nony no more wanted the mem coming down to the bathhouse, asking questions, sticking her nose in, than he did.

"Shut up!" she flashed. "Or your pelacur putih will hear."

Frank wanted to bellow like a bull or to roar like a tiger. But he wasn't so enraged he was beyond any hope of mastering himself, and with an effort so great it made his eyes bulge and his cheeks flame, he did indeed shut up. For a long beat there was stillness and silence in the bathhouse

Nony spoke first. She bestowed on Frank a look of gloating scorn, and she said,

"You'd better give me what I want, you know you can't negotiate when you're wrapped only in a towel."

Christ! Frank hated Nony then, he really, really hated her. But he continued to keep in mind the peril he was in, and though he snarled, he managed to do so quietly.

"This is disgraceful! Ambushing me in my bathhouse!"

"What? You didn't expect me?"

Frank's flush deepened and his bulging eyes glowed hotter. Nony smirked and then she said flatly, "You wouldn't give it to First Son, but you'll give it to me. The money. You own me one hundred and fifty dollars."

"You've got a nerve! I gave you five hundred."

"Last month. But now it's this month."

"Spent it already, have you?"

Nony had in fact stashed $150 of her hush money in a rice sack in her house, and the rest of the $500 she'd disbursed amongst her relatives.

"No need for that tone. You know what we agreed. And you're late with your payment."

"I never agreed to anything."

"More fool you."

Frank hesitated. Should he even now backpedal? Should he pay up and put off the reckoning another month? It was tempting … But no. No; this couldn't go on; he must be resolute.

"You've had your lot, d'you hear me? I'm not giving you another cent."

Nony laughed.

"You don't mean it."

"That's just where you're wrong. I mean it all right."

Frank's tone and his body language were as adamant as his words. Nony began to realise he did indeed mean what he said. Her laughter turned to a scowl and she spoke less confidently.

"I don't believe you."

"Not a cent more."

"Come on! You really want your pelacur putih to find out?"

Within Frank, in the ongoing struggle between anger and prudence, anger now prevailed; he shouted just as loudly as he had when he'd first entered the bathhouse.

"You've no right to come here! Get out! Get out! And don't come back."

Up on the verandah, Rose was straining her ears to catch what was going on in the bathhouse, notwithstanding both her official disavowal of inquisitiveness and also her inability to follow Malay. Though after Frank's initial bout of shouting, his voice had become low, she'd been able to hear he was furious – and no wonder, poor man! The Malay woman's replies were inaudible; Rose imagined her speaking in a threatening hiss. Certainly, she was engaging Frank in some kind of argument. Honestly! The natives should not challenge the white people. And what on earth could she and Frank have to argue about?

Now Rose was startled by her husband's roar: *Keluar*! That, at least, she understood: *Get out*! Quite right too! The Malay woman evidently did as she'd been ordered, because the next moment Rose heard the bathhouse door creak open and then slowly creak shut. Then she heard the bolt being shot – Frank was taking no chances, it seemed, he was locking out the Malay woman. She listened, but she could hear no footsteps on the path away from the bungalow – but then, she wouldn't expect to. The path was nothing but bare earth, and the woman, shoeless, would step silently. Nonetheless she must surely have gone. And no doubt gone for good this time, thought Rose. Although she'd had the sauce to defy her, the mem, by coming back, she certainly wouldn't defy Frank, the tuan.

Actually, Nony hadn't left yet. She was hovering just outside the bathhouse door, wondering whether to call Frank's bluff by storming up onto the verandah, there to grab the mem's attention in some dramatic way: dancing; simulating a seizure; flying at the silly cow with her fists. But keeping your options open was always better than closing them off, and what would be the point of such a display? What would it profit her? Baba must be in a state of some confusion right now. What if, on reflection, he changed his mind that he'd rather face the consequences of failing to pay up, than pay up? There was no rush, she could afford to wait a few days to see if he had a change of heart. And whatever he'd just said, she could surely encourage him to see sense, couldn't she? Granted, the little nudge she'd administered just now had failed to coax him into coughing up, but she could surely manage a harder shove in pursuit of the payment she so desired. So, no, Nony didn't bring things to a head by flinging up to the verandah; she walked calmly across the compound, and, after nodding to the gardener, who was pruning a banana tree, she let herself out of the gate.

With an hauteur that was entirely misplaced, Frank failed to realise Nony could so easily ignore his order to get lost, and instead tear up to the verandah to expose herself, and hence, inevitably, him, to Rose. But his arrogance didn't extend to thinking he was safe. After he'd shot the bolt he leaned against the bathhouse door for a few moments, trembling from mingled humiliation, and anger, and trepidation. Earlier this morning Rose had seen Nony; just now Rose must have heard him shouting, and given the thinness of the walls, no doubt she'd heard a woman's voice, too. At best she must surely smell a rat. At worst ... ? Christ! He told himself that now he really must speak, he must ... But, please God, not yet.

Though Frank dawdled over his bath, too soon for his liking he was back on the verandah, wet-haired and in fresh khakis. He was sitting at the table opposite Rose, who was looking at him archly through gleaming eyes, evidently itching to hear all about it.

Rose was indeed agog, but she knew Frank wouldn't speak in front of Boy. She waited while he served tiffin – rice, again, with yet another muddy river fish. Only after he'd withdrawn did she pinion Frank's gaze with her own and raise an inquisitive eyebrow: well?

Frank pretended not to understand. He began to eat his fish with a resentful expression on his face. Rose was disappointed, but she couldn't hold her husband's moroseness against him. She completely understood why her poor lamb was so glum. And it was up to her, of course, to jolly him along.

"I'm quite sure you could not even imagine being with another lady, no, not even imagine it." She teased – or anyway she told herself she teased. "Nevertheless, I can scarcely be expected to sanction your chattering with assorted female odds and ends in your bathhouse, and no matter if they're native."

Frank took a shuddering breath, steeling himself to speak – but no words came to him and so he said nothing. In the face of his silence, Rose soldiered on, still telling herself she was jesting and keeping her tone trilling.

"I'm a suspicious little woman, you know, prepared to be terribly jealous, if given cause."

Frank felt as if someone were grating his liver. He clattered his fork down and spoke peevishly.

"That mopsey! What nerve, cornering me like that!"

"Who is she?"

Frank swallowed, and then he swallowed again.

"She's ... She's ... Nobody. Just some woman from the kampung."

"Why did she want to talk to you?"

Frank prodded at his rice to give himself time to think.

"A confusing rigmarole. Fallen out with her husband. The entire family dragged in. She wanted me to adjudicate. Impossible, I told her. I said, don't waste my time."

Rose gave a burbling laugh.

"Her husband surely has right on his side if she's as brazen with him as she is with you," she added, with casual annoyance. "I should have mentioned it sooner: there was a Malay woman trespassing this morning."

Frank flinched so hard he dropped a forkful of rice down himself.

"Careless!" reproved Rose. "I thought she'd gone. I was going down to your bathhouse to check Boy had cleaned it properly and I saw a woman walk out." She paused. "No. Not just walk, madam may as well have been turning pirouettes. It must be the same one, don't you think?"

For a second time, Frank found he couldn't speak.

"Frank?" Rose repeated. "I said, it must be the same one, don't you think?"

Frank picked a few grains of rice from his shirtfront.

"Must be," he conceded, at last.

Belatedly, Rose now noticed her husband's discomfort – or else she could no longer ignore it. Either way, it unnerved her, so she felt a warning prickling at the nape of her neck. But then she remembered his long past in Kluanak. Was she perhaps now stepping between the shadows of old grievances she knew nothing about? She gave him a long and appraising look.

"Has she caused you aggravation in the past?"

Well, that was one way of putting it, Frank thought.

"They all have," he fudged. "All the villagers have caused me aggravation at one time or another."

"I suppose," said Rose, in an uncertain tone. "I tried to ask her what she wanted, but she didn't reply and we simply stood looking at each other for a moment or two. I thought her awfully bold. You'd think she'd be rather clandestine, but not a bit! Quite unabashed."

Frank whole-heartedly wished he'd strangled Nony earlier.

"You should have chased her off with a broom," he flashed. "I told her she's not to come back." He banged his fist on the table, making the crockery rattle. "Not to come back," he repeated.

Rose was further disconcerted by her husband's insistence. She gave him another assessing look, but then she reminded herself shadows of the past were, after all, only shadows. She again made her tone as playful as she was able.

"Come back?" she said. "I'd like to see her try, that's all."

After tiffin, Rose habitually went to her room for the lie-off, whilst Frank spent it sprawled in his favourite planter's chair on the verandah. Today, as they passed each other on their way to their naps, Frank caught Rose by the hand and he pulled her to him. He encircled her in his arms and he kissed her, in earnest; he kissed her hard and deep on the mouth. This was a kiss to banish misgiving, he yearned. But whose misgiving? Alas, it could not banish his own.

As Rose kissed Frank back her skin pricked to gooseflesh – but not for the usual reason. Notwithstanding she and Frank were newlywed, they were chary of kissing in full sight of prying native eyes in daylight hours. Of kissing like this, in any case. Pecks on the cheek, yes, before he went to the courthouse, or when he came back, but kisses like this were for the night, they tacitly agreed, and for behind her bedroom door. So what had prompted her husband's welcome, but unexpected, amorousness? Rose, stalwart, decided to think about it later. As she slipped beneath the gauzy jungle curtains draped about her bed, she told herself that indulging in wild speculation was a brainless thing to do. She reminded herself that all sorts of things could explain Frank's odd behaviour at tiffin. Indeed, she refused to conjure, even for a moment, bizarre complications to her happily simple life – and after all, no good ever came of dwelling on things. No, instead of dwelling, she must concentrate on … on … on whether to send to BB for a wind-up gramophone so she and Frank could have a bit of rag-time in the evenings. She managed it, and slept.

Meanwhile, for the life of him Frank couldn't nod off. He was relieved to have got through tiffin – his goose may be cooked, but it wasn't yet served up on a platter, that was something – but as he tossed in his rattan chair, his encounter with Nony replayed over and over in his mind. His responses to her had been so feeble; why had he said this, dash it, and why hadn't he said that? He should at least have pointed out she'd have nothing to gain from exposing him…Except she would of course; she'd have all the spiteful pleasure of seeing him miserable. All the venomous joy of causing mayhem. And it surely couldn't be long before she'd be back to indulge herself by spilling the beans … Unless he saw to it that she couldn't come back. What if he banned her from the property? By Jove! That was it! Why hadn't he thought of banning her before? After all, if she never again stepped foot in the compound, then he'd never have to confess a thing to Rose. Or so he hoped. And if he knew he hoped against hope, then even that, he told himself, was better than the hopelessness of no hope at all.

Wood deteriorated fast in the mildewed damp of the tropics. After the lie-off, Frank summoned Boy to the end of the landing stage, ostensibly to show him a couple of planks which had rotted and needed replacing, but really because here there was no danger they'd be overheard. It was a matter of moments for him to point out the routine repair, but even once it was done he lingered and hence so too did Boy. The two men, master and servant, the taller pink one in khakis, the fatter brown one in a navy baju and a paler blue sarong, stood side-by-side at the very end of the landing stage, under the full onslaught of the stinking sun. They stared out over the river. It was its usual slow-flowing calm and placid self; eddies swirled here and there; the fractured surface was speckled with decaying leaves; beneath, in the depths, long, narrow fish like needles stitched the water.

Hell, thought Frank, what a contrast with that other river, the turbid river of his own life, the turbulent river in which he swam. This was excruciating. It was torture, mental torture, to be forced to reveal himself to a servant like this. After all, it was one thing to know that all servants everywhere always knew everything about their masters, and quite another to acknowledge that this distressing generality applied particularly to Yours Truly. He was tempted to prevaricate, but he told himself grimly it was best to get the torment over. As usual with the servants, he spoke in Malay, notwithstanding Boy was reasonably proficient in English.

"Look, Boy, you know all about everything."

Boy had a name: Usit. And Usit did indeed know all about everything. It was by now common knowledge in the kampung that, so surprisingly, the mem was as blur as a belalang about the details of the tuan's past and in consequence Nony, ever the lucky cow, was blackmailing him to keep her mouth shut. The villagers found the plot unfolding in front of them easily as gripping as any in *wayang kulit,* the shadow puppet theatre. And naturally they were all rooting for Nony, despite their resentment of her good fortune. Even Usit and the other servants were rooting for her, notwithstanding relations between them had been decidedly strained when she'd been their mistress, of sorts, set over them in an equivocal way.

Usit kept his face a blank mask.

"Yes, tuan."

"You know Nony was in my bathhouse this morning."

"Yes, tuan."

"Making a terrific nuisance of herself. She's not to come back, do you hear me?"

Usit flinched and he blinked, twice.

Frank looked stern. He knew Boy wouldn't like it. None of them would, the servants. They'd jib at being forced to take his part against a Malay, but their loyalties were neither here nor there; they'd do what they were told if they knew what was good for them.

"Boy?" he warned.

Usit had recently lost heavily on the fighting cocks. He reminded himself that wages were wages.

"Yes, tuan."

"If she ever tries to enter the compound again, you must see to it she's turned away. And then you must come straight to me, to tell me what's doing."

"Yes, tuan."

Frank cleared his throat and he coloured slightly.

"And Mem is not to know anything about it. Understood?"

Some of the tension left Usit's body. He was too polite to smile, but oh, he thought, oh how they'd laugh about this in the kitchen hut later, and then later still in the kampung.

"Yes, tuan."

"You sure you've got that?"

"Yes, tuan."

"Any questions?"

"No, tuan."

Frank gazed down and he watched the river flowing past his feet a moment; it occurred to him it was quite indifferent who it drowned.

"Very well," he said. "That'll do."

OUTBOUND MAIL, FEBRUARY 1925
SENT FROM THE DO'S BUNGALOW,
KLUANAK, SARAMANTAN

From Rose to Beatrice

Dearest Bumbles,

My dear!!! THAT WAY!!! A honeymoon baby!!! I cannot say how pleased and excited I am for you, and for Edmund too. And your little stranger will arrive in the summer. How lovely. I think you are very wise to pay heed to the advice not to lift so much as a pin, although it's advice I could never follow, since here in the jungle one simply has to get one with things. I must say Dr Griffith sounds a most sensible and competent fellow – there are no doctors here closer than BB, seven hours away. And turning your thoughts already to finding a nurse? I think it's well done to plan ahead.

As to your idea you'll bore me if you cannot resist sharing all the details of your health: you need not worry. Your confidences, I trust, will soon enough serve me as a most relevant kind of education!!! Can you guess … ??? Yes, my dear, although I should probably say nothing yet, for fear of tempting fate, I feel I must burst if I don't share with you at least that if I cannot yet say I am certain I too am That Way, then I can in any case say I have had for the past month or so no evidence at all I am not That Way.

Oh, suppose I'm right! How marvellous that although we live half the world apart, we would in that case enter on motherhood near enough together, as near enough together we entered on wifehood, and come the day Frank and I return to England, our children could be playmates.

Do I need to say you are as yet my only confidante? Do I need to ask you to keep all to your own dear self? Mummy's latest is full of your news and she's as jealous as a Frenchwoman. It would be too cruel if even a hint of my Certain Suspicions got back to her, if then later I must write to tell her they were Groundless Suspicions after all – not to mention she would judge me a perfect daisy for making such a mistake and would no doubt fail to refrain from telling me so.

As for Frank, I do yearn to tell him, of course I do. But I will say nothing yet, for the same reason you delayed telling Edmund until Dr Griffith confirmed you could: fear he'd think me a most humoursome little woman if I were wrong.

This uncertainty! It's so frustrating. You'd think the medical gentlemen would be able to tell a lady much sooner than three months whether she was or wasn't That Way – not that I could consult even the cleverest medical gentleman, being hidden as I am deep in the jungle.

Still, I delight in imagining Frank's face, should the happy day come I must shyly announce: dearest, I have something to tell you...I thrill to imagine our shared excitement – his joy, his pride. But I am wary, too of adding to his burdens. He's always so dreadfully fagged and harassed from all he has to do, and he'll be so anxious on my behalf – no loving husband could remain sanguine to think of his wife That Way in the jungle – and I do not wish to add to his troubles by giving him cause to worry about me.

I'm so happy you remain in good health and I think you're a

perfect saint to soldier on with your Good Works notwithstanding your condition, you're angelic to say one cannot let others down, simply because one is *enceinte*. I think it's simply splendid you have progressed from delivering soup to codgers and crones in the village to volunteering every Wednesday with the Red Cross. Your weekly jaunt to Bury St Edmunds sounds ever such fun – although if Withers now insists on driving you no faster than walking pace, perhaps "jaunt" is not quite the word I want. In any case, I do envy you your tea with the other volunteers in a tea shop.

My dear, with that I must put down my pen, as Frank is calling me to drinks – he does enjoy his snifter and he says often we must watch it, as too many white people in Malaya turn into the most terrific soaks. (Yet another thing to keep from Mummy, do you think I am very awful?)

Your loving cousin, Rosebud

From Rose to Daphne

Dearest Mummy,

I was so pleased that at last you have received my letter sent from BB and also the first I wrote from Kluanak. How strange that you should have received them together, when they were not dispatched together. Frank says they must have gone off in the same ship from Singapore and that sometimes letters written Home arrive quite out of the order in which they were sent.

I'm sorry to learn you thought I made light of Miss Bellington's tale of Enid's murdering Walter and you quite took umbrage at my attitude. I cannot now remember precisely what I wrote, but I think I must have intended only gentle teasing of Miss B, not cruel, unjustified mockery. Honestly, Mummy, I think Miss B is a jolly good egg, notwithstanding I chaffed her.

As to your worry that I, like Enid, may be hiding things I refuse to tell in letters Home, I think your imagination here turns too gothic. I assure you I write Home of everything, it's just that nothing ever happens here. The days are much the same, slipping along peaceful and placid, like beads threaded on a necklace, each one as pretty as the last.

Yes, Beatrice did indeed write to tell me she's That Way, although she didn't mention you'd seen each other at Aunt Louise's. I'm sure you are quite wrong to say Beatrice has taken to simpering, although I do give you my word that come the day, God willing, I will indeed do my best to resist the same. As to Aunt Louise, I can imagine she's as excited as anything to think she'll soon be a grandmother and perhaps you're right she's lording it over you. Alas, I must yet again disappoint you; I still have nothing to report on that front.

Your loving daughter, Rose

From Frank "Langers" Langham to Charles "Slinger" Slightman

Heh-ho, Slinger,

So now Maude thinks I'm an alcoholic, does she? This on the evidence of one letter written whilst I was tipsy? Women! And my sincere apologies, her advice I must confess to Rose grows increasingly shrill, it pains me no end to think of your being nagged on my account.

Perhaps you should tell Maude I have more than once tried to speak. Last night, for instance, I was fully intending to tell the little woman a lot of bachelors out here solace their solitude with a native woman. But at the last moment I funked it. I couldn't prevent myself imagining how horrified Rose would look, so I changed tack, and started telling her about the fall in the price of rubber, instead.

The price of rubber! Oh, God, Slinger!

Meanwhile, I've told Nony enough is enough. I've told her I'm fed up with it; I'm simply not prepared to continue to pay her any longer for her silence. And from dread of what she'll do next, or try to do next, I've instructed my servants she must not in future be admitted to the property – the dipper was loitering in my bathhouse the other morning, just as if it were her right to take a bath.

Maude will no doubt say banning the brassy egg from the compound will be as effective as banning the rain from falling and I fear I think the same. Which is to say I suppose the jig is up while at the same time I hope it isn't. Disaster looms, old man, disaster looms, and yet I can't have my marriage withering before it has ripened.

Your miserable friend, Langers

8

It was mid-morning and Rose was again sitting on the verandah with the chicks lowered against the sun; in the dim light she was slumped over her desk desultorily studying a Malay grammar, as per. But then, with a start, she bolted upright: an incomprehensible cacophony of Malay had begun shrieking up from the lawn. It was Boy she could hear, he sounded frantic and there was a woman's piercing voice too, sharp, evidently hurling abuse, and also the plaintive wail of a child's crying.

Well! Rose guessed at once the brazen Malay woman who'd ambushed Frank during his bath the previous week must be hanging about again, notwithstanding she'd been told not to come back, moreover, she must have a child with her – her own presumably. She had a nerve! Such effrontery! What could be the meaning of this latest disgraceful intrusion? ... Mind you, whatever its meaning, was it one she wished to discover? Rose could not pretend to herself she was not uneasy, but she summoned her resolve and she told herself this was another of those annoying questions with only one possible answer: I'll think about it later. In the meantime, unless Frank showed up from the courthouse, she'd better take control, it would be expected of the mem.

Rose felt she had all the pomp of empire behind her as she

slapped shut her grammar. She stood up and she walked to the rail of the verandah, where she raised one of the chicks. Beneath her, on the hummocky expanse of coarse grass that formed only a rough approximation of a velvety English lawn, she saw exactly what she'd expected to see: Boy yelling in the face of the same dumpy little Malay woman who'd been loitering before, with, today, a bawling toddler balanced on her hip. Was it a boy or a girl? Rose really couldn't determine but certainly it was a grubby little scrap, scraggy and naked but for some sort of dirty, ragged loincloth or nappy, and surprisingly light-skinned for a native child, much lighter-skinned than its mother. Moreover, its hair was fine and mousy.

By George, thought Rose, here was another half-caste! That was four of them she'd seen. Perhaps the woman on the lawn was the mother of the other ones, too – those three boys who'd fled her the day she'd watched the bird catch a cobra in the coconut grove. It was most awfully odd, all these half-castes all over the place, most awfully odd and the woman haunting the place too was queer … But Rose again resisted suspicion. She would not imagine things. Certainly not. She reminded herself she was an Englishwoman and imagining things was not for her.

Just as Rose was channelling the redoubtable spirit of Britannia, Usit grabbed Nony's free arm and began trying to yank her towards the gate. But Nony wasn't budging; she dug her heels into the grass, so the two of them swayed to-and-fro on the spot, still shouting. Usit, a patient, gentle man, lost patience. He raised his own free arm, as if to strike Nony.

Rose was appalled. She'd never before seen such an outrage;

no English gentleman would ever hit a member of the fairer sex, even if she were not fair, but as dark as anything and twice as provoking. No, no decent chap would ever hit a girl. And however the awful woman had goaded him, Boy's ungentlemanly behaviour could only reflect badly on Frank, his employer and also on her, his mistress. Well! She must stop her wool-gathering! She must jolly well enforce the proprieties!

"I say!" she ordered, in her confident, ringing English. "I won't have this."

Her words cracked and ricocheted. Startled, Usit let go of Nony and dropped his risen arm. The two of them swayed apart; once separated they were shocked into stillness and silence. But First Daughter continued crying, oblivious to Rose's casual assumption of authority – indeed, her wails intensified.

After a fraught and quivering moment, both Usit and Nony slowly turned to the verandah. Nony made sure she had Rose's full attention; she locked gazes with her and stared at her through eyes just as malevolently blank as she could make them. Then she showily adjusted First Daughter on her hip. She'd been in two minds about whether to bring the child along today; the mem had seen her sons and failed to twig they were Baba's; she'd seen her and failed to twig she had anything to do with Baba; but if the mem saw both her and her fair-skinned daughter, perhaps she'd realise the truth? In which case Nony could kiss goodbye to any chance of more hush-money, that was for sure. But she anyway sensed the hush money slipping out of her grasp; she'd decided she may as well do something drastic. So here she was with First Daughter, risking it.

Meanwhile, Usit was in turmoil. Though they often deserved it, he never hit his wives. Never. He was shamed by what he'd so nearly done and grateful to the mem for saving him from himself, and mortified she'd witnessed this whole commotion and furious with bloody Nony. Granted, it was her right to cause as much trouble as she could for the tuan. Except her causing trouble for the tuan would also cause trouble for him, as she knew full well, since after the tuan had issued his instructions last week, he'd sent his second wife to tell her he could no longer tolerate either her or First Son sneaking into the DO's compound. Alamak! Why had she ignored his message, and barged in? Now he'd cop it! He was so angry that for a moment old resentments resurfaced, from the time when Nony had been his mistress, of sorts, and he sided almost wholeheartedly with the mem, and against her, for all she was a Malay. So, far from apologising for raising his hand to her, he leaned towards her and he hissed, "You've got what you came for. She's seen you. So, be off! Go home and quit making problems for me!"

Nony, who'd taken the odd knock from Frank now and again, mostly when he'd had one too many, didn't hold it against Usit that he'd so nearly hit her; a little slap was neither here nor there. To her mind, slapping never did much damage, neither to a woman, nor a child. And though she was sorry for the bother her trespass would cause Usit, she really was, she no more apologised to him than he had to her. What would be the point? Indeed, she gave no indication she'd even heard him: at his hiss, her blankly staring face did not change a jot – she continued to pierce Rose with her poisoned gaze, or so she hoped.

Rose felt Nony's gaze as an onslaught and she shuddered just as she had the first time they'd met each other's eyes; again she felt she was the object of the other woman's hostility. But today she couldn't quite convince herself there really was nothing personal between them – that this matronly little thing had no more reason to hate her than did the river flowing past the bungalow. She felt all at once as if she'd opened the door to a cold, dank coal cellar, and she was now breathing in chilly wafts of foetid air – which was too silly, since she was in the tropics. No! She must get a grip! She stood up straighter.

"If you wish to convey a message to my husband, tell me and I'll see he gets it."

Nony had no idea what the mem had said – not that it mattered, since she wasn't interested in holding a conversation. She continued to pinion the other woman with her gaze, but she coolly began to stroll away from her and from the whole scene, walking backwards at first. At last, she turned and she headed toward the path to the kampung.

Usit was determined to see Nony off the premises. He followed her all the way to the wooden gate, whispering at her angrily all the while.

"Come on! What do you suggest I say when the mem asks what's going on?"

Nony's only reply was to shrug, which was nothing more or less than he'd expected; she really could be an infuriating woman. And it was no consolation to think that whatever he said, the mem would in all likelihood think it was cock and bull – every Malay was aware the Mat Salleh thought them irredeemable liars.

Up on the verandah, Rose too wanted to make sure the Malay woman had really gone this time; there must be no creeping back today. Only once the intruder had passed through the gate of the compound and out onto the jungle path beyond, did she peremptorily call, "Boy! Boy!"

Usit could see nothing for it but to shuffle towards the bungalow. He climbed the steps as slowly as he could, dragging his feet as if they were a pair of heavy sacks. Once he reached the top, he stood stock still and he looked at the mem sideways, through half-closed eyes. What had he done, he wondered, to deserve all these problems the world kept throwing at him? Alas, though he hoped for inspiration, he still had no idea what he'd say when the mem asked him, as he anticipated she must: what was that all about? Why was that woman here?

Again, Rose couldn't quite convince herself of something she'd rather she could: this time that she found Boy's manner more impudent than disturbing. And once again she took refuge in the proprieties. For heaven's sake! There were standards to maintain. She did not attempt to hide her anger as she said, "Behaving like that! You'd have struck that woman if I hadn't intervened and don't try telling me you wouldn't. So what d'you think you were doing? Explain yourself, young man!"

Guilt and discomfort swirled in Usit, with relief that the mem hadn't (yet) asked the dangerous questions he'd expected. Nonetheless, he paused before he answered, wondering how much he would have been able to say, even if he'd had the English for fluency. He settled on, "Make her leave. Tuan say she never come here next time."

Rose blinked. It was only sensible, she supposed, that Frank had enlisted Boy into helping keep the annoying Malay woman at bay but why hadn't he mentioned he'd issued this instruction? Perhaps he'd simply forgotten. Yes, that must be it; he was so busy all sorts of things must slip his mind.

"It's no excuse!" she flashed. "And her child with her too. I won't stand for it and nor will Tuan when he learns what happened."

Usit blushed and he looked away. He was embarrassed not only for himself, but also for the mem, for her ignorance, for her blundering oblivion.

Rose assumed the boy blushed solely for shame at his loutish behaviour. Yes, she thought, yes, you may very well look sheepish! She gestured towards the kitchen hut.

"Dismissed," she said.

Rose returned to her Malay grammar. She would not shrink from her purpose and so she attempted to translate, from Malay to English, a passage about a wedding. But she couldn't concentrate after such to-do. Naturally, the morning's palaver had left her feeling irritable, she told herself, as she refused to notice, or tried to, her condensing half-sense that something not quite nice was stirring.

Still, Rose was sturdily working away when Usit returned to the verandah to prepare for tiffin. She ignored him, until all at once he clattered down the tray carrying the water jug and glasses.

"I take tuan's topee," he announced. He rushed to the top of the steps that led into the garden and hurried down them.

Although it was Boy's job to take Frank's topee, Rose surmised he wished to collar her husband, in order to proffer his version of the earlier flap. Oh well, she disparaged, it could not matter what he said; it would make no odds once Frank heard what she had to say about the way he'd threatened a defenceless woman.

Frank's morning had been grim; since nine, he'd been closeted with his clerks in a meeting room, hot as a furnace, as they'd attempted to balance the outstation's accounts. Now, on the lawn, he listened to Usit with a stony face. Christ! After such a scene Rose must surely have guessed the truth; how could she not have done? And was Boy a mental deficient? How could he have allowed Nony to trespass when he'd specifically warned him not to? He resisted boxing the simpleton's ears but he did give him a thorough dressing down, and only after he'd run through a whole dictionary of expletives did he climb the verandah steps to his wife. He did so as reluctantly as a man climbing the scaffold to his doom.

Rose was much taken aback when Frank, hatless, at last joined her on the verandah. His face was so drawn he almost looked ill. And she herself felt a little green to see him. She again felt she was breathing cellar air – air stale and chilly and dusty with dread. Though she warned herself, almost even only for form's sake, she must not succumb to some deranged temptation to mistrust her husband, she could not prevent herself blurting another of those questions she wasn't at all sure she wanted answered, "Frank! What's wrong?"

Frank peered at his wife closely. Her ignorance did not seem feigned, did she really not suspect? He squared his shoulders and his manner became blustering, "Why should anything be wrong?"

Rose was so disorientated, and so afraid, though she couldn't admit it, or wouldn't admit it, of what she'd hear if she pressed her husband, she found herself saying, "Oh, no reason at all, dearest, I don't suppose."

Still, the incident on the lawn was like an itch spreading over her thoughts, it was more maddening, even, than the mosquito bites which formed the background scratch of her life, so she almost felt in torment whilst Frank took forever, it seemed, to have his bath. Eventually, though, tiffin was served – corned beef from a tin, for a change. Rose waited until Boy had left them and then she took the plunge.

"Such a terrible commotion this morning. That woman turned up again. The one who ambushed you in your bathhouse."

"I gather," said Frank.

Rose thought him hurtfully terse. She looked at him levelly and she spoke slowly.

"She had a half-caste child with her, I assumed it must be her own." She paused. "And she must be the other ones' mother too, don't you think? Those three boys I saw in the kampung."

Frank found he couldn't look away. He toyed with the idea of denying he knew a thing about it. But there were lies, and lies, and times to tell them too. No, he daren't be quite so bald-faced.

"Yes," he said. "She is."

Rose continued to hold her husband's gaze, as she asked, at last, the questions that had been creeping up on them both like threatening shadows lengthening upwards along a staircase wall.

"Where is their father? Who is he?"

Frank looked down. He used his fork to mash the unappetising mess of his corned beef with much more force than was necessary. He wanted to answer: you're looking at him. Truly he did. But willy-nilly he found himself saying, "There are some questions we Old Hands on Saramantan think it best not to ask."

Alas, Frank immediately regretted what even he must call his weaselling equivocation. And Rose was shaken by it. For a long moment she continued to look at her husband through appraising eyes. But then she girded herself and she told herself mistrust was weak-headed. If there were some harmless little mystery surrounding the Malay woman, then it wouldn't do to pry. If Frank had something he didn't wish to tell her then that was his business. If it were something she ought to know, then no doubt he'd tell her in his own sweet time. She took a steadying breath and she retreated, for the third or fourth time that morning, to the proprieties.

"Boy would have hit her if I hadn't stopped him. I upbraided him and you'll have to too."

Frank was grateful for the reprieve, notwithstanding he knew it must be temporary.

"I told him if she trespassed again he was to turf her out."

Rose bit back the challenge: you could have mentioned it.

"So he told me. I told him: it's no excuse."

"You know servants. I suppose the excitement of it all went to his head."

"Excitement cannot justify his bullying." Rose paused. "The child was terrified – it was barely more than a baby."

"Oh, the girl will be all right."

Rose's eyes widened.

"Girl?"

Hell! thought Frank. He tried to tell himself there was no reason at all why he shouldn't know the sex of every child in his district, but, alas, it wouldn't wash. He felt himself redden.

"So I heard. Boy. Girl. It doesn't matter."

Rose saw that her husband's cheeks were blazing as hot and as red as pain. She felt her own cheeks blaze in response. But she would not be a daisy and she decided to decide that was quite enough of half-caste children. Nonetheless, when she spoke she couldn't keep a mocking, sceptical note from her tone.

"What was she doing here this time? The mother. Another row with her husband, d'you suppose?"

Frank felt his wife's doubt as fingers prodding an open wound.

"How should I know?"

"Didn't Boy say?"

Frank stabbed his fork downward into the pink sludge of his beef – once, twice, he stabbed. Instead of answering Rose's question, he said, "She's a frightful pest. A one-woman infestation. I won't have her swarming all over the place."

A stretched beat elapsed in silence. It would take an expansive and just slightly self-conscious, no-nonsense briskness for Rose to refuse to know, or else to fob herself off, but she reminded herself she was a sensible woman, and she summoned the requisite brusque obtuseness. She nodded and she again decided to decide for trust.

"No, swarming won't do," she said, with a smile that was only a little taut. "Anyway, madam's taken more than enough of our time. Never mind her, how was your morning?"

That afternoon, after the lie-off, a tropical storm roared across the darkened sky, a storm flashy and dramatic beyond any storm ever witnessed in England. A monstrous wind attacked the jungle trees; it lashed the canopy into a writhing mass of green, clawed leaves from whipping branches, ripped branches from swaying trunks. Thunder shuddered through the air. Lightening shredded the densely towering clouds. Warm rain roared down like a slobbering creature consumed by a fierce, fierce desire to dissolve the earth. The river surged from placid sluggishness into maniac frenzy.

Rose watched the tempest from the verandah, where, as every day when the heat began to fade, the chicks were raised in a prayer for coolness, despite the risk today of rain blowing in. She was most relieved tennis was out of the question; it worried her now that a woman who harboured Certain Suspicions should not exert herself to tennis and she'd taken to racking her brains every afternoon for some credible excuse not to play. Meanwhile, lack of exercise made Frank irritable – or rather, it made him even more irritable than he already was, under the stress of all he was hiding. Between one thing and another, after he'd finished at the courthouse he hurled about the bungalow, moodily abstracted. Unsurprisingly, he and Rose barely spoke to each other. He said little for fear of what he knew full well he must soon say; she asked nothing for fear of what she knew deep down she must soon hear; they each knew, really, why the other was so reticent.

The rain slackened during evening tiffin of mutton stew. Nevertheless, as Frank and Rose chewed the rather tough meat, it still drummed an insistently maddening tattoo on the roof and fell heavily enough to form a wavering membrane between the bungalow and the untamed wilderness of trees beyond.

After the meal, Frank could not settle, as usual, in his chair on the verandah, instead he was driven by restlessness and nervous anxiety to pace about like a caged bear. He knew he must summon all his courage – he must. He and Rose couldn't go on like this; they really couldn't, the time for prevarication, for evasion, for pretence, was over. He must do as he had so often resolved to do, he must speak. And this time he must not let terror shunt him into discussing the falling price of rubber or the failure of the coffee harvest on Sumatra or anything else, instead he must plough straight through his wife's horror and say what had to be said. In an attempt to calm himself he lit his pipe – the heft of it was so much more consoling than a cigarette – and he clamped it between his teeth. Smoke curled from the bowl in a tiny blue plume, which hung still and almost heavy in the damp night air.

Usually, Rose adored the intensely masculine smell of pipe tobacco, bittersweet and peaty, but tonight it made her feel queasy, which would have pleased her as a further hint she was That Way, but she was too much on edge for secret gloating. And in any case, her queasiness could very well be down to the greasy stew she'd eaten for evening tiffin. Or else to foreboding. But whatever the cause of her queasiness, she was loath to ask Frank to put out his pipe. Even he must know the possible significance of a heightened sensitivity to smell; she wouldn't have wanted to raise his suspicions, even if they'd been chaffing each other, with not a care in the world between them. She tried to read by the light of the paraffin lamp, which was, as usual, haloed by airy clouds of little flying things. But Frank's pacing was so distracting: up and down, he went, up and down until her nerves could barely stand it...Indeed, it was not to be tolerated. This could not continue ... this ... this ... this sense that something was crouching, ready to pounce with its jaws gaping full of teeth and its claws extended. There was nothing else for it, she decided, she must stiffen her resolve and face the predator. And so, her voice trembling, she forced herself to speak.

"My dear, what is it that troubles you?"

Frank was grateful for his wife's bravery and shamed by it too. He sighed and he stopped his pacing. He walked across the verandah and he perched on the edge of his planter's chair, next to Rose's. To prevaricate further, just a little further, he knocked the ashes out of his pipe and he refilled it. When he placed a match to the fresh tobacco, his hands trembled as badly as Rose's voice had done. He took a deep preparatory draw and he felt the smoke curl into his lungs, with its nicotine kick and its reassurance.

"Rose," he said unsteadily, "I must speak."

His voice was so low Rose found it hard to hear him above the rain on the roof and the background racket of the night-time jungle. Her nerves intensified, and although she had asked him to confide, now the time had come when all must be made explicit, she found she preferred, she desperately preferred, not to know what it was that troubled her husband. Or, rather, she preferred to be allowed to continue to pretend to herself that she did not know. And so she executed a complete *volte-face*.

"No. No. You don't have to say anything you don't want to say. Nobody ever does, remember."

"Yes I do," said Frank. "Dearest, I say again, I must speak."

There was now no possibility of turning back, they both knew that, and yet Frank lapsed into silence and Rose did not urge: go on! The paraffin lantern blew out but neither of them remarked on it. They sat in the darkness saying nothing for long moments more, each of them aware they must both soon face a dangerously changed world: a world in which secrets kept became shared knowledge.

At last, with effort, Frank gathered himself.

"It's hard to find the right words. It's a discreditable story, I don't want to varnish it, but I must explain." He paused and took another drag on his pipe. "I'm no loner, you know that. And when I was first stationed here – remember, I was only nineteen, not that youth's any excuse – when I first pitched up here, a callow boy, I discovered for me solitude's a kind of hell. Here I was, lost in this life without companions. Nobody to riot with. Nobody even to talk to, only trees whispering to themselves out in the jungle. I didn't mind in the daytime, you know how I enjoy my work. But what was I supposed to do after I left the courthouse each evening? No tennis, of course. Tramping through the jungle with my gun could fill an hour or so before dark, but, after, time dragged. Time became a trial. I tried drinking to take my mind off things but it worried me, drinking alone – where would it end? I could read, but my library was never exactly extensive. And of course I could talk to the servants. My chief houseboy back then was Boy's father, Boss Boy we called him, to distinguish him from Boy, Small Boy, who worked under him at the time – not literally small, you understand, a youth. Boss Boy and I often used to have a chat, and though he wasn't a real chum his voice was better than silence. But it was the same then as now: after evening tiffin the servants went home to the kampung. Once they'd headed off there was nobody but Yours Truly until morning. All I had to keep me company was the endless *geh-ko*, *geh-ko* up in the thatch, and the unearthly cries of the jungle filtering in through the walls – you know how it is. I tell you the howls and screams were enough to give any lonely fellow the jim-jams. Those nights! Intolerable! Interminable! If morning ever comes, I used to say to myself, if morning ever comes … I tried going to bed straight after evening tiffin but it was too early, a nursery hour. I used to thrash sleepless in the sheets, tossing and tossing in miserable frustration, hot, sweaty to no satisfactory purpose. It all seemed the limit, the absolute limit. And you know native servants. Impossible to keep anything from them. Of course Boss Boy knew all about it, of course he did, and that was my undoing, I suppose, the obviousness of my loneliness, of my need. One evening when it had been raining for hours, just like today, hours and hours, so I'd been unable even to go for a tramp, I felt dreadfully despondent. Boss Boy came to me after evening tiffin, and he asked if I wasn't sad without friends once he and the other servants had gone home. What a question! Not at all, I lied, I enjoy my own company. Boss Boy just stood there. Manifestly, he didn't believe me. Eventually, he said if I'd like to keep a girl about the bungalow he had one in mind. She'd do, he said, she was a nice girl, clean, neat, quiet, biddable – no bother to a man. He said her people would be happy enough to have me feed her, they wouldn't expect more than a token financial present. Give her a once over, he said, no obligation. If you don't like her, no need to keep her. He spoke as if she were already about the bungalow somewhere, so I suspected a set-up. Where is she? I asked. Boss Boy gave me a knowing smile, hang on, he said. He went to the edge of the verandah; while we'd been talking she'd been sitting on the steps with her mother, both of them in their glad rags. They came and knelt at the foot of my planter's chair. The girl was younger than I'd thought she'd be, but then adulthood comes so very quickly in the kampung – marry them off at 13, 14, sometimes. She was pleasingly timid and I thought she was fairly pretty – pretty enough to suit. She didn't talk much, just enough for me to hear her voice didn't grate and she laughed at my jokes. Flatteringly come hither eyes. Lots of sweet smiles. Her mother told her to come and sit on my knee: go, she said, sit. She hesitated but she came onto my lap, and then, after a nod from mater, she quickly kissed my cheek. Just a peck but gratifying. You see, she likes you, urged mater, all eager, do you want to keep her? I asked *her* if *she* wanted me to keep her. She covered her face with her hands and giggled. I took this to mean she'd be happy to come and live with me. I thought: to hell with the humiliation of it all! I decided I'd be happy enough to have her. Not exactly an ally but at least another human after dark. I thought she'd look after me, mend my clothes, darn my socks, that kind of thing as well as … the other. Very well, I said to mater, I'll keep her … Rose, my dear, I expect you can guess she's the woman who's been making scenes. She lived here for ten years …"

"Ten years!"

"Just shy. Until my Home leave, when I sent her back to the

kampung. But, please! You must understand ours was merely a practical arrangement, our liaison was only ever intended as a stop-a-gap until I married. No romantic feelings on either side. There were all sorts of benefits for her when she was living with me. Perks for her and all her family: food, little luxuries from the Chinese tinker, a dollar here, a dollar there. Pragmatism, that was why she stayed. The pragmatism of her race. As for me, I never thoroughly delighted in her, even in our earliest days. No infatuation. Nothing to cool to anything deeper than affection, if even to that. A calculation of interests, that's what it was, for both of us. *Both*. You're the only one I've ever loved. You know you're the love of my life, my darling."

At last, Frank fell silent. For long moments two hearts thumped like prisoners battering the doors of their prison cells, crazed with the idea of getting out.

Rose felt that the dripping tropical air was drowning her. Eventually, she said, half-gasping, "I trusted you."

"Of course you're shocked."

"That scarcely beings to describe how I feel."

"It's all so unexpected. I know that."

"I feel stupefied – I *am* stupefied." Rose cupped her hands over her ears. "Deafened. Made mute."

Frank resisted pointing out that claiming to have been made mute was as contradictory as claiming to be sleeping. His own ears and tongue were functioning well enough and as for his heart, it was by now returning to its usual pumping. Indeed, he thought he'd made a fairly reasonable fist of things; the worst was over, at any rate.

"Well, now it's all out in the open there's no rush to hash it over. No need for you to speak at all just yet, to say anything at all. Take your time – take all the time you need."

Time? All at once Rose heard loud the relentless tick-tock to nothing and she wasn't sure she wanted to squander on her husband any more of her precious seconds. She wanted to run away, right now; to flee, right this very instant. But how could she? She looked through the membrane of water wavering between her and the dark jungle stretching beyond, so immense it may as well have been infinite. She imagined she was running through the pitchy wilderness, lost and panicked, her scent being picked up by a tiger, so she was no longer a person, but prey.

Except where, truly, were the dangers? Abruptly, Rose turned back to her husband.

"*All* out in the open, Frank? *All*. What about the children? These half-castes I keep seeing everywhere. You said at tiffin they were hers. You knew the littlest one was a girl. It's yours, isn't it. They all are."

Frank inclined his head, minimally.

"Four children, Frank?"

Frank toyed with the idea of pointing out two of his brats were twins, and so perhaps should count against him in the scales as only one. But, prudently, he decided against. Again, he inclined his head, minimally.

"I trusted you," Rose repeated.

"Oh, my dear, you still can."

"I'm sure you're as reliable as you ever were."

Frank winced.

"You must be so very angry," he said. "I understand. I'm most awfully sorry."

Rose felt Frank's apology as an insult. It was as if they'd been back in London and he'd given her a bunch of flowers as he'd announced he'd got the housemaid That Way. Well, if that calamity had ever befallen her, she'd have flung the flowers back at him, that's all. As it was, she cast a haughty glance over her husband: his eyes gleamed with anguish in the dark, as if he, not she, were the injured party. She knew her own eyes gleamed too; she could feel tears massing at their corners. She remembered all those times Frank's eyes had shone to see her and her own eyes had shone with an answering light, and her tears welled further. But still she blinked them back. She had her proper pride. And, from proper pride, she was determined neither to weep nor to show in any other way her inner uproar. The Malay woman – Frank's little *midinette* – may do as she liked; *she* would not make scenes, *she* at least was an Englishwoman. She would not demean herself with creating and nor would she rail against her husband – in any case not in front of him and not yet.

"No, Frank," she said. "I won't accept your apology."

"Please, my ..."

"No." Rose stood up. "I'm going to bed. I want to be alone tonight."

She made a curt gesture with her hand to cut off any reply Frank may be tempted to make and then she crossed the verandah to her bedroom. Her eyes were adjusted to the darkness by now and she knew where the furniture was placed, so she walked as easily as she would have done at midday. Once she was inside her room and had lit the paraffin lamp, she did something she had never done once since marrying: she not only closed her bedroom door, she also bolted it.

Frank heard the bolt shoot home. Christ! It was a relief to have made a clean breast of things, of course, what a weight off his shoulders, but he felt so jumbled he almost couldn't think. Indeed he as good as gave up trying, he simply sat in the dark, finishing his pipe, his eye drawn all the while to the glimmer of light under his wife's door: it looked, to him, like a dainty finger, beckoning. Alas, he dared not stand up, to answer its summons...Was the little woman weeping in there, he wondered? He supposed she must be, tears must be expected of any egg, under the circumstances and yet he couldn't hear sobbing. So then: stifling her sobs in her pillow...Oh, hell! He almost felt a little weepy himself. Sniffling, he knocked out his pipe and lit another one. And then, as if not acting of his own will, as if at alcohol's command, he fetched the whisky bottle and a tumbler; he poured himself a tot so stiff it may as well have been starched. Yes, he saw nothing for it, but to solace himself tonight with companions far trustier than any woman: booze and tobacco.

Meanwhile, in her room, Rose's eyes remained perhaps the driest things in the whole rainy jungle. She was undressing. Usually, she'd next wrap herself in a towel and go down to her bathhouse for her final bath of the day. But tonight she was too distraught to bother and in any case she'd be sleeping alone, so what could it matter if she stank? For once she wriggled straight out of her clothes and into one of the high-necked white-cotton nightgowns she favoured in demure defiance of the climate. She extinguished the lamp and slipped into bed through the opening in the jungle curtains. As she lay on her back, rigid with misery, the gauzy net floated above her, pearlescent, like some pale ghost in the darkness, and all at once it seemed to her a mockery of a bridal veil. She was hideously aware that Frank's Malay midinette must be lying on her own bed – or rather, Rose corrected, lying on her own sleeping mat – not much more than a mile distant. Although she closed her eyes, she literally closed her eyes, she screwed them tight shut against what she did not wish to see, she saw it anyway: images of that woman and her husband at it. Brown limbs tangled with white; long ratty black hair tumbled across short blonde curls of chest hair; two bodies sheened with the sweat of lust...

No! Rose's eyes flew open so wide she almost thought they'd split. She bolted upright and she grimaced as she attempted to shove from her mind the images. Horrible images. Unbearable things. But she failed in her attempt to play the censor; even though her eyes were now open, she still saw images of Frank and la midinette flickering at the edges of her vision. Bits of body here. Bits of body there. It was as if she were being forced to watch scenes from some hellish moving picture, except in colour, and – horrors! – with sound. Rose attempted to block her ears and she told herself, firmly, to be calm. As so often she reminded herself no good could come of dwelling on things: it was pointless to torture herself by imagining the past. She should concentrate on the present and on the future; she must remember she was now Frank's wife; she was in all probability carrying his child, his legitimate child. She was the one with the power to make him joyful or to make him miserable; she was the one who could disarray and undo him. Or in any case she ought to be.

Rose scowled, but she nonetheless lay down again and she told herself that for the sake of the baby, if there was one, she simply must sleep. Except barely had her head touched the pillow, when it hit her where she was lying and once more she sat up. Her bed! *This* bed! Rose shuddered to think who had slept in it before; how many times her husband must have visited it before. Lying on it – lying *here* – waiting for him to slide through the darkness, she had so often felt tiny needles pricking all over her skin. Delicious needles of desire. But she felt now, everywhere, in every secret crevice and fold of her flesh, quite another pricking, one as if spiders were crawling all over her, their long legs hairy but metallic, like thorns where they walked.

One thin cotton sheet was all the bedding Rose needed in the heat. Now she slung it back and then she fought her way through the jungle curtains. There was a rattan *chaise longue* in one corner of her room. She knew it was hard and uncomfortable, nevertheless it was where she'd sleep tonight – or rather, she despaired, where she'd fail to sleep. As for the bed: she would never lie in it again. A gateway to delight? No, it was nothing but a shabby, tatty, hand-me-down; tomorrow, she'd have it burned.

9

The DO's bungalow, late February 1925

When Boy had knocked, to bring her cup of tea, Rose had called for him to go away. Now, out on the verandah, she could hear him laying the breakfast table – all the familiar clatter of a new day beginning to unfurl. But it was not a day she wished to face. She wasn't in the least hungry and though she ached everywhere from tossing all the endless night on the unyielding chaise longue, she refused to get up, to confront, just yet, her changed world, and at its centre her changed husband.

Frank no more wished to confront the day than did his wife – or to confront food, either, for that matter. Hell! As he lay in bed, his own cup of tea cooling on the bedside table, he berated himself he should never have let himself get quite so tight last night; despite the dimness of pre-dawn, the world felt to him as if it were stabbing him in the eyes, and it was blasting him in the ears and what's more his mouth felt full of feathers. Still, he was the DO and hungover or not, hungry or not, he must make an appearance at breakfast.

As should Rose, for that matter, she was the mem after all. But when Frank emerged from his room on to the verandah, he saw no sign of his wife. He checked that Boy was not lurking and then he walked over to her bedroom door, where he knocked with considerable trepidation.

Inside, Rose was still lying dully listless on the chaise longue. She presumed that this time it must be Frank who knocked, and she certainly had no intention of answering.

Frank's hangover did not improve his temper. Still: better grovel. He checked once again that Boy was not about and then he rattled the door latch. This produced no more response from within than had knocking. Frank pitched his voice loud enough for Rose to hear, but not loud enough to carry to the kitchen hut, or so he hoped.

"Darling?" he called, through the flimsy wood. "Darling? Are you awake?"

Silence.

"I'm going to have breakfast."

Silence.

"Will you join me?"

Silence.

"Don't go silent on me."

Silence.

"I should have explained last night, but I was so wound up, I forgot. It's the common thing out here. Concubinage. Six out of ten bachelors keep a nonya – that's what they're called, these watercolour wives who keep house for a fellow."

Silence.

"And I'm not sure if I made myself quite plain. Did you understand it was all over by the time I left for my Home leave? By then she'd long since become a millstone so I was jolly glad to send her packing."

Silence.

"I know it's all my fault. I understand if you're furious. But, please, do at least begin to forgive me."

Silence.

Frank sighed: evidently it would be a solitary breakfast for Yours Truly.

"All right. I'm going to sit down. Join me if you will."

Boy appeared suspiciously quickly after Frank had sat down at the table. Or in any case, so fretted Frank. He explained, unasked and with no expectation of being believed, that the mem was poorly and then he added, with every expectation of being understood all too well, that this morning he'd have coffee, not tea. Even for appearances' sake, he couldn't cope with his egg and he pushed it away, but once Boy had brought the coffee he downed four cups, one after the other. The coffee was black and sweet and grainy in the local style. It gave him the restorative kick he'd hoped for, and after he'd emptied the pot, he decided: nothing else for it, better try again with the little woman.

This time, after glancing around to check for watching native eyes, he rapped really hard on the door.

"Rose?" he called. "I'm off to the courthouse now."

Silence.

"Will you come out and kiss me before I go?"

Silence.

Frank shuffled uneasily: he'd never yet left for the courthouse without receiving from his wife his parting peck on the cheek and pecking her cheek in return.

"Please, darling."

Silence.

"It's all right. I understand. See you for tiffin then."

Only after Rose was certain Frank would be safely out of the way did she get up, bathe and dress. Then she went to her bedroom door and she called for Boy. When he appeared, she offered him no explanation of her pallor, nor of why she'd missed breakfast, nor of why she'd got up so late: let him think what he liked!

Actually, what Usit thought was the truth. Speculation in the kitchen hut this morning had been just as frenzied as was speculation on the stock exchange in London, and far less exuberantly irrational. Yes, the servants took the tuan's hangover and the mem's indisposition as evidence of exactly what it was: a marital bust-up. They argued, correctly, that after Nony's little display yesterday, the mem must have cottoned on to the facts of her husband's past, or else he'd cast to the chickens the chicken feed. But either way, the mem was no longer as blur as a belalang, indeed she was quite probably as knowing as a *semut* that was far too *sibuk* for its own good.

Now, as he waited for the mem to give him her instructions, Usit noticed, first, that she looked just as tired, drawn and wan as he'd expected she would, and second that she'd dragged her sheet off the bed and over to the chaise longue. Oh, it was delicious! For a moment he managed to keep his face impassive but the struggle was too much; he could not prevent himself from smirking and from bestowing on the mem a smugly knowing glance.

Rose saw Boy's smirk: how dare he! She felt a familiarly traitorous heat spreading across her cheeks. Still, she would not demean herself by otherwise acknowledging his insolence; she'd rise above his sauciness by ignoring it. So she did not command: wipe that smile off your face young man! Instead, she gestured peremptorily towards her befouled bed.

"Take it into the compound and chop it up! Then make a bonfire! Burn it!"

Usit's smirk switched into something of a rictus grin. It was fair enough the mem was upset to think the bed where her husband nightly fired his canon into her was the very same bed where formerly he'd fired it into Nony. But distress, he thought, was no reason for wanton extravagance and nor was pride. What? Burn the furniture? And this without the say-so of the tuan? Alamak! This could only lead to more trouble for him and he really didn't fancy another tongue-lashing after the one the tuan had given him yesterday.

"Mem … ?" he asked uncertainly. "Mem … ?"

"You heard me."

"But Tuan! What he say?"

"That's no concern of yours."

Usit gulped.

"Very expensive bed."

Rose drew herself up to her full height.

"Are you arguing with me? I no longer wish to see this bed. Chop it up and burn it. Then fetch one of the camp beds from the storeroom. Set it up in here. From tonight, that's where I'll sleep."

Usit cleared his throat.

"I go fetch axe," he lied.

With that he scarpered, and hotfooted it straight to Frank

Rose guessed that Boy had jibbed at taking her instruction

and, moreover, that he'd gone to consult with her husband about what to do. Inwardly, she was furious at this slight but she decided she had bigger fish to fry than a servant's refusal to submit to her authority. So, after he'd gone, she perched on her chaise longue and she waited, to all appearances calmly and passively, for her husband to show up.

Soon enough Frank knocked on her door with one hand whilst, with the other, he simultaneously raised the latch. He thought the little woman was being hysterical, but he was to blame, of course, and he was prepared to do all he could to appease her. He affected what he hoped was a jocular tone.

"What's all this about burning the bally bed?"

Rose ignored his question.

"My bed," she pointed. "The bed where we ... It's where you and your Malay midinette ... isn't it?"

Frank's cheeks glowed red.

"I see," said Rose. "And is it where she delivered your brats?"

Frank's cheeks flared even redder. He said, "Some fellows insist their nonyas sleep in the servants' quarters, but Kluanak is so isolated I saw no need for that."

For a moment, there was stillness and silence, and then again Rose pointed.

"That bed! It's an insult. Revolting. Even looking at it shrivels my innards."

Frank decided never mind the trouble and expense of a new bed, best indulge the little woman.

"I will replace it."

"I want it burned, just as Boy told you."

"All right. All right. It'll be firewood in an hour or two."

The servants were united in thinking the tuan was just as mad to order the burning of a perfectly good bed as was the mem to demand it, not to mention that a husband's bending to his wife's will like this was decidedly unmanly. Still, if the tuan wanted the bed burned, they had no choice but to jump to it. They lugged the mattress outside easily enough but the frame could not be fully dismantled; it was so large and heavy and unwieldy they had a devil of a job manhandling it out of Rose's room, across the verandah, and down to the lawn. It was a tiring, sweaty job in the gathering heat and one achieved only to the accompaniment of many curses. But once the bed was sitting on the lawn, Usit at last did what he'd earlier lied to Rose he'd do: he fetched an axe.

Soon the bed had been reduced to lengths of wood and the lengths of wood had been arranged into a bonfire, with the mattress balanced on top. Usit soaked a rag in paraffin and he shoved it under the higgledy pyramid of planks. The wood quickly caught and within minutes a fire was roaring: hungry flames licked the air with spicy tongues, sparks scribbled in all directions, smoke billowed skyward.

Rose was standing implacable on the verandah. As she watched the flames begin to gobble, she felt, already, nostalgic for the extremely recent past; the past, only yesterday, in which she'd been if not quite oblivious, then in any case oppressed by nothing but a smudgy sense of unease; an age of innocence, or so it seemed to her now, in contrast to the corruption of the present. She listened to the hissing crackle and spit of the flames; she watched sparks flaring and sinking, flaring and sinking; she breathed in the scent of smoke. This was not the sweetly melancholy smell of wood smoke, drifting blue-grey from autumn bonfires in England; this smoke seemed to singe her lungs and it billowed greasily black enough and thick enough and high enough to send a signal. A signal of an ending sent directly from fate to her, she thought melodramatically.

With great effort, she forced herself to remember hers and Frank's beginning. How unenthusiastic she'd been when her mother had suggested a month at Ryton Cove – and how glad she'd been later that Frank, in search of bracing English sea air after the damp of Malaya, had chosen the same resort in which to spend part of his Home leave. How relieved they'd been, each of them, to have found another young person amongst so many middle-aged and old ones. How quickly they'd fallen victim each to the other – or so she'd thought, back then. But had Frank ever been her victim? Had she ever been his prize? She remembered his proposal. *Oh darling, it is yes, isn't it.* Only now did she notice his presumption. *Of course it is.* She'd agreed. What a fool! She should have done as Mummy had wanted her to and turned Frank down. She so easily could have done. She'd half-persuaded herself Mummy was right it was unfair, selfish and disloyal of her even to think of waltzing to Malaya; she'd half-decided in advance of Frank's proposal that if he asked – *if* – she must refuse him. But then Frank had kissed her in the white marble rotunda and that blackbird had sung in the hedges behind and she'd clean forgotten Mummy; she'd quite lost her head, and accepted. And later, when, without actually saying anything, her mother had made it clear as gin she thought she was a most ungrateful daughter to abandon her to marry, she'd said – she'd actually said – she wasn't in the least sorry she'd accepted Frank; she should have been an utter daisy to have turned him down. She remembered the basilisk stare Mummy had bestowed on her then. She remembered how Mummy had upbraided her for being tiresomely headstrong and selfish, and had said again what she'd said before: that Frank was not to be trusted; never mind that he was a colonial, what about his charm? At the time, she'd dismissed this as the snobbish raving of a jealous, needy woman contemplating a lonely old age. But perhaps after all there was something damning about charm? Something mechanical and impersonal. So had she been gulled by Frank's flattering smiles and his flattering glances and all those flattering words she'd longed to hear? Had she been gulled when, after Mummy's outburst, he'd comforted her she wasn't tiresome at all, nor headstrong and that he liked her adventurous spirit: what a woman needed in Malaya was a bit of go? Had she been gulled during the voyage out? The P&O. Their little cabin. The joyful shock of carnal pleasure. Nights on deck. How thrilled she'd been by the romance of being a bride sailing under the glittering stars through a phosphorescent sea. Oh, the gaiety, the parties, the tipsy haze of Singapore and the jolly little club at BB. And then, when finally she'd arrived here at Kluanak, had she been gulled when she'd taken so contentedly to her new household duties? She remembered how she'd pitied Frank the life she'd mistakenly assumed he must have lived in the bungalow prior to their marriage. It must have been such a lonely life, she'd thought, a dreary bachelor's life in a dreary bachelor's den, so drably comfortless and grim.

Well, so much for that. So much for the memories she'd though would sustain her in old age; memories like jewels lifted from velvet, held up to the caressing light ... Rose watched her bed reduce further to ashes and she accused that all these months since they'd met, her husband may as well have been living the deceitful life of a spy. Everything he'd ever said to her was polluted by all the things he'd omitted to tell her. Not to mention by all those lies he actually had told her. *I haven't any family*, he'd said, at Ryton Cove. This, the man with four children running around the jungle. No, despaired Rose, nothing about Frank was as it had seemed until, yesterday, he'd revealed his secrets; now nothing about her life with him, her whole life as a wife, was any longer as it had seemed until then.

Meanwhile, after he'd given Boy instructions to burn the mem's bed, Frank had returned to the courthouse. His desk faced his office window, which itself gave a good view of the lawn in front of the bungalow. He was supposed to be documenting tax returns from the district, but this past hour he'd kept more than half an eye on goings-on on the lawn: the little gang of servants lugging out the bed, Boy chopping it up, the construction of the bonfire. Now Boy was setting it alight. Frank watched the flames begin their work of consumption and destruction. So it is done, he thought, *behold, the fire and the wood* ... Except this wood was in itself the burnt offering. Yes, the marital bed had been sacrificed on the altar of marriage. And good riddance, thought Frank. He felt positively disencumbered; as light as those sparks drifting like confetti through the air. He felt that this sacrifice must be an act of purification, and so now his sooty marriage, cleansed, could be made again as spotless as the tiny white orchids which abounded hereabouts.

When Frank returned from the courthouse for tiffin, the remains of the bonfire were still smouldering. But despite this insistent evidence of the discord between them, neither he nor Rose saw anything for it but to sit down at the table on the verandah, to eat together as usual. Where else should they have eaten? Out amongst the trees? One in the drawing room, one in the formal dining room? But wouldn't that have perfectly thrilled the servants, and neither of them felt inclined to give them the satisfaction.

In any case, Frank, for his part, still felt buoyed, just a little, by the hopeful idea that for him and Rose the burning of the bed would be a kind of purge, a ritual cleansing. He waited until Boy had served one of Cookie's dull river fishes, and then he girded himself, and he said, "No point bothering the PWD. I've already sent instructions down to the kampung. It'll only be a week or so until the carpenter can make you a new bed." He looked at Rose carefully. If she'd given him even the slightest encouragement he'd have said: in the meantime, I do hope you'll consent to share mine. But Rose merely looked at him as if he were going mouldy, and so he said instead, "In the meantime, take mine! I'll sleep out here, in my chair."

Rose poked at her fish.

"No thank you, Frank," she said politely. "Did Boy not tell you? I'm having him set up a camp bed in my room."

Frank recognised that his wife's politeness was intended to smother intimacy as a bucket of sand chucked over the bonfire would have smothered the flames, if they weren't already nearly out.

"A camp bed?" he echoed, all forlorn.

"Yes."

"Are you sure about that? A camp bed won't be very comfortable, even for a few days."

Rose had as yet eaten nothing. Nonetheless, prim, she dabbed at her lips with her napkin, before she replied, with significant emphasis, "It will do for *me*."

"For *you*?"

"For *me*."

Frank had as yet eaten nothing either. He dropped his eyes to his plate. So that was how it was to be, he thought. His wife was to deny him his bread and butter, *pro tempore*. Well, he must hope it wouldn't be too long before she got it all out of her system and decided to let bygones be bygones. In the meantime, he supposed he'd have to accept a few more nights in which his only consolations, and his only companions, would be booze and tobacco.

10

Rose knew her grim little camp bed looked pitifully swamped and spindly beneath the generous tent of the jungle curtains, and she found it barely more comfortable than her chaise longue. Moreover it wobbled, so once or twice as she'd tossed and turned through another tormenting night, she'd feared it would collapse. She'd several times considered telling Frank she'd changed her mind: she'd take his bed after all, until her new one arrived, and he could sleep in his chair. But she'd each time decided she'd rather be sleeplessly uncomfortable than to hand to her husband the slight advantage that would accrue to him if she'd asked him to put himself out for her. And despite the camp bed's rickety discomfort, she was as loath to leave it in the mornings as any bride the marital bed. Every day since Frank had tipped her world off its axis, she'd stayed exactly where she was when she'd heard him being served breakfast on the verandah and no matter what the servants made of her behaviour.

And every day since then, Frank had indulged his wife's need for solitude, but this morning he'd decided: enough. And so before he left for the courthouse, he knocked at her door with a particularly insistent and persistent knocking.

Rose knew this must be Frank; Boy would never knock like that. Despite her resentful irritation at being summoned by her husband, she answered at last. She was in her cotton nightgown with her hair all mussed, but Frank of course was looking trim in his khakis, and she felt bitter at his neatness. Still, his face was pale, just as pale as her own must be, she supposed, and the shadows beneath his eyes were as dark as bruises.

For a long moment husband and wife just stared at each other, but then Frank, optimistic, bestowed upon Rose the smile he knew full well she'd so recently found delightful. Alas, this smile seemed to her now both shallow and ingratiating.

"What?" she snapped.

Frank's optimism took a knock, and he spoke uncertainly.

"You haven't forgotten your new bed's to be delivered later from the kampung?"

"Of course I haven't!"

"A relief, no doubt, after the camp bed."

Rose spoke with feeling.

"I should say!"

Frank looked at his wife with yearning anguish. He didn't quite dare plead: I've missed reaching for you in the night. He'd didn't quite dare tempt, or cajole, or invite: I'm hoping that tonight, when you're sleeping once again in a proper bed ... ? No, he squared his shoulders, and he said,

"I've missed seeing you in the mornings."

Rose did not reply, as he'd hoped: and I you. Indeed, she said nothing at all. But her silence was better than a curt dismissal and perhaps she was willing to relent a little? Frank took a chance. "I've missed my kiss before I go to the courthouse too."

Rose stared into the middle distance. She imagined la

midinette's hideous sirih-stained mouth pressed to Frank's; she imagined that woman's stocky brown-skinned arms twined around his neck. But she couldn't imagine now brushing her own lips against his cheek. She shook her head.

"I'll see you at tiffin," she said.

Tiffin, when it came, was another drearily uncomfortable meal of bad food and stilted conversation. Afterwards, Rose and Frank took their lie-offs as usual, him in his chair on the verandah, her, for the last time, on the camp bed.

After the lie-off, Usit waited until the mem was occupied on the verandah, and the tuan had returned to his duties in the courthouse, as per his instructions. He then fetched a stepladder and took it into the mem's room, where he unhooked the jungle curtains, so they wouldn't be a hindrance later. He stripped and folded the camp bed; the bedding he gave to the water-carrier, for washing, and the camp bed itself he returned to the storeroom. Once everything was ready, he walked down to the kampung to tell Heri he could bring the new bed now – all the village men were excellent woodworkers, but it was always Heri to whom the tuan turned when he needed a skilled carpenter. The mem's splendid new bed, of dense mahogany, was standing in Heri's ruang. Usit, Heri and a small band of villagers loaded the frame, and also the new rice straw mattress Frank had commissioned from some of the kampung women, onto a raft, which they floated downstream from the kampung to the compound.

Frank often did his own typing. When, from his office window, he saw the bed being unloaded at the landing stage he was at his desk clattering away at a report for Mr Hollingworth on his efforts, so far unsuccessful, to persuade the villagers of his district to change their method of rice cultivation in accordance with the latest thinking from the agricultural gentlemen attached to the Colonial Office in London. He left his desk and he returned to the bungalow, so both he and Rose were on hand to supervise as the villagers and the servants manhandled the new bed into Rose's room – a job just as tiring and sweaty as that of removing the old bed, and accompanied by as many curses. Eventually, the bed was standing in its proper place, in all its sturdy wooden splendour, with its mattress atop it. The villagers then piled onto the raft and began to pole upstream, making slower progress than before despite now having no cargo, on account of having to battle the current.

Usit made up the new bed with fresh linen and re-hung the jungle curtains – he'd left the stepladder propped up against the bedroom wall, the while. When he had everything just so, he picked up the stepladder and carried it out of the mem's room, intending to return it to the storeroom. Outside, he found the tuan and the mem at opposite sides of the verandah. They were facing away from each other; the tuan was leaning against the rail, staring out over the river, the mem was sitting in a chair looking over the lawn. Usit put down the ladder and cleared his throat. Both the tuan and the mem turned to face him.

"Bed ready," he announced. "You look now?"

Frank nodded. He walked over to Rose and he held out his hand.

"Shall we?"

Rose wanted to say: certainly, we shall not. She had no

intention of yet readmitting her husband to her room, even in daylight hours, new bed or no new bed. But *pas devant les domestiques*, as Mummy would say; she felt she could scarcely create with Boy looking on. So she summoned all her skills as an actress and she too stood; she took Frank's hand.

"Of course," she said.

It pleased Frank no end the little woman had taken his hand, and it failed to occur to him that despite her compliance, Rose was seething, so he was both hurt and surprised when, the moment they were in her room, and the door had swung shut behind them, she immediately tugged her hand from his. He'd been about to remark on the new-furniture smell of shaved wood curling through the air, but now he didn't. In silence the two of them walked to the foot of the bed. The jungle curtains were tied back, and to each of them the bed, heavy, stolid and rustic, like all furniture of local manufacture, seemed to be crouching ready to spring. But to spring with what? A promise of delight? A threat of rejection? The certainty of mockery? What?

Well, thought Frank, there was only one way to find out. He took a deep breath, and he plunged in.

"Darling, I say it again: I know I've been at fault. I know I behaved badly. I beg again: forgive me."

Silence.

"I've been as miserable as anything ever since Hollingworth posted me back here, and you can be sure I haven't much liked sleeping by myself these past ten days."

Silence.

"I'm not some rotten adulterer, you know."

Rose granted the point: Frank had not committed adultery; it only felt to her as if he had.

Silence.

"I didn't betray our marriage vows."

Didn't you? thought Rose. She imagined herself in her husband's arms ... him kissing her ... him taking his leave of her ... him rushing straight into the arms of another woman. No, he hadn't done that, she supposed, he hadn't done that. But still, she felt she'd been sent sprawling by betrayal.

Silence.

"Surely you can understand?"

Silence.

Frank struggled not to feel resentful, but hadn't he stood for this damned bed? Huh! He felt like kicking it, and he couldn't help the thought momentarily flickering that the little woman was overreacting to what was after all pretty ordinary male misbehaviour – behaviour that was jolly well over and done with to boot. Furthermore, her silence was most peculiar; her coolness was not at all what a fellow would expect of an egg. If only she'd shout at him, slap him, start slinging things. If only they could have a proper quarrel they could properly make up. But how was he to make up with his wife while she seemed so ... so ... glassy? It would be like trying to make up with a window.

"Come on!" he begged. "Let's hear it! It's no good bottling things up."

Rose supposed he had a point, but a strangely confining restraint seemed to have clamped around her ever since Frank had revealed to her the facts of his past. She felt encased, as if by amber more chilly than warmly electric, so she seemed to be just barely living, just barely not dead, in a separate realm from the world beyond her skin, and also from the woman she'd been before she'd become entrapped.

But perhaps whatever held her was now crazing? In any case, she spoke angrily.

"Aren't you ashamed?"

"Well, now, I ..."

"Perhaps you're not capable of feeling shame."

"I say!"

"Ten years, Frank? Ten years and four children?"

Frank scowled and he said, "Not real. With her. Not like us."

"Not real? This whole other life you lived with a woman who wasn't me? A whole other life you wanted to keep secret from me. What was it then, a dream?"

"You know I meant it was not a real marriage. She was not a real wife." Frank paused. "More like a shadow." He paused again. "Or perhaps some kind of fake. Some kind of counterfeit."

"What? Like banknotes run off in an East End cellar? Well, you told me yourself: you bought her."

"I told you no such thing! I told you I made a present to her family. A present freely given, for the gift of their daughter; her mother was grateful to accept it."

Rose shrugged.

"Is that how you put it to yourself?" she said. "Well, whatever the arrangement between you, it must have been quite a surprise for her when I showed up."

"No ... Well, yes. A surprise I came back to Kluanak, I mean, neither of us expected that. But when I ended things I told her I was going to get married in England."

Rose's eyes widened. She remembered Frank telling her, the night he'd confessed, that his liaison with la midinette had only ever been intended as a stop-a-gap until he'd married. At the time, she'd been so overwhelmed the full force of his words hadn't struck her. But now his almost blasé admission positively assaulted her; she was stormed by a new understanding of her lurking worry she'd never been Frank's prize. She met her husband's eye and she held it as she accused, "What? We hadn't met then."

Frank found he couldn't look away. Willy-nilly, he made an explicit admission of one more sin against slush – an unwise admission this time, he suspected, but hey-ho.

"I told her I'd made up my mind to find a wife during my Home leave."

Rose flinched. Now, she remembered, again, her husband's proposal: *oh darling, it is yes, isn't it.* But this time she was struck not by his presumption, but by her own; she'd presumed they'd tumbled, romantically, headfirst to the altar, when all along, or so it now appeared, he'd never harboured in his heart anything more than the pragmatic desperation to marry. She'd thought she'd gambled all for love, whereas all she'd done, it seemed, was to take a foolish gamble with her life – even a tawdry gamble. When she spoke, she could not keep the bitterness from her voice.

"You must have thought I'd do as well as any other."

"Rose! You know how devotedly I love you."

"Oh, love." That glittering sham.

"Yes, dearest, love."

"You should have told me the truth before you proposed."

"With hindsight, yes. But I didn't think you'd much like it, I suppose."

Rose was frankly incredulous.

"*This* was a reason not to tell me?"

"I barely thought of her after I arrived in England."

"So?"

"I think I thought if I didn't admit it happened, then it never did happen – not for us. For you and me."

"Nonsense! You mean you hadn't the pluck to tell me."

Frank stared hard at his shoes. After a long beat he trotted out, lamely, the explanation, or the excuse, he'd tried to fall back on the first morning after his confession.

"I told you: six out of ten bachelors in Saramantan keep a nonya. I only did what everybody else was doing."

Rose looked at him with contempt.

"And if what everybody else was doing was wrong?"

"Wrong? Be reasonable! It's a sensible solution to a practical problem. The lack of white women in the East. In Malaya, anyway. And it's only natural the Malay women want to put rice in their rice bowls whilst they've still got the looks for it." Frank made an impatient gesture. "I told you before, she was never anything to me. Never."

"What you were to each other, or weren't to each other, is none of my concern."

"I told you, it was over ages ago. It never was, really." Frank paused. "We parted on the most dreadful terms. I should have told you that. She threatened to curse me, you know – she did curse me, I'm sure, or tried to anyway."

That jolted Rose.

"Curse you?"

"Black magic and all that sort of thing. Said I'd die at sea. I confess the thought haunted me on the Homeward run, though I clean forgot about it once I stepped ashore at Southampton."

Black magic? Rose was washed all at once by longing to be back in Kensington, where nothing strange ever happened, at least not to people she knew, and curses stayed safely in children's books. With effort, she gathered herself.

"What?" she said. "She's no threat to me? Not in the present. Is that what you mean? And so you thought I needn't know anything about her?"

"I knew you wouldn't understand."

"I understand all too well." Rose bestowed on Frank the sort of basilisk stare so often deployed by her mother. "You tricked me. You enticed me here under false pretences."

"Not at all. My darling, there's nothing false about my love for you."

"But you didn't tell me a thing. Not a single thing. Even when you were given this posting, you didn't tell me. You let me believe you were distressed to be coming back here because it was a drag on your ambition."

Frank's face became sullen and sulky.

"It was such awfully rotten luck being posted back."

"Bad luck justifies your lying to me?"

"Omitting to tell the truth."

"You see a difference?" Rose paused. "When I first saw your

sons, you let me believe they could have been fathered by a man in BB."

"I wanted to protect you."

"Protect me?" Rose thought it was as if Frank had handed her armour fashioned from tin foil, and all without even asking if she wanted to put it on.

Frank nodded.

"Listen!" he begged. "Listen! I've done my best to sort things out – to rid us of her, I mean. To rid you of her. As soon as we arrived, I offered her money to move to another kampung. She was in two minds about it until she guessed you knew nothing about her. Then she began blackmailing me: if you want me to keep silent, then … I tried to buy her off, but she demanded more."

Rose stared at her husband. Oh, the squalor of it all! She'd expect such venality from a Malay strumpet, but from the English gentleman she'd married?

"Buy her off?" she said. "Blackmail?"

Frank nodded.

"Yes," he said. "That day she ambushed me in my bathhouse, she wanted another payment."

"You told me she'd had a row with her husband."

"Then that flap with Boy. I realised things couldn't go on. They really couldn't. I knew I had to own up."

"Rather late in the day."

"I know. I do know I left it far too late to speak."

"And then only under the stress of her intrusions." Rose felt tears threatening. She stared hard at her new bed for a long moment and she mastered herself. Finally, she said, "When we first met you told me you had no family. I haven't a relation in the world, that's what you said."

"I meant I had no white people."

What? A brown woman, brown babies, were less deserving of attention, resources, even of compassion, than were white ones? Frankly, Rose agreed. Nonetheless, she said, "But four children."

Frank scowled.

"The brats? Why drag them into it?"

"Well we can't leave them out of it. We can't ignore them."

Now it was Frank's turn to stare down at the new bed. He remembered the first time he'd held First Son: the dark little baby had screwed up his dark little face and bawled. He'd thought: *that* is my child? He said, "Of course I wish them no harm, but I can't ... Rather heartless, perhaps, but I can't ... Well, I can't take much interest in them, I suppose. I grant that when they were babies they were rather appealing, in the way of all small creatures. But now they're bigger they're no more to me than any other kampung brats ... Do you think me pitiless? Perhaps I'm lacking in natural feeling, but there it is." He paused before he added, "The touch of the tar brush, you know."

Oh, Rose knew all right. Nonetheless, she rather thought she was appalled. Certainly, she would have preferred Frank to have said: it's strange how you come to love them; when they're your own it doesn't seem to matter if they're brown. But her distress was not on account of his first four children in the kampung, of their needs, fears, hopes, dreams, of the worlds that were them. She was instead thinking solely of her own child, the baby she was growing within her. Yes, there came a point in any pregnancy when doubt was banished. And though Rose was not yet showing, she was by now certain she was pregnant. If she hadn't started thinking of her husband as shoddy goods, she'd have told him already. Now, though, she was doubly glad she'd as yet said nothing. After all, was it only on account of their skin colour that Frank was so callously inattentive towards his first four children? Or did his smallness extend from what she thought of as the usual, into an indifference even she would judge to be culpable? Exactly how limited was her husband in imagination, in sympathy? How attentive would Frank be, could Frank be, to his fifth child? Her child. Would her child's whiteness make all the difference, as indeed it properly should, or would it not?

Rose placed her right hand on her belly. Notwithstanding it was still flat, she could feel a hard swelling under the thin cotton of her frock. She spread her fingers, as though to provide protective bars between the person-in-the-making she had developing inside her and the cruelty of the world. For the moment, Frank's presence seemed to her unbearable. She jerked her head towards her bedroom door.

"Go!" she said. "Go!"

OUTBOUND MAIL, MARCH 1925
SENT FROM THE DO'S BUNGALOW,
KLUANAK, SARAMANTAN

From Rose to Beatrice

Dearest Bumbles,

Wishing that something horrid could be avoided, does not make it avoidable. By which I mean I've had yours of February 2nd, and I assure you there was no need to apologise for not knowing whether to tell me, or how to tell me, and nor for being the bearer of bad news, neither. Of course I understand your kind uncertainty whether it was best to reveal to me what Mrs Dabney-Dent so casually revealed to you. I can understand you think it rotten luck you were both assigned to the Red Cross cake stall, and you may very well be right she is a hateful busybody; certainly her revelations put you in a hateful position. Nonetheless, I think you are wrong to regret you'd ever met her, or to chastise yourself you should never have asked if she knew Frank or me. Once she'd said she'd lived on Saramantan it was only natural that you should ask; any lady would have done the same.

In any case, Frank had confessed to me a couple of weeks before your letter arrived. I hope knowing that I already knew what it revealed when I read your letter makes you feel better about passing along what you'd learned. More, I'm in one way glad Mrs D-D chattered on over the buns and sponge cakes, with whatever silliness, or with whatever malicious relish, as your knowing already saves me the pain, the bitter pain, of telling you how things now stand here – something I fear I may not have had the courage to do if Mrs D-D hadn't.

Are you offended I may have kept the truth even from your own dear self? I beg you not to be, for though I'm accustomed to tell you everything, I never before had anything like this to tell, and the shame of it I hope excuses in your mind that I would perhaps not have told you of it, under other circumstances. No, I cannot deny it: I hate the thought of anybody knowing what Frank has done almost as much as I hate what he has done in and of itself.

Oh, I know the servants know, and they all know everything in the kampung, I'm horribly conscious of it, but I can't care over much what the natives think; it's the thought of white people knowing I find quite unbearable. Frank denies his debauchery is common knowledge in the colony, but he deludes himself, I fear. I'm not too new to the small, closed, and gossipy world of a handful of rulers far from Home to realise that if one British lady lately on Saramantan knows, then so too do all the other British ladies still here, and thanks to them so also do their husbands. It's too ghastly! I cannot help remembering something I rather would not: when I was staying in BB I got the feeling once or twice the ladies there were trying to tell me something. It's mortifying to think they must have realised I didn't know; it's more mortifying still to think what secret they were trying to impart. They must have judged me a perfect fool. I can't stand to think they were pitying me. I suppose all the time I've been in Kluanak they must have been speculating whether I'd found out. Now I quite dread going next to town – the horrors of conversations thick as cold cream with all that cannot be said.

And I shiver to think if this news got out at Home. Your solemn promise of silence to everybody debarring only Edmund was quite unnecessary, since I know you'd never tell – and I really cannot object Edmund is your confidante, since until so recently I should have made Frank mine. But I'm thankful you made him swear silence,* and your promise you wouldn't tell your own mother, knowing she would certainly tell mine, was a great relief. Only imagine if Mummy discovered all! Granted, she'd be kind in her own way, but I'd know she must be thinking: I told you so. She must be thinking: well what did you expect? Let's hope she never runs into some tattle-tale Mrs Dabney-Dent of her own, that's all.

Oh, my dear, I hope you never know the unhappiness I'm feeling now. I think at some moments I may as well throw myself in the river and have done with it all.** And yet at other moments I think I'm being hysterical. After all, plenty of wives – second wives, I mean – have to confront the lingering shadow of the dead first wife who preceded them. Is my predicament so very different from theirs? Then again, Frank was 30 when we wed, and though nobody ever talks of it – well, we are both married women, now, and we can confess, between us, that thing we of the fairer sex are not supposed to know or in any case to admit that we know: that young men always find an outlet for their energies. With other boys, yes, at school, and if later they pay some little midinette for their pleasure that's up to them. Something so cheap, so trifling could never threaten a wife. Which is to say: if I thought that, after, Frank had counted notes onto a table, or even onto some stretch of bare flesh, and then left, in the usual way, then, like any other sensible bride, I could have, I would have, consigned all that to the past***. But his Malay woman lived with him for ten years! Ten years! And four children!

I cannot just buck up and accept that woman, those children, are merely footnotes in Frank's biography. Indeed, they make me feel I am a footnote to his story – and also to my own. I feel now I never was, never will be, never could be, my husband's first in anything – and not just in the thing that makes a marriage a marriage. Do you think my desire for primacy is very horrible? Perhaps it is. Perhaps it is discreditable, this desire of mine, to be Frank's first, in time, in rank, in love – to be his template for womanhood, so to speak, existing for him in realms beyond the physical. Well, if it is: so be it; I cannot deny what I feel just because I perhaps shouldn't feel it.

She's not even a beauty. Oh, you should just see her! She's very ugly. I suppose, in her bloom, she must have had a certain native prettiness, the ordinary prettiness of youth anywhere around the globe, but these days she's a ruin: fat, with raddled cheeks, a mouth hideously reddened by sirih – a vile concoction all the native women chew – and coarse hair like a long black shock of matting. I tell myself it's something Frank cannot possibly have eyes for her now – not unless *she* exists for him in realms beyond the physical, and this I do not believe she does. He's been too disparaging of her, too casually belittling, for me to worry on that score. But instead of offering me relief, her ugliness humiliates me: if in the past Frank set the bar so low, then what does that say about me? I look at her, and I wonder: excepting only the colour of my skin, when he chose me, did he set the bar any higher?

And how Frank deceived me. So many truths omitted. So many lies told. Am I so easy to gull? I have to face that I am – this bitter humiliation of knowing I am a fool. It makes me so sad, miserable, to remember that once I would have said Frank and I told each other everything – I would have boasted we could tell each other anything, anything at all, even if it were barely proper. What a dupe! Sharing things? Intimacy? No. It's evident, now, Frank was never much concerned to reveal himself to me; I'm bound to wonder how concerned he ever was to know me. If he respected me so little he was prepared to keep such big secrets from me, then did he ever want to know me at all?

And the ordinariness of his betrayal – I find it so depressing. He seems to me now as humdrum as any other deceitful man; I seem to myself as workaday as any other silly woman deceived.

I confess it: a part of me now wants to escape the hall of mirrors that is my life, and without a word to Frank to boot – to vanish, wouldn't that be grand. But I know I could never bring myself to leave him without first asking his permission to go, as any wife should, of her husband. To love, honour and obey. I know I don't have the courage, the brio, the bravura, for disobedience. I'm not a wayward sort of person. Marrying Frank, a jungle-wallah, in defiance of Mummy, was the one wayward thing I ever did, and now I don't suppose I'll ever act waywardly again.

In any case, I couldn't just bolt through the jungle. To run from a place like this even the boldest wife would have to ask her husband for help. I could go to BB on the mail boat, but I'd have to beg Frank to give me money to get to Singapore and to pay for the passage Home, and to be horribly blunt, my dear, I doubt we could afford the expense.

But suppose we were rich, and suppose too I asked Frank if I may go. Wouldn't any husband think strictness quite the thing? Wouldn't any husband have his pride? Which is to say, though I've never yet given Frank occasion to be possessive, I fear if I provoked him by asking may I go, then possessive he would be, and he would say go I most certainly must not. And this before he even knows I'm deciding for two now, and that in refusing my request to quit the jungle, and him, he'd be deciding for three.

I assume you know what I'm talking about. I gather from your silence on the subject that when you wrote you still did not yet know of my Certain Suspicions. I hope you have read of them by now. Well, my suspicions have condensed to certainty, though from my disappointment in Frank you remain my only confidante.

I suppose I really should write to Mummy with the news, but I can't face writing to her at all at the moment, I just can't, not about Baby, not about anything else.

Oh, God, Mummy! Though she doesn't like Frank, in my mind's ear I can hear all too clearly what she'd say if she knew I'd ever entertained the idea of bolting: wives don't abandon their husbands, it's such terribly bad form. Your husband has a past? Forget all about it; sweep it under the carpet; pretend it never happened; buckle down and get on with your life as a wife; unhappiness is no excuse for moping; unhappiness is no excuse for anything at all.

Well, she may be right.

Your sad cousin, Rosebud

PS On re-reading my letter, some afterthoughts:

* Do impress upon Edmund I wish his silence too.

** Did I frighten you with talk of jumping into the river? Don't worry, my dear, I know I'll never do it – my lack of waywardness, again.

*** Do you think me very shocking to write of schoolboys' passions for each other and of grown men paying woman for the obvious? I suppose you do. I suppose my directness is indeed shocking, but Frank's revelations, I fear, have coarsened my sensibility and made me bold, and cold, and hard.

From Frank "Langers" Langham to Robert "Dandy" Dabney-Dent

What ho, Farmer Dandy,

It was good of you to break at last your long silence, and I thank you for your letter, although you hit the nail on the head that I must regret its contents – what dashed bad luck that your Violet and Mrs Marchmorant were both assigned to the cake stall at that dratted Red Cross jumble sale.

Cease blaming yourself instanter! I'd barely read three lines of your letter before I remembered Rose had a cousin somewhere in Suffolk, but I never anticipated any danger – after all it's a pretty large county. So I'm in no position to blame you in the least for failing to anticipate Violet would run into anybody who knew Rose, and thus for failing to forbid the little woman from discussing my affairs with all abroad. No fellow can be expected to think of everything, and it only goes to show that if disaster

can strike, then it always does strike, just as if fate had it in for a
fellow.

As to the vexing question of whether Mrs Marchmorant
would blab to Rose, I must confirm the rattler's done her worst.
There was indeed a letter for the little woman from her cousin in
the same packet that brought yours, and in response to a direct
question she conceded said cousin had through ill chance learned
all, and furthermore, had spilled the beans. But though you were
quite right to worry it may all come as a terrific shock to Rose, it
cannot matter now. No, old man, we're both quite out of danger
from women with loose tongues, for the very good reason that
even before your letter arrived I had myself confessed – sung like
a songbird, and twice as sweetly.

Mind you, I cannot pretend I'm not a little cross with Violet,
and I'm sure both of us of the Langham chapter hope henceforth
your little woman will be less free with her confidences. As to
her excuse she only said what any lady would have said, once
it became clear she and the lady to whom she was talking were
connected by connections as close as those between her and me,
and Mrs Marchmorant and Rose, it seems to me it was a pretty
poor one, and I cannot think you were wrong to give her what for,
for gossiping, although I suppose I'm sorry your rebukes made
her cry – certainly I can understand you were horrified to find
yourself mopping up her tears, and I'm only grateful you don't
hold the ghastliness of it against me.

Shall you write again next month? I hope you shall, though
I doubt it, unless you discover something else as incendiary to
report as that you feared your little woman's indiscretion had

cooked my goose.

Yours,

Langers

PS How goes the farm? I should have liked to have heard something of that.

From Frank "Langers" Langham, to Charles "Slinger" Slightman.

By my bloomin' eyebrows Slinger,

Was the news so exciting Dandy roused himself to write to you too? In case not, let me fill you in. Hard to credit, but in that sleepy back-of-beyond, Suffolk, Violet, drat her, ran into a cousin of Rose's and took it upon herself to enlighten the rustic relation about my past. The R.R., in turn, unable to keep her nose out, wrote to Rose ...

The cheek of woman! You can be sure I've told Dandy (more-or-less, not in so many words) to see to it Violet henceforth keeps her trap shut and stops interfering. I tell you I'd find it difficult to resist wringing that egg's neck, if she were any closer to me than half the world away. The same goes for Rose's meddlesome R.R. And both instances of neck-wringing notwithstanding I'd anyway made a clean breast of things before the mail arrived, like a cocked gun, all readied for spraying its bullets.

Yes, the deed is done: I've revealed all to the little woman. Do pass on the news to Maude, and I hope domestic peace reigns once more at Relunas, now she need no longer bend your ear about my reluctance to confess.

To be frank, Nony made herself such a bally nuisance I had no choice other than to speak. But though she rather forced my hand,

and though, too, confession was a ghastly thing, a grim quarter of an hour that seemed like twenty years, I'm glad, now, to have it all off my chest. Unburdened, that's what I am. Unburdened, and freed, thank God, of Nony. Evidently, the dipper's realised the jig is up, as she's quite ceased her pestering. Indeed I've had neither sight nor sound of her since I confessed, and I trust now she's done her worst she'll leave me in blessed peace.

As for Rose, there was a terrible tantrum about the marital bed – in days of yore the extra-marital bed – so I had to order her a new one, but otherwise, she's taken my revelations calmly, on the whole. Too calmly, I sometimes fear. I'm not sure it's quite normal. Still, I suppose I should be grateful I'm spared the horrors of her weeping.

Alas, the little woman's self-possession extends even where any fellow must regret it: notwithstanding the new bed, my dear wife has given up the prick, pro tempore. No bread and butter, old man, no bread and butter. I nightly tell myself she can't keep up the cold shouldering indefinitely, no little woman could if she were marooned in the jungle with no one but her husband for company, but she's taking her time about relenting, that's for sure.

Yours, Langers

11
The kampung, April 1925

Nony was feeling as flat and deflated as a dead puffer fish. It was so dispiriting being a failed extortionist, everything was such an anti-climax. When, the evening after she'd made her scene in front of the mem, she'd learned the bed she'd once shared with Baba had become ashes, she'd berated herself she'd over-played her hand. Baba had done exactly as he'd threatened to do: he'd called her bluff, he'd revealed all to his wife in preference to continuing to pay her. Damn! She'd known she never should have taken First Daughter up to the bungalow.

Still, despite her regrets, Nony had tried to feel smug that evening. I have begun it, she'd preened, or tried to. I have begun to cause whatever trouble it is I'm going to cause, now let's sit back and see what that trouble will be....

Gratifyingly, for a few days it had looked to her as if the trouble would be severe. Usit and the other servants had conveyed to the kampung that the tuan was nightly drinking himself stupid and the mem was sleeping alone on a camp bed. True, Usit and the others also said that during the day the tuan and the mem were treating each other fairly courteously, but everyone agreed it would be just like the Mat Salleh to put on a show. As for Baba ordering his pelacur putih a new bed from Heri, what else was he supposed to do? She could scarcely sleep on a camp bed forever, and certainly not on the floor like a Malay.

Now, though, the mem's new bed had actually been delivered. Happily, Usit, who changed the sheets, had reported there was as yet no evidence it had witnessed Baba firing his canon, but Nony couldn't help resentfully concurring in the general opinion that it surely couldn't be long. And, alas, she was losing confidence in herself as a trouble-maker. Alamak! It worried her that any difficulties she'd caused between Baba and the mem would soon be smoothed away, as if they were nothing more than lumpy clods of soil, smoothed to slick mud by the river.

Mind you, what had she expected? She'd previously assumed, she now belatedly supposed, that if Baba were forced to confess, his confession must be followed by some sort of excitement beyond the mere burning of a bed. She'd expected noise, she supposed, drums and xylophones and gongs, and performers in flashy, sparkly costumes. For sure she'd assumed Baba would have to deal with tantrums and tears and shouting and sulks, with nagging and scolding, with the opposite of a quiet life, a destructively unruly life, for a good long while and preferably forever. Yes, she now realised, she'd previously hoped that if Baba defied her, by refusing to pay her, and instead cast to the chickens the chicken feed, then, as the second best outcome of her little scheme, he and the mem would be condemned to live on together in the quiet violence of sex-free, sour-eyed unhappiness for years and years to come.

She certainly hadn't expected Baba and the mem would so soon appear to be edging back to roughly how things had been between them, before she'd flaunted herself and First Daughter up at the DO's bungalow. How could it be that by so manoeuvring things the mem had learned both of her existence and also of her role in her husband's life, she appeared to have achieved nothing at all? No, as far as she could tell there would be no long-term consequences for either Baba or the mem of the revelation, to one of them, that the three of them formed a triangle – only immediate consequences for herself in the form of lost income. Of course she felt despondent.

And she felt even worse to realise that lost income wasn't the end of it. Alas, it occurred to Nony that now she no longer had any hold over him, Baba may take it into his head to punish her for her various infractions, just as she'd so feared he'd do when he'd first returned from mysterious Kampung Inggris, and she'd been certain he'd want revenge for her failed curse. Yes, power and impotence had re-balanced themselves yet again, and yet again he, the DO, could make her life hell, if he so wanted. Dejected, she supposed she'd better revert to her original idea of dealing with his presence in her neck of the jungle by doing her best to avoid him altogether and hoping he'd avoid her too.

But what if he didn't? For that matter, what if he did? What if he punished her, and what if he didn't? What next? What now, for her, asked Nony, feeling all scratchy and out of sorts both with herself and also with the world, what did her future hold now it no longer held the possibility of either smashing down Baba's house or else of wringing money from him as easily as she'd wring water from a wet sarong, but only a high probability of being harassed and bullied by a DO who had it in for her?

Well, she knew a woman who could tell her, a woman who had privileged access to the future.

Nony no more held it against the pawang that her suggestion of blackmail had come to naught, than she had that her curse had failed – it was all Baba's fault everything had gone wrong. And so it was that, in trusting confidence, she was now once again squatting opposite the pawang in the middle of the old woman's unnerving, skull-hung, incense-scented, smoky ruang. She was addressing her quickly, in a low and urgent voice. As she did so, she could see out of the corner of her eye the big pan of silkily vitreous black oil the pawang used for divination. She'd brought along a basket of uncooked rice and another of plump purple dragon fruit to offer in exchange for a prophecy, and these sat between the two women on the mat. She'd also brought along First Daughter; the little girl was pottering about, picking things up, putting them down.

The pawang listened patiently, blinking in her froggy way as Nony told her of her dissatisfaction at the way recent events had unfolded. She knew that when the villagers came to her asking to have their futures told, they often wanted to talk things over, hash things out, clear the air, get things off their chests, just as much as they wanted to know what would happen next in the stories of their lives.

At last, Nony had run through her grievances. She sighed, heavily, and she pointed to the pan of oil.

"So, can you look what's in store for me?"

The pawang sucked her gums, before she said, "You

understand the spirits are capricious?"

As usual, Nony took a moment to unscramble the pawang's toothless mumble.

"Yes."

"Sometimes they reveal nothing in the oil. Sometimes they ignore the questions they've been asked, and answer quite other ones instead."

"Yes."

"Usually, they communicate in riddles. It's rare for them to give a straight answer to a straight question."

"Yes."

The pawang sucked her gums some more, but then, slowly, slowly, she creaked upwards – her spine was so curved she was bent almost double even when she was standing as straight as she could.

"Come," she said. "To the oil."

The pawang's pan of oil wasn't just a pan of oil, but a magic mirror. In the kampung all types of shiny, reflective surface were held in great awe. Could they not reveal to you your own face? Could they not expose the ghosts which were sometimes to be seen floating like dead fish in the not-real worlds behind them? More than this, could they not disorient ghosts, by confusing them about where the actual world ended and not-real worlds began, and thus offer to the living protection from supernatural malevolent intent? Above all, did they not reflect time in strange ways? Sometimes, it was true, they reflected only the present, but at other times did they not reveal the past, and at other times, by the grace of the spirits, the future?

Though the pawang had been grateful for the food Nony had brought her this morning, she'd been far more gratified to notice that First Daughter was once again quite unafraid, either of her or of the magic things in her ruang. Now the little girl was dabbling her fingers in the divination oil, where it brimmed sheeny-shiny in its big shallow pan. The pawang smiled at the child before she shooed her away. First Daughter toddled off to play with a pile of animal bones in the corner. The pawang and Nony then again squatted down, one to each side of the pan, on the bare earth of the floor. The pawang waited until the oil had settled back into sleek black blankness and then she commanded, "Be still! Be silent! You must be as still and as silent as a hunter about to let fly an arrow in the forest, else the spirits will be scared off as easily as the prey."

Nony hardly needed the warning; she was so afraid, and so excited, she scarcely dared breathe.

Both women stared into the looking glass of oil. The pawang took a few breaths, to compose herself, and then, in seeming disregard of her own demand for stillness and silence, she began rocking back and forth. Once a rhythm was established, she began to chant. Nony tried to make sense of the words. She couldn't do it. The pawang's chant didn't seem to be in Malay at all, she thought, but instead it must be in some other language, one reserved for magic.

Some time passed.

As Nony stared into the oil, she saw only what she'd expect to see: her own not-real face gazing back at her; shifting segments of the pawang's not-real face, parts of the not-real ruang. Ordinary reflections of everyday things. Which was all very well, but she hoped the pawang saw more than this.

Of course the pawang, this woman who saw everything, saw more than this. And this was because as she gazed into the brimming circle of flat unruffled black she wasn't looking through the eyes she'd use to look out on the world beyond her own self. No, as she watched shadows playing across the iridescent glaze of the oil like shadows cast by puppets playing across the puppet-master's screen, on the nights when, through his own variety of magic, he made the puppets come to life, to tell their ancient tales, she looked to the future inward, through shadow-adapted eyes adjusted to seeing things sunk deep below the level of conscious awareness

And it was through the eye of .hope, perhaps, that the pawang saw the first shadows the spirits deigned to show her. These spirits who co-mingled the ghosts of the dead and those of the as-yet unborn and all the immaterial animating principles of nature: of trees, rocks, caves, snakes, tigers, bats, clouds, rain, wind.

Naturally, it was just as the pawang had warned: the spirits were capricious, they communed in riddles. She'd asked them, in the arcane language they'd taught the very first pawang, to reveal glimpses of Nony's future, but they'd chosen not to do so – or not in any obvious way. They, of course, existed not just for all time, but also quite outside time, and at first they seemed not to have revealed a glimpse of the future as such at all – not the future as understood by humans – but instead of something else. Their own timeless realm, perhaps? In any case, the pawang saw shadows not of Nony, but of First Daughter; she saw her now as a little fish darting blue through the black, now as a fracturing shoal of fish darting gold and orange between the actual world she inhabited and all the worlds she didn't; between past, present and future; between here, there and nowhere; between the realm of the spirits and the human realm; between the dead, the living and the unborn, between the blessed and the damned.

But then the glossy black surface of the oil shivered and resolved into a new set of shadows. And now, perhaps, the pawang looked through the right eye of memory, and the left eye of experience. Or perhaps she looked through some third eye of surmising.

Whichever the eye through which the pawang now looked, the spirits remained capricious, so as she gazed into the oil, she saw, so unexpectedly according to human understanding, not shadows of the past cast onto Nony's future, but those shadows cast onto an entirely different woman's future: the mem's.

Granted, there hadn't been a mem at the DO's bungalow for well over a decade now, but what were decades to the pawang? She had lived for centuries. And, back in the day, she'd seen mems come, mems go. They'd always interested her, these exotic Mat Salleh women who were at once so rich and haughty and yet so pitiable. Yes, it had always seemed to her the mems led lonely lives of quiet desperation, aimless and isolated lives hemmed in by the jungle, by boredom, by the rains when they came. Some of their husbands had been drunkards. Some of their husbands had been bullies. Some of them had children to bring them joy, but only temporarily – Mat Salleh children were banished to Kampung Inggris when they were about 7. Either that or the spirits stole them, because their parents scorned the magic needed to stave off the theft.

In other words, with some part of her mind the pawang knew there must be a fair chance any mem consigned to Kluanak must ever and always be tempted to run screaming right out of her own life and into another one.

Not that the pawang knew she knew this. To her conscious mind, no mem would ever be stupid enough, or audacious enough, to succumb to the temptation to flee. After all, no wife either she or any other villager had ever known, would have been mad enough to leave a cushy life with a husband who could feed her and keep a roof over her head, for any reason whatsoever, let alone jealousy of another woman – and one in her husband's past to boot. No, no wife worth her salt would ever be caught dead allowing herself to be driven away by a rival, to let another woman triumph like that.

At last the pawang fell still and she stopped chanting. She was panting, a little, but slowly her breathing steadied, and she came back to herself from wherever she'd been, which certainly wasn't in her ruang. She became aware of Nony looking at her hopefully. After another moment or two she shifted her position and she began to circle her chicken claw hands over the pan of oil: three times to the right and then three times to the left she circled them. And then, in her prophecy voice, she began to speak of all she'd seen in her magic mirror.

Well, nearly all of it. She saw no reason to divulge the oil had flickered with lustrous shadows of First Daughter, splintered into a shoal of fish darting fire-bright between worlds. Those, she thought, had been shadows conjured just for her. And obviously here was confirmation the spirits had claimed First Daughter as their own. Already she was beginning to wonder why the spirits had chosen to reveal, unequivocally, that First Daughter was theirs now, today, when she'd asked them to illuminate Nony in their prophetic beam. Their revelation must have something or other to do with Nony's future, she assumed, but what? For the moment she could do no better than remind herself the mother's fate and the daughter's were ever entangled. Later, much later, she'd understand.

In the meantime, "This is what the spirits showed me: I saw the tuan and the mem on the landing stage below the DO's bungalow. It was early in the morning. Though it was still dark, the horizon tempted with a promise of light, and beneath the fading stars the river flowed ghostly under a drifting veil of just-visible mist. The mem carried one of those Mat Salleh suitcase things, just big enough to be packed with clothes she'd need for a short journey, and beside her stood a large trunk. There was a perahu moored at the landing stage. The crew stowed the suitcase and the trunk, both. The tuan stretched out his hand and the mem took it; they did that Mat Salleh thing of shaking hands – shake, shake, shake – and they exchanged a few words. Then the head boatman helped the mem aboard. He pushed off and caught the current. The perahu was carried downstream. The mem did not look back. The tuan watched from the landing stage till he lost sight of the perahu and then he returned to his bungalow, slump-shouldered."

Well! What a let-down! Despite the pawang's warning that

something like this may happen, Nony couldn't help feeling both bemused and bitterly disappointed. The mem would someday set off somewhere in a perahu? Here was a humdrum prophesy! And its workaday nature wasn't her only beef.

"What about me?" she asked, sounding whiney even in her own ears. "I thought you were consulting the spirits about me?"

The pawang was sharp.

"Child! I told you, the spirits reveal what they reveal."

Shamed, Nony hung her head.

The pawang sighed, and then she said, "Perhaps the spirits have chosen to tell your future slantwise."

"What d'you mean?"

"Think, child! Think of vines intertwined around a tree trunk."

Nony conjured the image.

"What? My future and the mem's are all in a knotty mass?"

Blink. Blink.

"But how? And how to untangle them?"

"These are for you to discover."

Nony did her best to resist thinking that from a seer, this was a tad unsatisfactory. She began to fish for clues.

"When will she leave?"

The spirits, existing as they did quite outside time, were notorious for having a distinctly casual attitude towards human dates and calendars.

"You know I can't answer that, child!"

Nony tried not to sound too forlorn.

"Where will she go? BB?"

The pawang sucked her gums a moment. True, it was strange this idea the shadows skimming across her oil had put to her, but she had no choice but to entertain it since it was spirit-sent. Or, rather, she had no choice but to accept it, since it was spirit-ordained. She said, confidently,

"Further. Much further. Kampung Inggris, I think."

Nony tried to imagine this distant place, but all she saw was an expanse of jungle transferred to goodness knows where.

"How long will she go for?"

"For good, I think."

Nony did a double take.

"Leave for good?"

Blink. Blink.

"But Baba waved her off."

Blink. Blink.

"So according to the spirits, Baba will stay here."

Blink. Blink.

"How can he, if she's gone? I don't understand."

The pawang let a long beat elapse and then she said, "I think the spirits are saying the mem will forsake the tuan."

Nony laughed. Women didn't forsake men; men forsook women. That was just the way of things – wasn't it? Her laughter died. It occurred to her the pawang had spoken in earnest.

"But why would she do that?"

The pawang shrugged.

"The mems can afford to be proud. These women who never go hungry, who are all as rich as queens, who know whatever they do they'll never have nothing to eat but bitterness."

Nony was incredulous.

"Pride? You think she'll leave Baba from injured pride?"

Blink. Blink.

"Injured by me, you mean?"

Blink. Blink.

"Really? You think the mem will let herself be chased away from Kluanak by me? Because she's found out about me? My past with Baba?"

Blink. Blink.

"Well more fool her. So much for worse for her."

Now it was the pawang's turn to laugh.

"The spirits are telling you you'll win," she cackled.

Wouldn't that be something, yearned Nony. Could it really be true she and the mem were destined to be intertwined as victor and vanquished? Could it really be true the mem had been so humiliated to learn about her and the children that from foolish pride she was now destined to upend her own life, with all its boons, with all its comfort, and run away? But what was she thinking? If the pawang said it was true, then it must be true. And so come the day the mem upped and left that would mean she'd not only had, but what's more, she'd exercised, the power to change the mem's life, and meanwhile the mem had never had any such power over her – not the actual mem, the flesh and blood woman now resident in the DO's bungalow, only the idea of a woman something like her, back before Baba had left for Kampung Inggris. Well! Here was winning, for sure! Furthermore, this coming victory over the mem would be a victory over Baba too. Yes, gloated Nony, by depriving Baba of his wife, she'd someday soon exercise the power to change his life as surely as she'd change the mem's. What a prophecy! Oh, it was grand! For a moment she felt happier than she had since Baba had dismissed her from his bathhouse.

But half a minute! Nony's happiness began to fade almost as quickly as it had arisen. Alas, this coming victory over Baba would be a pretty poor one. Huh! Even after she'd chased away the mem, she'd still have to live cheek-by-jowl with Baba, with this powerful man who hated her and who'd surely want to punish her for depriving him of his wife. Winning? Even after the mem had left, Baba would remain to her exactly what he was now: the sultan who treated his little people as he liked, and who may very well decide at any moment to haul her off to the courthouse, to charge her with blackmail, or if not with that, then with something or another else.

Disappointed, Nony wheeled back to her original peeve.

"Fine. But what happens next? What happens after the mem has gone and Baba has returned to the bungalow? What does the mem's departure mean for me?"

The pawang's wrinkled forehead wrinkled deeper in a frown, and she said, "I told you, this is something you must discover for yourself."

Again, Nony tried to resist thinking this really wasn't good enough. And in any case, before she had time to grow properly resentful she remembered something: Intan's dream. Yes, it occurred to her that Intan would think she knew the conclusion to the story the pawang had begun to tell. She heard her sister's voice loud in her head: *I've said it before, if only the mem could be got out of the way, you could slide back into your old life like a kris sliding into its sheath* And now it seemed the mem would indeed be got out of the way. So could the spirits be saying that after the perahu had taken the mem downriver, and Baba had returned lonely to the bungalow, then he'd want her back, to look after his creature comforts as she'd done before? If he didn't immediately summon her, she could present herself to him on the verandah. She'd do so humbly, without gloating, and it would no doubt be as Intan had wanted: Baba would nod and tell her, you can come back.

For a moment Nony felt she was almost brushing against the furniture up at the DO's bungalow. Hopefully she asked, "Perhaps when the mem leaves I can replace her in Baba's bed. Perhaps I'll be able to reclaim my old life and become once again his nonya."

The pawang didn't do her blinking thing. Instead she pursed her dried-leaf lips and she stared off into the middle distance.

Nony's lovely fantasy began to crumble; she should have known better, she berated herself. She pictured those two unmarried girls in the kampung, the ones who were as pretty as flowers and as juicy as ripe fruit.

"I suppose not. After all: Adik or Mahsuri."

Blink. Blink.

Nony flinched. So, it was not to be. Nothing was to be – nothing good for her. Mem or no mem, she was to remain a probable target of Baba's bullying. Her future was bleak; she was henceforth to be reduced to scurrying about the kampung like a hen trying to avoid the man determined to wring its neck. For a treasonable moment she regretted the rice and the dragon fruit she'd given the pawang, she really did.

12

THE JUNGLE PATH AND THE DO'S BUNGALOW
APRIL 1925

It was late afternoon, after the lie-off, and Rose's flesh was running rivulets as she slogged along the path to the kampung. It was so hot and humid even the insects sloshed through the wringing air. Worse even than the heat, the jungle itself seemed to be sneering at her. But she was determined not to turn back; she would march on in a spirit of defiance against the trees and the tyrant sun, as well as against everything else. She wanted to prove a point: to herself, to Frank, to the servants, to the villagers, to la midinette, to her son.

Her son! Yes, Rose was quite sure she'd got growing within her a little gentleman, and not a young lady; she didn't know why, feminine intuition, she supposed. But in any case the young wonder mustn't have a coward for a mother. Certainly not! For his sake, Rose would walk where she wanted to walk and no matter with whom she may collide.

Meanwhile, First Son was out with his slingshot, after lizards for the pot. He careened around a bend on the riverside path and got a horrible shock. He jibbed to a halt and stared: the monstrous mem!

Rose too jibbed to a halt, and the air quite went out of her defiance: here was Frank's oldest boy, the one she'd tried to speak to that day in the coconut grove. How mistaken she'd been to think there could be communion between them. She blushed now to remember their encounter. Her kind intentions! And all along the brat must have been laughing at her behind his hand. It was enraging. It was mortifying.

First Son panicked. What was he to do? Shout once more *pukimak kau*? But his teeth seemed to have become bamboo bars, preventing any words escaping his mouth. He had a pouch around his waist, it contained the clay balls he baked himself as ammunition for his slingshot; willy-nilly, he found himself reaching into it. He grabbed a fistful of the clay balls and, with all his might, he slung these imprecations made visible towards the mem. As soon as they'd left his hand he turned tail and fled back to the kampung, as fast as his legs would carry him.

The clay balls fell well short of Rose; she realised even if they'd hit her, they wouldn't have done her much harm. Still, she was outraged: what a heathen! That through good luck the brat's delinquent behaviour would have no ill-consequences was no excuse for it. Not that it was anything other than she'd have expected from a child of la midinette's; the woman clearly had no idea of morals, so how could she teach her children how to behave? She herself would never allow her son to throw things at ladies ... Her fingers fluttered to her belly ... Her own shining son ... Her shinning white wonder ... And, oh, it was not to be endured!

Indeed, it was not. Alas, Rose quite failed to consider that never mind Frank's life, his children by another woman could so easily enrich her own life and likewise her child's life. They could so easily bring all three of them delight. Instead she thought it was too bad that knowledge of the existence of Frank's by-blows would always now be part of her future. And, as she continued to gaze at First Son's disappearing back, it occurred to her it was even worse to think her child should ever have knowledge of them as part of his future. Brown brothers? A brown sister? How they would disgrace her son. How learning of them could so easily shift his sense of who he was; it could almost be as if he had a touch of the tar brush himself. Then again, how would he feel to learn his father was a man so weak, so degenerate, he'd succumbed to the pleasures of a Malay midinette before he'd married? How would he feel to discover he wasn't his father's firstborn? The shock he'd feel, and the sense of being displaced.

No, thought Rose, no, her son must not, and would not, be shaded by Frank's past offence against propriety, modesty and dignity; her child must not, and would not, be sullied by shaming connections. And it was her job to see to it that no such shading or sullying, no such reducing or traducing, ever took place. Children had to be protected from falling into fires, and from falling out of trees, of course they did, and they also had to be protected from all knowledge of their parents' folly. Children should respect their parents. *Honour thy father and thy mother: that thy days may be long upon the land which the Lord thy God giveth thee.* And if thy father had in fact behaved dishonourably? Well then, thy mother had better jolly well buck up and save the appearances, that's all.

After evening tiffin, Rose and Frank were yet again sitting next to each other, but not together, in uncompanionable silence on the verandah. The single paraffin lamp set on the table between them spilled a weak yellow chiaroscuro which was nearly all shadow. The past hour had seen another downpour of pummelling rain and, though the deluge was by now slackening, the swollen river roared unseen through the darkness and everything was watery: water drizzled from the sky, it dripped warm from every branch and vine and twig and leaf in the tangle of the jungle, it plopped from the bungalow's eaves, it oozed sweaty from the air.

Frank was trying to get his pipe going; the stem was clamped tight between his teeth but his matches were damp, so he was having problems. But finally the tobacco caught, and it began to smoulder in the pipe's bowl. He inhaled, deeply and then he exhaled a long smoky breath of satisfaction.

The smell of pipe tobacco again made Rose feel queasy, and tonight she had no intention of hiding it. She reminded herself, as she often did, she was deciding for two now, acting for two, and the time had come, she knew, that she must speak to Frank. She flapped her hand at the wisp of smoke hanging blue-grey in the spongy air between herself and her husband.

"It's making me feel sick. It stinks. Put it out!"

Frank was surprised.

"But you always say it: you like the smell of tobacco."

"I don't tonight."

Frank was not best pleased, but since he was still firmly in the doghouse he removed his pipe from his mouth. He was reaching for his ashtray from the table when something occurred to him and the force of it froze his hand in mid-air: I say! A sudden aversion to a smell an egg had previously liked? It was a well-known gestatory symptom. Certainly, Nony had become sensitive to smell each time she'd been in the pudding club. And, after all, he and Rose had been married almost six months before she'd banished bread and butter from their table. He cast over his wife an appraising eye: had she perhaps thickened everywhere since last he'd really looked at her? By George, he rather thought she had! Broadened. Coarsened. Her face was perhaps more moon-like than before, her waist less defined – and was it him or was her dress straining across the bodice? Well, well, well, was the little woman soon to become decidedly less little? His hand unfroze and continued its trajectory to the ashtray; slowly, thoughtfully, he began to knock out his pipe.

Rose watched glowing strands of tobacco crumble from the bowl of Frank's pipe and then cool to gritty white in the brass ashtray; she was grateful for these last few moments of absolute intimacy with her baby. We two and only we two. Now she was about to reveal her secret, she found she cherished it more than ever. Her precious secret. Her tarnished secret … No, that was wrong: her secret wasn't tarnished; breaking it would be. Oh, it made her as sad as anything to remember how happy and excited she'd been, so very recently, at the idea of making her shy announcement. She was washed by regret to think this revelation she'd always assumed she'd make from love, she would in fact make from calculation, as part of a strategy to manoeuvre Frank into doing what she wanted: she no longer even trusted him not to take the news shoddily; she'd thought he'd be so pleased, delighted, to be told she was to give him a child; she'd thought he'd be so concerned for her, his wife. Heavens, her vanity! How she'd boasted to Beatrice – well, to herself, really, she supposed – how she'd boasted her husband would be so worried to think of her That Way in the jungle. Well, so much for that. More likely he'd dismiss: you'll be all right, you've got the constitution of an ox. After all, making a new life was old hat for him; he'd seen it all before.

Frank had by now finished knocking out his pipe. He fiddled with it a moment, turning it stem-to-bowl, bowl-to-stem in his hands, waiting for Rose to say something. But she failed to oblige, and so, at last, he gathered himself, and he fished, or hinted, or both, "This sudden aversion to the smell of tobacco ..."

Rose looked over the verandah's rail out into the damp blackness where lurked her gaolers, the trees. At last she said, "You're not the only one with secrets."

Frank thought no end of mush was talked about children, even English ones, but it now occurred to him mush perhaps sometimes had its place. Certainly, he found himself ruffled with hope.

"R-o-s-e?"

Rose nodded.

"You're going to become a father," she confirmed, and then she added bitterly, "for the fifth time."

Frank winced.

"That's just where you're wrong."

Rose simply looked at him.

"You know what I mean. This one's my first proper one."

Rose did not challenge: a proper child? She said nothing at all.

Frank, the father of three boys, and two of them identical twins, such splendid proof of his virility, even if they were brown, regarded First Daughter as an aberration. Like Rose herself, he assumed she must be carrying a boy. What a bull! What a stallion! Mind you, his pride was not unmixed with love: love for his wife, love for the baby. His legitimate child. His son and heir. Grateful, he leaned forward and he successfully grabbed for his wife's hand.

"You'll make the most topping little mother."

Rose had all the usual doubts on that score. Again, she said nothing at all.

Frank frowned. Even in the face of her continuing crossness about his life as a bachelor far too gay, the little woman's sulky silence seemed to him quite at odds with her news. The first time Nony had told him the spirits had granted her an embryo, she'd been all pride and smiles – the pride and smiles of a woman convinced she'd now secured her future, he'd thought. But Rose, whom he'd have expected to be proud and smiling simply from the joy of conjuring a life from the void, seemed neither. Granted, they'd had a grim time of it lately, but, no, Rose did not now conform to his vague idea of how a lawfully wedded Englishwoman should look when she announced to her husband she was in the pudding club: there was no softness about her, no sweet vanity or shyness. Still, she'd not removed her hand from his; that was something, he supposed. He clasped his fingers tighter; even now she did not pull her hand away. Frank felt himself flare with optimism. And, dash it, if he and Rose didn't reconcile now, at this moment so drenched with hope, then when would they ever reconcile?

"Rose?" he begged. "Rose, please, a kiss?"

Rose too knew babies were offerings to the future. She again stared out at the imprisoning trees. Was it time for her to make her peace with Frank? Was it about time she ceased dwelling on things? Was it more than time to put grudges aside? Naturally, she'd have preferred to reveal to her husband simply that he was to become a father, and not that he was to become a father again, but perhaps it was churlish to think that word "again" was so important? La midinette and her brats. Frank's delay in revealing the truth. His pragmatic reasons to marry. All that. Had she perhaps overreacted? Perhaps it was foolish to have berated Frank for lying to her, both directly and by omission, about his past? Perhaps it was silly to worry his lies meant they could never really know each other? For that matter: what if they couldn't? After all, it was a truism: nobody ever really knew anybody else; not really, really. There were glass walls between people and that was that. There were glass walls even between sincerely besotted lovers tangled in each other's arms. And lying? The world couldn't turn without lies. Perhaps, indeed, there could be no love without lies; no marriage without lies?

Come *on*! Of course there couldn't, only the drifty-est girl could think otherwise – or so Rose now thought. But she didn't want to be drifty. She wanted to be a realistic sort of person. And the reality was: men and women who shared a bed lied to each other. The reality was: she was Frank's wife, he was her husband; like victims of a shipwreck, they must cling together or drown.

They both stood up. Frank let go of Rose's hand and he

opened his arms. She did not step into his embrace, but nor did she move away from him. Instead, she stood stock still and then, in a kind of compromise between his evident desire for her and her own determined desire to try to feel desire for him, she leaned forward and she tilted her face up. Frank didn't hesitate; he stepped forward and wrapped his arms around his wife. He couldn't pretend to himself she swooned against his manly chest, nonetheless, he closed his eyes and he sought her lips with his. Alas, Rose, wide-eyed, flinched; she felt sick and she knew the feeling had nothing to do with her pregnancy. At the last moment, she turned her head so instead of kissing her fully on the mouth, Frank kissed her cheek. Nonetheless, he began to slide his hands everywhere.

Rose blushed. She was embarrassed for Frank: for his desperation, the ease with which he must have convinced himself she'd be receptive. And she felt embarrassed for herself, too, for her fraudulence, for so nearly talking herself into kissing him, when the truth was ... the truth was ... Well, whatever the truth was, this was another of those things she'd think about later. She broke from Frank's embrace, and, forcefully, she pushed him away.

Frank flushed with mingled disappointment, frustration, humiliation and anger. He wouldn't have it! How could Rose do this to him? He wasn't some rotten cad, an adulterer, how often did he have to tell her that? He'd told her and told her: he'd only done what everybody else was doing; he'd finished things before he'd met her. Oh, he knew he should have confessed much sooner than he had, but he'd made a clean breast of things now, and wasn't that the point? Everything was above board now. Why couldn't Rose see? Why wouldn't she relent? How were they supposed to live like this? To share each other's lives? And carrying his son and heir to boot!

"I say!" he summarised. "I say!"

Rose shrugged and she sat down again.

"Let's talk about Baby," she said.

With effort, Frank mastered himself. He too returned to his chair and sat down. As he did so he reminded himself he must be patient; now more than ever he must be considerate. He must endure Rose's iciness however long it took until it thawed; for his son's sake, he must.

"All right," he nodded. "When can we expect him?"

"In about five months, by my estimate. Around about September."

Frank puffed out his chest.

"I call it ripping news!"

Rose glared at him.

"The problem is your kampung brats."

Frank was thrown.

"Them? What have they got to do with it?"

"Plenty."

"I've told you before they mean barely anything to me."

Rose made a dismissive gesture.

"That's as may be, but I went for a walk this afternoon. I encountered your eldest. He threw a handful of pebbles or pellets or something at me."

Frank said, not meaning it, "I shall talk to his mother."

Rose shrugged. "It doesn't bother me how he behaves. But it was the last straw. I don't wish that our son should ever be made ridiculous by him. By them, by your brown bastards. I don't wish our child should ever even know of them. They must be ... erased ... written out of your story."

"Absolutely!"

"And so also must their mother."

"I couldn't agree more."

"But we are living here." Rose swept her arm to indicate the world around her. "We are living here, in Kluanak, and she is living here, and her brats are living here."

Frank spoke confidently. "Oh, you don't need to worry about that, we'll be gone by the time Baby turns three. Four, at the outside."

"Too young to stumble on the truth?"

"Much too young."

"He'll learn Malay from the servants just like you did. He could hear things."

"Don't wind yourself up, old girl, nobody would dare breathe a word and I say again: we'll be long gone before he could even begin to understand a thing of what it'd be better he didn't."

"No. A child's never too young to notice things – to divine things. Never too young to be scarred by shame, to feel the sting of disgrace."

They both understood she meant an English child – or at a push a white one less lucky in its nationality. Frank was momentarily shamed to think both that his son, his legitimate son, may one day think of him as a disgrace, and also that he may be a cause of disgrace for his son. But then he rallied. Hang on! What if his son did one day learn all about Nony and the brats, would he really care? For himself, he thought it unlikely the young wonder would give a fig what pater had got up to before he was born, or with whom, or that there were brown half-siblings. Children were too self-centred to worry about anybody, or anything, but themselves.

"I insist if we're still here when Baby's old enough to look about the world, he'll be too entranced by monkeys and tiger cubs and snakes to bother about anything else. Animals. That's what grabs a young lad's attention. And don't worry: there'll be no fourth posting here, I can promise you that. Three times was unheard of."

"And yet it happened. You could be posted here a fourth time. You could, Frank, that could happen too."

"But it won't. Stop torturing yourself!"

Rose scowled at her husband. There was silence for a long beat until, at last, she said, "You told me you offered la midinette money to move to another kampung."

"If only she'd gone."

"Yes. But she hasn't. Yet. But now she must. She simply must. The risks of contact between our child and her, or between our child and her brats, are simply too great if she stays."

Frank sighed, and he rubbed his face between his hands a moment.

"All right. I'll try again to persuade her."

"Not good enough. You must see to it that she goes. This time, you mustn't take no for an answer."

"When I tried to get rid of her before, she made it pretty clear she didn't want to go."

Rose stared resentfully into the jungle. Frank had never told her how much he'd paid la midinette and she'd never lowered herself to ask. Gosh, the unpleasantness of it all! Still, needs must.

"How much did she extort from you?"

Frank hesitated before he lied, "Three hundred dollars."

Rose, cautious about money, kept a close eye on the household accounts. She transferred her gaze from the jungle to her husband.

"How did you come by a spare three hundred dollars?"

Frank blushed.

Rose thought she understood his embarrassment: it was at being unmasked as a spendthrift, of course.

"What a terrible waste. Still, write to the bank in BB for the same again. Offer it to her. It should surely be enough to make her change her mind."

"They can be very stubborn, the Malays."

"So?"

"So ..." Frank gestured, to indicate helplessness.

Rose crossed her arms and sat up straighter.

"Well, if she won't go, we must."

"Us? Go? Go where? What d'you mean?"

"I mean it's intolerable to think of Baby starting his life barely a mile from your by-blows. I mean if your strumpet refuses to move, you'll have to ask Mr Hollingworth for a transfer."

"Dearest, this is foolishness. White people don't put themselves out for Malays."

"I don't care about that."

"On what grounds could I ask?"

"Tell him the truth!"

Frank shook his head.

"You must've realised it's against the rules, concubinage."

"So tell him you broke the rules!"

"Think! He's such a terrific stickler. If he learned the truth, he may very well dismiss me."

"The lesser of two evils."

"But I'm an SCS man through and through."

"You can change."

Frank wasn't so sure. If he weren't an SCS man, then he couldn't think who, or what, he'd be. He snapped his fingers.

"Just like that," he said. "If Hollingworth gave me the sack, then where would we be? How would we live? How could I keep you or Baby? I can't just throw over my position. I can't be rattling round the Empire with a wife and a child in tow, with no job, no home and no prospects of either. No, I'm sorry, old girl, I can't tell the chief, it's the one thing I won't do."

"Won't you?" Rose stood up and she walked towards her bedroom door. "She goes or we go," she said flatly, over her shoulder. "You'll just have to engineer one or the other, that's all."

13

Nony was imagining the new sarong she'd soon weave for herself. She was standing at a wooden board in her ruang, extracting fibres from pre-softened banana leaves. These fibres, spun into thread and dyed, would form the cloth from which she'd make that sarong. As she scraped at long strips of leaf to get at the finest, silkiest innermost fibres, she was idly wondering which colours to dye her threads and whether she'd weave a design of flowers or a geometric pattern. First Daughter was curled up on the mat asleep, and as for First Son and the twins, Nony had no idea where they were or what they were up to. Still, she knew they'd show up in the kampung when they got hungry.

She'd just pulled a soft bundle of fibres from the leaf she was working on when Baba materialised in her ruang, as if from thin air. Naturally, he made her jump; worse, he made her afraid. Would he pounce on her now like a tiger on a chicken? Still, Nony didn't cringe. Instead, she defiantly reminded herself she knew a thing or two about Baba's future. She knew his wife would be leaving him soon enough. The knowledge felt to her as soothing as a cool cloth on a hot day and she used it to wipe away her fears, so to speak. She even considered taunting him with what he had coming, but on second thoughts she decided she didn't want him forewarned. Let him feel the full force of the coming shock!

"What d'you want?" she challenged, and her tone made the question sound like a spray of obscenities.

Frank was in a filthy mood. He'd hit the bottle so hard after Rose had gone to bed last night that this was another morning in which he felt the world as something pulsing too insistent in his head, not to mention he could smell the alcohol sweating off him. And he'd rather be anywhere than in Nony's ruang. Though there was no danger now the dipper could blackmail him, he felt as demeaned as he ever had to be coming to negotiate with her: the DO should command the natives, not negotiate with them.

He wanted to get the necessary over and done with as quickly as possible so he came straight to the point.

"The game's over, isn't it."

Nony said nothing, just looked at him sullenly.

"You know I confessed. You know Rose knows all about you now, I know you do. So no more blackmail, Nony, all that's over. It's done. It's finished. But the thing is, I still want you gone. Nothing's changed there. And I suppose you still want money off me. Of course you do. So, then, let's come to an arrangement." Frank paused. He was loath to admit to Nony that Rose was in the pudding club, since this was news any egg, anywhere, must find inflammatory under the circumstances. But, in the way of things, it wasn't intelligence a fellow could keep under his hat for long, the only surprise was that Boy hadn't already asked how it would affect the household now the spirits had granted the mem an embryo. So, reluctantly, he took the plunge. "It'll be obvious to everybody soon enough: the mem is going to have a baby. I don't want her upset by unpleasant reminders of my life before her – you, the children. And you won't like seeing her with a little one, will you. You know really it's in your own interests to make a fresh start somewhere. So, then. Let's pretend you never tried to blackmail me. Let's return to where we were before you got it into your head to pull that stunt. Remember my offer to pay you to leave? Despite everything, I'm prepared to make my offer afresh. Same terms as before. So what d'you say? Another five hundred dollars to shift. How about it?"

Nony barely registered Baba's offer, or even that, once again, he'd come to her as a supplicant. What? A *bayi putih*? A white whelp? This was scarcely unexpected news; she'd always assumed it was too much to hope the spirits had afflicted the mem with barrenness. She'd long anticipated she'd one day be caught on the raw to learn the spirits had granted the mem an embryo, she'd long realised her own children would one day have their noses rubbed in their father's indifference by the advent of a shiny new white child on whom he'd no doubt dote. But now one day was now, and Nony felt Frank's news like a punch in her own belly – her belly which was as flat as an empty water skin, her belly which in all likelihood would never again be occupied. Such was her distress, for a moment she even doubted the pawang. Perhaps the old woman had got the wrong end of the stick, as old women will, when she'd seen the shadows playing across the screen of her oil. Perhaps the mem wasn't destined soon to leave Kluanak for Kampung Inggris for good, on account of injured pride, but, more likely, she was merely destined to gad to BB for a few weeks to spawn.

When Nony finally spoke, her speech was a snarl.

"Why the hell should I put myself out for you? For that matter, why the hell should I put myself out for any of the three of you? You. Your pelacur putih. Your bayi putih."

Frank felt his face flush and his eyes bulge with fury. He balled his fists and he took a threatening step towards Nony – but then he remembered thumping her would scarcely help him further his end. So he shoved his fists in his pockets and he took a deep breath.

"Your family? The adat? All that. I know. I do remember, I do. But I'd set you up like a queen in a new kampung. You could settle down. Meet a topping man to marry."

Nony narrowed her eyes. Most village men now saw her as spoiled goods. Even if she'd spent only ten weeks with Baba and escaped before she'd begun cooking a dumpling it was unlikely any village man anywhere on Saramantan would ever have taken her on, even as a junior wife. As to a mother trailing four mixed-blood bastards after living for a decade with their father? Pull the other one.

"You know that won't be so easy."

"You'd soon get used to things in a new kampung."

"I'm not going. I won't go. You and your pelacur putih will just have to get used to having me around."

"All right. Five hundred dollars sent along a few days after you've left, and another hundred once you've been away a month."

"It's too late for bargaining."

"Come on, Nony, do the right thing. It's a generous offer."

Nony folded her arms across her chest.

"This is not about money."

We'll see about that, thought Frank.

"Two hundred, a month later."

Nony hesitated. But if after all it was about money, then it wasn't only about money, and she was resolute.

"It's about where I want to live. My life. Not being pushed around to suit you, or that hag-sister to Raksasa Wanita you call your wife, or your hag-spawn. So that's that. As I said, you and yours will just have to get used to having me around."

"Now look here!"

"I'm not some counter in a game you're playing."

"That's rich! What were you doing when you blackmailed me, except trying to make me into a counter in your games?"

Nony shrugged.

"You have my decision: no."

"What about your duty to your family? That sister of yours. What would she say to learn you'd turned down my offer?"

"I have three sisters."

"You know the one I mean. The youngest, I believe. The one who was always running up to the bungalow, stealing things all over the place – don't think I didn't notice."

Intan's pilfering? Now who was being rich? To Nony, it was as clear as rice wine vinegar that the Mat Salleh were the most audacious thieves in all Malaya, stealing the very land and everything in it, even down to the air and water. But she had to acknowledge Baba had a point: it was indeed her duty to acquire for her family as much wealth as she could, in any way that she could, to ensure for her relations full rice bowls now and in the future. So could she be so selfish? Could she flounce away from providing for her family another $500 and more? And for what? For her own happiness, that's what. No, it just wasn't right. It wouldn't be right to put her own interests above everyone else's in her family for something so trivial. She must give herself over to something much greater than herself: the group.

But though giving yourself over to something greater than yourself could give life such depth and strength and meaning, it wasn't always easy; part of Nony didn't really want to do it at all. And, fortunately, there was more at stake here than just her own happiness – or so she now argued. What about Baba's unhappiness? If she rejected his offer she wouldn't just be doing what was best for herself, she'd also be doing what was worst for him and for his family, his second family, that other insulting little group. And also for that bigger insulting group: the Mat Salleh. So, no, Nony didn't pause to remind herself her future could so easily be a bleak one of being harried by a vindictive DO She didn't backpedal. She didn't say: give me a few days to think about it. Instead, she burned her boats.

"No," she said. "No, Baba, I'm not going. I'm really not."

OUTBOUND MAIL, APRIL 1925
SENT FROM THE DO's BUNGALOW,
KLUANAK, SARAMANTAN

From Rose to Beatrice

Dearest Bumbles,

I do understand your frustration that when you sat down to write to me your last, you couldn't even know whether I had yet received your previous letter containing news of what Mrs Dabney-Dent told you, nor what's doing here, nor how I got along, for this frustration at the slowness of the mail is one I fully share. Oh, it would be too marvellous for words if we could each pick up a telephone and talk to one another, just as if we were both in Kensington – it makes me feel so lonely that I have no one to talk to, other than Frank.

It was kind of you to write me a cheerful letter, full of things to distract me. Though it was clear when you wrote you still had not received mine to you giving news I suspected I was That Way, let alone the one announcing my suspicions had condensed to certainty, you really must know by now, I think, and you can be sure I read your letter with great and particular avidity.

Nurse Simpkins sounds quite a treasure and your account of readying the nursery left me desperately jealous. Your lucky baby! As for my baby, its nursery will be rudimentary indeed, with no pretty yellow paper on the walls, with or without a pattern of ducklings. And a perambulator? If I buy one at all, which I think unlikely, then I shall have to make my choice from what's available in BB, when it comes time for me to travel there to the nursing home, for my confinement.

Mind you, my jealousy of wallpapers and perambulators is as nothing compared to my jealousy of your happiness with Edmund. By rights Frank and I should be so happy now – I have at last told him I am That Way, and what a thing for newlyweds to welcome their firstborn. But we are not very happy at all, as I am sure you can imagine.

My dear, will you resent me – I hope you will not – if from wretchedness and from the bonds of love and friendship between us, I now burden you by confessing something perhaps I shouldn't. Something I should perhaps keep as secret as the grave. It is certainly something you must not share, not even with Edmund – please do not show even him this letter, I beg you.

When I told Frank I would soon be presenting him with a son, God willing, he tried to kiss me, and such was the portentousness of the moment that for the first time since I learned the details of his life before he met me, I didn't immediately rebuff him. But when I felt his mouth approaching mine, it's no exaggeration to say I was revolted. I couldn't help myself: I twisted so Frank slobbered on my cheek and then I pushed him away. He was hurt, I could see that, but I couldn't care. And, oh God, that disgusting near-kiss has awakened in me the fear I'll never again be able to bring myself to touch my husband in any significant way. Which leads me to ask a most dreadful question: if I cannot bring myself to touch Frank, then though I am his wife, how am I to continue to live as his wife? What if I can never again with joy permit my husband to do what husbands do? What if I can never again submit to him as I have done in the past?

Since I'm haunted now by this idea I'll never again be able to feel for Frank as I ought, I find myself thinking more than ever of escape, and even more hopelessly than before. I know there is no chance at all he will ever now agree to my going – not now he knows I am soon to present him with a son and heir. What man would tolerate a desertion that was at the same time a theft? And even if by ill chance I only got a daughter she'd be his, and thinking of that would be enough, I fear, for him to want to keep me close.

Until death us do part. Like so many before me, I suppose, and so many yet to come, I now understand those words quite differently from the way I did when I spoke them in front of the parson. Then: the terror of that inevitable eternal separation so dreadful to lovers. Now: the terror of an eternity spent waiting for that separation – his death or mine, either would do.

Oh, I know there are other ways than death to end a marriage. In any case for some people. I know that in these modern, enlightened times the law can sometimes intervene to slice the knot the parson tied. But I'm far from sure the law would allow me to ask Frank for a divorce. Do you know anything about it? I don't suppose you do. I don't hold out many hopes you are any clearer on matters legal than am I. Hitherto, I think divorce must have seemed to both of us a subject just as distant as the composition of the sun. But will you contradict me if I say that even in Belgravia the only grounds for divorce are violence and adultery? And Frank has neither hit me, nor, strictly, betrayed our marriage vows – not in a way any judge would understand.

I suppose you'll tell me that these things can be managed,

and I grant the point. I know dukes and actors may pretend – that pretence may be the common thing amongst those kinds of people. Aristocrats, and members of the faster set, people like that. But for people like us? I've never even met a divorcee, and I don't suppose you have, either, have you, my dear?

Then again, even had Frank and I lived somewhere civilized, some place where the concoction of a bogus case were possible, I don't think he'd ever have agreed to it. No, I can't imagine him sitting up all night in a hotel with a lady provided by an agency, solely to furnish a lawyer with suitable "evidence" of "adultery". And for once I don't mean this is something I can imagine all too well, but instead that I am certain Frank would refuse to endure such indignity, and no matter that all abroad would see through the tawdry little piece of theatre. He simply couldn't summon the requisite devil-may-care casualness to put his reputation on the line like that.

So, I must grin and bear it, as they say. Mustn't wallow – but, oh, when I remember I once thought it would be impossible for me ever to feel cross with Frank for long …

I trust you have kept your promise to keep all this from Mummy – I know you have. I'm about to write to her she is soon to become a grandmother, so next time you see her I hereby grant you permission to make my little stranger the first topic of conversation.

Your cousin Rosebud

From Rose to Daphne

Dearest Mummy,

Did it distress you I failed to write last month? I do apologise, but when the March mail arrived I was feeling peaky. And I'm sorry too, to learn from your latest that Aunt Louise becomes insufferable on the subject of grandchildren. But perhaps now you will be able to forgive us both, on account of becoming just a little insufferable yourself? Yes, I write today with news to delight you: you too will soon have a child you can teach to call you "Granny" – or in any case you can do so come the day I first bring the young wonder for a visit Home.

I do know distance will deprive you of your grandchild and I'm sorry for it, for your sake, and for Baby's, but other than saying I regret it, I see no benefit in dwelling on the separation, and I hope and trust that on this we are of one mind.

I expect my little stranger sometime around about September. Frank thinks it's ripping news. He is as pleased and as proud as Punch and he says I will make a topping little mother.

I remain mostly well, although I'm now often much tired, and I don't relish at all becoming the size of a house, in this heat – oh, what a heat! It's like toothache, I sometimes feel. And I find now the violent rains of this climate oppress me with their endless battering on the roof, and everything always mildewed – clothes, shoes, bedding.

Still, mustn't grumble. I will go to BB for my confinement. Frank assures me the medical gentlemen there are as good as any you'd find on Harley Street. Our spare bedroom will become the nursery, although it's barely bigger than a cupboard. I will find a native girl to act as nurse and we must hope she is not so clumsy and careless I may as well not have bothered.

I anticipate getting a little gentleman. If my hopes are fulfilled, I intend to name him George, for father – if by ill-luck a girl, Grace, with Daphne as her second name, for you.

I do hope this letter finds you in continuing good health.

Your loving daughter, Rose.

From Frank "Langers" Langham, to Charles "Slinger" Slightman

What-ho Slinger,

So Dandy did indeed write to you and Violet wrote to Maude and so it goes around. It seems to me we live in a goldfish bowl so enormous a man is on view to mischief-making women everywhere, whatever the distance between him and the meddlesome female all and sundry, especially if her name is Violet. As to our far-from-shrinking flower demanding of Maude to know how things now stand here, perhaps you should tell your little woman to make up a host of details so lurid they would force even the nosiest of nosy parkers to put a sock in it.

More happily, I'm glad Maude approves I've confessed to Rose at long last, and under whatever provocation. It's a boost to learn she thinks now it's all out in the open any sensible egg must soon be reconciled to the truth and cease creating. I'm sure she's right and you can in any case tell her this: though I cannot claim to be back in the little woman's good graces quite yet, I think I soon must be, for she's confided most ripping news: she's in the pudding club.

I'm as proud as anything and it's common knowledge: as an

egg grows fatter, she grows more content. No little woman could remain cross with her husband whilst growing within her his son and heir. It all makes me doubly sure Maude must be right, Rose won't have the vim to keep up her current impersonation of the Snow Queen – especially in the tropics.

One fly in my ointment: on account of the S & H, Rose now insists she cannot live so close to Nony and the brats. She fears the boy will inevitably discover my quondam connections and that she insists is something she cannot allow. I've tried my best to convince her we'll be gone long before any such danger could arise, but she's hysterical on the point and refuses to listen to reason – I tell you I'd worry the little woman were going off her onion, if she didn't have the excuse of being in the pudding club. Nony must go or we must go, she said. Women and their ultimata! I'm getting thoroughly fed up with the old do this or else palaver.

Naturally, I've tried once again offering Nony money to move. Alas, the dratted egg's having none of it – she's dead set against toddling, whatever pecuniary inducement I offer. In consequence, and more to appease Rose than in hopes of success, I've written to Hollingworth, pleading for a transfer. Do you think me an ass? Certainly, I think myself one. I've been quite unable to give the chief any grounds for my request, except that my wife is unhappy here and not forgetting to mention she's in the pudding club. But you and I both know even if I could come up with a blinder of a reason why I must move instanter, Hollingworth would in all probability give me short shrift.

Yours, Langers

PS How fares your own S & H? Here's hoping your Peter and my young wonder will be the best of pals.

From Frank to Mr Hollingworth

Dear Sir,

I trust this finds you well and I hope you'll forgive me if I raise with you now a rather ticklish question. You may remember that when you posted me here to Kluanak, I asked if I may instead be used elsewhere, as I worried my wife may find it lonely and difficult on such an isolated outstation.

Alas, my worries were not unfounded. Rose is terribly unhappy here and what's more, she is now expecting a baby. And so I am writing to ask if there is any chance at all that I may be transferred to BB, or at least closer to BB?

I do know my request is unusual and I hope you understand I make it solely out of concern for my wife, and not out of any unhappiness, dissatisfaction or insubordination of my own.

I remain, sir, your obedient servant, Frank Langham

14

Government House
and the Pinners' bungalow, BB, April 1925

The fan above Mr Pinner's head barely moved the soupy air and he was sitting sweaty at his desk outside Mr Hollingworth's office in Government House, feeling horribly agitated. His secretarial duties included screening the chief's mail. Now he re-read Langham's note for the third or fourth time.

When the Langhams had departed upriver, they'd been taking bets in BB on how long it would be before Mrs Langham discovered the truth about her husband's past. At the time, Mr and Mrs Pinner had agreed the best hope she would remain in blissful ignorance was if by good chance when Langham returned to Kluanak with his bride, his erstwhile nonya happened to have moved to another kampung or else she quickly did so. These had seemed improbably optimistic scenarios, even then – and now this!

Mr Pinner could read between Langham's lines all right: the coming baby had nothing to do with it. Mrs Langham had found out, there had been a scene, words had been exchanged, she had set up a most awful stink. Hence this note, begging for a transfer. But what, now, was he to do about it? Mr Pinner glanced at the closed door of Mr Hollingworth's office: the chief was in there working at a speech he was to deliver to the merchants of BB next week. He imagined interrupting him, sliding Langham's note across his shiny mahogany desk ... But was that the right thing to do? The kind thing to do? Mr Pinner sighed heavily and he decided before he did anything at all about this bally note he'd take his problem home and chew it all over with Mary.

Like all the married men of the SCS, even those posted to BB and not some jungle outstation, Mr Pinner habitually returned home for tiffin and the lie-off. Now he and Mrs Pinner were at the table on their verandah – it was similar in design to Frank's and Rose's, but more agreeable and roomier, and furnished more smartly. Their view was over their tidy garden and beyond it the sleepy road. Their little girls, Emma and Harriet, were eating with their amah in the nursery. Boy – their own boy – had just served them a chicken curry. He'd now withdrawn to the kitchen hut.

Mr Pinner stirred a spoonful of curry into his rice and he plunged straight in.

"Langham's sent a note from Kluanak. It's as we anticipated. His wife's found out."

"Awful for her," nodded Mrs Pinner calmly.

"You sound as if you knew already."

"I've heard rumours."

Mr Pinner clattered his fork to his plate.

"You have? When? Who's the source?"

"Mrs Alford."

"Ah. Our dear newsmonger. And where's she got it from?"

"Mrs Slightman at Relunas, I gather. One of her many correspondents. Langham writes confiding letters to Slightman, apparently, and Mrs Slightman shunts those confidences straight to Mrs Alford – garbled, no doubt. The latest in Chinese whispers is the nonya bounced Langham into confessing." She paused before she added gloomily, "There is thrilled chatter even of blackmail."

"Blackmail?" echoed Mr Pinner, just as gloomily. "To be expected, I suppose ... And you only now think to tell me all this?"

Mrs Pinner shrugged.

"I can't pass on every morsel of gossip I pick up at the Club." She paused and looked at her husband. "Anyway, he told you this? Langham. That he'd told his wife?"

Mr Pinner shook his head.

"Not in so many words, no – and not me, either, come to that. Hollingworth. He's asked the chief for a transfer. It seemed clear enough, even before the latest headlines from Relunas: Mrs Langham has discovered all."

They each stirred their curry a moment.

"So," said Mrs Pinner at last, "What did Mr Hollingworth say about it?"

Mr Pinner looked glum.

"I've not yet passed it along to the chief. Langham's note. D'you think I should?"

"Why wouldn't you?"

"The consequences for Langham."

"Which would be?"

"Ridicule, at best."

Ah, thought Mrs Pinner, ah, no, it didn't do for an Englishman to look a fool. An Englishman couldn't risk being laughed at, not so much by his countrymen as by the natives he was supposed to rule, for it was rare indeed for a clown to be king. And it was them, she inwardly sighed, it was them, the natives, who were supposed to be so amusingly concerned with face – with saving it and losing it, with giving it and receiving it.

Not that Mrs Pinner could ever admit such a disloyal thought, even to her husband.

"I suppose," she conceded.

"I mean, the booby gives no grounds at all for his request, apart from his wife's unhappiness. That won't cut the mustard." Mr Pinner paused. "He said she's expecting a baby, by the way."

Mrs Pinner stared at him wide-eyed.

"Expecting a baby? What? And you accuse me of being miserly with gossip?"

Mr Pinner smiled at his wife.

"I gather this is so far unknown to Mrs Slightman and Mrs Alford?"

"Well, it's the first I've heard of it."

"As if it would have any bearing on Hollingworth's thinking."

Mrs Pinner used her fork to poke at a piece of chicken. It was the perfectly normal thing that the SCS should be blind to the domestic concerns of its staff, let alone of their wives.

"Dearest, if it ever came to it, I do hope you'd take your chances with Hollingworth rather than condemning me to misery, especially if I were expecting."

"I hope I would too," said Mr Pinner, although his tone betrayed he was not quite certain on the point. He chewed a mouthful of curry. "And I can't tell him, can I. I can't tell

Hollingworth the real reason Langham's so keen to quit Kluanak is his wife's found out he formerly kept a nonya, and what's more she's living in the local kampung, along with the kiddies."

"Indeed you can't. These are not your secrets to reveal."

"Mm. And imagine being the one to bring it to the chief's attention his finger's not quite as much on the pulse as he supposes."

"Shoot the messenger and all that?"

"Absolutely."

Husband and wife exchanged a glance and they each speared another piece of chicken. Mrs Pinner wafted her freshly laden fork, and she wheeled back to ridicule and face.

"Embarrassment's a potent force," she said. "But would the simple fact Langham had requested a transfer really be so damaging to his long-term prospects?"

Mr Pinner nodded.

"I fear it would. Sometimes people *get* transferred – incompetents and misfits bunged in the treasury, that kind of thing – but I never heard of any fellow upping and asking for one on no sensible grounds whatsoever. I'm sure Hollingworth would consider it the most frightful cheek – judge Langham not at all a fellow to be trusted to show the flag."

Mrs Pinner imagined the Union Jack, waving red, white and blue from its flagpole over the roof of Government House, waving of fighting spirit, fortitude and selfless service. Or in any case waving of these things to the Britons of BB, to the natives it must wave of other things entirely, she supposed – mind you, this was another thought best kept to herself.

Mr Pinner interrupted his wife's mild and inward sedition. He said morosely, "I tell you, I'm tempted to burn Langham's bally note."

Now Mrs Pinner imagined one lowly servant of empire holding a match to a letter from another lowly servant of empire, to an imperial Grand Pooh-Bah. She met her husband's eye.

"Perhaps better to lose it instead," she suggested. "Then later, if need be, you could always find it."

Mr Pinner exercised something of a *volte face*.

"Either way, burn it or lose it, I suppose Langham would only write again."

"I suppose he would," agreed Mrs Pinner. She thought a moment. "Why don't you write to tell him not to be a damned fool, and only then, ahem, lose his note?"

"It's an idea."

It was, but, half a minute, Mrs Pinner couldn't help realising it perhaps wouldn't be terribly fair on Mrs Langham. Now it was her turn to exercise something of a *volte face*.

"Although on second thoughts poor Mrs Langham may not judge it to be a good one; she must so badly want to leave Kluanak."

Mr Pinner groaned.

"We're going round in circles. We're back to Mrs Langham's unhappiness and that not cutting the mustard."

Mrs Pinner told herself it was scarcely her husband's fault if the bureaucracy of empire found it difficult to accommodate the needs of one unhappy woman on an outstation. She reached for the spiciest sambal and helped herself to a spoonful. As she stirred some of it into her rice she said, "Why don't you sleep on it and decide things after the lie-off?"

Mr Pinner, never averse to prevarication, again smiled at his wife.

"What an eminently sensible suggestion, dearest."

15

THE DO's BUNGALOW, KLUANAK
THE END OF APRIL 1925

Frank was at his desk, drafting a report on a recent explosion in the local population of wild pigs when, in the late afternoon, Usit barged into his office and started speaking in a rush of Malay.

"Tuan! Tuan! There's a perahu come from BB. The head boatman's got a letter for you. He won't give it to me. He's under strict instructions to give it to nobody but you."

Frank frowned: unscheduled mail runs from BB usually spelled an increased workload for him. Perhaps a forestry officer was soon to pay him a visit, entailing all sorts of domestic palaver? Perhaps Government House wanted an explanation instanter of why tax receipts from his district were declining? And perhaps Hollingworth had replied to his note asking for a transfer. Christ!

Frank opened the note right there on the landing stage, the moment the head boatman passed it over. As he extracted the paper from the envelope he was horribly aware he had quite an audience: Boy, the head boatman and the perahu's crew were all watching him intently, as were a pair of workmen who happened to be on the landing stage making yet another of the endless repairs to its structure. Well, there was nothing to be done about any of them. Frank unfolded the note. It was not typewritten, like most missives from Government House, but handwritten in black ink, in neat, precise writing. It was only one page, so he read it quickly.

My dear Langham,

Forgive me if I reply to you myself, in an entirely unofficial capacity. If you want to make a stand on it, I will of course put the matter of a transfer up to Hollingworth, but I think you would do a great deal better to let it go. More, I hope that on reflection you will come to agree you are fortunate indeed that I see all the mail coming in before it goes to the chief. I do understand your wife at present finds life on an outstation isolated and lonely, but I think she will with time become accustomed to the lack of company. I don't deny it's admirable for a man to be uxorious, I hope and trust I am an uxorious fellow myself, but I must say I think you are a little too inclined to attach importance to personal matters when considering the administration of our Empire. Never forget an SCS man should be reliable, competent, hard-working and uncomplaining. I think if you and your wife will exercise a little patience, you'll both soon be getting on splendidly at Kluanak.

Yours very sincerely, John Pinner.

Though Frank had expected his request to be turned down, he was infuriated: Pinner was a condescending, patronising fathead! He swore and then he ripped the sod's letter into pieces. These he tossed into the river, which flowed placidly today, its surface flecked here and there with splashes of creamy-yellow foam. The scraps of paper fluttered downwards into the muddy water, where they looked like flecks of foam themselves. Frank watched them eddy a moment and then he wheeled about and marched towards the bungalow, not caring two hoots what the watching Malays made of things.

Rose was resting in her room. She spent a lot of time resting now, her condition provided an easy excuse for avoiding Frank, the servants, everybody. She was lying on her bed, fully clothed, staring up at the jungle curtains and trying, unsuccessfully, not to think. Though she was displeased to hear knocking at her door, she didn't call out for whoever it was – Boy, she supposed – to come back later. No, she heaved a martyred sigh, and then she went to her door and opened it.

Frank and Rose stared at each other a moment. Frank both played for time and also tried to soften his wife, by holding out the prospect of a minor boost.

"Got any letters you want to send out tomorrow?" He asked, faux cheerily.

Rose looked at him blankly.

"But it's only a few days since the last packet went."

"BB sent an extra perahu between regular mail runs. Happens sometimes."

"Why now?" asked Rose. As if she needed to ask. "It's a reply to yours to Mr Hollingworth, isn't it?"

Frank nodded.

Rose momentarily flared with hope.

"He has given you a transfer?"

Frank shook his head.

"As I anticipated. Sorry, old girl."

"We can't leave here?"

"Pinner replied."

Rose had talked to Mr Pinner once or twice at the Club; a weedy, droopy sort of man, she remembered, and as skinny as a candlestick.

"On behalf of Hollingworth, you mean?"

"No. He sifts the chief's mail. He was so appalled by my request he didn't even put it up to the presence. I'd like to write to tell him to go toast his bloomin' eyebrows, but you know I can't." He paused. "I did my best."

"It seems to me your best is a pretty poor one."

Frank shrugged.

"I'm sorry. But it's Kluanak for us, for the foreseeable, you'll just have to get used to things, that's all."

Rose wrung her hands, and her voice was anguished.

"This is too unfair for words. I can't be expected to live like this, in such close proximity to your strumpet and her brats, and it won't be any good for Baby, either."

Frank, already put out by Mr Pinner's letter, grew still more irritated. By George, he was getting fed up with this! With feeling guilty all the time; with contrition. He simply couldn't have it! He was a patient man, but he must by now call his wife's stubborn intransigence jolly petulant and her refusal to see that Baby would never come across his kampung family was positively unhinged. Truly, was his wife mentally unstable?

"Rose, please, this can't go on."

"What? You think I should be reconciled, by now, to ... to ... everything?"

Yes, thought Frank, yes you jolly well should. With effort, he reminded himself that when an egg was in the pudding club, a heightened degree of hysteria was only to be expected. He repeated, with exaggerated patience, "This can't go on."

"What can't? Why not?"

"You know very well what. You know very well why not."

"I wish I did."

"We're married, aren't we."

"Indeed we are," agreed Rose. "Man and wife." She added, in a tone just as insulting as a slap.

Frank winced.

"Not that you'd know it," he said bitterly. "We barely touch each other now."

They each thought of their bread and butter – or, rather, of its lack.

Rose was absolutely thankful that come what may, she'd be let off the hook these next few months as her body swelled grotesquely. And after that? After that, she supposed, she'd have to train herself to lie back and stare at the ceiling and will her husband to get it over with, as quickly as he could.

Frank thought he'd been so good about giving up the prick and all that, awfully good. Rose couldn't say he'd pestered her or pawed at her. He hadn't tried even to press his lips to hers since she'd so hurtfully rejected him the night she'd told him he was soon to welcome his son and heir. No. He'd restrained himself since then to chastely kissing her cheek – something he did every night now, as a point of principle, before they went separately to their chilly beds. And of course he wouldn't force things while the little woman was in the pudding club – he wasn't a monster – but after Baby arrived, how were they ever supposed to begin to feel their way back to their former intimacy, if she insisted on living in a permanent flounce?

Rose broke the stretching silence.

"You said you'd give me time. All the time I need."

Frank thought: you've had time; any sensible egg would by now have come around to my way of seeing things.

"Yes. But how long do you expect me to indulge you?"

"Indulge me? What, as if I were a child?"

"Well, it's certainly childish to be so preoccupied with the past."

Rose slammed her bedroom door in Frank's face. With that, she returned to her bed, lay down and once again did her best not to think.

UNSCHEDULED OUTBOUND MAIL,
THE END OF APRIL 1925
SENT FROM KLUANAK

From Rose to Beatrice

Dearest Bumbles,

Are you surprised to receive this unexpected letter written not a week after my last? I can send it from the circumstance that the government in BB today sent a boat between regular mail runs to convey to Frank most crushing news.

Did I tell you before I had put to him an ultimatum? No matter, I tell it to you now. Yes, my dear, I told Frank I could not live in proximity to his discarded trollop and her mixed-breed brats, so he must see to it that either she left the kampung or we left the DO's bungalow. Alas, she point-blank refused to go, notwithstanding he promised to make it well worth her while, so he wrote to his chief in BB asking for a transfer. But he is not to be given one; BB sent this boat today specifically to convey a note telling him so.

So now I must stay here, crammed close to her, and I don't know what to do. I feel so trapped. I find it difficult to remember that once, in Frank's presence, I felt suspended amongst the stars, whereas now he makes me feel I'm suspended cold and still and mummified in bluely groaning ice. And this despite the wretched heat. Yes, it seems to me that in this torrid jungle world nothing changes and nothing changes and nothing happens between us, me and Frank; no communion, no exchange. There is no movement to our lives, no flow, only the relentless flowing of the river, and how long can I watch the river and not go mad?

Still, there's nothing to do except to resign myself; I must acquiesce to my fate and try to make the best of things. And things, I suppose, are not so bad. I have nothing to complain of. I am English. I am Frank's only ever legal wife – polygamy is the common way here, did I ever tell you that? I am not starving, illiterate, beaten, enslaved. I have a house, servants. Pretty dresses, even, although many of mine are now too tight for me to wear. I am not a spinster; I will never suffer the indignities that befall an Old Maid. I will soon, God willing, have a child. I have you and other friends in England. I have Mummy, for all she's a mixed blessing.

But, oh, my dear, isn't counting ones blessing's a miserable thing to do. I am Frank's wife and I have vowed to obey him. That is that. The end. *Finis*.

Your unhappy cousin, Rosebud

From Frank Langham, to John Pinner

My dear Pinner,

Thank you for declining to pass my request for a transfer up to the chief. On due reflection, I find that your kind intentions align precisely with my own best interests. My wife and I have had it all out and she is now quite sure she can make a go of things here. Henceforth there will be no distractions of a domestic nature to sway me from my service, which service I intend to render with the assiduity and diligence of a D.O who bows to none in his desire to be effective.

Please find enclosed with this packet my report on reducing the wild pig population of Kluanak.

Yours very sincerely, Frank Langham

16

It was the hour before tiffin when in those past happy days at once so recent and so distant, Rose and Frank had been accustomed to play tennis. But now Rose was standing by the verandah rail, staring out over the river flowing relentless to the sea and Frank was watching her from his planter's chair, where he was sprawled with a cigarette and a whisky.

As he smoked, Frank felt no apprehension. Until now the thought his wife may get a notion to up and leave him had no more crossed his mind than it had crossed the pawang's before the spirits had led her to think of it, or Nony's before the pawang had, in turn, led her to think of it. He would have agreed with Daphne that wives just didn't leave their husbands, it was such frightfully bad form. He would have seconded what Rose herself half-believed even now: bolting was for duchesses and actresses and people like that, not for ladies like her.

But what kind of lady was she? Well, in any case, ever since Frank had uttered the words *this can't go on*, she'd been the kind of lady who was unable to get them out of her head. Now, as she watched the river, her inner ear heard them again; their repetition sounded somehow metallic. She knew Frank had been right, of course: this really couldn't go on. She didn't mean her anger couldn't, or their not touching couldn't; she meant her own pretence could not. Oh, she may have been able to keep it up – pretence may slowly have become unnecessary – if only she and Frank had been able to make a fresh start in a new place. But now she knew there was no hope of a transfer, Kluanak felt to her as a green grave and she didn't think she'd be able to maintain it, this silence about what she really thought and felt. This silence about who she was. She must do what Frank had been too cowardly to do. She must reveal herself. She must speak. She must, to save herself. She must admit it was a pretence that ... That what was a pretence? She couldn't finish the thought.

Meanwhile, Frank, watching his wife staring over the river, was thinking it was high time to insist. By George, it was too ridiculous he only ever now got to kiss his little woman on the cheek. Whatever she thought about things or thought she thought about things, he was her husband and he must remind her both of the delights of a proper kiss, on the mouth, and also of the wilder delights promised by such a kiss, even if they could not, alas, partake of those delights for the few absurdly fat months ahead.

Frank ground out his cigarette and put aside his whisky. He stood up and walked over to join his wife, so they stood shoulder-to-shoulder a moment, both of them now looking out over the river: it was carrying nothing this evening but occasional swirls of leaves and the odd branch or log. Frank decided Malaya must be cheering for him: everything was so beautiful and so peaceful. The background noise of the jungle was not intrusive but soothing, and the river flowed with a lullaby murmur. The sky was beginning to flaunt its sunset glory; the sinking sun put Frank in mind of a mango, dribbling its golden juices into the clouds.

He cast a sideways glance at Rose. The little woman had a wistful expression on her face. Perhaps she was feeling just as fed-up as he was? Just as yearning. He waited a moment longer and then he snaked an arm around her shoulder, drew her to him and kissed her neck.

Rose jumped a mile and pulled away from him.

"What are you doing?"

"Please!" said Frank. "A kiss? A proper kiss."

Perhaps I should steel myself, Rose thought. But then she decided perhaps she'd better not. She stepped away from her husband and she blushed as she said, "I expect I'm just one of those awful neurotic women who're a trial to all abroad."

Frank had often recently thought something similar, but now he was thrown. He said, "What?"

"I expect you'll say I'm wound tight as cotton on a reel, but … even when your lips only brush my cheek … and when last you tried to kiss me on the mouth … I almost … it almost … frankly, it made me feel … I don't know … and when I think of … you know, bread and butter…when I remember … when I anticipate, I feel … I feel … violated, I suppose."

Frank was aghast.

"Violated? Rose! I'm your husband."

"You so badly misrepresented yourself to me."

"I did no such thing!"

"I feel as if I never consented."

"Didn't consent? This is absurd!"

"Not to you. The real you."

"I'm as real as … I tell you, my name's stamped all the way

through me. Frank Hector Langham, from head to toe."

"As if I couldn't consent just now."

"Consent to what? I merely kissed your neck. I've asked nothing of you. Nothing at all since I confessed."

"Yes, but what of the future?"

"Exactly. For the sake of our future, we have to draw a line under this nonsense."

Rose looked directly at her husband; she felt she was looking at him across a chasm.

"I don't think I can." She paused. "I can't."

"What d'you mean?"

"We both know full well what I mean. I don't think I could ever again allow you to ... I don't think I could ever again bring myself to ..."

"But I'm your husband."

Silence.

"You're being ridiculous. Unfair."

"Unfair? Don't you think it was unfair to entice me out here, without telling me of your former life as a family man?"

"I understand why you blame me."

"This is not to do with blame."

"Then what is it to do with?"

Rose's blush deepened, but she didn't lose her nerve. She said, "Attraction, I suppose you'd say. It's to do with attraction." She paused. "Attraction, and its lack."

What, his wife, no longer attracted to him? Frank didn't really believe it.

"Come on, old girl, we're man and wife."

Rose watched a large stick bob past in the river and then become snagged on a submerged root. She confronted the thought she'd earlier tried to evade: it was time to admit it was a pretence she and Frank could share a future. She summoned all her courage,

"That's as may be," she said, and her voice was shaky. "But I want you to release me."

"Release you? What the hell d'you mean?"

Rose's vision smudged. She blinked, and she told herself she mustn't cry – and she didn't.

"Not divorce," she said.

Frank looked and sounded as shocked and incredulous as he felt.

"Divorce?"

"I wouldn't inflict that indignity on you."

"I should think not! Ludicrous!"

"I just want you to release me to go Home, that's all."

"Home?"

"Yes. I want to go Home."

"This is home."

"I want to return to England."

"A visit? What, six months?"

"I don't mean to visit, Frank. I mean for good."

Frank remained flabbergasted. It was one thing, he thought, for a little woman to sulk after a row, quite another for her to flee her marriage; there was no end of difference between the cold shoulder for a few weeks, and desertion. And would even a duchess dart from her duke while she was in the pudding club?

"You'd bolt?" he said.

Rose hesitated.

"Not that dramatic. It's just ... it's just we wouldn't live together. Not so unusual, really. I'm sure plenty of disappointed, disillusioned husbands and wives live entirely separately, in separate houses, separate towns, separate counties and, yes, sometimes even in separate countries, too."

"Disappointed ... disillusioned ... separate countries." Frank felt the words spin around him, so he almost felt dizzy. "What? As if they were not married at all?"

Rose ignored the question.

"I could leave with the next mail boat to BB."

"Don't be silly! What about Baby? You'll soon grow as large as the house."

"I suppose it wouldn't be wise to undertake a long sea journey in my condition, but ..."

"No doctor would sanction it."

"... but I could wait out my time in BB and then after Baby was born I could sail with him for Home."

"This is madness!" Frank momentarily dropped his head into his hands. But he reminded himself this sort of thing was only to be expected when a little woman was in the pudding club. He raised his head again and he said, more gently, "Why such a rush? Why don't we wait until after Baby is born and talk it all over then?"

"I see no point in prolonging things."

"Is this because I won't press Hollingworth for a transfer? Dearest, if it means this much to you, to hell with the risks, I'll do as you want me to: I'll write to Hollingworth to tell him the truth."

Rose shook her head.

"It's too late for that."

There was silence for a beat or two and when at last Frank next spoke his voice was hoarse.

"But I love you."

"Oh, I know that. I know you love me, in your own way, and I loved you too, Frank, I loved you deeply."

"This is unreasonable. Hysterical."

"I dare say."

"Was my transgression really so grave? I've told you and told you: when I took a concubine I was nothing but a lonely boy. I only did what any other lonely boy would've done, what any man would've done. Would you punish me for that?"

"I already said none of this is about blame. It's not about punishment either. It's not even about her. It's about ... it's about ... what it's always about."

Frank looked at his wife: and that is?

"It's about who can be known, who can be trusted ... Who is worth knowing, who is worth trusting."

Frank flushed, and then he scowled.

"Of course I can be trusted. Come on! It seems to me there's something overdone in your refusal to believe me."

Rose shrugged.

"Overdone? That's what you say."

Frank spoke in a voice of iron.

"It's what your husband says."

Silence.

"I am your husband."

"So you keep saying."

"I have my rights. What if I say you cannot go?"

Rose stared hard at the river for a long moment. Her husband's word was law, she knew. She turned and met his eye.

"Then I cannot go. But if you refuse to set me free, I'll die."

"Don't be melodramatic, Rose! For God's sake! I'm no tyrant. Of course I don't want to keep you here fettered, in manacles, b–"

"Then I may indeed go? You'll give me money? I'll take only my own things. I'll leave all our wedding presents."

Frank threw up his hands.

"I don't give a damn about our wedding presents! Look here. I say again I don't want to keep you here by main force but of course you can't go. Of course you can't. I never heard anything so ridiculous in all my life – too idiotic for words. What? Not yet a year married and you'd run off? Deserted by my bride? Abandoned? You'd almost make me into ..." Frank had been going to say, *you'd almost make me into a cuckold.* He imagined himself a laughing stock with everybody all over Saramantan. Indian. Chinese. Malay. Dayak. British. They'd all be in stitches. He blushed and he said instead, "It's not from pride I'll have you stay, you mustn't think that. It's ..."

"You'll force me to stay?"

"... it's from concern for you. Imagine it! The pinched life of a nearly-spinster in a grim little bedsit in Clapham or somewhere. And I ask again: what about Baby?"

"We'd manage very well, however grim our bedsit."

"I didn't mean that. Although come to think of it, my son and heir in a bedsit with gas on the meter? It wouldn't do."

"You sound like Mummy."

Frank remembered Daphne treating him with mocking condescension; furious resentment of his mother-in-law now mingled with his anger with his wife. He shouted, "It couldn't be in Baby's interests for you to waltz Home. How can you even think of leaving when doing so would mean not only depriving me of Baby, but also depriving Baby of me. We'd be strangers to each other, that could be no good for the little lad."

What, thought Rose, a mother must not put her own interests above those of her child? A lady may choose to prioritise her husband over her children or her children over her husband, but not herself over either? She supposed she agreed. And she supposed, too, Frank had a point: Baby may never know himself if he never knew his father. But on the other hand she felt dead certain if she couldn't leave Frank now, then she'd stop knowing herself; that she'd become disconnected from her self. Whatever that was. But whatever it was, this thing that was her self, if she were not connected to it, then how could she ever hope to connect to Baby, to anybody at all, to all humanity? And if she couldn't connect to Baby then how could he, in turn, connect to her? He couldn't. And if he couldn't connect to her, to his mother, then how could he connect to his self, to anybody, to all humanity?

Mind you, Rose backpedalled, motherless children managed it. On half a minute's reflection she acknowledged motherless children could flourish. Children whose mothers had died, children whose mothers were madwomen, children whose mothers were lost to gin or to social climbing or to good causes. More to the immediate point, children could thrive in the absence of their fathers. Had not both she and Frank thrived without theirs? You had to believe that for the sake of all those children whose fathers had been killed in the War. Most of them would be happy; scarred for sure, but most of them would lead lives that were successful according to their own ideas about what counted as success. Yes, damage could always be overcome. Or so Rose told herself now. Nothing was irreparable. And what about all those children whose fathers were positive dangers to them? She didn't mean fathers who were simply remote from their children – so many fathers were as remote from the nursery as from the moon. She meant fathers who bullied their children, or disparaged them or beat them, fathers who were wantonly cruel. Surely children were better off without such fathers than with them?

Rose glared at Frank. She said, confidently, but with a confidence that was perhaps founded on nothing more than wishful thinking, "I'm quite sure Baby would be perfectly all right without you."

The words hung for a long beat. Frank felt them as splashes of acid sizzling through him. This was intolerable! How could Rose be so blind, so selfish? He slapped his palms hard against the verandah rail and he said, "I've had it with this! Absolutely had it! I'll brook no further argument about it. You really are making a terrific fuss about nothing, you really are, Rose. It's vulgar to create about what I did before I met you – although I grant I was wrong not to confide in you before I brought you to Saramantan. Now, come on! No more discussion about leaving, about any of it. Nony? We've said all we have to say about that little madam, it's not seemly to go on and on. And we can't have Boy finding us at each other's throats when he comes out with evening tiffin. Let's sit down and have our sundowners like civilized people."

17

It was once again the festival of Bulan Penuh. The inky heavens were cloudless and the lovely full moon was shining enormous now, casting her chilly quicksilver abundantly over the jungle. Rose and Frank had finished their evening tiffin, and the servants had by now all returned to the kampung for the coming hours of music, feasting, firecrackers and wayang; as usual even the night watchman had gone off to enjoy his portion of fun and meat on sticks.

And as usual on Bulan Penuh, Rose was a little afraid that in the watchman's absence, a tiger may wander in from the jungle, not that she said so, since she and Frank were barely talking at all now. She and he were sitting side-by-side on the verandah, each of them nursing a drink – it was common knowledge gin was an excellent tonic for women who were That Way so Rose's was a gin pahit, and Frank's was a neat whisky. They were reading by the light of that puny shadow of the moon, their insect-buzzed paraffin lantern. Rose had on her lap a copy of *The Lady*, two months out of date, open to an article about dresses to pack if you intended to take the boat train to Paris. It made her feel terribly dowdy; she was wearing an old frock, her plain navy, let out at every seam, and sensible brogues. Not the sort of clothes to have adventures in, she sighed, even if there had been any adventures to be had in Kluanak.

Meanwhile, Frank was reading a detective novel. Out of respect for Rose's current sensitivity to smell, he had not lit his pipe and on account of his own unhappiness, he was drinking hard. He'd already knocked back two generous whiskies and he'd just poured himself another tot; his tumbler now contained three or four fingers of syrupy 110 proof.

Rose didn't care how much her husband drank: let him damage his liver! If he wanted to drink himself into an early grave, that was his business.

They heard gamelan music start up: it rippled downriver from the kampung as if it were water itself. The liquid notes were soon followed by the gunfire rattle of firecrackers. Frank turned another page and then he glanced up from his book, drink was making him maudlin so he more than ever regretted the ghastly row he'd had with the little woman the other day. And no matter that they'd almost been as strangers to each other since then, it was after all Bulan Penuh ... He couldn't help remembering how, on previous nights of Bulan Penuh, he and Rose had invariably gone down to the landing stage to see the full moon reflected in the water ... Shared memories. Happy times ... Right-o, despite the frost patterns spreading between them, he decided there could be no harm in making an effort.

"They sound like they're having a jolly time."

"Jolly, yes." Agreed Rose.

They lapsed into silence, again.

Frank finished his whisky and stood up to pour himself

another one. He walked over to the cluttered drinks table, where the array of bottles, his inanimate accomplices to debauchery, winked and beckoned.

"A top up?" he asked Rose.

She shook her head.

Frank shrugged and then he poured himself a whisky that was even stiffer than the last one – two thirds of his tumbler now sloshed amber. He returned to his chair, where he put aside his novel – it couldn't hold his attention, he preferred to drink than read tonight. He didn't sip his whisky but took great gulping slugs; within ten minutes he'd drained the tumbler; within another ten he'd drained another one and his face had become all red and sweaty. He looked at Rose through glassily unfocused eyes.

"Thefullmoonishmakingmeshentimentalmydarlin," he slurred, all mawkish.

"What?"

"The moon. Mooooon. Mooooon."

"What about the moon?"

Frank made a huge effort.

"Itsh making me shenti … shenti … shentimental."

Rose glanced over the verandah's rail to the moon hanging in the sky. She too remembered, with regret, standing on the landing stage, hand-in-hand with Frank, her body inclined to his, the two of them looking down on the moon's reflection in the river. The scene so beautiful and so romantic. Oh, well.

"That's as may be," she said.

"Rifer," slurred Frank. "Mooooon, in the rifer." He levered himself to his feet with a slow dignity which was itself an indignity; he was just about as drunk as a man could be whilst still being able to stand. "I hash a mind I sh-sh-sh-should like to shee it again." Swaying, he held out his hand to his wife and in a voice he misjudged to be as beckoning as a crooked finger, he said, "Come!"

Rose sighed, rather as a mother would when faced with the whims of a wilful toddler. And like a harassed mother trading effort now for peace later, she heard herself saying irritably, "Oh, all right."

She didn't know why she'd accepted. She didn't know why at the time and she'd never know why later, though this was a moment she'd replay in her memory again and again: if only Frank hadn't made his drunken invitation; if only she hadn't indulged him; if only she'd told him not to be an idiot, he was in no fit state to go moon-gazing; if only she'd said she was disinclined to view the moon with him at all, but especially whilst he was as tight as a boiled owl. If only. Those two saddest of words. But as it was, Rose accepted. Perhaps, she'd later theorise, she'd accepted out of nostalgia; perhaps she'd hoped if only they could be rinsed by the loveliness of the moon's light she and Frank could be purified, magically, allowing them to start afresh in dazzling cleanliness; perhaps she'd wanted to see again the beauty of the moon reflected in the river; perhaps she'd simply wanted to stretch her legs; perhaps she'd accepted as casually, as unthinkingly, as she'd once have accepted a cup of tea from her husband over breakfast. In any case: she accepted, and by accepting, she condemned them both.

Still, it was with no sense of foreboding that Rose accompanied

Frank down the steps off the verandah and across the lawn. They left the paraffin lantern on the table, so the moon alone lit their way. The two of them walked a couple of feet apart. Frank lurched and staggered but Rose did not offer him a steadying hand, let alone slip her arm around his waist so she could support him as they went. Indeed, she held herself stiffly and tilted a little away from him.

They reached the landing stage. The perahu was tethered about halfway along it. After they'd passed the boat, Frank moved a little ahead of Rose. He reached the very end of the landing stage and he swayed there alone, staring down at the moonlight making a pathway on the water, one leading to the moon's reflection. His vision was so blurred, so bleary, it seemed to him the edges even of solid things bled into each other, or else that even solid things were slowly dissolving as he watched. As for reflections and fractured pathways of light? He could barely get a bead on them at all. Nonetheless, as he stood at the end of the landing stage, looking down, he did at least, and at the last, recognise beauty: he saw a wavy-edged circle of silver, gorgeous, radiant, rippling silkily in the water. He was moved by such loveliness, notwithstanding it was swimmy. He became fascinated by the circle's ripples. He swept his hand in an expansive, drunken arc.

"Itsh all moving," he slurred. "Everyshing. Moving."

Rose, still standing behind him, heard him mumble but she couldn't understand what he'd said. And here were more moments that would haunt her: if only Frank hadn't walked ahead of her; if only he'd turned around as he'd said whatever he'd said; if only he hadn't been silhouetted so temptingly against the sky. Above all, if only some careless workman hadn't left a forgotten hammer lying where anybody may find it and put it to vilest use.

Rose first became aware of the hammer when she knocked it with her foot. It had a sturdy wooden handle and an iron head, rusty, so it didn't glint in the moon-silvered dark. She didn't bend to pick it up. She was quite sure she didn't. She didn't even move, she didn't think.

And nonetheless.

And nonetheless, the next moment she saw the world as if through an evaporating fog; a white fog of blindness, coldly clammy and swirling.

And through this thinning fog she saw Frank lying quite still, face down in the lapping water.

And across the back of Frank's head there was a messy-looking wet gash oozing with a sticky liquid that looked tar-black in the moonlight, and which spread through the muddy water cloudy like ink

Sound which for long moments had been just as muffled as had light and time, again rushed in on Rose. She heard again the plashing of the river and the din of the jungle. She realised she was now at the end of the landing stage. She had the workman's hammer in her hand. She was panting hard – and her heart was pounding as if *it* had a nail to bang in. A hammering heart. She understood what that meant, now. She screamed a scream just as animal as any of those echoing from the jungle, and she pleated to the landing stage's wooden planks.

What had happened? Rose really couldn't think. Which meant she could think all too well. She could imagine all too well. Without giving herself time to calculate or Frank time to process what she was doing, let alone to react to it, she must have snatched up the hammer and crashed it down as hard as she could on the back of her husband's head. She screwed her eyes tight shut against the battering images. But she saw them in any case. She saw her arm swinging the hammer lightning fast. Perhaps the blow had landed just where the base of Frank's skull met the top of his spine? She imagined metal connecting with flesh and bone with a sound somewhere between a thud, and a crack, and a thwack, and a slam. At the point of impact, blood would have splattered, the bone would have pushed into Frank's brain, where, almost in the same instant nerve cells started going haywire, they would have ceased firing; they'd have shorted into oblivion, and with them, Frank. Through her mind's eye, Rose saw her husband topple forward, rigid and ramrod straight, and then plop soundlessly into the river, which at once began to swirl and lap around him. He wouldn't even have had time to cry out, she supposed. One moment he was, the next moment, he wasn't; the hammer fell and time and space stopped for him. There could have been no dread, no fear, that was something; it was something that Frank, quite literally, could not have known what had hit him.

But it wasn't much. It wasn't anything, really, in the face of a crime Rose knew, even as she slumped on the landing stage, she must never attempt to rationalise or to justify, let alone to excuse, whatever the provocations that had led to it, and however unpremeditated it had been. Life had screwed her into a vice so secure she'd thought it would never budge? Too bad. She had put a stop to another person. She had committed the worst of crimes; ergo she was amongst the worst of people. She just was. That it was only through bad luck – through the force of unlucky circumstance – she had joined their ranks, had nothing to do with it. What about Frank's bad luck in making himself vulnerable to her tonight? What were her husband's lies, his betrayals, his domineering pride, his swagger, his bullying, his arrogance, his conceit in the face of what she'd done? So what if Frank had made her think, even before she'd swung the hammer, that the past, to her, could never be consolation? She had put an end to his chances of ever making things right, of his chances of anything at all, of chance itself as it related to him, of all possibility for him, of all the possible futures he must have imagined for himself. She had brought Frank to the end of the line in everything … She must have been possessed … This demonic wildness … Oh, Frank! And, oh God, the guilt!

Still, even as Rose told herself her life henceforth would be forever dimmed by shame, she realised she would acquiesce to no other dimming and certainly to no snuffing out. Murder. Manslaughter. However they classified her crime, she must not swing for it. Granted, by obliterating Frank's world, she'd changed her own world forever, but she did still have a world and she intended to keep it. Her punishment must be guilt, the cat o'nine tails lashes of remorse, there must be no noose. Oh, they wouldn't hang her while she was That Way. Even in her first distress, Rose recognised her condition would offer her temporary reprieve. But after Baby was born: what then? Then, she panicked, they may very well hang her, if only they could convict her. She imagined herself blindfolded, the noose descending round her neck, the trapdoor opening beneath her feet …

Rose gasped and she scrambled to standing. To her surprise, she was still holding the hammer. Avoiding looking down, indeed keeping her eyes fixed on the further bank, she flung it as far out into the river as she could. It curved through the air and splashed into the deep water halfway across. Nobody would go looking for that hammer, she thought, and so nobody would find it. But if they did? No matter. Nobody would ever connect it with Frank's death. It would be assumed some workman had knocked it off the landing stage, not that it had become a murder weapon and then been thrown away.

Or in any case, corrected Rose, nobody would ever connect the hammer with Frank's death in the absence of a body with its head staved in. She steeled herself to look down again. The box that had so recently held her husband was still floating where it had fallen in the lapping water by the landing stage. Well, it mustn't stay there much longer. Rose couldn't have that. She walked back to where the perahu was tethered and, with movements made graceless by the gathering bulk of pregnancy, she clambered down into it to fetch the pole. It was unwieldy but it was light, being nothing but a length of bamboo. Rose easily lifted it onto the landing stage and it was no struggle to carry. Once she reached the end of the landing stage, she used it to prod her husband's body out into the fast flowing water at the centre of the river's course, where there were no roots or rocks to snag it.

The thing that was no longer Frank was very quickly caught by the current and it began to be swirled away downstream, like a log, like any other piece of debris; just more flotsam and jetsam, more wreckage, more rubbish to be carried by the river, Frank's temporary grave, to the deeper, final, grave of the sea.

At first, Rose followed the progress of her late husband's corpse easily enough in the mercury light but perhaps five hundred yards downstream it bobbed out of her view. She stood a while longer, staring at the water with unseeing eyes. But then, slowly, she became aware of what, she supposed, must have been the last thing Frank had ever seen: the moon's reflection. She stared down at the beautiful silver disc floating below her; she glanced up to its source, the beautiful silver disc floating above her. The moon and her reflection were like a pair of eyes, she thought, a pair of eyes watching her, silver eyes, knowing eyes shadowed and secret with grey.

Frank's eyes?

Rose told herself to get a grip, she really couldn't be doing with unearthly eyes. Not now. She peered along the river's course, to confirm for herself that Frank's corpse was already long gone; she glanced to roughly where the hammer had landed in the water; she returned the pole to the perahu. And then what was there for her to do? Rend her clothes and hair in mourning for Frank? Smear herself in ashes and wail in mourning for herself? But what would have been the point of such histrionics with no witnesses to them, debarring only the moon? No, Rose told herself firmly, if ever there were a time to keep a cool head, then it was now.

As Rose walked back across the compound she couldn't help staring, with a shudder, at the cell attached to the courthouse. And as she climbed the steps onto the verandah she couldn't help thinking that this was the very same bungalow from which she and Frank, two of them, had departed, but to which only one of them would ever return. She was shocked almost, by how little the outward world of things and happenings had been changed by the death she'd brought about – indeed nothing at all had changed in the outward world, it seemed to her, except that Frank was no longer in it. But then what had she expected? Thunderbolts flashing down from heaven to smite her?

Once she reached the verandah, Rose extinguished the paraffin lamp but she did not pause to clear away the glasses – the tumbler that had been the very last thing Frank's fingers had touched. To do so could only rouse suspicion. Boy could clear the things in the morning, just as if this had been an ordinary evening.

After Rose entered her room, she lit her own paraffin lamp and then she stood an appraising moment in front of her pier glass: her hair was dishevelled, but the tangles were nothing her brush couldn't smooth. Her face was red and shiny but that was quite as per in Malaya, she had sweat patches spreading dark under her arms, but that too was nothing but the usual. She hadn't suddenly transformed into an ugly hag, no telltale marks or blemishes had appeared on her face. She didn't look criminal, she didn't think. Mind you, what did criminal look like? Well, not like her, in any case. Not like a pregnant woman. Having reassured herself on the point, Rose stripped and put her clothes in the laundry hamper. She then went down to her bathhouse for her bath. Afterwards, she slipped into one of her demure high-necked white-cotton nightgowns but she didn't go to bed. Instead, she paced her room.

Back and forth she went, back and forth, and as she paced she became aware of some thought flickering at the edge of her mind ... But what was it? What? ... Back and forth she went again. And then, in a swoop, she caught the thought in the net of her conscious mind. She halted and she wheeled about to walk over to her chest of drawers.

Rose kept her letters from Home in the top drawer and now she opened it. Her letters were neatly arranged according to date and sender, so she quickly found the one she was looking for – it was from her mother, the one she'd found waiting for her when she'd arrived in Singapore. She'd not really believed the sensational content the first time she'd read it and she'd not been best pleased by it either, thinking her mother had intended an unfair jibe against Frank, a warning against him. But now she thought she might just as well have taken Mummy's yarn as a warning against herself – and what's more, she hoped the tall tale was true. Yes, though she usually reread her letters from Home to provide a link with her lost life as the sort of rooted Englander who never went anywhere, this letter, she now hoped, contained not a bridge to her past but one to her future.

Rose collected the paraffin lamp from the little table just inside the door and she carried both it and her mother's letter over to the chaise longue. Here she so placed the paraffin lamp on the floor that when she sat down, she could angle her letter to the spilling circle of yellow. Her mother habitually wrote in forceful black ink on thick, creamy paper, and her spikey hand was all bold strokes and slashes. Rose, accustomed to it and anyway remembering now the gist of the letter, found it easy enough to read.

Dear Rose,

I suppose it's understandable you are now so busy with your new life you can find little time to write Home to Mother, but I confess myself disappointed I have received no letter from you except the one from Marseilles. I enjoyed your description of the port, and now daily anticipate something similar from Aden, although I rather think Arabia must be altogether too exotic for my taste.

Sadly, I must report Miss Bellington's cousin Jane died a fortnight back but since I never knew her, I cannot much regret the loss, and her death did at least free Miss Bellington to return from her nursing duties on the Isle of White. Almost her first call on returning was to me. I had of course written to tell her about your marriage and your departure for the East and I knew she'd want to hash things over. But I must say the nature of her hashing caused me something of a surprise. She was less interested in hearing about your dress and more interested in telling me about another bride who went out to the colonies back in the 1890s. She said it wasn't a very polite story, which I must grant; indeed, it's decidedly impolite but I retell it now in the hope it's instructive.

Miss Bellington can be a confusing narrator, but evidently it all began when one Enid married an Old Africa Hand posted to some frightful nowhere or other – British Somaliland, I think she said, not that it matters.

Enid's Walter was considerably older than your Frank, being over forty when he took what was destined to be his final Home leave and met Enid. Meanwhile she, I gathered, must have been plain or else approaching 30, so spinsterhood loomed. In any case, when she was introduced to Walter, she quite set her cap at him, not that Miss Bellington put it quite so indelicately, but I don't doubt that's what she meant to say.

After they returned to wherever it was, Enid and Walter lived on an isolated station miles out in the desert. Some hot and sandy oubliette where even the sanest people could go doolally, I shouldn't wonder.

Alas, Enid had been a wife barely two years before she became a widow. The story she told the authorities was that Walter had shot himself. Meanwhile, the story she told her family, in letters Home, was that Walter had died of a fever. Naturally, they all believed her – why on earth shouldn't they have done?

She returned Home to live with her parents, and this story of fever was the one she stuck to until her own dying day. But the real truth was even more shocking and shameful than a self-administered gunshot: Enid was a murderess!

Mind you, she'd suffered sore provocation, as if it were any excuse. Walter drank! Drank like a fish! Enid of course knew nothing about it before she arrived at the desert station; Walter was always very abstemious in England and the stakes were so high he even managed to maintain his abstinence during the voyage out. But once he'd got her trapped amongst the sand dunes, he was always more or less tight as a boiled owl. He hid a bottle of whisky in his wardrobe, another in his gun cupboard, another in his desk at the courthouse; he started drinking before breakfast and he took regular nips throughout the day. When challenged, he denied he drank to excess, even when Enid waved empty bottles under his nose. But he couldn't deny he was subject to attacks of the DTs. The DTs, Rose, imagine!

Naturally, Enid was horrified by her husband's weakness – thoroughly disgusted and revolted. Drunk, she found him despicable. Even sober, she began to detest him. Everything he said irritated her and his presence was at all times annoying. What's more, he was neglecting his duties; she began to fear he'd be dismissed and then what would happen to them?

Then dawned the fateful day. Walter was even later than usual in dragging himself from bed, so Enid went into his bedroom, suspicious. And with good reason: he was snoring face up on the bed, shockingly naked, dead to the world; overnight he'd drunk himself into a sweaty, grunting stupor.

Enid tried to rouse him. She shouted at him. She shook him and shook him. She slapped his face. But he remained inert, like a corpse. He stank of liquor and, worse, he'd soiled himself. She tried to drag him off the filthy bed, but he was a big man and she couldn't budge him. She was overwhelmed by loathing and repulsion, so angry she almost forgot she was human.

There was a revolver on the table by the bed; the area was not immune to banditry and Walter kept it there in case of intrusion in the night. But then the revolver wasn't on the table, it was in Enid's hand and the blood spurted from Walter's chest. There was a gaping hole bubbling right above his heart.

Enid realised the red mist had descended and she'd shot her husband, hence all the red blood. But she didn't panic; she had the presence of mind to place the gun in Walter's hand and to close his still warm and pliant fingers around the grip. She flung open the bedroom door, as if she'd just rushed through it. Only then did she scream. She was in the nick of time – the servants had heard the bang and they'd come running. She showed them Walter's corpse, she said he'd shot himself. Of course, the simple blacks all fell for it and they too started screaming. Indeed, they ran out of the room even quicker than they'd run in. You never heard of people so in thrall to superstition, Miss Bellington said, scared to death, the lot of them, dreadfully afraid of ghosts and all that kind of thing.

Enid got hold of a coffin from somewhere and she paid a couple of the braver, more sensible blacks a handsome sum to dig a grave. She had Walter buried before sunset. Nobody batted an eye at the speed as in Africa you have to bury people quickly on account of the corrupting effect of the heat. Or so said Miss Bellington and I see no reason to disagree.

Enid was horribly aware, by now, that her husband's dipsomania was no secret at Government House in Cairo or wherever it was. Once he was buried, she wrote to the authorities saying she'd found him dead with a revolver in his hand; there was no doubt he'd shot himself in a fit of *delirium tremens*, either accidentally or from despairing drunken shame at his degeneracy, who could ever tell. Our people no more questioned her account than had the darkies, which I must say seems to me a poor show.

Anyway, as I said, Enid told those at Home the different, less degrading story that Walter had been carried off by fever. Once she returned to live with her parents she stuck to her line – she guarded her secret for years and years. But she confessed everything on her deathbed: her wicked act, her wicked lies. Well one would, I suppose, wouldn't one, hoping for absolution before one met one's maker. According to Miss Bellington, Enid's confessor was her sister, whose verdict on matters was: she must suppose Enid wasn't truly guilty but then she didn't know who else was.

There, Rose, what do you think of that? Frightfully bad form, isn't it, and it only goes to show you never can tell about people.

Alas, I now find this unedifying tale has filled so many pages I have quite run out of paper, so I must put down my pen. I trust you will reply with greater alacrity than you have yet shown in your correspondence.

Yours &c, Mother.

Rose re-read this letter twice – this guide to conduct. Yes, she must take Enid as her template. Enid hadn't swung. Enid had got away with things. And she'd got away with things because she'd kept her cool. She'd been clever and crafty and cunning and cautious and careful and calculating. Well, she, Rose, would be no less. And like Enid, she'd have some powerful allies when it came to misleading. First, she was English; there was not a magistrate in the Empire who'd jump to conclude one of his own had committed murder. Enid must have relied on that useful prejudice in Africa the 1890s, thought Rose, and she could certainly rely on it on Saramantan today. Then again, she was a woman and a respectable one to boot. Disgruntled maids in Midlands towns may do in their mistresses sometimes, but respectability and her feminine nature had acted like protective cloaks around Enid and they would do the same for her. Moreover, she had the advantage over Enid: she was That Way. Nobody, nobody at all, would ever suspect a lady in her condition of killing, she was confident of that.

Then again, Enid had had to explain away a body and a gun to servants who'd actually seen blood splattered on the walls behind Walter's bed and soaking into the sheets beneath his corpse. But she was quite alone in the bungalow tonight and she'd already seen to it there'd be no body to find and no murder weapon either.

As for the authorities, it was a comfort Enid seemed not to have worried anybody at Government House may think Walter's drinking provided her a motive for murder. Which was fair enough, since even for Sherlock Holmes it would have been an almighty leap from suspecting a wife was disappointed in her husband, to suspecting she'd killed him. And no, thought Rose, no, it needn't overly worry her all the gossips of BB knew full well about la midinette and Frank's by-blows, or so she'd assumed ever since she'd learned Mrs Dabney-Dent was privy to the facts. So what if they knew? So what if they assumed, correctly, that she too by now must know what they had known all along? They would none of them think her sense of betrayal could have led her to do away with her husband; more likely they'd all pretty quickly forget she'd had reason to be angry with him at all. Or at least they'd assume that in the face of his death she'd put her anger aside. After all, death changed things. Frank's death changed things. Once it were known he was dead then everyone, would assume the immensity of her loss had erased her resentment – had washed it right away, as a wave washes away a message in the sand. Suspect her? No, everybody would feel sympathy for her – a bride become so soon a widow, and That Way too.

Or so argued Rose, to whom wishful thinking, whether

justified or not, had by now become essential. And, she told herself, and after all, she only had to come up with a plausible story. A story to convince and to mislead, first the local Malays – her servants and the villagers – and afterwards the white people in BB. Granted, she'd never before thought of herself as a skilful liar – except, perhaps, to Mummy, she'd certainly told some half-truths there – but she was sure she could lie as fluently as a horse trader to spare herself the noose. Yes, with her life quite probably at stake, she could surely, surely, come up with a better cover story to explain Frank's disappearance than Enid had provided to explain the bullet hole in Walter's chest. Shooting himself in a fit of delirium tremens indeed! On first reading her mother's letter, Rose had been quite unable to believe Enid had ever persuaded anyone to swallow such nonsense, and she remained just as incredulous now; she was quite confident she could do better.

18

The pre-dawn darkness was tinged with grey and Rose could tell from the light that it was well past six. She'd barely slept. She'd been kept awake by memories and, when once or twice she'd nodded off, she'd been prodded back to wakefulness by the beginnings of tormenting dreams. But now morning had arrived at last, as mornings generally did, although they never again would for Frank, and here was Boy, knocking. She sat up in bed, irreproachably decent in her white night gown and she took a few deep breaths, readying herself for performance.

"Come in!"

Boy entered her room, carrying the tea tray.

"You're late."

"Sorry, Ma'am."

He was clearly on edge, thought Rose, whereas her own watchful wariness was, she trusted, well-disguised. She reminded herself it was not the servants' place to question either her manner or what she told them. If she remained self-possessed, Boy would remain deferential. Meanwhile, should she ask him what was the matter? She decided against; better to wait for him to speak, she decided – to tell her what she already knew.

Usit was indeed agitated, and as he set down the tray and opened the jungle curtains around Rose's bed, he struggled to keep his face its usual impassive mask. He poured her a cup of tea, handed it to her with a distracted air, and cleared his throat. He summoned his best English.

"Talk, please."

Rose looked at him, all faux innocence.

"Yes? What is it?"

Usit blushed.

"Is tuan here?" he mumbled. "In room. With you?"

Rose laughed gaily.

"You can see he's not."

"In night?"

Rose bolted upright against her pillows; she had no need to act that she was affronted.

"I say! Where he was earlier is none of your concern."

Usit was mortified. And yet, stubborn, he persisted.

"In bathhouse?"

"What d'you mean? Are you asking me if the tuan is this very minute bathing in my bathhouse?"

Usit nodded.

"Don't be ridiculous! You surely know where he is. If he's not already at breakfast, then he's still in his own room, and if you've not yet taken him his cup of tea you'd better jump to it, young man."

Usit gave up trying to keep his face a mask. He looked as he felt: miserable and anxious. It didn't help that he knew by now the spirits had granted the mem an embryo – all the servants had learned it, within a day of Nony's knowing, and in any case she was beginning to show. Alamak! Nobody would want to frighten a woman who was cooking a dumpling.

"Tuan gone," he said.

"Gone? What d'you mean, *gone?*"

"Not with you. Not in room. Not in bathhouse."

Rose frowned.

"But what's the time? Quarter past six?"

"Half past."

"This is most irregular."

Actually it was entirely unprecedented, but Usit didn't know how to say so in English.

"Gone," he repeated forlornly.

"Gone where?"

In reply, Usit merely looked at the mem blankly.

"Perhaps he went early to attend to business in the courthouse?"

Usit shook his head.

"Never do that. Never last time."

"Never before? Well, there's a first time for everything, go and check!"

It took under fifteen minutes for Usit to establish that Frank was nowhere in the courthouse, but by the time he returned to inform the mem of this, she was bathing, so, on his own initiative, he organised the servants to conduct a thorough search of the entire compound.

When Rose emerged onto the verandah for breakfast, Usit was hovering.

"Tuan not in courthouse," he blurted.

"Not at the courthouse?"

Usit shook his head,

"All looking everywhere for him now. Water-carrier, night watchman. All looking all over compound."

"Jolly good. I'm sure they'll find him."

Before he and Cookie went off to help with the search, Usit served Rose her breakfast: two poached eggs coated with a jungle approximation of hollandaise sauce. They seemed to Rose to gaze up at her from the plate like jaundiced eyes and, as with the moon and her reflection last night, she briefly wondered: Frank's eyes? But no. No. Though she was nominally a Christian and observed the pieties, she hadn't a scrap of faith; now she told herself not to be a daisy. The dead were not just gone beyond reach but gone. Gone beyond all possibility of earthly contact, gone beyond looking, gone beyond being seen, gone beyond the bounds of reciprocal bonds – bonds of love, bonds of loathing. Gone.

Rose didn't have much appetite, nonetheless she forced herself to eat her eggs for appearance's sake, and by the time she'd finished them Usit was back to report what was scarcely news to her.

"Tuan not in compound," he said. "I look-look everywhere. All look-look everywhere and no see."

Rose affected not to understand.

"What d'you mean, he's not in the compound?"

"He not here. I also help look. We all look. Me. Cookie, water-carrier …"

Rose cut him off.

"Yes, yes." She paused. "Well where is he, then?"

Usit shrugged unhappily.

"Gone."

"Don't be silly! There's nowhere for him to go to." Rose drummed her fingers on the breakfast table, a moment. "Go and ask in the kampung! Perhaps he had some business there. Perhaps he's holed up in one of the houses, investigating a theft of chickens or something."

Usit shook his head.

"Bulan Penuh, last night."

"What has that to do with it?"

"Everyone very party-party. Nobody steal chicken last night."

"How can you be so sure? A party? The perfect cover for a thief."

Again Usit shook his head.

"No thief last night, all drink palm toddy, not steal." He paused and he added, "Tuan know not do business in kampung today. No business after palm toddy."

Rose made a dismissive gesture.

"Go and ask in any case. Even if you all have thick heads, somebody may have seen him."

The kampung was unusually quiet this morning, as the villagers slept off their hangovers. Despite – because of – what everybody knew to be their requited loathing, Usit reasoned that if anybody had seen the tuan then it would be Nony, so he first went to her house. It was still closed up for the night; he had to yell from the ground to rouse anybody.

Nony was cross to be woken. She didn't hurry as she changed her sarong and when she eventually opened up her house and clambered down the ladder to answer Usit's summons, her irritation was plain.

"What is it?"

Usit, fluent of course in his native Malay, didn't beat about the bush.

"Have you seen the tuan this morning? Or perhaps after the celebrations last night?"

Nony hadn't clapped eyes on Baba since she'd told him she wouldn't leave the kampung. She suspected Usit was mocking her and she was most put out.

"Is that a serious question?"

Usit nodded.

"He's nowhere about the compound. Not in the bungalow. Not in the courthouse. I thought perhaps ... ?"

Nony scowled, and she snapped, "Well you thought wrong."

Usit shuffled.

"The mem sent me to check for him in the kampung."

"Go and check then!" said Nony, and with that she climbed back up her ladder and replaced the panel in the entryway. For the next few hours, until she learned Baba was well and truly missing – indeed probably never coming back – she more or less forgot all about him.

When Usit returned to the DO's bungalow, he found Rose sewing on the verandah. It was too complicated to give her a full account of his investigations in English and so he summarised his searches, "Tuan not in kampung. Nobody see him."

Rose affected exasperation.

"Well I can't think where he is."

Usit was becoming more and more afraid to speculate. He stared straight ahead of him, saying nothing.

"He mentioned a bit of a rum do upriver," Rose lied. "A dispute between the headmen of two adjacent kampungs – something to do with the death of a water buffalo greatly prized by one of them, apparently. Perhaps he went to sort it all out."

Usit pursed his lips. It was beyond him to point out in English that the tuan would never leave without telling anybody, and certainly not in the night. He contented himself with saying, "Perahu still at landing stage."

Rose flinched at this mention of the landing stage. She warned herself to keep her voice steady and her gaze open and frank.

"Perhaps the buffalo people sent messengers who arrived in the night and insisted he must go with them to their kampung at once, immediately, to deal with the emergency, and he went with them in their perahu."

Usit noticed the mem flinch; it was with distress at another dead end, he assumed, and this talk of a buffalo was surely nothing but a fairy tale she'd conjured to keep her courage up. He spoke gently, "Malays not travel far at night. Short and know the path only. Know well the way."

"I'm not talking about taking an unknown path. I'm talking about floating down the river. Or up it, I suppose."

Usit shook his head.

"*Hantu. Ponitanak.* Many danger. Too much keep an eye out, in the dark."

"Hantu? Pontianak?"

"Hantu ghost," explained Usit. "Pontianak …" He hesitated. Ponianak were female ghouls who killed their male victims by ripping off their genitals. He rather wished he hadn't mentioned them to the mem. "Pontianak also ghost."

"Ghosts!" dismissed Rose. "Perhaps he took his gun, like he does, and went for some sport in the jungle?"

"In night?"

"The full moon. He'd have been able to see the prey well enough."

Usit again shook his head.

"Trees make roof. No light under leaf roof. Bulan Penuh same-same every other day."

"Perhaps he took a lantern."

"Many danger," Usit repeated. "Hunter hunted, in night."

"That's as may be," said Rose. "In any case, go and see if his gun's in the gun cupboard!"

Usit very quickly confirmed what both he and Rose had anyway known all along: Frank had not gone for a spot of night time sport in the jungle.

"Gun in gun cupboard," he told Rose, after he'd made the pointless check.

By now it was getting on for tiffin, and Rose decided enough of the sensible briskness, she'd better start showing a little wifely concern.

"Well, I just can't think where he can be," she said, with a brave, and quite deliberate, quiver to her voice. "Wherever he is, let's hope he turns up for tiffin."

Frank, of course, did not turn up for tiffin. And nor, afterwards, did he turn up for the lie-off. Rose wrung her hands as she instructed the servants that notwithstanding the absence of the tuan, they should take their rest. She said there was nothing anybody could do for the next couple of hours, except to hope that the tuan strolled into the compound, oblivious to the worry he'd caused. She said, too, that there was simply no point in everybody becoming exhausted. She herself then went to her room for her own lie-off.

As in the night, Rose did not sleep, but this time it wasn't memories and the threat of tormenting dreams keeping her awake. As she lay on her bed, her rounded belly ever so slightly bulging, something radiant happened: Baby quickened. She felt, she thought, a fish wriggling inside her – inside her most secret hollow. But it wasn't a fish. Rose knew at once what the strange sensations meant: they meant that joy, for her, was even now not out of reach. Yes, she rejoiced to feel her baby move; she rejoiced as she would have done if she hadn't just killed his father.

And, thought Rose, Baby's quickening meant something else too: it was a reminder from fate, as if one were needed, that she must not swing. If she swung, Baby would be orphaned. If she swung, Baby, defenceless, would be left all forlorn. Not to mention if she swung, then it would be because the truth had been revealed to a court, to court reporters, to newspapers, to the world at large. Hence in all probability Baby would one day learn of it, no matter how those around him – Mummy, probably – no matter how Mummy tried to shield him from it ... Oh God, how Mummy's life would become a void if she swung ... But she must not distract herself by imagining her proud mother's crumpling. Her concern, now, must be all for Baby. And Baby must not learn the truth. Not ever. So then, there must be no judge in a black cap pronouncing her death sentence, for Baby's sake, there must not. Hadn't she once argued it was her job to see to it he was never disgraced by his father's shaming behaviour? Well, then, the same went for her own behaviour, too, his mother's behaviour. Baby must never be disgraced, shamed, tainted or sullied by it. He must never be belittled or dishonoured by it. And so he must be protected from all knowledge that his mother was a killer, just as, she'd argued, he must be protected from all knowledge of his father's debauchery. Furthermore, if her child learned the truth, he'd feel such revulsion for her, such disgust. Well! That was something Rose simply couldn't allow; she couldn't have it, her child despising her posthumously. Granted, if she were dead, she'd be unable to feel the lash of her child's disdain, but to anticipate it now, whilst yet she lived, was torture enough. Her child must judge her a wonderful woman, wonderful, the best mother any child could ever have. And for that to happen, she'd have to live. No, she reiterated, no, she mustn't swing, for Baby's sake, she must live to keep her secrets.

After the lie-off, Rose decided it was high time to get her story out. It was a very simple story and it's simplicity, she trusted, would help keep her safe. She summoned Usit to the verandah. Mistress and servant faced each other across the planter's chair where Frank had been wont to sleep in the afternoons and to booze in the evenings. Rose wrung her hands and she spoke, she hoped, with anguish.

"I've been thinking and thinking what can have happened to the tuan."

"In kitchen also, Ma'am."

"I've got an idea."

"Yes, Ma'am?"

"You know there was nobody here last night but the tuan and me, because of bally pinoo. I wonder if after I went to bed, the tuan heard some noise and thought it was either an intruder, or a tiger? Perhaps he went to investigate. Perhaps he took a lantern, and perhaps he didn't. Perhaps he let himself out of the compound, thinking he'd only go a little way beyond the fence. Perhaps he followed the noise just a little way off the path, down an animal track, thinking he knew the area so well he couldn't possibly get lost. Perhaps he followed the noise, just a little further, a little further and … and …" Rose stuttered into silence, hopeful that Usit would catch her meaning.

Usit did. Rose's story aligned almost exactly with speculation in the kitchen hut. Just as Rose claimed to do, the servants thought it likely Frank had last night gone to investigate some disturbance, some animal grunting or crashing, just beyond the compound. This they judged reckless behaviour, given the dangers of the night – not to mention the previously full, now almost-empty, whisky bottle he'd left on the verandah indicated he'd been tipsy. Still, this sort of thing was nothing less than they'd have expected from the crazy Mat Salleh. As to what had happened next? The villagers didn't often lose someone to the jungle, but about every third or fourth year, a lurking forest hantu, jealous of the living and spiteful, lured an unfortunate child, or a man out hunting, deep into the great maw of the swallowing green, and then deeper, and then far too deep for escape. And if the tuan hadn't fallen victim to a forest hantu, then perhaps he'd been caught by a river one. After all, river hantu were more dangerous, even, than the crocodiles which shared their home. Perhaps one had spotted the tuan on the riverside path and had whipped out a watery arm-tentacle thingy to pull him into the water, to pull him under, to drown him just for the fun of it. But whatever the precise details, the servants were of one mind: the tuan had paid dearly for his silly drunken swagger in leaving the compound, alone and unarmed at night. And if by some miracle he wasn't yet dead, then he very soon would be, unless he were found double quick chop-chop.

When Rose stuttered into silence, Usit swallowed, and he nodded gravely.

"Perhaps do search party. Village men go look-see in jungle."

Rose wished she could weep at this ominous suggestion. But, alas, she seemed unable to weep for anything. She felt quite numb; she was numbed to callousness, she supposed; numbed to nothing. She managed to inject into her voice a tremble.

"Yes. A search party. I suppose it's time."

"And men in dugouts look-see at riverbanks."

Rose's stomach spasmed with terror as it occurred to her, for the first time, that Frank's corpse could have washed to the bank a little downriver after she'd lost it to sight last night. If it had, would it be found? Probably not. The obscuring vegetation. Probably it would already have been dragged into a tiger's lair. But if the worst happened and it were discovered complete, or nearly so, she'd postulate to the natives that Frank must have fallen and split his head on a rock, before slipping unconscious into the river. Still, tears now at last welled at the corners of her eyes, and, as she dabbed them away, she was no longer acting.

Usit was moved to see the mem dab her eyes like that. How brave she was to resist weeping at the terrifying prospect her husband was lost. For himself, he struggled to remain composed – indeed, as he thought of the tuan scrabbling in the jungle, he found tears spilling down his own cheeks. He didn't wipe them away and as his tears fell he told himself precisely what Rose had hoped he'd tell himself: that whatever troubles there had been between the tuan and the mem, and the spirits knew there had been plenty, they must all have been erased for the mem now. They must have been rubbed away by the immensity of her husband's disappearance – of what might have happened to him, and probably had. He thought her courage was most affecting; it was most affecting, such self-possession in a pregnant woman who was probably no longer a wife, but a widow.

UNSCHEDULED OUTBOUND MAIL, MAY 1925

From Rose to Mr Hollingworth

Dear Sir,

I have today ordered the perahu sent to BB and in it our most trusted native clerk, that he may deliver to you this note.

I have most distressing news to report: my husband has vanished. He disappeared three days ago. I last saw him the night before on the verandah where we'd been sitting together; it was a perfectly ordinary evening and I went to bed as usual, leaving him to sit up a little longer, reading. When the boy went to wake him in the morning, he was not in his room. Indeed, he was nowhere in the compound, nor in the local kampung. He was absent all morning and when he had not reappeared by late afternoon, it seemed the only thing was to suppose that for reasons obscure he must have left the compound, in the night or very early, without breathing a word to anyone. And then he must have got lost in the jungle. So in any case we presumed, my servants and I, and it was decided to get up a search party. At sunrise the next day, a group of Malays commenced looking for him in the forests hereabouts. They kept up their searches all that day and yesterday, but there is nowhere any trace of my husband and, though they are looking now, I have been made to understand the Malays will not search again tomorrow as they think it's hopeless.

I cannot accept their pessimism and I confess myself worried to death. I ask now for your guidance about what next to do. You will perhaps think it is not relevant, but I am with child, as perhaps you know, and I feel quite overwhelmed and alarmed here without my husband.

Yours faithfully, Mrs Frank Langham

19

The heat was simmering, as per, and Mr Pinner was stewing at his desk in the anteroom outside Mr Hollingworth's office. A worker had recently run amok on a rubber estate about 50 miles along the coast to the west, and the planter, Mr Kemper, had shot him dead, thus sparking all his other workers to riot, so Mr Hollingworth was not in his office today; he was out at Kemper's place, showing the flag – along with a contingent of soldiers dispatched from BB's small cantonment. Mr Pinner was grateful the chief was absent; once again, he found himself holding a letter from Kluanak – indeed, a bombshell. This time he could scarcely reply with a brush-off. This time he could scarcely rip up the letter and toss the scraps in his waste-paper bin; after much dithering that was what he'd eventually done with the recent notes from Langham, both the one to the chief and the subsequent one to him. Moreover, as he reread Mrs Langham's plea for help, it occurred to him he may be implicated in this bad business at Kluanak. Such was his distress, he decided he'd slip out of the office for half an hour and take this note home to Mary, to see what she made of things.

Mrs Pinner was most surprised when her husband came home in the middle of the morning and interrupted her as she was doing the flowers – her weekly pleasure, for she most enjoyed flower arranging and loved to fill her rooms with vases of ginger lilies and other blooms. She had this week's fresh flowers piled on a work table on the verandah. When her husband arrived, she was trimming the tough stems of torch gingers. She put aside her secateurs, wiped her hands and took the note he proffered.

Mr Pinner watched her read. Stricken, he said, "I'd like to think it's all a mistake. That Mrs Langham's got everything wrong and Langham isn't lost at all. But it's not crossed wires, is it. He probably is lost, isn't he. And if lost, the Malays know it well enough: he's dead."

Mrs Pinner continued reading a moment and then she lowered the note.

"Lost, yes. Dead? Surely he may still turn up?"

"Three days he'd been missing, before Mrs Langham wrote ... four days now." He paused and counted in his head. "Or even five."

"Four, five, six, seven, he knows the jungle well, he'll be able to find water, food."

"True ... perhaps he's built himself a shelter?"

"Perhaps he has."

Mr Pinner swallowed, and shuffled where he stood.

"But if he is dead ... It couldn't possibly be a deliberate act, could it? Langham's losing himself like that?"

Mrs Pinner flinched. Suicide? she thought, with a shudder of mingled horror and distaste. She understood at once what her husband was thinking: from kindness, he'd thwarted Langham's attempt to leave Kluanak; he now worried his well-intentioned meddling might have been the final straw that had pushed a fellow at the end of his tether over the edge – or, rather, into the jungle, with the intention never to re-emerge.

But, thought Mrs Pinner, if in fact Langham were dead, and if, too, John bore any blame for this, then so did she. If one of them were guilty of having a hand in driving a man to his death, then they both were. After all she was the one who'd suggested John write to tell Langham not to be a fool and then to lose his note. Should she feel remorse about her advice? Oh, she felt remorse all right that her suggestion had perhaps been unfair to Mrs Langham, that side of things bothered her still, but should she also feel remorse that the way she and John had acted together to foil and frustrate poor Langham's quite understandable desire to quit Kluanak had led him to feel such despair he'd taken his own life?

Mrs Pinner couldn't think she should, for even if Langham were dead she couldn't think this was suicide. Not at all. Suicide was so ... so ... final, so terminal. Except for those left behind. Those left wondering. For them it was so definitively not-terminal. And however unhappy Langham had been at the mess he'd made of his life, specifically, perhaps, at his inability to remove his wife from the vicinity of his former nonya, she couldn't think he'd have acted so rashly or so cruelly as to kill himself, and leave his wife beset, forever, by questions. She was in the family way, for heaven's sake! He'd had so much to live for.

Mrs Pinner met her husband's eye, and she spoke at last, "The closeness with which Langham's getting lost followed on your dashing of his hopes about a transfer must be coincidence, that's all."

"You think so?" said Mr Pinner miserably. Oh, he knew well enough suicide was a jolly poor show, servants of empire didn't fall on their swords – or plunge into the jungle – on account of things like letters telling them to pull their socks up and stop making loony demands, but he felt grim about all this, he really did.

"Of course I think so!"

"But that note I sent him, I can't help worrying I came over more pompous, more censorious than I'd have liked."

Mrs Pinner, who'd not seen her husband's note, thought this possible. Still,

"I'm sure you didn't. And from what you said, Langham's reply scarcely suggested desperation. If he'd been distraught about staying in post, he'd have written again to Hollingworth in the teeth of your advice."

"I suppose."

"John!" said Mrs Pinner. "It's only common sense. Has Langham ever shown signs of mental instability?"

"Not to my knowledge."

"Well there you go, then."

"Although living in the jungle could cause anyone to snap."

"Not a level-headed fellow like Langham. If he took himself off into the jungle in the middle of the night, he must have thought he'd heard intruders, or a tiger perhaps."

Mr Pinner groaned. He said, "Whatever happened, I'd better own up. When Hollingworth gets back tomorrow I'd better tell him I wrote to Langham quite off my own bat. No doubt he'll tear a strip off me."

Mrs Pinner spoke patiently.

"You're his secretary. It's your job to spare him trouble, to screen his mail. He'll thank you for dealing with Langham's request sensibly and briskly, he'll not accuse you of anything."

"Thank me?" said Mr Pinner. "I can't see it, somehow. And I'll have to tell him about Langham's nonya. His jungle family."

"You don't need to mention them, surely?"

"I'd better. If Langham's dead, then, as investigations are launched and recriminations fly, even our oblivious chief must soon enough discover that as a bachelor he kept a nonya. Since it's inevitable someone will say something, I suppose it had better be me – best, in the long run, if I speak up now."

Mrs Pinner frowned.

"If Langham's dead, then out of respect, even Mrs Alford will stop her tattle. And Langham didn't confess to Mr Hollingworth when he so easily could have done – when it would have been better for him, perhaps, to have done. But he didn't. If he's still alive he'll thank you for not confessing on his behalf either, so to speak, and if he's dead all the more reason not to have said anything. A man no longer able to defend himself, no longer able to explain." She paused. "Anyway, if Hollingworth did discover all, you could always lie the nonya business was as much news to you as it was to him."

Mr Pinner shook his head.

"You think he'd swallow that? Easier to imagine him barking how long had I known it for and why the devil hadn't I told him." He scowled down at the flowers heaped on the table and he said to the torch gingers, "Blast it! One way or another, I'm in for a most awful roasting."

All the rest of that day Mr Pinner willed another boat to come from Kluanak, in quick pursuit of the first, saying Langham had turned up after all. But it didn't. Which was too ghastly for words for Langham and Mrs Langham and, frankly, not all that much better for him. He slept badly that night, and first thing the next morning he steeled himself to share Mrs Langham's note with Mr Hollingworth. Though, with the rational part of him, he knew Mary was probably right – his had been a trivial administrative intervention – and though too, in the matter of spilling the beans about the nonya, his dear wife thought best not to, he remained convinced it would be in his own best interests both to reveal to the chief what he'd taken it upon himself to do and also to enlighten him about the gaiety of Langham's bachelor days.

Mr Hollingworth re-read the note from Mrs Langham with mounting irritation. He felt affronted that one of his DOs had disappeared. Causing such a terrible flap was scarcely showing the flag. And lost in the jungle indeed! Leaving the compound at night? Wandering about? Highly improbable. Mrs Langham may believe her husband could have been so irresponsibly deranged, but he had a hunch this was not a simple case of a man getting lost in Kluanak's wretched wasteland of thoroughly excessive vegetation. Call him cynical, say, if you liked, he had the cynicism of an Old Malaya Hand, but far more likely, to his mind, Langham had been lured from his bungalow by men with murderous intent.

Natives, and their vendettas! And Langham had been nothing if not cocky. He remembered their last meeting: had the fool not dared to argue over his posting? Yes, he always had been an uppity fellow. Chippy, like any so-called Englishman born in the colonies. Well then, the Saramantanese, though childlike, didn't take too well to cockiness. Made them as reckless as schoolboys. Led to all sorts of jiggery-pokery. And his gut now told him he was confronted at Kluanak with a dangerous case of native dark dealing.

Alas, though Mr Hollingworth's gut was correctly suspicious of Rose's version of events and though too it was quite right a crime had been committed at Kluanak, it now thoroughly misled him. It wasn't hard to do, since he had the smugly misplaced trust in his own superior gut feeling of any tyrant, whether of the petty variety or one strutting his arrogance on the world stage. So if is his gut told him, as it did now, that his upstart DO, Langham, had come to a sticky end courtesy of resentfully disgruntled Malays, or one of their number at any rate, then that was what had happened, as far as he was concerned.

And, by God, if a native had murdered a white man, then, debarring only the rape and murder of a white woman or a white child, it was the worst, most barbaric, wickedest of crimes. An outrage. Abominable. Certainly, in such cases justice must always be seen to be done.

Or, rather, justice must almost always be seen to be done. But dispensing justice sometimes conflicted with the immediate needs of the Empire. Or so thought Mr Hollingworth. And obviously, he thought, obviously when justice and the immediate needs of the Empire clashed, the immediate needs of the Empire took precedence. Yes, to his mind, in a far-flung colony such as his own, a colony where troops were so distressingly few in number, doing the right thing could be construed sometimes as a kind of sedition. Contradictory? Perhaps. But although Mr Hollingworth was sincere in his belief that no Englishman should surrender to native ways, he couldn't have remained in charge as long as he had if he didn't have his little inconsistencies. In his opinion, dressing correctly for dinner was one thing and preventing an uprising quite another, meaning he was prepared to be supple sometimes, even when, on the face of it, a public hanging was required. And, as he reread Rose's note, he couldn't avoid noticing this business at Kluanak had come exactly when the restiveness of the natives on Kemper's estate could so easily become general. So now more than ever hanging a Malay – either the guilty party or any other badmash would do – hanging some or another Malay for any crime at all would be risky. As to hanging a Malay for murdering a white man? Right now, right here on Saramantan, it would be putting a bally spark to a bally powder keg.

Right-o. Mr Hollingworth decided it was not worth risking a revolt, for justice for such as Langham. After all, if his whole bally colony went to blazes, then so too would his own good name, his own reputation for calm and competent management. Still, he mused, it was incumbent upon him to appear to act in the matter of Langham's disappearance; he'd better be seen to be doing something about all this. Indeed, he had no choice, he must send someone to Kluanak to cow the natives. But he'd better not send anyone too effective, that's all. He'd better send somebody unlikely to uncover the truth (the truth according to his gut). Or else a man so pliant he could easily be persuaded to hush up the truth – (ditto) – if he happened to stumble upon it.

Mr Pinner, sitting nervy on the wrong side of Mr Hollingworth's tidy mahogany desk, was becoming more and more agitated by the chief's long silence. He cleared his throat.

"Sir?" he prompted.

Mr Hollingworth looked at him over the top of Rose's note.

"Damned fool!" he said. "Langham."

Mr Pinner decided best not to add fuel to the fire by mentioning he'd recently received a most extraordinary note from the booby, in which he'd only gone and requested a transfer. Since he couldn't think of anything else to say, either, he made an inarticulate sound, intending what he didn't quite know.

Mr Hollingworth interpreted this sound as an expression of agreement. He said, with an exasperation he made no attempt to hide, "Lost in the jungle? Bosh!"

"Sir?"

"Been out here long enough to know never to take anything at face value. And you know the Malays, fine fellows some of them, but their own ways of doing things."

"Sir?"

"It's obvious what's happened."

"It is, sir?"

"A pretty piece of rascality, I call it."

"You do, sir?"

"Your Malay's a touchy creature; takes offence as easily as pie. And Langham could have about him a certain … roughness, shall we say. I'd lay any money he wasn't silky enough in his handling of the natives in his charge. He offended one of their number, ridiculed some fellow in public perhaps and, in consequence, he's now received a kris in the back. He's lying dead on some jungle path, I shouldn't wonder."

Mr Pinner winced to imagine a crinkly-bladed dagger flashing silver through the darkness. Murder? Surely this horrible possibility was a most outlandish one? Mind you, if it were murder, then it couldn't be suicide, which was something – despite Mary's reassurance, he remained troubled on the point. And if the chief's theory were right, and Langham had been murdered by a Malay brooding on injured pride, then it was clear as gin which of the Malays he'd offended: his erstwhile nonya. Or so Mr Pinner now jumped to conclude. Yes, he decided, if Langham had succumbed to skulduggery then there could be little doubt the vengeful nonya had asked one of her brothers, or male cousins, to strike as soon as chance arose, or else one of them had taken it into his head to defend her honour by killing the man who'd defiled it.

Hell! Mr Pinner knew if ever there were a time to alert the chief to the nonya's existence, it was now. He took a deep breath.

"Sir," he plunged. "Sir, I ..."

Mr Hollingworth cut him off by tapping Rose's note. He flourished it to eye-level and he read aloud, "*I ask now for your guidance about what next to do.*" He lowered the letter again. "I'll have to send someone to investigate." He stared directly at Mr Pinner. "I'll have a devil of a job sparing anyone."

Mr Pinner swerved from what he'd intended to say. He asked,

"Will you send Gregson?"

Mr Hollingworth affected astonishment.

"What? The chief inspector of police himself?"

"Perhaps excessive."

"Gregson's got his hands full with miscreants on Kemper's estate."

"A bad show that." Mr Pinner thought a moment. "Braddle? Nobody more thorough."

Mr Hollingworth said nothing, he simply looked Mr Pinner up and down: once, twice, he looked him up and down. Mr Pinner supposed he must feel rather as a sheep must feel as the butcher approached it with a knife.

"Braddle?" he repeated nervously.

Mr Hollingworth shook his head.

"We're so damnably short-handed," he said.

"Sir?"

"All hands to the pump. Men doubling up duties, if needs be. You know how it is."

"Sir?"

"May as well be you, I suppose."

For a moment, Mr Pinner failed to understand. But then he cottoned on. He forgot himself sufficiently to show his surprise.

"Me?" he jibbed. "Me? Investigate what's doing at Kluanak?" By Jove, he simply couldn't think of anyone less suited to the task.

Mr Hollingworth was facetious.

"Come, come, you think you're indispensable here, do you?"

"Not at all, sir. It's just I rather thought you'd want to send a police officer and I've no experience of police work."

Mr Hollingworth smiled at Mr Pinner his smile that wasn't a smile. He said, "Part of ruling well is realising that sometimes, as the rulers, and being so few in number here on Saramantan, we Britons must be more pragmatic than we would be at Home – indeed almost as flexible and fluid in our thinking as those we rule."

Mr Pinner entirely failed to keep up. He looked at the chief blankly.

"Sir?"

"I told you: Langham took a kris in the back for offending one of the Malays. We'll never get to the bottom of it. You know Malays, vague at the best of times and scarcely averse to lying. In a case like this they'll close ranks whatever it was all about and whomever I send. All you'll have to do is show the flag and put the frighteners on them, so they know they can't make a habit of this sort of thing."

"Put the frighteners on them?" echoed Mr Pinner, thinking how the deuce was he supposed to do that?

Mr Hollingworth nodded and then he tapped his nose.

"But best keep it hush-hush," he warned.

"Sir?"

"Best not to let on for now we think Langham's been murdered. Later, perhaps, but in the meantime, don't want to rile the natives." He paused. "Further rile." He paused again. "Don't want to frighten the horses, either."

"Sir?"

"Don't want to put the fear of god into our ladies who'll all go thinking they'll be next. Don't want to stir up some of our hotter fellows into shooting a few natives in retaliation."

Mr Pinner merely stared at Mr Hollingworth, his mouth a little agape.

Mr Hollingworth nodded again, this time solely to himself.

"May as well remain at Kluanak," he said. "Just until I can find a replacement for Langham."

Mr Pinner hated being separated from Mary and his daughters. He swallowed, making his Adam's apple bob, and he risked saying, "I do hope it won't be too long, sir."

"Shouldn't be more than a few weeks." Mr Hollingworth slid Rose's note back across his gleaming desk. "That'll do."

By the devil! When Mr Pinner left Mr Hollingworth's office he felt thoroughly wrung out. And his day didn't get any better as news of what was doing at Kluanak gradually oozed like lava along the corridors of Government House. All sorts of fellows stopped by his desk to chew things over, and some of them were senior to him, so he could scarcely refuse their requests to read Rose's note. He felt all at sea as he fielded questions. It jangled him he couldn't go against the chief's express wishes and let on to the doubtful idea Langham's disappearance could have been down to foul play. Furthermore, since he'd failed to spit out to the chief anything about it, nor did he feel he could mention Langham's recent request for a transfer.

The walls of Government House could not stop the lava flow of gossip. By the next day it was all over town that Langham had disappeared into the thick green air of the jungle and that Pinner, Lord love him, was to be sent upriver to investigate. And notwithstanding her pregnancy was merely domestic news of little interest to any of the men who'd actually read her note, it had also got out that Mrs Langham was pregnant – intelligence Mr and Mrs Pinner had previously kept to themselves.

Mr Alford, head of the Forest Service, was currently doing field work in the north of Saramantan. Mrs Alford, the colony's arch rattler, thought it too bad Gerald was off with his trees just when she needed him most in Government House. Still, Gerald or no Gerald, she had her sources and she was confident she now knew something none of her friends did.

Mrs Gregson, wife of the chief inspector of police, was a fading blonde whose intelligence had never been shining. Today was her birthday and she was throwing a little tea party on the verandah of the Club to celebrate. Mrs Alford was the first to arrive. The two friends exchanged greetings and knowing looks; immediately they set to discussing the sensational developments at Kluanak. Mrs Langham's pregnancy! Mr Langham's disappearance! Craftily, Mrs Alford refrained from yet mentioning the tidbit of extra information dear Maude had sent her; revelation would be wasted on an audience of one, she felt.

Nearly an hour later, Mrs Pinner was the last to arrive. She'd rather have cried-off entirely, but to have done so would have been horribly rude. The moment she joined the other ladies, she confirmed, from the shiver of excitement in the air and the avidity of their expressions that it would be exactly as she'd supposed – she'd now not only be forced to endure discussion of poor Langham's fate, she'd also have to face a grilling about John's unexpected, unfortunate and temporary redeployment as a police officer.

After the usual gushing pleasantries, Mrs Alford returned to the topic of the hour. She looked at Mrs Pinner through her sharply observant eyes and she smiled at her a toothy smile.

"So your husband's off to see what's what at Kluanak?"

Mrs Gregson gestured with a large hand and she relayed, without any regard for Mrs Pinner's feelings, her husband's opinion, "William thinks Hollingworth's decision is an absolute stinker."

"I cannot disagree," said Mrs Pinner.

"Not at all," said Mrs Alford. "A chance for him to shine. The clever detective solving things."

"If there's anything to solve," said Mrs Pinner.

Mrs Alford shook her head.

"There are always little mysteries to solve. And I'm sorry but I do call it fishy. Surely there's more to this – Langham's vanishing like that – than meets the eye?"

Mrs Pinner reached for her cup and took a sip of her tea. Though he'd sworn her to silence, John had of course confided in her the chief's idea that in Langham's disappearance they had an insoluble murder on their hands. He'd added that in the unlikely event the chief was onto something, then the blasted nonya must be the prime, indeed the only, suspect. Far from being scared out of her wits by the thought of natives slaying white men and, more particularly, white women, Mrs Pinner had dismissed the whole idea of murder as perfectly ridiculous. She'd said never mind the nonya, it was all too sensational for words; impossibly lurid.

Still, even if she'd been free to, she'd never have dreamed of telling Mrs Alford any of this. She replaced her cup on its saucer and she said, "It was probably exactly as Mrs Langham surmised: Langham left the compound at night for some trivial reason unknown, stumbled off the path and couldn't find his way home."

Mrs Gregson looked doubtful.

"Trivial reason? William says Langham probably got lost on his way to an assignation of no innocent purpose."

Debarring only Mrs Pinner, who stared straight ahead, the ladies exchanged looks of conniving archness, as they all imagined Langham creeping into the jungle at night to meet his former nonya, the brassy strumpet.

"Perhaps he did," agreed another lady. "Perhaps, from misguided kindness, Langham had decided to tell the nonya his wife was expecting and he got lost on his way to, or from, their rendezvous."

Mrs Alford gave a self-important wriggle, "Or if not that, perhaps he wanted to tell her something else."

There was an expectant hush for a beat.

"What else?" obliged Mrs Gregson.

Mrs Alford was determined to drag things out. She smiled around the group.

"I assume you all know Parkin's back," she said.

Parkin was a man all the ladies, including Mrs Pinner, considered quite mad. An Australian naturalist, he'd come all the way from Sydney to investigate the bats of Saramantan. He'd been staying with the Slightmans at Relunas this past fortnight investigating a colony of bats out there, supposed to be particularly interesting if you liked that sort of thing, which none of the ladies did.

"He got back last night, didn't he?" said Mrs Gregson.

Mrs Alford nodded. She said, "Though he's generally too absorbed by bats to pay much attention to humans, he called on me this morning. Brought me a note from dear Maude."

There was another expectant hush.

"And?" prompted Mrs Gregson.

"She's been poorly. Tummy. Could scarcely eat. Unable to leave her bed. Barely able to read, unable to put pen to paper. But nothing to worry about. She's perfectly all right now."

The ladies waited, sure that Mrs Alford had more up her sleeve than Maude's uninterestingly recovered health – a decline was always so much more satisfactory. At last, with relish, their oracle revealed what she knew.

"She mentioned, in passing, Langham had written to Slightman that he was intent on leaving Kluanak." She paused. "At his wife's insistence no doubt. Well, we can all can imagine the conversations between them, can't we."

This morsel had fully the effect Mrs Alford had hoped it would. There was a moment of fizzing silence and then questions began rippling round the group.

"Leave Kluanak? How could they?"

"Where would they go?"

"What would they live off?"

Mrs Pinner shuddered to think what John would make of the ladies of BB gossiping about Langham's desire to leave Kluanak.

"Surely just wishful thinking on Langham's part," she quashed.

One of the other ladies, Mrs Talbot, nodded. She said,

"Leaving sounds most unlikely."

Mrs Alford was having none of it.

"I can't agree." She looked directly at Mrs Pinner. "I gather your husband hasn't mention anything? I mean, Hollingworth's secretary, he'd know if Langham wanted a transfer."

Mrs Pinner lied smoothly. "John hasn't said anything."

Mrs Alford looked regretful. "No?" she sighed. "Well, I expect Maude will tell me all about it in her next. My point now is: perhaps Langham had an assignation with the nonya to tell her he'd be going?"

Mrs Pinner was relieved by Mrs Alford's vagueness – and by Maude's presumed vagueness, too. She decided she needn't mention to John something hazy had seeped out about Langham's request for a transfer. Why worry him further when he already had so much on his plate? After all, rumour was merely rumour, even when it happened to be true.

"An assignation?" she said. "An assignation, my foot!"

Mrs Alford was irritated. Oh, Mrs Pinner did so like to put on her superior airs! "Come, come, my dear!"

Mrs Pinner shrugged.

"Isn't this needlessly complicating what was probably horribly simple?"

"I think it is," agreed Mrs Talbot. "Alone in the jungle at night? Perhaps poor Langham stepped on a cobra."

"Met a tiger."

"Fell and bashed his head."

"Speared himself on a fallen branch."

"Fell in the river."

Mrs Gregson suggested, "Whatever happened, perhaps he drank more than was good for him the night of his disappearance. A man with a thick head wouldn't do very well in the jungle in the dark."

Mrs Alford looked at Mrs Gregson with shrewd intelligence.

"Drunk? Perhaps he was." She swivelled her head and attempted to meet Mrs Pinner's eye. "Do you remember we once saw him decidedly squiffy here?"

Mrs Pinner looked away.

"No," she lied.

"Really? I'm surprised. It was the day he learned he was posted back to Kluanak."

Again, except for Mrs Pinner, the ladies exchanged looks of conniving archness. Mrs Gregson said, "To think of the trouble awaiting him there!"

"Yes," nodded Mrs Alford, "I don't want to speak ill of the ..." She caught herself just in time. "Although it's possible he's still alive, of course. But, I'm sorry, I simply can't help wondering: did he solace the domestic complexities of his life at Kluanak with far too many tiddlies, d'you suppose?"

Tomorrow, Mr Pinner would be leaving BB for Kluanak, taking with him all his worries and uncertainties, all his biases, prejudices and wrong-headed ideas. He and Mrs Pinner had just finished a gloomy evening tiffin, during which he'd made pointed remarks about wild goose chases and she'd expressed considerable unhappiness that she was soon to be deprived of her husband for an unknown length of time. Now they were sitting together in the dark, in rattan chairs they'd pulled to the very edge of their verandah, so they could enjoy the stars sprinkled like salt across the heavens. They were saying little, each of them sunk in their own thoughts, but they held hands across the small space which separated their two chairs.

Eventually, Mr Pinner broke the stretching silence.

"By Jove! I fear lives as operatic as Langham's and Mrs Langham's will be too much for me."

Mrs Pinner transferred her gaze from the stars to her husband's anxious face and she gave his hand a comforting squeeze. He continued,

"I dread seeing Mrs Langham. However angry she was with Langham before he disappeared, now that in all probability she'll never have anything to feel angry with him about ever again she must feel ransacked. And I can't shake the idea she'll blame me for her misery. What if the moment I arrive she lunges for me and accuses: if only you'd put my husband's note up to Hollingworth, he'd never have gone wandering in any jungle. Hell! How will I be able to look her in the eye?"

"Ssh!" said Mrs Pinner. "She may not know Langham ever wrote to Hollingworth, let alone that you replied."

"In the way of things, she must do, surely? And what if ..." Mr Pinner hesitated. He was worried if Mrs Langham knew about his intervention, she could decide to tell tales to Hollingworth. But this was a childish worry, and beneath him. "Oh, nothing."

Mrs Pinner let it slide. She said, "Langham could have been hoping to surprise her with the good news, come the day. When it became evident said day would never arrive, perhaps he simply kept silent?"

"I do hope so," said Mr Pinner, not very hopefully. "But don't forget she seemed unsure whether Hollingworth knew of her pregnancy."

"So?"

"I can only think she knew her husband had written to him of it but that I'd intercepted his note, and with it, probably, her news. She's bound to think if I'd not stuck my oar in, she and Langham could have left Kluanak by now and be getting on with new lives somewhere else."

"Stop it, John!" said Mrs Pinner, and not without a trace of irritation now. "Let's suppose Langham had managed to win for himself a transfer – which he never would have done, I'm sure you were right about that, but let's suppose he had – well then, it wouldn't have happened for months yet. Months and months. He'd be lost now just the same."

Mr Pinner wished he could be convinced. He sighed, and he said, "Lost? He really must be dead by now, either by natural causes or by foul play."

"Foul play? Don't be silly!"

"But what if the chief's right and it's murder?"

"Murder! If Langham's dead, then it's because of his own ill-luck and foolishness not because someone disembowelled him with a kris."

Mr Pinner looker even more mournful than usual. He said,

"Whatever happened, I suppose I'll have to interview the nonya to see what she says about it all." He paused, and then he added, "Even if nothing seems fishy, I suppose I'll have to have a word with the blasted woman."

Mrs Pinner begged to differ.

"If nothing seems fishy you needn't interview anybody at all," she said stoutly. The word *fishy* set off a train of thought. With her inner ear, she heard again Mrs Alford saying *I'm sorry but I do call it fishy. Surely there's more to this than meets the eye?* "Mrs Alford's full of it," she veered. "Langham's disappearance."

Mr Pinner nodded abstractedly.

"Of course she is."

"She's putting it about drink may have had something to do with things. I hate to say it, but I suspect she may be right. If Langham was tipsy when he stumbled into the jungle, then it's perhaps no wonder he's as yet failed to stumble out again."

Mr Pinner now gave his wife his full attention.

"However am I supposed to ask Mrs Langham: was your husband a toper? Was he befuddled by drink when he went and got himself lost?"

Mrs Pinner looked directly at her husband, and she was clear and firm.

"No need to say anything at all about anything at all, unless she does. His drinking, if indeed he did drink more than the usual. His nonya. The children. No, unless she says something, you should pretend to ignorance of everything. It's only polite, and it's only fair, and it's only kind. Poor Mrs Langham! What a rotten time she's had. The humiliation of knowing her husband's former nonya is in the kampung, not to mention seeing light-skinned children running around. And now she must face her husband's probable loss – in the family way, too. No, John, when you see Mrs Langham, unless she chooses to talk about things, then from common decency you must resist alluding to what you know, you must resist alluding to any of it."

Mr Pinner withdrew his hand from his wife's. He kneaded his eyeballs a moment.

"Oh, God!" he said. "Oh, God!"

20

The kampung, Kluanak, May 1925

It was around midnight. In BB, Rose's note to Mr Hollingworth was lying in Mr Pinner's in-tray, in the dark hush of his office, waiting to detonate. In the kampung, where most of the villagers were now sleeping, everybody knew that today the mem had written to Tuan Besar Hollingworth, Great Tuan Hollingworth, to tell him Tuan Langham was lost and that tomorrow there would be no more pointless search parties sent into the jungle to look for what must be, by now, the body.

Nony and First Son were both lying wide awake on their sleeping mats. Neither of them knew the other one was awake. They were both breathing quietly and evenly, and lying as still as they could. Nony shared her sleeping mat with First Daughter, First Son shared his with the twins, and all three of the others were restless sleepers, wriggling and snuffling like puppies, but neither Nony nor First Son thought that was any excuse to risk waking them by tossing and turning. Outside the waning gibbous moon shone bright, but inside the house it was pitch black – once the removable panel had been installed in the entryway very little moonlight and even less starlight sifted in. Likewise, there was no breeze, only warm drafts wafting through the various gaps in the roof, the walls and the floor, so the room was stiflingly hot and the air was soggy and still, and whiffy with the yeasty smells of four people. Cockroaches scuttled, mosquitoes whined and house lizards chorused *geh-ko, geh-ko* up in the roof.

Mind you, it wasn't any of these discomforts or annoyances keeping First Son awake. No, he was worrying and worrying about Baba. He knew, or rather he thought he knew, that three nights ago, on Bulan Penuh, Baba, for some inexplicable Mat Salleh reason, had gone for a walk in the forest alone and he'd not yet come back. Perhaps he was still alive and he would turn up tomorrow. First Son tried to kid himself he may. But he knew what the adults were saying: Baba had been captured by a hantu, either a watery river one or a leafy forest one. Either way, Baba was dead. His poor father! *Baba*, he breathed into the felted air. Now, when it was too late, First Son thought he began to understand just a little bit what the word meant – what it meant about connection to another, and about safety and about belonging. Tonight, for the first time, he had an inkling of what was never to be his and what was never, now, to be his father's either – a loving relationship, or, indeed, any relationship at all, between them. Other boys went fishing with their fathers or learned woodworking from them. Such ordinary things, but when First Son thought of all that may have been, but wasn't now ever to be, he was washed by a sorrow of loss he'd never felt before. He rolled onto his stomach and he let his tears plop silently onto the sleeping mat.

But even as he cried, First Son remembered that earlier time when Baba had gone – when he'd left last year for far-off, unimaginable Kampung Inggris. He remembered that back then he'd very soon realised he had something better to belong to than an indifferent father: a gang. He thought of his gang now, the

gaggle of village children with whom he mostly spent his days, out
of sight of adults. He thought too of his uncles and aunts in the
kampung, of all his kissing cousins amongst the grown-ups. He
listened a moment to the people breathing and snuffling around
him: Bu, his brothers, his sister. He wiped his eyes. He'd be all
right, he thought, with only a hint of a wobble, he'd be all right,
and so would the twins, and so would First Daughter. They'd
be fine as they all four went wheeling into their futures without
Baba.

Nony wasn't worrying about her children, she was worrying
about herself. To think she'd once fretted her life could be made
miserable by the petty retaliations of a vindictive DO. A living
man? The dangers the living could impose on each other were
nothing compared to the dangers the dead could impose on the
living. And now she must face those dangers, so she dreaded the
future, the possible brevity of hers. She roiled with a terror that
had started to swell within her the evening after Bulan Penuh,
when Usit had got together a search party of village men and told
them to be ready to set off next morning at first light to look for
the tuan. By now her fear was such she felt always on the edge of
screaming.

It was obvious to her what had happened: her curse had
succeeded after all. Baba had got his just desserts for dumping
her. But his death now could not make her happy. Alas, she'd
remembered too late that thing she'd quite forgotten when she'd
cursed him: the spirits were not chained by time, the spirits existed
outside time, the spirits could not be expected to notice time

as divvied up, and as experienced, by mortals. Granted, it was over a year now since she'd called down her mirthless, merciless laughing curse on Baba, but did the spirits recognise years? For that matter, did the spirits recognise now? No, thought Nony, no, the spirits had acted in their own sweet obliviousness to time, but acted they most certainly had, so when Baba had gone wandering alone in the forest at night his behaviour hadn't been explained simply by Mat Salleh craziness and he hadn't encountered any old, opportunistic hantu either. Instead, he'd been hounded from the DO's bungalow and into the forest by maddening spirits, ones who'd marked him as doomed, ever since she'd begged them to make him their target.

Oh, the horror! Her desperate peril! If only Baba hadn't died so close to home. If only he'd died where she'd wanted him to die, somewhere at sea, the watery barrier, the salty cage, which would have contained the danger and prevented his ghost from returning to wreak vengeance on her. But he hadn't. The spirits were as oblivious to place as they were to time, it seemed. The spirits had chosen to take Baba now, not then, and here, not there. Meaning his ghost was hanging about somewhere in the vicinity, the non-stuff stuff of it stained dark with the desires for revenge, and for a return to how things had been, but a few days ago. Yes, thought Nony, Baba's jealous ghost must long to find itself once again embodied, so it may live once again in the sensual blaze of the human world and not in the greyly chilly world of the wandering dead, the hungry dead. It must be on the look-out for a body to snatch, a body to occupy. And whose body would Baba's vengeful, resentful ghost occupy, if only it could?

Hers, obviously. Or so trembled Nony. Baba's ghost, she argued, must rightly blame her for its recent change in metaphysical status from person to shadow; for certain it would judge she ought to be the means by which it switched back again, from shadow to person. She was in no doubt Baba's ghost must want her body, in compensation for the body it had lost, thanks to her, and once her body had been occupied by Baba's ghost, then she herself, thus disembodied, would become a ghost. Alamak! Only a fool could have delayed so long – how stupid she'd been to tarry. She needed protection from the supernatural, fast; come the morning, she'd do her utmost to secure it.

It was barely light when Nony set off through the coconut grove towards the pawang's house. She'd got up early to prepare a fish porridge, now she had a big basinful balanced on her hip. First Daughter was toddling along with her. As she walked, Nony remembered with a kind of dull interest that the last time she'd visited the pawang the old woman had said Baba would soon wave the mem goodbye as she left Kluanak for Kampung Inggris, for good. And never mind the little question of whether the bitch had in fact been heading to BB only temporarily, to spawn, clearly there'd been a deeper muddle somewhere: Baba had waved his last and the mem was still in the DO's bungalow. Still, thought Nony, it was not for such as her to ask the spirits, or the pawang, to explain themselves. For that matter, it was not for her to protest if the pawang had failed to predict her curse would work over a year after she'd set it loose and miles and miles off its proper course.

Like everybody, the pawang knew the tuan was dead and, like Nony, she thought she knew why. The morning the search party had set out she'd consulted the oil about his fate and she'd seen no future for him. She'd understood immediately that the curse she'd taught Nony had done the trick, belatedly and in the wrong place by human reckoning, but exactly in its proper place and at its proper lack-of-time by the spirits' reckoning. Notwithstanding her important role in bringing about the tuan's death, she was not especially afraid of his ghost, however near and vengeful. After all, if a man ran amok with a knife, nobody would blame the smith who'd made the knife. Nony was the one with the motive, the one who'd intended the tuan harm, all things being equal. Nony was the one at risk, not her.

But what was the meaning of that risk? The pawang thought she had an inkling. Unlike Nony, she had a few ideas about how to answer to those interesting questions: Why here? Why now? Why had the spirits, in their wisdom, chosen to act here and now, rather than there and then? The pawang was prepared to speculate and she'd done so these past couple of days with both mounting pleasure and with mounting certainty that she'd understood.

And now here was Nony bringing with her that jewel, First Daughter. Though it was early, the pawang was already busy; as mother and daughter came closer, she was standing just outside her ruang, brewing a draught to settle the villagers' upset stomachs. She'd suspended one of her pans on a tripod over a fire and she was using a wooden paddle to stir the bubbling contents; though she didn't stop stirring at the pair's predestined approach, she stared at them through her froggy eyes and she smiled a greedily triumphant and intimate smile.

When Nony arrived by the fire she glanced around, nervous that even here, so close to the pawang and to the many protective amulets stored nearby, Baba's ghost may at any moment pounce, for it must be lurking somewhere hereabouts. Her hand trembled as she silently held out to the pawang the basin of fish porridge.

As she agreed to her payment of food with a nod, the pawang, still stirring, kept her gaze on First Daughter – by the spirits, how she was growing! The little girl, the shining treasure, had already pulled away from the adults, she was making straight for the ruang, where she made a beeline for the pile of animal bones she'd played with once before. She took two long bones, leg bones from a tapir, and began waving them around, one in each hand.

Abruptly, the pawang paused in her stirring and transferred her attention to Nony.

"I've been expecting you," she mumbled.

As ever, Nony took a moment to unscramble her words.

"Because you know I'm in danger," she said, hoping against hope the pawang would say: don't be silly, child, what dangers does life hold for you? But the pawang said nothing at all, instead she did her blinking thing.

Blink. Blink.

"The curse worked. Late, but it worked."

Blink. Blink.

"I killed Baba with witchcraft."

Blink. Blink.

"But his ghost is not held far away, lulled by the rocking cradle of the sea. His ghost is wandering the kampung."

Blink. Blink.

"It wants revenge on me."

Blink. Blink

For a moment the world swirled around Nony and she thought she'd faint. But in fact she didn't even drop the basin of fish porridge. She took a deep breath.

"Can you protect me?" she begged.

The pawang's face remained impassive, but silently, joyfully, she praised the spirits, those most skilful of weavers; those weavers who conjured every pattern of every life, the patterns of life itself, the patterns too of death. The spirits were twisting the threads into a single golden strand – the threads of the tuan's union with Nony, their begetting of First Daughter, his abandonment of her, her curse working only once he'd returned to Kluanak. All of it. It had all been leading to this moment, and to this the only possible outcome, and where had it all begun? With the dawn of the world probably, thought the pawang.

Nony begged again, "Can you protect me?"

The pawang hung the wooden paddle with which she'd been stirring her brew from a hook on the tripod. She jerked her head toward her ruang.

"Come!"

The two women crossed the border of coloured stones and lumps of milky quartz that marked the edge of the pawang's ruang. Inside, they squatted on the mat, where Nony placed the basin of fish porridge between them. First Daughter wandered over and scooped out a big dollop, which she then took back to the pile of bones to eat. Neither her mother nor the pawang minded.

Nony couldn't help sliding her gaze to the trunk where the pawang kept those most precious heirlooms, her funerary amulets. The pawang followed her gaze.

"You're thinking of the skeleton of the two-headed cobra, child."

Nony shivered with mingled hope and hopelessness.

"Perhaps if I could sleep with it in my house … ?"

Though the cobra was one of the most deadly creatures of the jungle, it was at the same time, thought the villagers, by far the most powerfully protective. And of all the powerful amulets in the pawang's locked trunk, the most powerful of all was the skeleton of a two-headed cobra; it was a very old skeleton, said to be a 1000 years old. After funerals, the pawang placed it in the house formerly occupied by the newly deceased, where it guarded the living against the ghost's return and kept at bay as well all those other spirits which thronged to a death, however peaceful.

But now the pawang shook her head.

"Not even that can protect you against the ghost of a man you've murdered with witchcraft."

Nony was so terrified she couldn't speak, she simply stared at the pawang with dumb and pleading dread.

The pawang sighed. "There are things I can do." She paused. "Secret things."

Nony knew better than to challenge: secret things? What secret things? She checked instead.

"They will keep me safe?"

Blink. Blink.

Nony was too wound up to feel much relief.

"When can you start them? Now?"

"No. You must first purify yourself. Have you eaten this morning?"

"I tried, a few mouthfuls of rice. I couldn't manage more."

"A pity. However little, it means we can't start the preparations until tomorrow. You don't have a husband, so no need to worry about no sex. But no food, and nothing to drink but water, from sunrise tomorrow until I'm done with you. Done with the ceremony."

"What ceremony?"

"I can't tell you. And you must promise not to reveal the details afterwards. Not ever. Not to anybody. On pain of death."

"I promise."

The pawang jerked her chin towards First Daughter.

"If you dare ever to breathe a word of the secret rituals, the spirits will crush you as easily as you'd crush a nit plucked between thumb and forefinger from her hair."

"I promise."

Nony and the pawang exchanged a look and then the pawang pursed her lips.

"I will bring three bundles of herbs to your house tomorrow morning. Each sunset, between then and the ceremony, you must burn one bundle and stand naked in the cleansing smoke."

"I can do that."

"You must come here, hunger-scoured and smoke-cleansed, at midnight of the third day. You must be dressed in a white sarong." The pawang pointed upwards, to the room above their heads. "You will remain with me from midnight to midnight, and then to midnight again. Two nights. By sunrise of the next day all shall be accomplished, although you'll be fit for nothing until the following sunrise."

"I understand."

"I can at least tell you this: you will smoke the weed which sends the dreams and drink the fermented juice which fills the world with impossible colour. Nonetheless, there will be pain."

Nony didn't flinch.

"So be it."

"Come the morning of the sixth day, you'll be protected. Once I'm done with you, the tuan's ghost will find you as slippery as an oiled fish; his barbs of black magic will bounce off you like rain bouncing off the river."

"Thank you," said Nony humbly.

The pawang looked crafty.

"There's just one thing," she said.

"What's that?"

"Payment."

"Food? Palm toddy? Cloth? A parang? Anything you want. Name it." Nony remembered the $150 still stashed untouched in a rice sack in her house. That money had come from Baba. Was he determined to deprive her of it from beyond the grave? "I have money," she said, with resignation.

The pawang looked dismissive. She didn't bother to say she had no use for dollars. Instead, she paused to prepare herself to take that golden strand the spirits had spun. She prepared to do as the spirits had ordained she should do. She pointed to First

Daughter, who was now stacking animal bones one on top of the other to make a tower.

"Her."

Nony did a double take.

"What?"

"First Daughter."

"You want my daughter?"

"In return for saving you from the tuan's ghost, yes."

"To look after you?"

"Yes and no. No and yes. I'm getting on. I need to train up my successor before I die, and the spirits have chosen her. I saw it in the oil and you can see it for yourself. Look at her playing with those bones! Remember when she slapped her palms on my trunk, as if it were a drum? Remember she dibbled her fingers in the oil in my divination pan? Your girl. She's the one the spirits have chosen to serve them long into the future."

Nony rocked back on her heels. She was surprised, of course, but she was not hostile to the idea of First Daughter becoming the pawang's apprentice. Indeed, it would be a very great honour to be the mother of a pawang. And the honour would not accrue just to her. If First Daughter became a pawang, she would be as a lamp burning in all her relations' houses – her whole family would be burnished.

Alas, Nony saw a snag.

"But she's a half-caste."

"She's not properly one of us," said the pawang. "I know. I know. Her skin. Her round eyes and her funny nose. She doesn't fit, it's true, but nonetheless the spirits have chosen her. And if the spirits have chosen her, that's all there is to be said about it; everybody will have to accept her or answer to the spirits for it."

Nony let that sink through and then she said, "She's still little. Are you saying she must come to live with you at once?"

"Yes. You'll be able to visit her whenever you like and she'll be able to run home to you whenever she wants, but once I've guided you through the secret rituals, you must bring her to live with me here, that I may begin to teach her magic and the ways of the spirits."

Nony couldn't help wishing the spirits were less impersonal in their attitude to maternity. On the other hand, everybody in the kampung lived so much on top of everybody else she need not be much bothered in which house her daughter officially lived, she supposed, and this way she'd at least have one less mouth to feed. She looked at her daughter – her tower of bones had just fallen down and she was patiently starting to rebuild it. How astonishing that her child – hers! – should be spirit-chosen for an exceptional life. True, if First Daughter became a pawang she'd forever be set a little apart from other people, who'd naturally be in awe of her skills in magic, their awe shading into fear, and she'd probably prove harder to marry off than other girls, but she'd prove harder than others anyway, on account of being tainted with white. In any case, Nony reminded herself, she was in no position to quibble. Really, what choice did she have? And it was after all a fair exchange: the daughter's life for the mother's.

"All right," she said. "All right. You initiate me into the secret rituals and thus protect me against Baba's vengeful ghost, and you can have First Daughter to train up as your successor."

21

The DO's bungalow and the kampung Kluanak, May 1925

Rose knew the administration of Frank's district, or rather, of what had been until so recently Frank's district, must go on regardless of his fate. When she'd sent her note to Mr Hollingworth, she'd trusted he'd think her husband's disappearance an open-and-shut case of misadventure and so she'd hoped he'd send, in response, only an administrator to take over his duties, and not somebody – an official, a police officer, or even officers – to enquire into the way he'd vanished, so bafflingly, without even a trace of a trace.

But she felt dreadfully apprehensive, when, in the late afternoon, Boy came to tell her a perahu had been spotted coming upriver towards the DO's bungalow. Still, she reminded herself, even if she now had to face a whole platoon of police officers, she'd have nothing to fear unless she lost her head and gave herself away. Thus she battened down her nerves, and it was with outward calmness that she was waiting on the landing stage, now become, to her, another sort of stage, to greet Britannia's representative, or representatives, whomever he, or they, turned out to be.

Britannia, it turned out, had sent only one man. And Mr Pinner had never been, so far as Rose was aware, a police officer, which was something. Nonetheless, her nerves resurged as he clambered out of the perahu, it gave her the willies to shake his hand and to exchange with him the customary how d'you dos. It was terribly awkward, too, that this was the man who'd taken it upon himself to dismiss Frank's request for a transfer. She was unable to avoid asking herself whether, if Mr Pinner's meddling had not dashed her hopes of escaping Kluanak, then she would never have bashed Frank with the hammer? If he'd acted differently, then, in turn, would she have done? But who could ever know? And after all, if he'd passed Frank's request upwards, Mr Hollingworth would probably have turned it down. In any case, she could scarcely challenge: what on earth made you think you had the right...She wanted Mr Pinner to feel for her sympathy, not a hostility she'd provoked with her own hostility – hostility may lead him to ask pointed questions. In short, it would be prudent, she decided, to allude neither to Frank's note, nor to Mr Pinner's reply, unless he did so first.

It did not occur to her that Mr Pinner may himself feel miserable and guilty about his note, but such was the case. He was as nervous as she was and, as they shook hands, he prepared to defend himself against angry accusations of interfering. But, thank God, he didn't need to. To his great relief, from the off Mrs Langham spoke to him perfectly politely and pleasantly. No, he reassured himself, she appeared to hold no grudge against him. Perhaps Mary's idea Langham had never told her he'd written for a transfer had been the right one after all? If, on the other hand, she knew all about it, then they'd evidently reached a tacit understanding to draw a veil over the whole matter of the blasted notes, Langham's and his. Moreover, Mrs Langham didn't seem like a lady hell bent on shopping him to the chief for going beyond his remit. The poor creature! Evidently she hadn't slept or eaten properly for days, she looked so pale and drawn.

Mr Pinner certainly didn't want to add to Rose's anguish. And yet how could he avoid doing so? As he haltingly explained to her, it was his lot to try to discover what had happened to her husband and thus he must interview her; he must press her on what, if anything, she knew.

He began his timid questioning, in civilized fashion, when he and Rose were having gin pahits on the verandah before evening tiffin. He was in fresh khakis and she was again wearing one of the floral cotton frocks she'd let out wherever she could. She was attempting to flaunt her little bump, not out of vanity, but because she trusted it must be affecting. She'd been careful to ask Mr Pinner not to sit in Frank's chair, as seeing another man there would have been too painful for her, she'd said, and not untruthfully either.

Golly, Mr Pinner was uncomfortable. The swampy smell and the threatening trees! He really didn't know how anybody could stand living in the depths of the jungle like this. And though he was doing his best, he felt as thoroughly out of his depth as he'd all along expected to feel. It didn't help there was so much he couldn't mention, and which therefore constantly tempted him to mention it.

Meanwhile, Rose was grateful Mr Pinner was sticking to the rules of society by not admitting to what he surely knew: that before she'd been mistress here, the DO's bungalow had housed Frank's nonya. But better even than his discretion was his diffidence, his general air of ineptitude. A bloodhound? No, she thought, if Mr Hollingworth had had to send somebody to see about Frank's death, then she couldn't have hoped for anybody less investigative, less forensic, than Mr Pinner. She looked at her hapless interrogator with the same kind of frankness Frank had so often looked at her, the kind Mummy had warned her against back in another lifetime, or so it sometimes seemed, a kind of frankness she now knew to be so frank it could only be false.

"I'm afraid that's all I can tell you," she sighed. "Nothing more, really, than I wrote to Mr Hollingworth. Frank and I had drinks together and I went to bed. Overnight, he vanished. As I explained in my letter I can only think he left the compound for some mysterious but compelling reason. Went into the jungle. Ventured too far off the path and disorientated in the dark, he ... he ..." She stuttered into a showy silence.

Mr Pinner did so hope Mrs Langham wasn't going to cry; he'd rather be up on the mat in front of Hollingworth than dealing with a lady's tears.

"Yes, yes," he said hurriedly. He considered asking Mrs Langham: how did your husband seem in the days before he vanished? But it was such an intrusive, impertinent question and could so easily lead to the bogs of all those things that couldn't be mentioned. He tried to think what Gregson would want to know, or Braddle. He adopted what he hoped was a ponderously policeman-ly tone.

"I'd better take a look at your husband's papers," he said. But even as he spoke, he regretted his suggestion. What was he thinking? Going through a man's papers was a thoroughly rotten thing to do.

Rose got a fright, although perhaps an unnecessary one. Either way, she thought she'd been too quick to dismiss Mr Pinner's nose for guilt. It occurred to her that even in the ordinary way of things any widow would want to burn those of her late husband's papers she didn't want others to see, but since all that business with the hammer she'd been nowhere near the desk in the bedroom she still called Frank's. Indeed, she'd barely been inside his room at all – a kind of horror of encountering his lingering atmosphere, she supposed. Had she been foolishly squeamish? She tried to tell herself there couldn't possibly be any paper trail leading from heaven knows where, to the idea she'd kill her husband – but what if there were? A diary? But why should it be incriminating and in any case he hadn't kept one – had he? Letters? What if his desk contained correspondence that could somehow damn her?

She pulled herself together and adopted a stern expression.

"His private papers? I can't see they could shed light on anything."

Mr Pinner flushed.

"Quite. Quite."

Rose hesitated before she said, with what she hoped was touching reluctance,

"I suppose I could go through them for you, and see if there's anything of significance?"

Mr Pinner was most relieved at this helpful suggestion.

"Awfully good of you, if you can bear to do it." He slapped at his forearm to swat a mosquito. "I assume you sent boats to all the kampungs hereabouts to ask if anybody has any leads?"

"Yes, to every kampung up or down river for fifty miles, but that's only three of them, not including the kampung here, and the enquiries all drew blanks."

Mr Pinner nodded. He cleared his throat. "I suppose I'll have to talk to your servants. I do apologise."

"Of course, but none of them saw a thing. They weren't here, you know. They live out. And in any case, it was the night of the full moon – do they celebrate it in BB?"

"Bulan Penuh? Yes, they do."

"The servants were all in the kampung, having a party."

"What about the night watchman?"

"We always give him a holiday on the night of billy penoo."

Mr Pinner frowned. Langham had been a damn fool to let the night watchman go like that as a regular thing. Any Malay with a grudge would have known he could safely approach the bungalow on Bulan Penuh – and, Oh Lord, Malays with grudges! The blasted nonya! There could be no shirking his ghastly duty to have a word with the woman, or to go through the motions of doing so at any rate.

"I see," he said glumly. "Well, then: this kampung. I supposed I'd better walk down there tomorrow to ask a few questions."

Rose, so guiltily aware of the truth and so concerned to keep things plausibly simple, unthinkingly assumed Mr Pinner must think la midinette irrelevant to his investigation of Frank's fate, so she neither blushed to think he was now thinking of her late husband's discarded strumpet, nor tried to throw the blame where it didn't belong – not unless she were some kind of automaton and the spirits had used her as their tool for carrying out that wicked Nony's criminal curse. Not unless the sensible world really did supervene on an invisible framework of magic which both affected our lives, and, in turn, could be affected by those who knew how to do it. In which case, sure, Nony would be in it up to her neck.

But no. Rose, practical, simply said, "The morning after Frank went missing, I sent Boy to ask the villagers if they'd seen anything. But I told you: billy penny. Drinking and so on. Nobody knows a thing."

It was rather charming, Mr Pinner thought, that Mrs Langham would trust a Malay to question other Malays on such a serious matter. In her innocence she must never have considered questioner and questioned would collude to pull the wool over her eyes. Not that he was entirely confident his own eyes would be resistant to Malay wool-pulling but never mind.

"I'll ask again. Somebody may have seen something and not realised its significance, at the time."

"We can only hope so," said Rose. She sighed heavily. "As for me, I suppose I'd better start packing tomorrow." She took her handkerchief from her pocket and dabbed at her eyes.

Mr Pinner shifted uncomfortably.

"You could leave on my perahu, if you want. I could delay its departure an hour or two, while you pack."

Though Rose was keen to be off, she thought she'd better not show it.

"To depart without Frank ... I feel I must wait here a little longer just to see if ... if ... he scrabbles out of the jungle, gaunt and dishevelled, but alive."

Mr Pinner didn't know what to say. He swallowed, twice, and then he settled on, "Then I suppose you'll leave next week on the regular mail boat."

"I suppose I shall."

"Mary trusts you'll become her guest whilst you're in town."

Rose tried to picture Mrs Pinner, but all she could summon was a nondescript smudge. Still, she remembered playing bridge with her at the Club. She remembered, too, the other woman looking at her with eyes full of anguish on the day Frank had told her their first home would be in Kluanak. Back then, like a simpleton, she'd found Mrs Pinner's anguish puzzling, but now? Now, well! She dreaded to think of the coming weeks she must spend in BB, of the avidity with which the women there would greet her, of the difficulties of avoiding them, and of parrying their beastly attempts to fish. And worse even than their nosiness would be their tactfully conveyed sympathy, the kindness they'd show her. She'd just have to put up with it, she supposed, just as she'd have to put with the strain of worrying some slip would give her away.

"How very kind," she said.

At first light, Mr Pinner's perahu had set off back to BB with the crew carrying chits from him to Mr Hollingworth and to Mrs Pinner, saying nothing more than that he'd safely arrived. There was nothing from Rose to the outside world; when Mr Pinner had asked if she'd anything to send she'd tremulously explained she couldn't face writing Home of recent events, just yet.

Nonetheless, letters were now very much on Rose's mind. Straight after breakfast she'd steeled herself to enter Frank's room, where she'd tried to ignore his rustling presence. She'd settled herself at his writing desk in order, belatedly, to go through his possibly traitorous papers. There was no sign of a secret diary, but within five minutes she'd found his letters; they were in the top drawer, along with a plentiful supply of stamps. Like her, Frank kept, or had kept, his letters neatly organised by date. She'd extracted them, and settled back to confront correspondents who had perhaps known more about her husband's life than she ever had.

By now she'd read the letter from Dandy and all those from Slinger twice, in sequence. She was holding the most recent of Slinger's letters, the one in reply to Frank's of March. Her cheeks were flaming and she felt quite sick. She re-read a couple of sentences: *Maude expresses herself thoroughly satisfied you've spoken, at long last, and never mind you were only bounced into spitting it out by the nonya's brazen boldness. She says to tell you any sensible lady must now accept there are worse things husbands can do to wives than take watercolour wives before they were married and Rose surely now won't have the vim for sustained resentment* ... Assuming Frank had replied to this letter, what on earth had he said? And whatever he'd said, Maude, the cat, must think she was a perfect fool. As, indeed, she was. It was too bad! Had Frank had no sense at all of the value of privacy? She felt now as if he'd stripped her naked in front of a crowd of strangers ... Still, she must hang on to the thought she was not endangered by these letters, that was the main thing; they merely offered further confirmation of what she'd already assumed: everybody knew. And that everybody knew was no reason for anybody to find in what they knew any reason at all to accuse her of killing her husband, she remained convinced of that. As to these horrible letters? They must be allowed no afterlife, not even as waste paper. She'd do as she should have done already and burn them.

Mr Pinner had spent the time since breakfast holed up with his thoughts in the tiny spare room, but now he emerged onto the verandah. He checked that Mrs Langham wasn't about. Though he realised Malay could have been to her a code she hadn't cracked, he was wary of having her as a witness now it fell to him to interview her boy about issues of such painful delicacy. Satisfied the coast was clear, he made his summons.

"Boy!" he called. "Boy!"

Mr Pinner judged his own Malay to be pretty good, nonetheless, now Boy was standing in front of him, he found himself silenced by the thought anything he said must be so tawdry. He hummed and hawed and decided he may as well grab one of the many stampeding bulls by the horns and start with the idea that Langham had been far too fond of a tiddly.

"Look here! How much did Tuan Langham drink?"

Mr Pinner's accent was terrible. Usit took a moment to understand. Once he'd got it, he kept his face impassive.

"Quite a bit. Anything up to a bottle of whisky a night, I suppose." He paused, and he blushed for the late tuan. "Sometimes more."

"Had he been drinking the night he disappeared?"

"Yes, sir."

"I see. So if he wandered off into the jungle his sense of direction may have been impaired."

"Yes, sir."

"And if he were attacked, drink could so easily have undermined his capacity for self-defence."

Usit assumed Tuan Pinner didn't mean attacked by a hantu.

"Attacked, sir? By a tiger?"

Mr Pinner fixed Usit with what he hoped was a gimlet glare.

"Possible, I suppose, but I wasn't thinking of a tiger. It's no secret in BB that Tuan Langham had a nonya living with him before he married."

It took a moment for that to sink through, but when it did, Usit flinched. By now, of course, everybody in the kampung was as certain as Nony and the pawang that rather than falling victim to some gleefully haphazard hantu, Tuan Langham had been hounded to his death by grimly purposeful spirits Nony had summoned. But everyone knew British justice concerned itself with natural causes, not supernatural ones; after all, the foolish Mat Salleh could never even think of black magic as a murder weapon. So though everyone knew Tuan Pinner had yesterday turned up to take over, for now, Tuan Langham's role in policing their lives, and to poke his long Mat Salleh nose in places where it wasn't wanted, none of the villagers had yet thought to worry Nony's obvious and unquestionable guilt meant she was at risk from such as him. No, everyone agreed she was endangered from quite another direction.

But hang on a minute! Usit was aghast. Against all the odds it appeared Tuan Pinner did indeed suspect Nony had exacted revenge on Tuan Langham for scorning her. Had he somehow or other heard whisper of her curse? Did he intend to investigate Tuan Langham's death by hexing as if it were death by poisoning or stabbing? Alamak! Nony could be worse than irritating, but she was, after all, one of his own, she must at all costs be spared the retribution of the British. But could she be spared such retribution? It now rushed in on Usit, at the speed of jumbled, frightened thought, that Tuan Pinner, the *kepala butoh* – the arsehole – may put Nony on trial. The outcome would be a foregone conclusion – odds on he'd have found her guilty even if she'd been innocent. And with the verdict delivered, he'd surely hang her. Usit imagined Nony's body swinging from a gibbet. He found himself unable to reply to Tuan Pinner's question.

Mr Pinner thought the boy typically shifty and he wasn't having it. He said, in a tone intended to indicate he brooked no nonsense, "I need you to take me down to the kampung, to introduce me to her."

Usit barely managed to whisper, "Now?"

"Now."

"To Nony?"

"Speak up, Boy!"

Usit pulled himself together.

"You want to meet Nony? I'm sorry, sir, it's not possible."

"She goes by 'Nony' does she?" asked Mr Pinner, without any interest. "What d'you mean it's not possible?"

Usit struggled with himself. Two nights back Nony had

gone into the pawang's hut, there to be initiated into the secret mysteries which would protect her from Tuan Langham's vengeful wandering ghost. This morning, before he'd left his own house for the DO's bungalow, he'd been speculating with his wives what kind of state she'd be in when the men who'd fetch her home from her ordeal went to collect her – which they would have done by now. But he really didn't want to mention the secret mysteries to Tuan Pinner. He considered lying that Nony no longer lived in the kampung. But the lie could so easily be exposed and what then? In the absence of anything to say, he said nothing.

Mr Pinner was scarcely surprised by the boy's obduracy, but he was disappointed in himself that he'd failed to intimidate him out of it. He said, with uncharacteristic sharpness, "Come on! Let's get going!"

"She's sick," said Usit. "She can't see anyone."

Mr Pinner raised one eyebrow.

"Infectious is she?"

Usit's only reply was to blush.

"Something to hide, have you?"

Usit decided there was nothing else for it. He squared his shoulders and hoped for the best. "These past two nights and days, she's been with the pawang. She can only just have returned to her house. She'll need to recover."

Mr Pinner thought: Oh, these pawangs!

"Recover from what?" he asked.

"The rigours of the secret mysteries."

"What secret mysteries?"

"They are secret."

"Well, yes. But what are they?"

"Nobody knows, except the pawang and the initiates."

"What d'you mean, nobody knows but them?"

"Nobody can tell the secrets, on pain of death."

Mr Pinner let a beat elapse before he asked, "Well, why's she being initiated into them?"

Usit hesitated. How on earth to answer, without incriminating Nony? But then, in a flash, it came to him, "She's pledging her daughter to the pawang today."

"Her daughter? You mean Tuan Langham's child?"

"Yes, sir."

"What d'you mean *pledging*?"

"Nony is giving the pawang her daughter, so the girl can be trained up as her successor."

Mr Pinner did a double-take.

"Tuan Langham's child will be the kampung's next pawang?"

"Yes, sir."

"But she's half-white!"

"Yes, sir."

A rum do, Mr Pinner thought, a rum do, but the fate of Langham's mixed breed child was none of his concern.

"I see," he said. "And so her mother needs to perform the secret rituals, does she?"

Usit was firm.

"That's it exactly, sir."

Mr Pinner was even firmer.

"Well, never mind any of that. Come, come, man. I just want to ask her a few questions. I'm sure by the time we've walked down to the kampung she'll be recovered enough from these bally mysterious mysteries to see me."

Usit shook his head.

"How about I take you tomorrow?"

Mr Pinner was a patient man, but he was becoming thoroughly exasperated by the boy's attempts to obstruct him. He again spoke sharply.

"Tuan Langham is missing in the jungle, presumed dead. I need to interview anybody at all who could cast light on the matter and that includes his former nonya. Not tomorrow. Not this afternoon. Now. Come on!" He paused, and he assumed a severe expression. "And unless I say otherwise, not a word of this gets back to the mem, you understand me?"

Usit led Mr Pinner up the bamboo ladder and through the entryway into the musty dimness of Nony's one-room house. Inside, Nony herself was sprawled on the bare wooden floor, sleeping off the effects of who-knew-what. She was dressed in the same white sarong she'd worn for the past two days, so it now looked slatternly: in some places it was smeared with ochre pigment, in others with blood. Her hair was hidden under a length of white cloth, wound tight in a turban around her head. Her arms and her legs were scratched. The pawang, who would watch over her until she awoke, was squatting next to her with First Daughter cuddled in her lap. The little girl was calmly sucking her thumb; the old woman was crooning to her, to her sleeping mother and to the spirits the words of an ancient incantation. But she was shocked into outraged silence when two male heads appeared in the entryway.

Mr Pinner was dripping from the short walk through the humid jungle. He removed his topee and tucked it under his arm, thus revealing that his sandy hair was slick with sweat. Though his work now mostly kept him in BB, in his day he'd been in these gloomy native huts often enough – there was never anything in them except a few pots and baskets here and there. Sacks of rice in the corners. No furniture to speak of. The foetid air was always too hot. Not to mention the moment he stepped across the threshold, he always began itching from fleas, real or imagined. Still, at least the roof of this one was high enough that he could stand. It was a strange sight before him: the woman lying there, looking like some sort of cocooned moth; the raggedy mixed-breed child staring at him through owl-wide eyes – Langham's daughter, he supposed, the one being pledged today to the local pawang. And the tiny, desiccated crone? She must be that very pawang.

Usit shuffled uncomfortably. It must be as clear to Tuan Pinner as it was to him that Nony wouldn't be answering any questions just yet, but he daren't turn to the other man and dismiss: I told you so. And he barely dared look at the pawang. It was a terrible transgression, intruding like this. He could feel fury beating hot off the ancient shaman, so hot his face felt as if it were melting. He didn't give any explanation of the stranger – neither of his identity, nor of his purpose. Notwithstanding she'd been shut up inside her house these past two days, he assumed the pawang would be aware not only of who the visitor was and of what he was doing in Kluanak, but also of the shocking fact he seemed to have Nony in his investigative sights; she had, after all, her ways of knowing.

The pawang did indeed assume this must be a tuan arrived from BB to enquire into Tuan Langham's death. And, to her horror, she immediately guessed why he'd now appeared in Nony's house. Despite his Mat Salleh blindness to magic, he must suspect the child. But she was no more in awe of Britannia's representatives than she was of flies. And as to British justice, it was as irrelevant to her as the weather today in Kampung Inggris. She trusted in a higher justice, the justice of the spirits. And – praise be! – the spirits showed her now how to keep Nony as safe from this living tuan as she would be henceforth from Tuan Langham's ghost. Yes, this tuan may suspect, but had he abandoned entirely the Mat Salleh's vainly vaunted rationality? Had he abandoned the Mat Salleh belief Malays were incorrigible liars? The pawang thought no and no again. Well, then, she'd turn against this twit both his trust in reason and also his mistrust in Malays. Suspicion? She'd confuse him so badly he soon wouldn't know a suspicion from a scorpion. She'd confound him so thoroughly he'd mix up yes and no, right and wrong, night and day, east and west, fact and fable. Then she'd laugh to see the perplexity on his face. And her weapon? It would be (as she believed) the truth.

Mr Pinner's respect for the irrational extended no further than raising his hat to clergy of the Church of England. As for pawangs, though he didn't like to call them frauds, he couldn't think of a better way to put it. Still, old fraud or not, he'd expected Langham's boy to make some sort of introduction to the pawang now actually in front of him. But it seemed the mental deficient may as well have been struck dumb. Mr Pinner let the silence stretch a little longer, and then he decided it was high time for Britannia to take charge.

"I've come from BB," he announced.

The pawang smiled condescendingly at Mr Pinner's appalling Malay. Still, she understood him well enough. She nodded: yes, I know.

Mr Pinner flapped his hand at Nony.

"I want to ask this woman some questions. Wake her!"

Usit shuffled and looked at his feet. But the pawang wasn't angry. No, with satisfaction it occurred to her that the tuan's intrusion now, whilst Nony's being was still stretched thin between this world and other ones, was as much spirit-ordained as anything else. It would only make it easier for him to step onto the misleading path she planned to lay before him. Nonetheless, her enormous eyes hardened. She blinked a couple of times at Mr Pinner and she shook her head: no, that's something I can't allow.

Mr Pinner was tempted to bend down and shake the woman awake himself but he restrained the impulse; he was here as a police officer, he wasn't some domineering bully.

"I won't need to talk to her for long. She can sleep again afterwards."

The pawang's expression was frankly dismissive.

"She drank the drink. She smoked the weed. Now she must sleep. But don't fret, I can tell you everything you need to know."

Mr Pinner took a moment to unscramble the crone's toothless mumble and he was not best pleased once he'd understood.

"Madam ..." he began.

The pawang cut him off with a sharp gesture of her hand.

"You want to find out who's responsible for Tuan Langham's death. Well, I can tell you: it was this child here." She indicated Nony. "You must know she used to be the tuan's nonya, otherwise you wouldn't be in this hut. When he told her he was returning to Kampung Inggris to marry, she called a curse down on him. It …"

Mr Pinner interrupted her, "A curse?"

"A curse. It worked this past Bulan Penuh, belatedly according to human understanding but exactly in its proper time according to higher understanding." She again indicated Nony. "That night the spirits took the tuan, at this child's behest. That's all you need to know."

Spirits? Mr Pinner thought. Curses? He should have predicted it, he supposed. Still, what rot! Although, half a minute, was all this, on the contrary, a crafty kind of smokescreen so typical of the Malays? And if so, then what was it hiding? As if he needed to ask. Blow me down, was this vindication of Hollingworth's idea Langham had been murdered? Did the chief perhaps have his finger on the pulse of things after all?

"I see," he said. "A woman scorned. You mean one of her male relatives avenged the dishonour the tuan did to her, by knifing him on a jungle path."

Usit started. So did the pawang. It was one thing to so thoroughly confound the tuan he'd give up on harassing Nony and quite another to set him off chasing mad ideas. It had not previously occurred to the ancient shaman her testimony could be taken as a disguised description of murder by natural means. As to this idiot framing, so unjustly, one of Nony's innocent male relatives, it was unconscionable, abhorrent.

"I mean no such thing!" she said forcefully. "No man in this village is responsible for the tuan's death, I promise you that. If he were stabbed, then it was by a knife which flew through the air at the behest of the spirits and found its mark likewise thanks to them."

"A magic knife?" echoed Mr Pinner. "So you admit he was killed?"

"Admit it? I praise the spirits for it."

"You admit he was stabbed?"

"He might have been. He might not have been."

"Let's say he was." Mr Pinner jerked his head towards Nony. "To be clear, you're telling me you think the spirits wielded the knife because this woman cursed him after he scorned her?"

"Yes."

"She didn't wield the knife herself?"

"No."

"She didn't ask one of her male relatives to wield it?"

"Certainly not!"

"Where is the knife?"

Mr Pinner hoped to throw the pawang with this question, which he thought something of a pounce, but she merely shrugged.

"If there was a knife, a magic knife, a spirit weapon, it could be anywhere. It could be nowhere. It could be invisible. It could have turned into a snake and slithered off into the undergrowth."

Though it occurred to Mr Pinner that between damp, heat, insects, fungi and carnivorous animals, the jungle was horribly efficient at destroying corpses, meaning Langham's was quite possibly no more, he attempted another pounce.

"And where is the body?"

The pawang shrugged.

"That is something we should all like to know – everybody in the kampung." She didn't add what she thought was obvious: that a corpse not made safe by the funeral rites could be a dangerous thing if it fell into the hands of someone intent on black magic. "I did consult the spirits on the point, but they chose not to tell me. When I poured oil into my pan, all I saw was a pan of oil. It happens sometimes."

Mr Pinner, losing confidence in his Malay, thought he'd misunderstood.

"A pan of oil?"

The pawang nodded. She said, "Like the knife, if there was one, his body could be anywhere. Taken by the birds to a high mountain. Washed by the river down to the sea. Carried by the wind across to the mainland. Anywhere."

Mr Pinner, still wondering about the oil business, felt somewhat as if he were floundering in a pan of oil himself.

"Yes, yes," he said. "In short, you don't know where the knife is and you don't know where the body is?"

"No human knows these things."

Right-o. Mr Pinner heard Mr Hollingworth's voice scoffing loud and unwelcome in his head. He imagined him saying: *I'm sure the natives know where Langham's body is well enough, they'll retrieve it from the jungle in their own good time or let it rot in place as the mood suits them.* By the devil, it was too bad! In glum despondency, he indicated Nony.

"Does she know?"

"Only the spirits know."

Now what? Mr Pinner thought he'd asked all the questions a sensible fellow, a sane fellow, could be expected to ask. As he wondered, resentfully, how to proceed, he used his free hand to scratch at a mosquito bite on his cheek. After a moment or two it started to bleed. As he irritably swiped his hand across his face to smear away the blood, he became aware that Boy and the pawang were both staring at him through shining eyes, and for that matter so was the urchin sitting in the pawang's lap. Blast it! They were all three waiting for him to speak, but what on earth could he say? Thank God Hollingworth had such low expectations of him. Thank God he wasn't actually expected to get to the bottom of things, he was merely expected to show the flag and somehow or other to put the frighteners on the natives.

Mr Pinner squared his shoulders and he nodded down at Nony,

"I'm not done with her yet. When she wakes up tell her I'll be back to talk to her before too long. I've got my eye on her. I've got my eye on all you villagers – your men, in particular. You make sure you tell them that. For now, though, that'll do."

He turned on his heels and stepped towards the welcome rectangle of light spilling into Nony's house from the outside world, it was something, he supposed, to be leaving with his dignity intact.

Usit had cottoned on to the pawang's game. Now he and she exchanged an exultant look; they allowed themselves the briefest moment of shared gloating at the way she'd bamboozled Tuan

Pinner. But then Usit obediently turned to follow the disbelieving kepala butoh down the ladder to the ground. As for the pawang, she circled her scrawny arms tighter around First Daughter, pulled her closer and returned to singing her ancient incantations.

22

Rose, a woman changed forever by her seven months in the jungle, was taking away with her much less than the mountains of barang she and Frank had jointly brought to Kluanak: just her smallest suitcase and a trunk. The suitcase was packed with toiletries and those clothes she'd brought from England and let-out so that they still fit. The trunk contained better dresses she'd not wanted to let out, and her personal things: a framed photograph of her mother; her silver dressing table set. None of her wedding presents. She didn't want them and she was leaving, too, just as Frank had done when he'd left on his last and fateful Home leave, assorted items of the clutter that silted any home.

Though it was barely six thirty in the morning, Usit had already stowed Rose's scanty barang on the perahu and returned to the bungalow. Now Rose and Fitri, the senior native clerk, were taking their leave of Mr Pinner on the landing stage. Fitri never took any barang on the mail run but, as usual, his well-worn leather mail satchel hung across his shoulder. For once it didn't bulge; today it contained nothing but a couple of dry administrative reports begun by Frank and completed by Mr Pinner, and the letter Mr Pinner had written for Mr Hollingworth – the letter he'd written to his wife he'd entrusted to Rose to deliver.

The horizon tempted with a promise of light, and beneath the fading stars the river flowed ghostly under a drifting veil of just-visible mist. The head boatman and two crew lounged in the boat. Fitri, who was portly, lumbered down into it, leaving Mr Pinner and Rose alone on the landing stage.

Mr Pinner turned to Rose and he proffered his hand.

"Well, goodbye, Mrs Langham," he said. "I do hope you settle in comfortably with Mary."

"I'm sure I shall," Rose nodded and then they shook hands.

Rose joined Fitri in the perahu. As she settled herself on the rough wooden seat, she thought of the miry river flowing beneath her, washing her out of the jungle, just as it had washed Frank's corpse out of ... But no, she would not think of that. She twisted around to look one last time at the long, pile-raised bungalow. When she'd arrived she'd expected it to be the setting for her happy ever after and now it was nothing to her but a crime scene. She promised herself once she turned downriver she would not again look back. And she most certainly would not imagine that her husband was still alive; that he and she were happy; that he was seeing her off to BB to have her baby. He would have stood on the landing stage till he lost sight of her, she was sure of that, he'd have been waving and waving, she supposed, waving and waving ...

And now, at last, Rose properly wept. She wept sincerely, with abandon, so Mr Pinner, Fitri and the perahu's crew exchanged glances and wondered what to do, and tacitly agreed to do nothing. She was wracked by sobs so strong they disrupted the bellows of her lungs and the pump of her heart. She wept in a delayed reaction to killing, to the tearing shock of it, and the violence. She wept for herself, a woman previously well-behaved and docile now become untamed, even savage. She wept for the emptiness inside her, despite the fullness of her belly. She wept that Baby would never know his father. She wept for Frank; for the loss of him, of all that was lost with him, the enormity of those losses, the pity of it all.

Everyone in the kampung knew the mem would be leaving this morning. Nony wanted to watch her go. First Daughter was already living with the pawang and she'd left her sons sleeping on their mats. Alone, she'd slipped through the darkness and she'd crept down the path to the edge of the DO's compound. Here she'd stepped into the jungle a little way and found a spot that gave a good view of the landing stage, but which was itself obscured behind a fringe of vines hanging from one of the towering trees – each strand was almost as thin as a human hair.

But though Nony had wanted to come, now she was here, she felt uneasy to be so close to Tuan Pinner, even if he were unaware of her presence. She knew, of course, that whilst she'd been sleeping off the effects of the secret mysteries, he'd given the pawang a grilling. Indeed, he'd returned to the kampung a couple of days afterwards to grill her in her turn. It had been an experience almost as terrifying as submitting to the secret mysteries, but it could have been so much worse – almost as bad as losing your body to a ghost – except the pawang had forewarned her what was afoot, and had reassured her if she told the truth she'd be quite safe from British justice. And so tell the truth was exactly what (she believed) she'd done. Though she'd been so nervous she'd gasped for air and jumbled her words, she'd confessed to Tuan Pinner she'd killed Baba with black magic. But he hadn't immediately arrested her and carted her to the cell in the compound. Instead, just as the pawang had promised, he appeared to have lost interest in her since then. But, Nony now trembled, but what if appearance deceived? What if Tuan Pinner still had an idea she was guilty and intended to hang her for her crime?

Mind you, she rallied, she should not doubt the pawang. It was not for her to probe the secret things of omniscience, and though she couldn't understand why Tuan Pinner had let her off the hook, she could see for herself it was in the end all happening exactly as the beloved seer had predicted. For sure, it was Tuan Pinner who'd just shaken the mem's hand, and seen her into the perahu, not Baba, but confusing one Mat Salleh with another was a mistake anyone could have made when consulting the oil: the Mat Salleh all looked alike; it could be hard to tell them apart even in sunlight, when they were full-size and right in front of you, so if they were seen in shadowy miniature, swimming across a screen of oil, it was perfectly understandable that errors would slip in.

Nony had just reassured herself, only slightly incompletely, that Tuan Pinner was to her no threat, when she heard footsteps coming along the path. She turned: Intan. She hissed her sister's name and beckoned her behind the fringe of vines.

"I knew you'd want to make sure she'd really gone," said Intan. "Me too."

Nony nodded and both sisters turned to the landing stage. Rose was sobbing by now but neither of them was perturbed by her tears. Now the mem's disappearance could be of no possible benefit to her, Intan was indifferent to her fate and also to that of the bayi putih she carried in her belly. Meanwhile, Nony wished the pair of them ill; let mother and child be equally wretched! After a moment or two, Intan gave Nony a sharp dig in the side to regain her attention, and she said, "Remember when I thought if the mem left you could get your old life back?"

"I told you it was a pipe dream."

Intan shook her head.

"I know the tuan's dead. I know you'll never again use a thunderbox. I know from now on it's rice for you every meal, my girl, just like it is for the rest of us, and you'll think yourself lucky to have it, too. Granted, I can never again expect little presents of this and that from the tuan's kitchen. But I still think you can do it."

"Do what?"

"Get your old life back."

"Don't be silly."

The villagers quite often changed their names, either as their circumstances changed or to change their luck – for names were intimately connected with luck, of course. Now Intan made a little moue: *Nony* was not the name her parents had bestowed on her sister; it was the one the tuan had given her when she'd become his nonya.

"Silly?" Intan echoed. "But you're nobody's nonya anymore and the man whose nonya you were, the man who named you

Nony, isn't a man anymore. Well then! You must tell everybody: stop calling me *Nony*! You must tell everybody you'll no longer answer to that."

"What, choose myself a new name?"

Intan shrugged.

"If you want. But I meant you must tell people to address you again as they did when you were a girl, by the name Bu and Baba gave you."

For a moment Nony felt the world settle soft and still around her and she sighed with sadness; she never had mourned the passing of her girlhood, of herself as a girl – there had never been time in all the busyness of living.

"What's that got to do with getting my old life back? I can never return to being that girl. I can never live the life that girl would have lived, if she – I – hadn't gone to the tuan."

Intan was airily dismissive.

"You know what I mean," she breezed. "Reclaim your name and you reclaim yourself." She paused. "I suppose what I mean is: shed the name the tuan gave you and you'll get a self that's nothing to do with him."

Nony stared through the fringe of vines with unseeing eyes. She wasn't convinced. How could she ever now have a self that was nothing to do with Baba? A self that was nothing to do with her own past, her own children ... A new self, even ... But no. No, there could never be any such thing.

On the other hand, there could be new versions of yourself; the world could reflect you back to yourself in new ways. Nony imagined staring down into the pawang's pan of oil, and seeing her not-real face staring up at her. She imagined turning her head, so she saw her not-real face in three-quarters, and then in profile; here was a face that shifted, moment-by-monent, not only with the shifting of her head, but also according to the shifting of the light. This shifting, reflected face was indubitably hers, but she semed to see it faceted, like a rough-hewn lump of salt come straight from the saltpans of Saramantan's northern coast. She saw her reflected face as one of glittering planes and angles, each of them at once both familiar and unfamiliar to her. She smiled, and her imagined reflected face smiled back.

But then, with her mind's eye, she saw the oil shiver. Her not-real face faded from its black satin depths, to be replaced by images of her children's faces. And no, she thought, she'd never liked the stupid, pretentious Mat Salleh names Baba had bestowed on their own children – names so strange and difficult to pronounce everybody else had quickly given up on them and begun referring to her children numerically, by birth order, as had she. It was not an uncommon practice – there were other First Sons in the kampung and other First Daughters too – but she'd always felt uneasy that children so-named received in their rice bowls less than their full measure of rice.

Nony returned her attention to Intan.

"And the children too," she said. "No longer show-off Mat Salleh names. No longer First Son, Second Son, Third Son and First Daughter, either. I could give them new names, couldn't I."

Intan nodded.

"Proper Malay names," she said. She reached out and she stroked her eldest sister's cheek, almost as if she were her mother and not her little sister. "Mutiara," she said. "Our precious Ara."

Mutiara – Ara – hadn't heard her name in so long the world felt all distorted by spangles.

"Ara," she agreed.

23

Government House
and the Pinners' bungalow, BB, May 1925

Since the perahu taking Rose, Fitri and the mail to BB was travelling downriver with the current, by mid-afternoon of the same day it had pushed off from the landing stage in Kluanak, it arrived at the much bigger, busier quay in town.

Mrs Langham looked just as unhappy as you'd expect. Or so thought Mrs Pinner, who met her off the perahu and immediately whisked her into a fly, to take her back to the quiet sanctuary of her bungalow, where she hoped the poor young pregnant widow could begin to recuperate a little from her ordeal, if such recuperation were possible.

Fitri didn't mind that the two women more or less ignored him as they greeted one another: he'd delivered many messages, many letters, in his time, and had rarely been thanked for it. Once they'd gone, he uncomplainingly set off into town on foot, to deliver the official correspondence from Kluanak to Government House.

But who would receive it? Usually, Fitri delivered the correspondence to Tuan Pinner, but now everything was topsy-turvy and he was worried on the point. He'd barely arrived at Government House before he discovered, to his dismay, that Tuan Besar Hollingworth had no acting secretary to assist him whilst

Tuan Pinner was at Kluanak, meaning he'd have to hand the mail packet direct to the demigod himself. Alamak! He'd never before even spoken to him and he felt jittery to his liver as he knocked on the Tuan Besar's office door.

When Mr Hollingworth saw that yet another cringing Malay clerk had come to interrupt him with yet another packet of mail from yet another outstation, he couldn't help regretting, again, his lack of an acting secretary. He felt positively affronted at the indignity of opening the mail, and no matter the affront was a necessary one, consequent on his own decision to deploy Pinner as a police officer. He was brusque to Fitri and he didn't thaw even when he learned where he'd come from, notwithstanding he'd been keenly anticipating the mail from Kluanak. Once he had the packet in his hands, he dismissed Fitri with casual rudeness – not that Fitri minded, he was too grateful to have escaped without a mauling.

Mr Hollingworth withdrew from the mail packet the monthly report that was nothing less than he'd expected, even if the man who'd begun it was dead, and an assessment he'd asked for on the feasibility of eliminating stagnant ponds from the kampungs until so recently under Langham's charge. But he didn't let these humdrum administrative documents detain him. Instead, he turned straight to the much shorter letter addressed to him, from Mr Pinner.

Dear Sir,
I have concluded my investigations into Langham's disappearance

and though he is by now undoubtedly dead, I trust you will not take it amiss if I report I found no evidence to substantiate your idea of murder.

Mrs Langham repeated to me what she told you in her note: that Langham left the compound during the night for reasons unknown, and subsequently became lost in the jungle. It happened to be the night of Bulan Penuh and the servants were all of them attending the festivities in the kampung. In consequence, they could tell me nothing, other than that from the bottles they'd found on the verandah they knew Langham had been drinking on the night he vanished. Enquiries amongst the villagers in the kampung drew a blank, as you warned me they would. By the time I arrived boats had been sent to all the kampungs up-and-down river 50 miles, and they all brought the same news. Which is to say: no news. Nobody had seen or heard anything of Langham.

I am myself convinced Mrs Langham was broadly correct in her surmising. I think that after she went to bed on the night in question, Langham drank more than was wise, as a man will do on an outstation. He heard some noise at the edge of the jungle, just beyond the fence of the compound and he went to investigate. He then either became lost and his body is now lying somewhere in the jungle, or else he fell in the river and drowned, in which case his body may very well be in the sea by now.

In short, sir, I think we have no choice but to declare his disappearance: case closed, unsolved.

Mrs Langham is as drained and exhausted by all this as one would expect. She will tomorrow travel back to BB with the mail boat and when she arrives she will stay with my wife. I trust all in BB will treat her kindly and I hope you will not judge me to overreach myself if I express the hope the government grant her a pension.

I wonder if you have yet found a man to replace Langham, as I am anxious to return to BB as soon as he can be sent to relieve me.

I remain, sir, your faithful and obedient servant, John Pinner

Mr Hollingworth stared a moment at Pinner's neat signature, and then he lowered his letter with a complacent grunt. For himself, he remained convinced his hunch was right: Langham had been killed by a native bearing a grudge, and never mind there was no evidence to substantiate his idea. He'd said all along this murder would remain unsolved. Of course the Malays had closed ranks against the white man; of course they'd kept to themselves what they undoubtedly knew. But they must have got a nasty jolt when Pinner had arrived from BB to show the flag. And with the villagers cowed by the red, white and blue, so to speak, there would be no more native rascality in Kluanak for a while, of that he was certain. What's more, the natives elsewhere on Saramantan would not now be provoked into dangerous paroxysms of wildest mania because one of their own had been accused of killing an Englishman. Then again, none of his countrywomen would be needlessly alarmed for their own safety and likewise none of his more fanatical countrymen would be tempted to exact upon the natives a most unwise revenge. And not forgetting his own reputation for running a tight little ship would now be preserved. All in all, most satisfactory. Yes, Mr Hollingworth congratulated himself, it had been nicely done, to send to Kluanak a man as pliable and lacking in experience of policework as Pinner. He could have chosen no better pawn, notwithstanding the inconvenience of losing his secretary for the duration. Of course, things may have been different if he'd had more troops at his disposal. But as it was? Doing nothing by appearing to do something, that was the trick.

Almost the first thing Rose and Mrs Pinner had done, after they'd arrived on Mrs Pinner's verandah, was to exchange letters. Rose had given Mrs Pinner the envelope Mr Pinner had entrusted to her, and Mrs Pinner had given Rose the latest packet of private inbound mail for the Langhams – the one the mail boat would have delivered to Kluanak yesterday, if only life hadn't become so disordered. How terrible it would be to open it, Mrs Pinner had thought. How terrible to read letters that must assume a dead man was still alive. She'd said she knew Rose must want to read her letters, and her husband's, immediately and in private. She'd then shown Rose to the guest quarters, where she'd left her to her tears, and to what she'd hoped would be soothing solitude.

The guest room was cool and airy, much pleasanter than any of the rooms in the bungalow at Kluanak, and Mrs Pinner had placed vases of flowers here and there. By now Rose had bathed and changed. She was relieved to be on her own and relieved, too, to have left Kluanak. But she knew she couldn't yet say, for sure, she'd got away with things, only that she most probably had, and she could see no reason why she shouldn't. So though she'd rather have slept after her long journey, and though, too, she'd rather have tossed the latest mail packet into the waste-paper bin unopened, she was sitting at the writing desk by the window, preparing to open it. She'd gone through with her decision to burn all the letters she'd found in Frank's desk in Kluanak, and for good measure she'd burned all her own letters from Home to boot. But now she felt she'd never be free from infernal letters.

It didn't take Rose long to read everything, both the letters to her, and also the letters to Frank: two from London, one from his lawyer, one from his bank, one ostensibly from Mr Slightman at Relunas, although Maude appeared to have directed his pen. She resolved she'd better reply to the lot of them at once, Frank's letters as well as her own, to get the grim business over and done with. Moreover, she'd better write too to Mr Dabney-Dent. She'd kept a note of his address against just this moment; the moment she must wield her pen as if it were a horse crop and take him for a ride.

Without further ado, Rose took a sheet of writing paper from the pile laid out for her, filled her pen with blue ink from the pot, and plunged in.

Dear Mr Dabney-Dent,

I am Frank Langham's widow, Rose, and you will gather from that horrible introduction the news I must impart: Frank is dead, or anyway presumed dead. He vanished into the jungle over a fortnight back, and nothing and nobody can explain it.

On going through Frank's papers, I found a long letter from you to him, so I'd have known the two of you were close, even if Frank hadn't talked of you often, and fondly, which, in fact, he did. Since you were friends, I hate even more to be the bearer of such shocking bad news. And though it too is rather difficult, I must say straight out this letter of yours concerned Frank's domestic arrangements before we married, so I know none of that is any secret in your household.

Indeed, as perhaps you know from Frank, I have known for weeks that you knew how things stood at Kluanak. This I learned from my cousin, Mrs Marchmorant, who some time back wrote to alert me to her conversation with your wife, which conversation formed the subject of your letter.

I should like both you and Mrs Dabney-Dent to know Frank and I had put all that behind us by the time he died. We had resolved not to let the past fester, but to look, instead, to the future and to the arrival of our child – for yes, I am expecting a baby.

Please forgive me if you think me blunt, but I must beg that out of respect for my husband's memory you will both henceforth keep to yourselves what you know of the scandal of his former connection. I should hate for him to become the subject of gossip at Home and he should have hated it too; he always did value discretion.

I hope you are comforted to think Frank will have a child as his legacy.

Yours sincerely, Rose Langham

Rose sat back and read through her letter. Had she said enough to shame Mrs Dabney-Dent into silence? She shuddered to imagine this unknown woman whispering to a friend: you're the only one I can tell … Well, she had no choice. She had to trust this letter would put a stop to her chatter. She straightened and jutted her chin, and then she placed her letter in an envelope, addressed it and put it to one side for stamping. She then picked up and reread the letter ostensibly from Mr Slightman. As she did so, she scowled to imagine Maude, this woman who was just as much a stranger to her as Mrs Dabney-Dent and just as much a busybody, it seemed. She was still scowling as she began to write, in her looping, girlish hand, a guileful reply.

Dear Mr Slightman,

Condole with me. I am Frank's widow, Rose, and if you don't already know it from others, you will gather from that horrible introduction the news I must impart. Yes, Frank is dead, or anyway presumed dead. He disappeared into the jungle two and a half weeks ago now, and no trace of him has been found, although search parties were sent out and Mr Hollingworth sent Mr Pinner to take charge of enquiries.

I am now removed to BB, where I am staying with Mrs Pinner, but before I quit Kluanak I went through Frank's papers and I found your letters to him. My husband in any case often spoke of you, so I know you were close; you must be terribly upset by developments and I am sorry for your distress, although not as much as I am for my own.

I gathered from your letters you were Frank's confidante in the business of his native concubine. Thank you for all the wise counsel and patience you showed Frank on this delicate matter. I gathered too your wife had been advising Frank; please pass on my thanks to her for thinking of me so often and so kindly.

I have by me your reply to his last of April. Let me assure you that before he vanished, Frank had quite come round to your way of thinking that he was being foolish in the matter of a transfer, and let no more be said about that, as I hate to think of him being laughed at now he is beyond responding to mockery.

Thank you for your congratulations and your kind good wishes in the matter of our baby. I suppose Frank told you of his pride and delight at the thought he'd soon be getting a son and heir. Let me add that in the way of things this baby wrought its magic between us – I mean that in the days before Frank disappeared he and I were reconciled. I told him I accepted his past; we had resolved to turn our faces away from all that and instead to look to the future and to the arrival of our child.

It saddens me enormously that this child will never know his father, and I feel guilty now I ever held it against Frank he had a watercolour wife before me. What can any of that matter, in the face of his death? I am only pleased my husband and I were all smiles again when he vanished and despite what must be such a ghastly shock for you, I hope you are comforted to know your friend was content – indeed, that he was happy – in his final days.

Yours sincerely, Rose Langham

As before, Rose sat back and read her letter. It too would do, she thought. She folded the letter, put it in an envelope, and wrote the simple two-line address that was all the local mail required: Mr Charles Slightman, Relunas.

Now that she'd dealt, as best as she was able, with both Frank's correspondence, and also with his correspondents, she started thinking about her own. She read again her latest letter from Beatrice, before sliding another sheet of writing paper towards her, and beginning another necessary, and necessarily dishonest, reply.

Alas, she found this letter more difficult, more troubling, to write even than the two she'd already finished. It was so hard to deceive her cousin. Truly, she hated to mislead her; she'd never deliberately lied to her before. She wrote *Dearest Bumbles*, and then she paused and stared into space for a long while. Eventually, she screwed up the sheet, tossed it in the waste paper basket and began again with more determination.

Oh, My Dear,

So you know at last I am That Way and I should be so pleased you are brimming with excitement on my behalf, and with joy to think of our children as playmates, but I cannot linger on all that just now.

There are no words to say what I must except brutal ones, and so I shall say straight off that over two weeks ago now Frank became lost in the forest, and all say he must be dead, so I think I must come to believe it, though I wish I could deceive myself it is not true.

He vanished from the bungalow in the middle of the night. I sat up with him the evening before, but after I went to bed, I never saw him again. And neither did anybody else. When Boy went to wake him next morning, his room was empty – the bed had not been slept in. He was not in the bungalow, not at the courthouse, not about the compound at all and nor was he visiting the local kampung. I was not too worried, at first, as it seemed he must have left very early to attend to some urgent business in a more distant kampung, although why he'd not mentioned he'd be going was a mystery. But he'd not reappeared by nightfall and I became frantic. I ordered the Malays to get up a search party. They could do nothing that night, but at sunrise twenty men set out from the kampung and beat the jungle to a distance of ten miles in all directions. For three days they looked, but no trace of Frank could be found, so I sent to BB for help, and one Mr Pinner duly arrived, charged with conducting enquires to see if he could establish any better than I could what had happened, but he could not fathom it at all. Since there was no longer any point in my staying at Kluanak, I have now come to BB, where I shall remain until after Baby is born and I can travel Home.

Though with your customary sensitivity and understanding you did not mention it, in what was after all a happy letter of congratulations, you know as well as any that my Frank and I had some disharmonies in our marriage, some little problems which needed to be faced and to be dealt with. But now all that seems to me as ephemeral as mist – something that evaporates, something trifling compared to Frank and me, and the cool solidity that was us.

What a wrench to leave Kluanak. How it distressed me to leave the place where last I saw Frank, the house where all the servants knew him and where his things were all about me, the things he touched and used – his clothes, toiletries, books, his gun.

I think I now feel more keenly my dear husband's loss even than I should have done if we'd never exchanged a cross word. I feel I let him down by being too strict about things that required fluidity of thinking, and not rigidity. I feel I love him all the more now, for having hated him just a little when I learned of his other woman and his other family – for I did hate him a little, you know it, and I confess it frankly. How could I not have done? And yet my past hatred now shames me. How could I ever have hated my husband who loved me? How could I ever have been irritated by him? His past was past; I was his present, I was his future – and Baby, too, the son Frank will never know, the boy who will never know his father. Baby and me, we were Frank's future and now he has no future and how am I to stand it?

Excuse my scrawl, and possibly too my incoherence, but I'm all in agitated disarray, and I'm sure you will forgive me if I only now think to do as I ought to have done before: send wishes for your good health and for your confinement, which I suppose may be behind you by the time you read this.

I cannot today call myself Rosebud I feel too withered for that.

Your sad cousin,

Rose

Tears trickled down Rose's cheeks as she reread this letter. The sentiments it expressed were not entirely a pack of lies and though her tears were self-pitying, they were salty too, with mingled regret, grief and remorse. But her sadness at simply everything was neither here nor there: she could rely on Bumbles, that was the thing. She could rely on the dear, with her kindness and her trusting nature, not to be suspicious. She reached into her pocket for her hanky and wiped away her tears. And though she felt positively sick as she addressed the envelope and added this letter to the growing pile of her outbound mail she did not waver in her determination to send it.

Finally, Rose steeled herself to write to her mother – who certainly did not have a trusting nature at all. Far from it, she was capable of being just as suspicious as … as … as a corpse floating in a river, with its head smashed open. Mind you, if Mummy's suspicions were aroused, she'd keep them to herself, Rose was fairly sure of that. Weighing the social humiliation that must follow if it got about her daughter were a killer would almost certainly be enough to prevent her making a public accusation. But social humiliation was scarcely the end of it. And, thought Rose, she must spare her mother from being laid waste by the truth. Yes, it was to protect her mother, rather than herself, that she must now deceive – or so she told herself, as she again began to write.

Dearest Mummy,

I cannot announce some dreadful news except bluntly for the most terrible thing has happened. Frank is lost in the forest, by now presumed dead. He vanished into the green after leaving the compound alone at night, for unknown reasons. I wrote to BB for help and the authorities sent a man – Mr Pinner – but he has had to close the case, unsolved, and now I have come to BB, as there was no reason for me to stay on at Kluanak.

I hope you are not made ill by this shock. As for me, despite events I keep myself as well as I am able, on account of the being

I have growing within me. I will book the nursing home for my confinement in the next few days. After Baby is born, I will return to England as soon as is possible. And then I suppose I shall live again with you, so from saddest circumstance, distance will not after all deprive you of your grandchild.

I cannot for my tears write more than this, except to say that I hope now Frank is dead you can agree with me he was a good man and a good husband, and he would have made a good father, had he lived.

So now we are both widows, and what a sad word is *widow*.

Your daughter, Rose

As Rose was spinning cobwebs of deceit in the guest room, out on the verandah, Mrs Pinner was opening the letter from her husband. She was sitting in a high-backed cane chair by the rail, the last of the afternoon sun fell on her and she could hear birdsong in the garden as she extracted the letter from the envelope – it was long, four pages. She smiled to see her husband's beautiful writing and she could almost imagine he was sitting by her as she began to read.

Dearest,

Langham is still missing and there can now be no question in anybody's mind that he is dead. Accordingly, I now send Mrs L to you. Despite all my worries on the subject, we have been these past few days the best of friends and I know you will treat her as tenderly as if she were your sister – the poor creature certainly needs a little touch of my Mary. She is quite worn out and ill with grief, and from her delicate condition. I trust you will do all you can to shield her from the circling gossips – I am sure you will. Leaving her husband somewhere in the jungle hereabouts, whilst she travels alone to BB, must be ordeal enough without adding to her unhappiness by forcing her to confront, when she gets there, the indecent eagerness of all abroad for all the details.

Alas, my skills as a police officer turned out to be no better than I expected and I confess I have been in quite a quandary about what to do. Oh, that you were on hand to give me your sensible advice! If I've done wrong, may God forgive me, and may you forgive me too.

Let me explain. I quickly established from poor Mrs L she could add nothing new to what she'd told Hollingworth: that her husband had vanished overnight in the jungle. I myself still thought mischance the most likely explanation of events and so I didn't perturb her by mentioning Hollingworth's idea he'd been murdered. And when it came to the prime suspect, if indeed it transpired he were murdered, on her I remained as silent as the grave. Yes, I was just as discreet about the nonya and all that as you wished me to be, and since Mrs L chose not mention her either, she remained between us quite undiscussed.

But though I was stealthy about it, I did of course have to interview the nonya. As soon as I could, I hotfooted it down to the kampung to see about it. But you know what a strange land this is and when I got there I found her in a stupor after participating in some rites so secret nobody would tell me a thing about them. Still, it wasn't a wasted trip. The pawang who'd conducted the rites was on hand so I talked to her instead – a toothless hag, who looked to be about 103. Somewhat to my astonishment, this crone immediately revealed that Langham's former nonya ordered him killed in revenge for being spurned – Hollingworth is a slyer dog than we are accustomed to credit, it seems.

Mind you, the pawang didn't speak plainly. She didn't point to our comatose suspect and say: she's the guilty party. Far from it. She put it all in terms of spirits, and curses, and magic knives and what have you. Her story was that from bitterness the nonya cursed Langham, and then as a result the spirits killed him, possibly with a magic knife, possibly not. Naturally, I saw through the wretched flimflam to the cold, hard truth: murder.

Two days later, when the nonya had recovered her senses, I went back and asked her all about it. Shameless, she gave me the exact same rigmarole, in the exact same terms as the pawang had used.

Alas, it's scarcely a confession they'd admit at the Old Baily, is it. And hoodoo won't cut the mustard in a British court out here either. So though I'm quite positive the nonya is guilty of ordering Langham's murder, if not actually of wielding the knife herself, I can't see a hope in hell of pressing charges. Nothing could ever be proved, there's not a shred of what you'd call actual evidence to be had anywhere, no murder weapon, no body, no physical clues. Beyond reasonable doubt? There's nothing even the wiliest lawyer could put to a court.

So here's the dilemma that's been tormenting me: if the nonya can never be brought to trial, let alone convicted, then what on earth is the point of stirring up a hornets' nest by revealing her role in Langham's death? Isn't it better to hush things up?

On balance, I think it is. After all, as you yourself once gently reminded me, Langham is no longer able to explain. He is no longer in a position to defend his reputation. Doesn't it follow that those of us in a position to defend it for him should do all we can to do so?

Except: perhaps it doesn't follow at all. Are you horrified I could even entertain the idea of subverting the course of justice? Do you think your husband is becoming as pragmatic as any native? Am I failing myself here? Perhaps I am. But in my defence I cite something Hollingworth told me: sometimes, as a tiny band of rulers, we Britons must be more pragmatic than we would be at Home; as flexible and fluid in our thinking as those we rule.

Think, dearest!   So much is at stake beyond justice for Langham. You know the Malays – so touchy, so quick to be roused to fanatical frenzy. And Hollingworth specifically warned me against riling them. It's obvious, isn't it: if a native woman were accused of a crime as heinous as murdering an Englishman then we could be faced with riots island-wide. It would be like the trouble at Kemper's place multiplied by thousands and I don't much fancy having a hand in anything like that.

Moreover, I have tried to think what's best for Mrs L. How could it benefit her to know responsibility for her husband's death lay with his erstwhile nonya, if no punishment were ever possible? She surely in any case loathes the woman and it could only torment her further to know she'd got away with murder.

Not to mention if my conclusion became widely known, then trial or no trial Langham's murder by his former nonya would be the sensation of Saramantan: everybody would be talking about it. Mrs L would be unable to maintain even the shreds of her dignity by pretending to ignorance of her husband's past and nor would anybody be able to pretend to her, kindly, that they did not know of it.

Then again, what of matters pecuniary? Consider this: if Hollingworth knew his late DO had once indulged in concubinage with a native, then he may very well decide not to offer the fool's widow a pension – or anyway to offer her a reduced pension – to set an example to other fellows. That would be too bad, both for Mrs L and for her child.

Above all: this child. Mrs L will want to avoid scandal at all costs, for her child's sake – its father, Mary, its father. But if the scandal of pater's murder by the concubine he'd cast aside got about at Home, as it surely would if there were a trial, however pointless, then even worse than being harried and hounded by the gossips herself, she'd find it dashed difficult – impossible – to prevent the little lad or lass from learning the unpalatable facts, despite the thousands of miles between Saramantan and Old England.

And so, dearest, I confess it, I have written to Hollingworth to say that according to my investigations, Langham vanished into the jungle just as Mrs L said he did. The only extra item of intelligence I added is that drink surely played some part in the affair – as you suspected he drank far more than was good for him, it seems. Apparently, he'd been boozing heavily on the night he disappeared, although I trust you'll keep any hint of that from Mrs Alford.

In upshot: case closed, unsolved.

Understand that despite my pragmatism, I do not deny the seriousness of the crime. I keep imagining Langham lying face down on the jungle floor, half hidden by undergrowth, with a kris in his back and with his open mouth chocked with mud and leaves. Or else floating on his back in the river with a kris sticking out of his chest. It's a bad show, this, and no denying. But nothing can bring Langham back to life, and I say again: it seems to me that whatever I do, or don't do, the nonya and any accomplices will get away scot free.

Thank God I'm an administrator and not a police officer. If I've learned anything these past few days it's that sleuthing's not for me.

Kiss the girls from Daddy, and I send a kiss to you too, and I miss you, and I will miss you worse, come the night.

Your own John

PS perhaps for safety you'd better burn this letter once you've read it.

PPS I wish I could believe divine justice would sort it all out in the next life.

Mrs Pinner finished reading and she lowered her husband's letter in shock. What? Murder, after all? Oh, the horror! And she was all for discretion, but John, her mild and indecisive John, conniving in letting a native off a terrible crime – a native and all her accomplices? It was almost as if he'd become an accomplice to crime himself. Moreover, if she didn't take John's letter straight to Mr Hollingworth, she too would be little better than an accomplice to crime. It was impossible! How could she tolerate pretending to ignorance of a crime, of the perpetrator of a crime, if she knew it had happened and who had done it? She stood up and, in some agitation, she walked twice around the verandah, still holding her husband's letter – clutching it tight in her fist. But at the beginning of her third circuit, she stopped and she stood stock still for a couple of moments. Would she really shop her husband to Mr Hollingworth? That too was impossible. Yes, both things were impossible: speaking up or keeping silent.

Except what was she thinking? It was an illusion, this choice, this appearance of choice. Do this or do that? In truth, she couldn't put up much of a fight with herself. Indeed, no fight at all really. Right or wrong, life had chosen for her; marriage had chosen for her. Now John had put aside what he knew, she must do the same. Wifely solidarity was the thing. The only possible thing. Of course it was.

And this was no time for second thoughts; there must be no turning back. With no further prevarication, Mrs Pinner walked into the drawing room and over to the shelf where her husband kept his smoking paraphernalia. She reached for a box of matches, this she carried back onto the verandah. She walked over to the rail, where she did as John had suggested she do: one by one, she burned the four pages of his letter. She touched a corner of each sheet in turn to a lit match, each time the fire caught easily, each time she held the sheet gingerly until it was consumed. In a few moments all that remained of her husband's letter were scraps of charred paper, fluttering like sooty butterflies about the garden.

Epilogue

Almost a year to the day after she'd first arrived in BB, Rose was leaving. She was going Home – although Home, she'd come to suspect, was an unattainable ideal even for those who'd never left it. She went with no husband by her side but with her baby daughter in her arms. Grace. She'd been so surprised when the midwife had said she'd got a young lady and not a little gentleman, she'd thought the woman must have made a mistake. But no. As she walked across the gangway onto the coasting steamer which would take them to Singapore, Rose looked down at her daughter, whom she loved, now, just as she would have done a son. Grace seemed blankly mesmerised by something above her. What it was, Rose couldn't tell: there was a stiff breeze, so the clouds ripped across the sky and the one or two strands of bunting strung across the gangway whipped and snapped; clouds or bunting, one or other seemed to have captured her daughter's attention; her enormous eyes, too large for her pocket watch face, were fixed upwards and staring.

Oh, what eyes! Rose was grateful they were already turning brown; they were not remaining blue, like Frank's, nor would they be green, like hers. Grace's eyes, thought Rose, were all her own, they were vessels to be filled up with memories all her own – mind you, it was a mercy she'd remember nothing of BB. As for herself, Rose was relieved beyond measure to be leaving. She was eager to be Home, where nobody but the Dabney-Dents and the Marchmorants knew a thing about Frank's watercolour wife, his watercolour brats, and those four she must trust to be discreet. Bumbles, she was sure, would never breathe a word – and what a comfort it would be not to have to pretend to the dear that Frank had ever and always been an ideal husband, even if she could never say a thing about the business with the hammer. Mrs Dabney-Dent remained a worry, but she'd written a sympathetic note saying the last thing she wanted was to cause embarrassment, and that would have to do. As to the men, they must have lost interest in her life by now, she supposed, if ever they'd been interested in it at all. Suffolk wasn't Saramantan; neither Edmund nor Mr Dabney-Dent was caught in a colony like a rabbit in a trap, they had more to occupy them than tattle. No, in England she surely needn't worry people were whispering about her, and about her marriage, behind her back. Oh, she'd be a sensation for a while, she knew that, and there was nothing to be done about it, she didn't suppose, but once her family, and her friends, and her mother's friends, had got over the novelty of having in their midst a widow whose husband had disappeared in the jungle, no doubt everybody would forget all about her. Obscurity couldn't come soon enough. What a hell it had been, to be such a focus of attention these past few months. Rose paused in her progress across the gangway and she turned back towards the quayside, where her acquaintances were now gathered to see her off. She was absolutely thankful she'd never see any of them ever again. She took a deep breath of the humid tropical air, and for the first time since the business with the hammer, she allowed herself to believe, to wholeheartedly believe, to believe definitively, that she was safe.

Or in any case, as safe as anybody ever could be. What lay ahead for her – for the two of them, her and Grace? How would they get on in England? How would it be returning to live with her mother, as though she herself had become once more a child? The future, sighed Rose, was so unknowable, and, perhaps, so chaotic. Still, at least she did now have a future. That was the thing. She hadn't swung. Her punishment now not only must be guilt, it would be guilt – remorse, and the loneliness of living with herself. Nothing deadlier. And probably you got over things, even things like the thing she'd done with the hammer. Either way, she'd now, God willing, live to see Grace turn from a baby into a girl, and then into a fine young woman.

Smiling now, Rose held her daughter up to the crowds, took her arm in hers and, holding her small hand in her larger one, caused her to wave. She was well aware that she and Grace, mother and child, must make a most affecting picture.

All along the quayside men were waving their hats at departing passengers, but Mr Hollingworth was not himself of the hat-waving fraternity. Still, when he saw Mrs Langham making her little girl wave like that on the gangway, he raised his topee. He was glad for her she could now at last depart for Home. He thought her admirably stalwart – as fine an Englishwoman as was to be found anywhere between Saramantan and Old England. By George, it was difficult to credit that damn fool Langham had ever worried about taking her to an outstation, for fear she'd be lonely and miserable. A lady who could remain as composed as Mrs Langham in the face of tragedy could surely never have been fazed by the hardships of life upriver. Mr Hollingworth wished her all the luck in the world, and he was jolly glad he'd been so generous in the matter of her pension.

Mr Pinner had been back in BB a month by now. He and Mrs Pinner were standing hand-in-hand a little apart from the crowd, and though neither of them would ever admit it to a soul, they were united in thinking they were glad Mrs Langham was going. Other than being a tad moody, as was only to be expected, she hadn't been a difficult houseguest, and they hadn't minded the to-do of a baby, but it would be a relief to have their home to themselves again. Not to mention that her presence had been a daily reminder to both of them of their equivocal role in allowing (as they believed) a native to go unpunished for murder. Kind hearts and good intentions were all very well, but what about justice – ordinary, human justice? What about morality? When Mr Pinner had decided to hush up (as they believed) a Malay woman's frightful crime, had he been right to evaluate solely the feasibility of pressing charges, the political consequences of his action, or inaction, practical matters, people's pragmatic interests? Had Mrs Pinner been right to go along with his well-meant subversion? Neither of them was entirely confident on either point. Neither had admitted as much to the other, but the unspoken worries lurking in both their minds had caused the atmosphere between them to become a little strenuous of late.

They both looked forward now to forgetting the whole hideous matter entirely, once Mrs Langham was gone.

Mrs Alford was standing with Mr Alford, the pair of them surrounded by a little group of the gossipy ladies who ever orbited her as planets orbit the sun. Mr Alford was smiling benignly, but vaguely, in Mrs Langham's direction, and Mrs Alford was waving her lacy white hanky towards the steamer – but she was looking, with disapproval, at the Pinners. Holding hands, indeed! So horribly boastful, after the honeymoon. Moreover, she wasn't at all surprised they were keeping themselves aloof from everybody else, even at the best of times they were such a standoffish couple and he'd been worse than ever since returning from Kluanak. Decidedly strange in manner – shifty, she may even say. Jumpy. It only added to the fishiness of it all; the idea she'd never quite been able to shake that there was more to Langham's disappearance than met the eye. As if what met the eye wasn't vulgarly plenty. Yes, there was more than enough scandal to require covering up. The nonya. Half-castes. Boozing. But was known scandal the end of it? Mrs Alford had an uncanny feeling it was not; that she was missing something somewhere.

It was infuriating! She couldn't be doing with doubt, it was so namby-pamby, so why this nagging doubt about … about … well, she was sorry, but she couldn't help thinking the Pinners and Mrs Langham all three knew more than they were letting on, that's all. Mrs Alford slid her gaze to the grieving widow, the unfortunate young mother: she was standing there on the gangway, cool as a cucumber, holding her daughter up to the crowds, leaving at last, just as she'd so manifestly desired. Honestly! She needn't have made it so hurtfully obvious how keen she'd been to be gone. Although, in fairness, she must think of this departure as an escape; anybody would, under the circumstances. Mrs Alford granted that, and she didn't wish to be unkind, unsympathetic, it was just she couldn't help thinking that from the moment Mrs Langham had arrived in BB her behaviour had seemed decidedly off. Off! Iffy! The photograph, for instance. It was known from Mrs Pinner's amah, who'd told Mrs Gregson's amah, who'd told Mrs Gregson, that Mrs Langham didn't have even a single photograph of her late husband in her room, which wasn't on even if their marriage had had its little troubles. And though Mrs Langham lost the thread of conversations, and though too at social events she often stared into empty space, as was only to be expected of a woman recently bereaved in such a dreadful way, otherwise her mourning was so undemonstrative a suspicious person could almost suppose she wasn't mourning at all. Of course, there was no grave to keen at, but where were her tears? True, a stiff upper lip was quite the thing – except when it wasn't. Then again, Mrs Langham really shouldn't be so ... so ... elusive, thought Mrs Alford. Yes, elusive, that was the word. Or did she mean evasive? Either way: to her nose, it stank. Mrs Langham never wanted to talk about her dead husband – never at all. She quite blanked even the most direct of questions. Mrs Alford huffily remembered how Mrs Langham had stared through her when she'd asked whether it were true that just before his disappearance her husband had asked for a transfer. Yes, yes, Mrs Langham must have been cross with Langham when she'd discovered his various debaucheries but surely her crossness hadn't survived his death? In any case: did crossness justify outright rudeness to ladies in BB? Sorrow took people in different ways, Mrs Alford supposed, but it was such a pity Mrs Langham so blatantly discouraged the sympathy she for one would have been so willing to show her, given the slightest chance. And it would have done the poor young widow a power of good to hash things over. Her reluctance to do so, her silence, seemed to Mrs Alford so peculiar it was practically criminal, so to speak.

Mind you, when she'd mentioned to Gerald she detected some undeclared mystery lurking beneath all the known mysteries of Langham's disappearance, her husband had put his fists on his hips and told her, in no uncertain terms, not to go pestering poor Mrs Langham, nor inventing intrigues neither. Gerald rarely put his foot down and though Mrs Alford was unaccustomed to obeying him, she'd been shocked into promising discretion. And she'd not broken her promise; say what you liked about her, she was a woman of her word.

Nonetheless, it gnawed at her, this idea that something or other more than usually shady was being hushed up about events at Kluanak. She suspected secrets were being kept. And secrets, felt Mrs Alford, really wouldn't do ... Well, she had a few little secrets of her own, of course. Not even Gerald knew absolutely everything about her; it wasn't possible for him to; it wouldn't be proper if he did. But her own secrets were neither here nor there, their existence didn't change how she felt about secrets in general. And Mrs Alford felt, she very strongly felt, that secrets were in general to be discouraged; secrets, she thought, were in general as unhealthy as bad air, or bad water, or wet woollen socks in winter at Home.

Surely no sensible woman would disagree? Mrs Alford frowned as she kept her gaze steady on Mrs Langham. For goodness sake! If she were indeed keeping secrets, then you'd have thought she'd bloomin' well have learned her lesson when she'd belatedly discovered her husband had withheld from her the truth about his past. Oh, a nonya was the common thing, but on learning her new husband had kept one, even the most redoubtable bride must think here was something it would have been better if she'd known all along. It was too bad! If only she could speak to Mrs Langham now, she'd say she wished her to remember a simple truth: that secrets kept are always more powerful and more powerfully destructive than secrets told.

Still, the baby at least was as yet unsullied by secrets. Mrs Alford flicked her gaze from Rose to Grace, and her face softened; she allowed herself a smidge of tenderness when it came to dogs and children. Poor little scrap. Poor little poppet, fatherless even from before her arrival. Fatherless and, even on the face of it, Daddy's fate so ghastly. What a thing! To learn Daddy had been lost in the forest! Even she, an adult who didn't care much for fancy, could sometimes fancy the jungle was determined to strangle itself and everything in it. But a child? Dear little Grace would no doubt imagine Daddy falling prey to fanged and hairy monsters, to hungrily grabbing trees with devouring howl-eyes, to vines with python faces hissing with intent to throttle the unwary. Yes, in the way of children, Grace would no doubt terrify herself imagining things that were far worse than reality.

Except: could the reality of Langham's disappearance be worse than any child's imagining?

As this question reverberated around her head, it seemed to Mrs Alford that the bustle and noise all about her stopped, for a moment. My days! Could she all too easily conjure theories about how Langham's disappearance might indeed have been worse than a child's nightmare?

But no! No, of course she couldn't. It was absurd! It was utterly preposterous! Or so insisted Mrs Alford. Instead of pursuing a question which gestured in a direction so shocking, she resisted examining it or even entertaining it at all. To protect herself from its abhorrence, she took refuge in her own realistic, commonsensical nature. Honestly! What on earth was she thinking? Never mind criminal undemonstrativeness, iniquity was an entirely different kettle of fish. It was unspeakable! Too vile for words! Not to mention it was all a lot of nonsense. Mrs Alford glanced at her husband standing beside her, looking like he wanted to bumble off somewhere. Dear Gerald had been quite right, for once, when he'd warned her against inventing intrigues. It was one thing to gossip, pleasantly and cattily, about one's acquaintance; it was quite another to go inventing things. Terrible things. Dreadful things. You fool! Mrs Alford self-accused. Making things up! She gave her hanky an especially vigorous wave and she narrowed her eyes against both the harsh dazzle of the sun, and also the harsh hot light of the truth. After all, she felt, she very strongly felt, that making things up just wouldn't do.

Would it? Mrs Alford glanced between Rose's face and her

husband's. It was too silly, but, despite herself, she couldn't help wondering whether, after all, she should say: Gerald, I have the funniest idea, I don't know why, but just listen a moment ...

Acknowledgement

Circumstance was partly inspired by William Somerset Maugham's short stories set in Malaya. Copyright in Maugham's work is owned by The Royal Literary Fund, in London. *Circumstance* is published with the agreement of the Royal Literary Fund, but it is not endorsed or authorised by the Fund.

I am grateful to the Trustees of the Royal Literary Fund for allowing publication of this novel.

But above all, of course, I am grateful to William Somerset Maugham - in particular, for writing the short story *The Force of Circumstance*. There are echoes of, and references to, *The Force of Circumstance* throughout *Circumstance*.

The Force of Circumstance was first published in *The Casuarina Tree*, in 1926. It concerns an English bride, Doris, who has recently arrived on a jungle outstation in Malaya with her new husband, Guy, and who soon discovers his former mistress, an unnamed Malay woman, is living in the local kampung with their three children. I took this tangle into *Circumstance*. Doris, Guy, and the unnamed Malay woman were my starting points for Rose, Frank, and Nony. However, the plot of *Circumstance* does not unfold in the same way as the plot of *The Force of Circumstance*.

If you haven't already read *The Force of Circumstance*, I urge you now to do so.

If you are not yet a Maugham fan, I hope you now become one. If you want to read his stories set in Malaya you can find them, for instance, in two collections, *Far Eastern Tales* and *More Far Eastern Tales*, published in paperback by Vintage. I also urge you to read others of his works exploring Britons' encounters with Asia, such as *The Painted Veil*, *On a Chinese Screen*, and *The Gentleman in the Parlour*. These too are published by Vintage.